GOODBYE BABY BLUE

Goodbye Baby Blue is the first of Frank Ryan's acclaimed thriller trilogy, which continues with *Sweet Summer* and *Tiger Tiger*, all featuring Sandy Woodings. With his perceptive eye for background and character, Ryan has created a thriller master-piece.

"Magnificently tense . . . "   *The Sunday Times*

"The page-turning and spine-chilling ability of a good novelist."   *The Sunday Telegraph*

"Powerful atmospherics . . . Impressive storytelling throughout."   *The Literary Review*

"A riveting thriller."   *Publishers Weekly*

"Well written . . . Recommended for libraries."
Library Journal

"The twists and turns from which he extricates his characters are very clever. To call (this book) a psychological thriller would be to understate it. The novel is a work of genius."   *Liverpool Echo*.

"A riveting book . . . "   *Elle*.

Frank Ryan

One of today's more exciting and gifted of writers, Frank Ryan is equally adept in fiction and non-fiction. He came to widespread international acclaim with thrillers such as *Goodbye Baby Blue*, and his ground-breaking non-fiction, *The Greatest Story Never Told* and *Virus X*. His books have attracted front page reviews in the *New York Times* and *Washington Post*, in addition to lead reviews in the *Daily Telegraph*, the *Sunday Telegraph, The Scotsman* and *Irish Times*. They have also been translated into a dozen languages and have been the subject of features in many television documentaries in Britain and America. A play, based on *The Greatest Story Never Told*, featured the Oscar-winning actor, Jason Robards. More recently, he has added fantasy to his fiction repertoire, with the publication of *The Sundered World*.

GOODBYE
BABY BLUE

FRANK RYAN

—

GOODBYE BABY BLUE

SWIFT
PUBLISHERS

GOODBYE BABY BLUE

A Swift Book

First published in Great Britain by New English Library 1990

Swift Edition published 1999

1 3 5 7 9 8 6 4 2

Copyright © Frank Ryan 1999

A catalogue record for this book is available from the British Library

ISBN 1–874082–26–X

Typeset at The Spartan Press Ltd
Lymington, Hants,
Printed in Great Britain by
Caledonian International Book Manufacturing Ltd.
Glasgow

Swift Publishers
PO Box 1436, Sheffield S17 3XP
Tel: 0114 2353344; Fax: 0114 2620148; website: swiftpublishers.com

I am grateful to my agent, Bill Hamilton, and to my original editors, Nick Sayers and Vanessa Daubney, for their help in the writing of this novel. Special thanks to my brother, Tony, for his encouragement – also to my friend Craig Dent for the courtesy of his time and technical advice.

Hadja no more to do? Was your work all done?
Had ya seen your first son?
Why 'dya leave us all here?
Has the battle been won?

Elegy for Neal Cassidy: Allen Ginsberg

For My Son, John

1

The leaves fall in a pattern, all off one branch together, so that there are whole branches black and bare with others in the same tree with plenty still left on them. He notices these things as he smells them and he senses the touch of the leaves on his skin. Even to their dry crackling death under his feet as he walks on them, he senses them and he sees them in his mind's eye, the fresh fall on the path behind him, he is aware of them blown into an agitation by his passage. *And in the vine were three branches: and it was as though it budded, and her blossoms shot forth – .* How certainly he feels things like that today, how alive are all his senses. He could be overpowered by the aniseed smell of crushed ferns as he watches from his hiding place in the thick bushes. He can see the children playing and there is a hard quality of touch to his eyes as there is the quality of patience.

Emotion has made his face peculiarly blank and the staring quality of his expression is heightened by the very light colour of his eyes, which are a uniform ash grey. He stands so still and silently it is as if he were immune to the simple human comforts, to the need for blinking and to the cold – for it is certainly the coldest autumn afternoon so far, proven by the dense puffs of steam that blow at excited intervals from the mouths of the children.

"Here! Look at this – I found this. This'll burn right well."

"Hey! Let's have a look. Hey, Bobby – come and look what Chris's found!"

Their voices have a lucid musical quality, almost as pure as the note of the male blackbird which has flown up out of the leaves and shrieks a warning.

There are three of them, all boys. They are collecting twigs and odds and ends of wood from amongst the withered nettles and big rusty seed-spikes of docks, putting them down carefully in a pile for their bonfire. Everything about this activity fascinates him: their little dashes here and there, their intimations of adult complexity, the hierarchy, already clear, amongst them. Yet it is only one of them who is really the focus for his eyes. This is the one who is obviously their leader, the tallest of them, with dark wavy hair and brown eyes. The others keep on calling out his name. All the time they want to please him. When he moves they follow him, eddying round him, asking his opinions on things and vying for his attention. He is a little king amongst them and in regal fashion he watches what they do and he is spare with his replies. How calm the world is seen in those big brown eyes.

Bobby! Bobby!

The memory comes without warning: the knowledge that she too is here, that her face hangs in the air, with death in her eyes and her blood has become a thick oil, gushing from the fork of her thighs into the dust.

For a moment the memory is unbearable. For a moment the pain of that memory blots out the world. He has to shake the vision from his head, he is aware only of the need to tear himself clear of the image of her welling blood. He can hide himself no longer. Suddenly there is the bright flash of phosphorescent light. How surprised they all look, as he walks out from where he was hiding, as he smiles and walks amongst them, holding three burning sparklers in his right hand. They are all afraid of him but he calms them quickly with the softness and the calmness in his soothing words.

"Here! The's not fritt'ned on't, eh?" He crouches to come level with the smallest of them, who is wearing a blue parka with the hood partly covering his neck, blond hair and a gap in his top teeth.

The boy's hand trembles slightly as he accepts the burning sparkler.

Still frightened: he stands up tall above them, his eyes close in a prolonged blink and when he opens them again, he is staring up at the gnarled branches of the autumn trees.

The second of them has a plump face, cheek-heavy, with a sensuous surly mouth and a flattened nose. Their eyes meet but he accepts the sparkler.

"Here!" he says calmly, "here you are – last one for Bobby."

"I don't want it."

"Why doesn't the' want it?"

The tall man's teeth show white against his heavy blue stubble: he is smiling: the grey pearls of eyes are glittering. A face that seems younger now, in spite of the unshaven cheeks and chin and in spite of the dialect. He laughs and seems to enjoy the steam of his own breath, bathing his face, warm and moist, as he cups both hands in front of his lips and he blows heartily to warm them.

"Thee mates are not fritt'ned on a couple o'sparklers."

"I'm not afraid neither."

Superior even in the way he is dressed: a grey bomber jacket, with black patches over the shoulders and elbows, blue and white mittens in the colour of the Wednesday football team, jeans with horizontal zips over the knees.

"Oh, sparklers aren't good enough for thee, are they not? I suppose the'd expect rockets?"

"Hey, Mister – have you got any more fireworks? Hey, he's got more fireworks. Hey, Mister – what kind of fireworks have you got? Go on, show us then if you've got some better ones." The younger two boys are excited, shouting, but he keeps his smiling grey eyes on those suspicious brown eyes.

"Aye. Happen I have some more. But I were goin' t'save them for bonfire night proper."

"I'd just love to see a rocket. I'd love to put the light to it myself."

"Only the'rt not big enough, art – !" He laughs and ruffles the blond wisp of hair that has fallen over the apple-downy cheeks poking out of the hood. "The'rt nobbut a snip on a dog's tail, that's what the's up to."

"Bobby's big enough."

"Aye. He's big enough. But I don't reckon he's of a mind to."

"Oh, go on, Bobby. Go on. I dare you."

Still the smile shows through the dark mouth and those eyes are shining. Underneath his feet he feels the crush of beechnut cases while the ground, strewn with tansies and dandelions, is a celebration.

"All right."

He nods calmly: for he was always certain. "Now then – thee two guard t'fuyer whilst me and Bobby comes back with the rockets. Okay?" He raises his eyebrows humorously at the middle boy, whose sulkiness has never left him. He can still see the pair of them as he takes Bobby in the direction of the embankment, wide eyes in faces pale with the cold, and the little one's left hand clenching and unclenching.

2

Standing close to the large uncurtained window, Sandy Woodings gazed through his own reflection into a garden that was illuminated as bright as day by a powerful arc light. The light was brilliant because the woman who owned both the garden and the apartment in which he was standing, had a morbid fear of burglars; an understandable fear given the wealth of antiques that decorated every room, even the bathroom. But Sandy Woodings wasn't very interested in antiques. He was interested in the little things. Like a first tooth, or the loss of that first tooth. Or that first concentration in four small faces, the sandcastles on the beach at Croyde Bay, the drawings which followed the colouring books.

When he lit a cigarette, the lighter solidified his reflection. A tall man, dark curly hair, medium blue eyes. Athletic, more than fit for his age, but not young looking. He was aged thirty-nine but he knew that he looked two or three years older.

Josie, on the contrary, looked younger than her thirty-six years. Maybe it was the individual woman in her – feminism appeared to have completely passed her by – or maybe it was because she had a good sense of humour and things didn't worry her for long. He liked that about her, he liked her irrepressible sense of humour, almost as much as he felt curiously a part of this twilight world of the widowed and the divorced. Not love, no – neither pretended that. In that sense they were honest with each other. Just a good evening out and afterwards . . . Yes, he was looking forward to the afterwards. But the telephone call spoiled all that.

He took it in the bedroom, although he was well aware of the main extension, hidden in a Japanese lacquered cabinet in the lounge. "Chief Inspector Woodings," he announced quietly into the receiver, and as he waited for the connection he watched Josie's antics in the mirror, how she had fallen back onto the black satin counterpane, the carmine sheet lipping it at one angle like a tongue, one hand splayed backwards against the pillow, and the other hand, finger wagging an admonition in his direction.

Listening to the desk sergeant's voice without taking his eyes off her, he watched her form kisses with the half made-up mouth, the dog's-tongue expressiveness of her face, the dyed blonde hair, the widely spaced pale blue eyes.

"A young lad has gone missing," he spoke calmly, his eyes still on the reflection of her face.

"How do you mean, missing?"

"Kidnapped. I'm sorry, Josie."

He turned to look at her, at the wilful posturing against the counterpane, the sort of woman's body that was popular in the sixties. Josie would have been a teenager in the sixties.

"I can see why Julie left you."

Their eyes met but he said nothing.

"I shall go out without you. I'm going to dress up and I'm going to go out without you."

"Suit yourself." He had stood up and was distracted momentarily by the Watteau vignettes that decorated her ivory-coloured wardrobes.

"Go on then – not even a kiss. Not even a teensy weensy one – you pig!"

He came back over and sat on the edge of the bed and he allowed her pale blue eyes to search his face. "I'll be in touch. Give you a tinkle."

"You don't care." She kissed him miserably, but with wet lips and long enough for the kiss to linger. She left her scent about him like a talisman and the weight of her breasts seemed to have impressed itself onto the memory of his left arm.

A detective sergeant called Tom Williams opened the car door for him and then led him across the wet tarmac road until they stood facing a long and dark slope, illuminated by floodlights. Behind them, with noses directed like bloodhounds against the grey brick terrace of houses, were a dozen squad cars with blue lights asynchronously flashing.

"Have we got an accurate time for when it happened, Tom?"

"Four fifteen – give or take a couple of minutes."

He looked at his watch: already 7.36. His eyes performed a low wide sweep of the site of abduction, which, to judge from the position of the lights, was about two thirds the way down the slope, close to where it terminated in a wooded coppice, parallel to a busy main road.

"It's some playground, Tom."

"How do you mean?" asked Tom.

"Were you never a kid yourself?"

"Never," said Tom, sniffing.

Something about this scene had an immediate and powerful impact on Sandy Woodings – something about it, even in the dark, as they now made their way past wild grasses, docks, what was left of the nettles and the big flat pancakes of butterbur – it was one of those islands of wild nature found in the waste areas of any large city, a wilderness fighting a festering war against humanity's rubbish.

"What's the lad's name?"

"Stephens, Robert. Eight years old – closer to nine. Taken from the company of his two small pals when

7

they were making a bonfire down here, close to the trees."

Thoughtfully, Sandy led Tom in negotiating some old prams, pieces of garden fencing and some other rubbish, walking with hand-held torches across a fissured lake of old pink mortar, until they came to a part of the slope where it met the road and bloomed, completing the transformation back into primeval forest.

"Four fifteen – so it all happened in daylight?"

"Look up there, in the direction of the houses, and you can see the row where he lived. Four hundred yards away."

Sandy Woodings took time to look, he picked out the house from the degree of police activity about it.

"Four hundred yards," Sandy mused still, then suddenly they came on the spot where a sergeant was working under spotlights, knocking hooked pins into the ground and watched in open-mouthed admiration by two boys, the older and plumper of whom was wearing a police officer's helmet. Tom introduced himself to their two witnesses, then extricated his handkerchief and blew his nose with a trumpeting, staccato relish.

Children make good objective witnesses. The two young boys gave Sandy Woodings a very clear description of the man who had taken their friend Bobby. A tall man, unshaven, with funny eyes. They weren't altogether clear what they meant by funny eyes but Sandy Woodings thought it unusual. Standing over the spot above a sheer embankment leading down to a main road – the spot where their kidnapper's feet had left ski marks from his heels on sliding down to where he must have parked some kind of vehicle – Sandy thought again about the strangeness the children had remarked in those eyes. But they had not recognised him, the man was a perfect stranger to them. And yet . . .

Sandy Woodings felt himself invaded by a sense of strangeness. A menacing bewilderment that caused the hackles to rise slowly on the back of his neck.

Disturbed by that same sense of foreboding, he climbed the hill, leaving Sergeant Tom Williams to liaise with the Scene-of-Crime constable, while Sandy entered the terraced house where Inspector Jock Andrews had already taken down the statements from the Stephens family. Quickly reading through these, he sat in the living room of their home, keeping a curious awareness of the dark-haired woman who was the boy's mother.

Mrs Stephens must have been interrupted in preparing the tea – her fingers were red and shrivelled, as if recently in water, and there were traces of flour across the belly of her open-necked red dress, decorated with small green leaves.

Either they found her son alive and well or Mrs Stephens would never recover. There would never again be a normal day. Sandy Woodings chose his words, his tone of voice, with care.

"We need your help, Mrs Stephens."

She nodded. She blinked her eyes wide several times, then appeared to withdraw somewhere deeper, her neck fallen forwards, ahead of the line of her shoulders.

"This man – " he hesitated, because he thought she needed time to take it in, "you've heard his description – does anything about him seem familiar?"

She shook her head. She was sitting at the far end of a red dralon settee, close enough to the window for the intermittent flashes of blue light from the cars to illuminate her face. Her attractive brown eyes did not look back at him, but stared in a distracted way at the floral hard-wear carpet under her feet.

"Think again, if you can, Mrs Stephens. A man perhaps hanging about the street? Somebody watching the house? Maybe something Bobby said to you – perhaps he was approached by this man recently?"

It was an enormous effort for her to speak, her voice husky, tremulous. "You'll find him, won't you, Mr Woodings?"

"We'll try very hard, Mrs Stephens."

"You won't find him, will you? You're just saying you'll find him but you won't find him. You read about it in the paper, children going missing . . ."

He passed her the photograph Jock had chosen for circulation. "Please look at it, Mrs Stephens." It was a picture of a slim boy with dark hair like that of his mother. In the photograph he was leaning against the trunk of an oak tree, his hands in his pockets and his head inclined slightly downwards. He was wearing black jeans with white stitching down the sides. She lifted her eyes to the photograph as the blue lights stopped flashing.

"He wasn't wearing these."

"What was he wearing then?"

"Grey – his grey jacket, with black over the shoulders. And blue jeans."

"Do you have any photographs of him wearing the same clothes as today?"

"No. The bomber jacket and jeans were new. He's – Bobby is – quite fashion conscious for his age."

"What were on his feet, Mrs Stephens?"

"Trainers." She allowed the photograph to fall loosely in her hand. "Black and white trainers. Size threes. They were a present from his grandmother."

A policeman brought in two mugs of coffee. Mrs Stephens made no response so one of the mugs was put on top of the sideboard, in case she changed her mind. Sandy Woodings accepted the other, gazing at the photograph again. Out of what depths had this character emerged? He inhaled deeply, added, "I've got four of my own, Mrs Stephens. My son is only a year older."

Suddenly something erupted inside her. All the time she had been living a few feet in front of her eyes, now she

10

discovered her real self an infinite distance behind them. She screamed.

Her husband brushed aside the comforting hand of Jock Andrews, to throw his arms about her.

"For Christ's sake, why aren't you out there searching? Nothing but damned fool questions. Questions and more bloody questions."

"I have more than sixty men down the slope already, Mr Stephens. Before the hour is out, I hope to double that figure. Every road is blocked. We'll make it our business to search every street and every house in every street. I want you to believe me, we're searching."

"But you've found nothing, have you?"

"Think, Mr Stephens. You're angry but it isn't helping, is it?"

"We can't take any more of it, no more of these useless questions."

"Why – why, in heaven's name, did Bobby go with this man? He seems to have gone willingly. That's what the two boys told us. This man, a perfect stranger, approached him and Bobby just went along with him without a struggle."

A shortish thickset man, his greying black hair back from his temples and a large circular bald patch on the crown of his head: Mr Stephens' face was a livid red and he was sweating heavily. "You said you had kids yourself, I heard you."

"Yes, I said that, Mr Stephens."

"Then you damn well know, don't you?"

"What do I know, Mr Stephens?"

"You know they don't do as they're told."

Sandy Woodings stood up abruptly, studied Mr Stephens a moment, then put his hand reassuringly on Mrs Stephens' shoulder. "Allow Inspector Andrews here to call in your doctor. He'll give you something. Try to keep calm – get a little rest."

*

11

At 10.00 p.m. Sandy stood once more at the scene of crime, a habit of his since he had first taken charge as an inspector. They had failed to find either the boy or his abductor.

It had happened here – *here*.

This crime had erupted from some human depths, not incomprehensible, something understandable if you could never sympathise. In that understanding must lie the clue, the explanation. Sandy thought about that: he stood alone for many minutes thinking hard.

He detested what he was thinking because he was thinking sex offender and this aroused an instinctive revulsion in him. He thought about it, and was revolted or changed his mind and instead was baffled, all night; and by dawn he still wasn't certain. In this job nothing was ever quite that certain.

Sandy Woodings had consumed several cups of coffee in those uncertain hours and he had climbed to his feet on many an occasion, to stretch his legs, or step out of doors and bruise his lungs with the ice-cold night air, or to smoke a cigarette outside, where cigarettes always tasted ten times better.

But there were peculiarities, weren't there?

And peculiarities, he nodded, bringing a freshly lit cigarette to his lips and inhaling, were interesting. He saw the pair of them now, in his restless mental eye, the two boys, fidgety and tired. He listened again to their precise answers to his questions, registered the posture, the tilt of their faces – the tone of bewilderment in their voices.

Here you are . . . last one for Bobby . . .

Bewilderment. But did it mean anything in two children? Maybe. Maybe it did. And that was the first inkling of the unusual. But then something even more striking was the degree of intelligence – planning even – about the kidnapping. Now he considered the nature of that plan, while continuing to smoke his cigarette, until his thoughts were interrupted by the radio sergeant, who drew him back into the incident Portakabin and where, with cigarette stubbed out in a saucer, he listened to Inspector Andrews' voice over the radio set:

"Do you want me to just collect the files together and bring them out to you?"

"No – I'll come in," he took a sidelong glance out of the aluminium-framed window, to witness the smoky wash of dawn illuminate the distant trees, even as yet another mug of strong and burningly hot coffee was deposited on the Formica-topped table next to his elbow. "We should get together on this, Jock. Let's meet up for lunch."

Andrews hesitated, then agreed.

Through the window of the Portakabin, he saw a uniformed chief inspector arrive, Charlie Earnshaw, who had a team of trained searchers with him and a man in a buff-coloured overcoat who was a forensic technician down from North Yorkshire.

"Another thing, Jock – I've been giving it some thought. We'll concentrate on boys. Put boys missing in a separate file – collect all missing children, but put boys separately – have you got that?"

Earnshaw saw him through the window and waved. Sandy Woodings waved back with the hand that was holding the receiver. The radio was a temporary link-up while they were waiting for a proper telephone to be installed. He made a signal to Earnshaw because he wanted him to wait, but the uniformed officer didn't see it. Jock said, "I've got you then – separate out boys – shall we say under the age of fourteen. Boys reported missing in the last couple of years?"

"That sounds about right."

Even before the moment of real daylight, Earnshaw's team set about it. They had unloaded metal detectors and were now making their way down the slope.

"Can I ask you, Chief, if we can get together on this a little earlier than lunchtime?"

"If you like – say ten or so." It was a good idea; he knew the reason Jock was worrying. But he felt impatient. "Listen – with regard to headquarters – let's just hold what we've got until the actual meeting. Keep out of people's way – got it – until we can sift through the files."

As he replaced the receiver, he saw a new van arrive with the sniffer dogs. He left the comforts of the Portakabin to catch up with Earnshaw and then he insisted on dragging him away from his treasure trove of tin cans, pull tabs and milk bottle tops, to talk.

"That's fifteen hours missing now, Charlie," he said, blowing between his cupped hands and wincing with the cutting edge of the cold.

"If you ask me the poor little devil's done for," said Charlie phlegmatically.

Sandy Woodings scratched at the unshaven side of his neck without a change of facial expression. Charlie had a long face, which he needed to accommodate a very flat and lengthy nose. Now Woodings looked Charlie directly in his overmoist half-mocking hazel eyes, the purse of the underdeveloped upper lip under the strong black moustache.

"We don't know he's dead, unless you've found something?"

"No," said Charlie, "we've found nothing."

"But?"

"I just don't fancy the odds, that's all."

Charlie was a man who liked a flutter more than he should. That was part of the reason Georgy Barker didn't like him. But Georgy didn't like a lot of people – detectives didn't make good friends, not with each other. Suspicion had been developed to too high a degree, like an overworked muscle.

"Five to one on," Charlie gave him his considered opinion on the odds calmly, and without the slightest intention of disrespect.

But Sandy Woodings was already hurrying with an athletic springy step up the slope to where he had caught sight of Sergeant Tom Williams. And even before they were within speaking distance, Sandy knew that they hadn't been able to spot any definite vehicle.

Tom said, "I've got reports varying from a Ford Granada, orange, green or blue, a Sierra with stripes, a motor-bike with side car and one extra-large furniture removals van."

"Parked on the road at the bottom?"

"Either parked on the road or nearby or seen prowling about the streets at the right time. And there will be many more, by the sounds of it."

"Perfect!"

Dawn had brought out a gaggle of reporters, who were held at the top road by some uniformed men on duty, and the photographers were giving the constables the run around, trying to get close enough to take better pictures of the policemen searching. While they watched, they were joined by the scientist from the forensic science laboratory, who had realised the unlikelihood of finding anything useful but felt obliged to wait until the searches were completed.

At the time of the telephone conversation he had felt something hard to describe – a kind of debilitating surge of excitement. Now he was thankful for that because it primed something deep inside him, something to do with that same conversation with those two boys. *Bewilderment!* He didn't know why he was so suddenly overwhelmed by it, except that there was something more to it than was obvious, a recognition that was a stirring of painful memory, something deeper still.

They had a clear twenty minutes before the rain started. Then, trudging the way back with Tom to the Portakabins with their familiar navy and white cross-hatching, he cleared aside the reporters with a firm courtesy, while refusing to talk to them.

15

"I could have told you they'd find nothing," said Tom, sitting comfortable, adding whisky to his own mug from a pocket flask.

Watching through the window, the dog-handlers caught Sandy's attention, putting the fur-soaked shapes back into their van. He could tell they were mad, because he would have been mad in their place, finding himself called out this morning after a hundred pairs of boots, knees and clawing hands had ploughed up the ground.

He called him Bobby!

"Get Jock for me in records, will you, Tom," he must have squeezed his own tension into his voice, because Tom looked at him and he laughed back at Tom.

Inside the Portakabin, there was a deafening increase in the patter of rain as he waited on the telephone. "Bloody hell, Jock! I asked you to call me."

"I would have done to," said Jock cautiously, "but there were reasons."

"I asked you to call me back straightaway, that was what I asked."

"Well there was nothing to tell you anyway. I found absolutely nothing. No similarity with any previous kidnapping."

"You didn't look hard enough."

"I looked pretty hard, I can tell you." Jock was a mouth breather, which you only noticed when he was on the other end of the telephone. "It's a one off, Chief. That's what I think – and if you ask me, it's something a bit peculiar."

"Why do you say that?"

"I feel it in my big toe, the same way you do," said Jock, while Sandy watched, through his window, a headquarters car pulling into the place vacated by the dog-handlers' van. There was a monstrous contortion as a balloon-like figure fought to clamber out.

"Tell me why peculiar, Jock. Make it snappy."

16

There was a pause, the mouth breathing again. "The two kids seemed to trust him."

"Go on – "

"I thought they somehow believed in him." Jock coughed with embarrassment. Sandy saw him with that perfectly clean handkerchief, the nervous mascot, a clean one, pressed into four every day.

"That's all?"

Sandy watched the big man take the felt hat which was passed to him from the passenger window of the car, then his eyes made a long sideways sweep, taking in the slope, the glance in the direction of the incident centre. He appeared to swirl, on remarkably dexterous feet, a dancer's lithe movement, called something into the yawning car window, another graceful swirl towards the party still searching with their metal detectors; a matt of wire-wool hair, with the remains of its original red showing for all the world like an early rust, that large squarish head elevated turtle-like over the slow-moving carapace of a body.

"I think there was something odd about the character's voice."

"What about his voice?"

"I don't know."

Sandy Woodings nodded: he had felt something very similar. He considered what he and Jock agreed on: that the two boys had trusted the man and there was something odd about his voice. Sandy noticed the second figure, the figure of a woman, which had made an appearance, now dawdling about the top of the slope. Even as he registered that great square untidy head nodding up and down, the long, tree-trunks of arms windmilling one way, the hands pirouetting to make some point, and perhaps a ninety degree clockwise turn of the whole upper trunk in Sandy's direction, he observed how the woman stood absolutely still and stared hard for a moment in his direction.

"You're worrying me, Jock."

17

"I know I am."

The big man was starting to walk the last few yards in the direction of the incident centre, limping slightly – you had to know about the arthritis in his hip joint.

"I want you to talk to Mrs Stephens again, Jock."

"Thanks a lot."

His heart suffered a delicate somersault

He was in the act of putting the phone down quickly. "Talk to her and let me know, Jock."

The big man was in the same room with him; he had to bend his neck, incline his body sideways, to squeeze through the small door. Now he just stood inside the doorway, statuesque, with his Michelin-rubber-man smile, waiting for Sandy to replace the telephone. Sandy remained seated.

"Woodings – you're a caution."

"You're up early, Georgy."

Sandy had already guessed the reason for Jock's failure to telephone, a reason now emphasised as he heard that beefy fist slap twice into the palm of the other hand like a sound like a flat shovel smacking wet sand.

Superintendent George Barker had got to Jock and indulged in one of his little games, which might have taken Sandy by surprise if he hadn't phoned Jock on the suspicion. Yet the presence of Georgy at this early stage was something he hadn't bargained on. It wasn't that he didn't get on with his boss – of any detective he had ever met, Georgy had the most profound understanding of warped human nature – but Georgy and he had such different ways of going about things. And he had taken Georgy's active service position after the big man had been bounced upstairs on account of the effects of age and eighteen stones weight on his hip joints.

Georgy put his felt hat down in the centre of the table immediately opposite Sandy Woodings.

"Now come on, Sandy, for the sake of these aching bones,

tell me what we've got. I'm waiting to hear it. What have we got on this character, eh?"

Broad daylight: it wasn't even an exaggeration. Sandy found it easier to focus on the hat than on that corned beef face. If Georgy played it dramatic, then you had to be careful not to underestimate the intensity of his feelings on the matter.

"We haven't much, I'm afraid. If I am to be honest about it, we have sweet nothing." He hesitated, his eyes lifting from the hat to gaze calmly into those of Georgy Barker. "All I have is instinct and one slight puzzle."

"What slight puzzle?" Georgy had the ability to focus on three things at once: Tom – who had managed to conceal himself out of the firing line, now adding another tot of whisky to his coffee – the sergeant in charge of provisions, who appeared without apparent prompting, with a full pint-sized mug of cocoa, and Sandy's eyes. All the time he had never stopped searching for something in the depths of Sandy Woodings' eyes.

"He knew the lad's name. He called him Bobby."

Margaret Stephens was standing on the grass verge by the side of the top road, overlooking the slope where policemen were still conducting their searches. She had got this far but her legs would not carry her further. Yet there was a desperate need in her to go further, to go down there and just to look, and the need contracted in her, a torturing spasm that would have driven her except for the weakness that debilitated her legs above and below the knees.

All night long people had tried to console her, to press alcohol on her, and sleeping pills, and empty words, affection, well-meaning but totally misplaced rationalisations.

There was no rational explanation for her presence here at the top of this familiar slope, for the difference in her that had taken place in the short space of twenty-four hours.

19

First she simply could not believe it, and that had been the most difficult thing, simply believing it, and then there was the coming to terms with the fact that the explanation would not be reasonable or rational.

3

In Bolton, Lancashire, a man called Reynolds watched in
his rear-view mirror as the old Rover pulled into the
kerbside immediately behind his four-months-old Vaux-
hall Cavalier. For early November it was bitterly cold –
unseasonably cold. The cold was part of the reason that
Reynolds was inclined to watch in his mirror as Gill
emerged, a man of above medium height, squarish build,
with a thick sandy-red moustache. He was wearing an
open-fronted sheepskin overcoat. Reynolds timed it to
the last second before getting out of his own car to meet
him.

They were parked in Bridgeman Street, adjacent to the
railings of Heywood Park, and now, huddled against wind
and cold, they edged by the brown-painted railings until
they could enter through the gate next to the Labour Club.
In a slow torment of walking, with the wind howling in the
leafless trees, they crossed the park at a diagonal and as they
walked, Reynolds, who was tall and mousy-haired with
steel-rimmed myopic spectacles, described the manhunt
that was taking place in Sheffield.

The story appeared to affect Gill emotionally. Throughout the walk his face had adopted a thick-lipped half smile
which owed more to the non-stop high speed drive from
London than humour. Reynolds thought that Gill looked
puffy and unhealthy and the combination of florid skin and
lines had deepened into a suggestion of hard-boned drink-

21

ing. Sicker and older than when they had last met and the thought didn't worry him one bit.

Gill muttered a profanity in full view of the statue of Jesus.

Reynolds asked him, "So where do we go from here?"

"We keep our mouths shut."

"They're bound to make the Bolton connection sooner or later. And we're talking about a kid, for pity's sake."

"We wait. We watch. We listen."

"I think that's crazy."

"Shut up, Reynolds."

Reynolds made no attempt at all to contain his antipathy. "My responsibility isn't just to you. Half of my job is liaison. I think this is stark raving mad. And I know it's a mistake."

"I hope you haven't been so daft as to mention Bolton to the cowboys already?"

Reynolds ignored this, glancing at his watch, which was strapped to the inner aspect of his wrist. "If we walk back to the club, we can catch it on the news," he muttered hoarsely.

"Did you hear what I said?"

"Yes, sir!"

Reynolds had abruptly turned on his heel so Gill was forced to walk back to him.

"Keep your mouth shut. That's an order. We tell the police bugger all."

Reynolds had to wait for the ITN news on his own because the very notion of entering a Labour Club was anathema to Gill. And during the ten minutes or so of reflection, while downing a quick double Scotch, he sensed it again, a feeling he would have had difficulty in describing to his superiors: that glimpse both interesting and disturbing of something secret. Something which would normally be locked away in the darkest pits of a man's soul but which fatigue had ill-concealed.

It was the main item on the news and it nearly caught him

napping, standing at the bar waiting for a pint of bitter to be pulled. He had literally to run back to his chair in front of the big colour television, with his heart pounding. He knew the petite brunette, Police Inspector Jennie White, who had been given the honour of presenting it. On a better day he'd have enjoyed the sensation of fancying her. The pounding of his heart got progressively worse as she described the actual details, showing a picture of the missing lad and then a video of the grieving parents. Then he saw the identikit picture. "*Jesus Christ!*" he whispered.

He too watches the broadcast, although the police inspector's charms are not material to his gaze. His television is an old Phillips 21inch, with the cover torn off the tuning box and a picture which fades and refocuses at will. He has taken it all in, the time, the policeman leading the hunt, *Chief Inspector Woodings* – he laughs when he inspects the picture of the boy closely – the clothes, the two black and white trainers. Patrick Stabil trainers, because our Bobby is very particular when it comes to clothes, very fashion conscious. He takes a close interest now in that identikit picture, as it happens on the out of focus blink, and he waits until they have read out the full verbal description, tall, dark-haired, heavily stubbled, blue eyes. Baby blue eyes!

He chuckles aloud, switches off the set, and then he stands at the bottom of the stairs and sings, in a soft and humorous murmur, the Dylan song:

> Well it ain't no use sittin' wonderin' why, babe
> If'n you don't know by now
> And it ain't no use sittin' wonderin' why, babe.
> It'll never do no how.

Then he calls out, in a boisterous voice, as he ascends the stairs, with a lively deliberation.

23

"I'm here, Bobby lad. I'm back. Now then, aren't you glad to hear that?"

He has given over his struggling now but he hasn't given up. No, not a one for giving up, is our Bobby, curled into his ball on top of the yellow counterpane, when he had been put nice and snug under it, with his hands and feet tied with women's tights, his mouth partly open behind the plaster, which he must have managed to dislodge with his tongue, and now with his face turned in towards the wall. The tall man clucks disapprovingly on taking in this scene, so much of a struggle has taken place, six hours of struggling, so that the left foot is without shoe or sock and the toes and the end of the foot are swollen and blue from cutting off the blood. A good little fighter is Bobby and the fight is still in him, although not so much a struggling now as a stiffening of every muscle and sinew as the man lifts him bodily from the counterpane and then, with a playful tap in the solar plexus, makes him bend in the middle so he can sit him back against the pink-flowered bedroom wall. Now he can pull the resisting legs out so they jut over the edge of the bed, ready for his rolling up of the two legs of his blue jeans and then to start the patient and rhythmical rubbing.

"Footballer's legs, these. Good at football, are we then?"

First the calves, which are hard as ivory with the grimly contracted muscles, and then the rolling round of the ankles, the long strokes over the feet, like a whistler, blowing into his cupped hands to warm the frozen flesh.

"If the'll behave theeself I'll tak' plaster off thee mouth."

Brown eyes in a tear-blackened face regard him for an instant, terrified yet defiant, then the massaging fingers, but there is no nod of agreement.

"Me, Bobby lad – the' may call me Mag the Magician. To magicians time is elastic so I've got all the time in the world."

He paces to the window, bending his head slightly to look

24

out. A landscape of backyards, walls, one dilapidated elderberry still with its drooping leaves. There is a mist hoary enough to blur the edges at thirty feet.

He turns back to put on the sock and the shoe, which lie on the floor under the bed, and then he ties the feet again, leaving the mouth only half-sealed, and he drips with a dancer's feet down the uncarpeted stairs and into the kitchen, where, whistling that same song "Don't Think Twice, It's All Right", he inspects the beans which have been soaking overnight.

The ingredients are now tipped into a large green saucepan and he gives this a good stir on top of the single large hotplate, agitating the saucepan for several more minutes until it is thoroughly mixed and has started to sizzle. Through the window, the mist has lifted slightly: the green of ash over the red brick wall at the end of the yard, a deep and sensual blue-green, a royal green, against a haze of yellow-gold which is the turned sycamore.

Caressing the head of a black and white mongrel dog, which has been lying watchful under the table, he takes the stairs two at a time, so that within seconds he is gazing onto the miserable ball that is Bobby.

"The's wet theeself." His voice is calm, consoling. He inhales gently. "Never mind." Then, picking up the boy, he removes the plaster from his mouth and then he considers the binding on wrists and ankles. Already there is a delicious savoury smell of soup drifting upstairs. He decides against undoing the bindings for a moment, picking Bobby up like a sack, over his shoulder, then down the stairs, counting one two three – all the way to thirteen, his lucky number, and they are on the floor.

With the boy still over his shoulder he inspects the bubbles popping in the soup, and then, hardly pausing, he takes him out to the toilet off the back entrance and he pushes him in through the unlockable door and then he waits for him, with the door partly open.

The voice is calm and deep and has completely shed its dialect. "Hurry up, Bobby. There's soup and chocolate biscuits."

From the toilet comes no sound, still playing awkward.

He checks the back door and then walks back into the kitchen, knowing the boy is listening to him. Switching off the heat under the big flat plate, he moves the saucepan to the edge of it, then with his ears attuned to the lavatory, his eyes perform an inventory of the room. A puzzling curiosity, for surely the contents are familiar to him. There is the big white porcelain sink with one tap of brass and one chrome, with the plaster bulging in the wall over each of them; a double line of erratically placed white tiles, cracked where the screws for the taps have been forced through them; the square heavy table with the boxes of tins neatly stacked under it. He hears the tinkle of water. No flushing of the chain. His gaze is fixed absent-mindedly on the legs under the sink, which take the form of individual steel balls and claws, now rusted red.

He has just poured soup into two bowls when, predictably, he hears the scuffling.

"Though you'd escape through the back door?"

He laughed, picking up the writhing body once again. He carries him struggling, back into the kitchen, and there sits him down in front of a bowl and a spoon by the table.

Bobby's voice is jittery with terror. "I won't eat it."

"Then you'll starve."

There are tears in Bobby's eyes now. "I'll starve myself to death."

"There's no need to go looking for death. Believe old Mag the Magician. Death has a habit of introducing himself."

Tears were running from Bobby's eyes, making clean tracks through the night-time's dirt. "You can't make me eat – or drink."

The man's face crinkles with a hard lively humour. This is

merely a factual time, a time for explanations. But he isn't yet sure about such things as explanations.

"Eat up, Bobby. You and me, we're setting out on a journey."

The boy's eyes strike towards the window, drawn by the clinking sound – the milkman. But he brings them back again and stares hard at the green-patterned oilcloth over the table.

"I can't eat no soup with my hands tied."

"I'll fetch it to thee mouth for thee."

"No."

The man starts to eat his own soup, which is thick and home-made with big red kidney beans and whole rings of courgettes in it, breaking bread from the single plate he has placed in the centre of the table. He eats slowly, watching the boy, the downturned grubby face.

"I'll free thee hands if the'll promise me something."

No reply. Only the sniffling posture.

"If the'll think on the words I have to say. Think on the fact there's more truth in feelings than words. Trust thee feelings, Bobby lad."

The boy says nothing but all the same, after several more minutes of contemplation, the man removes the tights that bind the hands together.

"You're . . . you're going to kill me."

"Why would I do that?"

"You said that – about feelings. I feel that – that you're going to kill me."

"If I were going to kill thee, why would I give thee soup?"

He doesn't know the answer to this and tentatively he picks up the spoon, prodding at the soup. The man, who calls himself Mag the stupid Magician, picks up a buttered slice of bread and drops it so that its corner hangs into the bowl.

"Where are you taking me?"

"The'll see soon enough when the' gets there."

27

He is still crying as he takes a little soup, just the edge of a spoonful. Yet the soup tastes as delicious as it smells and he is starving. His stomach picks this moment to growl a reminder of just how starving he is.

4

Four days and they had found nothing. Detective Chief Inspector Sandy Woodings had suddenly stopped walking. Up to this moment he had been hurrying towards the second city centre police headquarters at Castle Hill, which housed the computers for suspect elimination, together with the offices for a proportion of senior officers, the divisional intelligence officer and the emergency switchboard. Now his hands gripped the pedestrian rail rammed into the pavement's edge, his slightly hooded eyes wandered uphill, across the four-lane highway of West Bar, congested with bumper to bumper Saturday morning traffic, to the dense jungle of streets opposite. The heart of the city was nearly all modern, the architects forced to keep to the old plan because prime city centre lots became vacated one at a time, so that even the new red brick buildings followed the organic twists of the old, taking his eyes now even higher upwards towards the jarring tall glass and concrete office blocks. The old city centre had been a rabbit warren of coral-red Georgian brick. He remembered much of it. Not the sandblasted fragment that peered out here and there now, preserved for the professional smart set. Paradise Square and the streets about the cathedral, tarted up to serve solicitors, architects and estate agents.

Four days!

He inhaled now as if to clear his mind. He was hurrying on again, across the panda crossing. During those four days a squad of detectives every bit as large as a murder squad on house to house enquiries had collected six hundred-odd statements which were at present dumped in piles on the office floor in the building behind him.

From experience, Sandy Woodings knew that those four days might as well have been four years. In a case like this they knew where they were going within twenty-four hours or else they knew they were in serious difficulties.

Four days – and we know nothing!

In the city of Liverpool a woman was peering from the windows of a metallic blue Ford Fiesta with an expression of patient intensity. The subject of her scrutiny was a small detached house. She had been watching the house for rather longer than Sandy Woodings had been gazing at the cathedral spire, a full three quarters of an hour in fact. Which was all the more surprising since the house was painfully ordinary, built from the same soot-stained red brick as the swarming old district of Kirby about it. There was something comical about the design of this house, a design common enough in these northern parts, which appeared as if it had been chopped neatly from the middle of a red brick terrace, with eighteen inches between its gable and that of the neighbour on one side and a narrow tarmac path winding past the sharp corners of the other.

The woman had now stepped out of the car and was peering into the house through its single front ground floor window.

Her appearance was different enough to arouse the curiosity of a fat middle-aged lady, laden with two shopping bags. What the fat lady saw was a woman in her early thirties, her hair cut boyishly short along her neck and the back of her head, hair indeed too uniformly black for natural until you realised that her skin was coffee-coloured and her features were half-Asian. She was wearing navy cords under a matt-black leather jacket. A man would have found her sexy, in a mildly sadistic fashion: the fat woman thought her hard-faced.

Ignoring the woman's backward glances, she walked round the side of the house and knocked gently on the back door. So very quickly, she could not have anticipated a response to her knock, she let herself in using a brand new Yale key.

The cold alone told her the house was empty.

Before anything else, she picked up the telephone and checked it was working perfectly. Only then did she remove her black leather jacket and matching gloves. She clearly intended to take her time. Under the jacket she was wearing a man's overlarge sports shirt, pulled in at the waist by a two inch brown leather belt, and under the shirt and fashionably exposed in its big open vee, an air force blue polo-neck jumper. She started her search in the bathroom.

Since the house was owned by a single man, what she was looking for would be distinctly female. She found nothing. From the bathroom, she moved into the bedroom, stopping to inspect a reproduction of Lowry's *St John's Church, Manchester*.

The print was more the subject of curiosity than interest to her and she quickly moved on to inspect the wardrobe, the chest of drawers, under the bed – extra-long, she noticed, to accommodate an exceptionally tall man. She inspected the bed itself, between the sheet and neatly folded continental quilt. Nothing struck her as at all unusual. Not even a photograph. She was plainly disappointed.

Monkish was the adjective which came to her mind: she nodded in a wry amusement when she thought of this.

In the dining kitchen she seemed very interested in the contents of the freezer. She made a mental inventory of frozen peas, oven chips, beefburgers, a two-litre tub of ice-cream, eight choc ices, four pork chops and two sliced steaks, in addition to several ready-made meals for two. *For two*, if that meant anything at all when applied to a large man with a large man's appetite. Back in the lounge, where she had deposited her leather jacket over the back of an easy chair, she sat back thoughtfully in its twin and smoked a cigarette.

Picking up the telephone and after dialling only a single digit, she spoke into it in a tone both familiar and business-like.

"Jacky here. Tell Gill – the place is dead." Her voice was most certainly not Merseyside, closer to the Home Counties than Lancashire. "Plenty of food in the freezer – but if you ask me, I'd say he's been leading us a merry dance." There followed some discussion during which she studied the modest print which decorated the wall between the tele-phone table and the door into the dining kitchen. This was a Brueghel and gradually, during the course of her conversa-tion, it dawned on her that its theme was the Parable of the Sower. It appealed to her rather more than the Lowry. She spoke once again, it seemed to the cold and empty house, after she had replaced the receiver and donned her jacket prior to leaving.

"It's a cell. This whole house is a bleeding cell."

A battery of rockets tracered the navy darkness as Sandy turned up at his former home, arriving late and carrying his box of fireworks round the back and onto the elevated patio he had built with his own hands. There was no sign of his estranged wife, Julie, and he wanted to avoid just walking into the house, so he gave each of his kids a hug and then stood with his hands in his pockets, watching two families of children cavorting round the fire.

If he had been smart, perhaps even a little selfish, he would have gone to see Josie. It was his first evening off since the start of the enquiry. Josie was nervous – she had never really got over the premature death of her husband – and she needed somebody close to her.

"How's the world treating you, Mary?" he accepted a kiss on the cheek from the woman who had once been Julie's best friend.

Mary looked momentarily surprised and then wistful, gazing down at her own brood. "What can one expect – the world is crazy, Sandy."

He laughed in tandem with the single musical note of a Catherine wheel. But he was baffled to find Mary here with her children. Mary must be controlling her loathing for Julie and Sandy wondered why. "It's a good fire," he handed over his presentation box of fireworks to the organiser, Jack, who was Mary's husband, and Julie's lover.

"Bugger of a thing!" retorted Jack, pretending the polite laugh. "Had to drench it in paraffin before it would take."

A necklace of bangs, one expensive rocket, a milk bottle stagnant with white smoke: nothing made sense tonight. The two families all together, as if it were old times.

"Always rains on bonfire night."

"Not always. It wasn't bad last year. Not as bad as this – only bitterly cold." Mary shivered exaggeratedly in order to make her point.

He liked Mary's voice, because it had such a lively banter to it: he found himself agreeing with her, remembering last year particularly well.

Julie: oh come on! She had made such an issue of inviting him here tonight and now she wasn't even here to insult him with the platonic kiss.

"I presume," enquired Mary, "that you're still searching for the little boy and that monster who took him?"

"While you're interested, perhaps you could tell me Jack's movements on the night in question?"

She whinnied with delight, at the impossibility of it, but rather wickedly. "Then surely you've made the assumption that the poor child is dead?"

"I haven't made any such assumption, Mary."

He had no real desire to talk about the hunt with Mary.

Four days and nights had been filled with it and he needed a rest. Then he caught sight of Julie out of the corner of his eye, slipping out of the side door so she could approach him and Mary from behind. She wore blue jeans under a quilted anorak with its red hood pulled firmly over her fair hair and she was carrying a tray of disposable cups containing black peas – black peas because, like Mrs Stephens, Julie was a Lancashire girl.

"How about you, Jack?"

"See to the kids first."

Sandy eyed Jack contemptuously and Jack returned a monk's purse-lipped benediction.

"Sandy?" She enquired, with wary politeness.

He manufactured a smile of his own, taking the spoon and cup and attempting to place some distance between the pair of them and Jack. Her eyes were avoiding his. She said, softly, "I want an uncontested divorce, Sandy."

His eyes picked out Jack, hurrying away towards the side entrance.

"Surely you want it as quickly and painlessly as I do?" she asked urgently, so vehemently he wondered if she was in fact angry.

He could say nothing, which probably infuriated her further.

Julie looked as if she wanted to say a good deal more but the smell of food brought the kids trailing up the steps.

"I want a hot dog," wailed Marty, their youngest daughter, dragging one leg after the other, in exaggerated fatigue. He ran his fingers through her wet hair and felt a thrill of fright, like a hand clawing at the pit of his stomach.

"Say something, for heaven's sake!"

"What did you expect me to say, Julie? You can't hurt me. That's history now."

"You don't care because you've got what you want now, haven't you?"

"What's that?"

34

"They say she's built like Bardot and just as loaded – your tramp down the Riverdale Road."

He actually laughed, at the irony of her anger. What did all of this little outburst mean? Nothing. She didn't love him. She cared about him, in that absolutely useless way a woman cares about a man she once loved. She cared about the fact she had had four children by him. But she didn't love him. So talking was a waste of breath. Anything he had to say, could say, might have said, was all a waste of breath. She needed to be angry with him to make herself feel better. A year ago, almost to the day, it had given him sleepless nights and an irritable bowel syndrome. That year had shown him he was a survivor. Julie didn't love him but Josie did – or at least she cared about him in the way a woman cared about a man, she cared about him in a sexual way, which as far as he was concerned, was the only worthwhile way. So why not try to be reasonable? He had no doubt they would end up trying to be reasonable.

"Come home early for *her* do you?" she pressed him bitterly, as he maintained his silence, and another small voice trailed past them. "Ooh, chestnuts! I can smell chestnuts – "

Mary seemed to time it, coming out of the house with a hot potato pie balanced on one outstretched hand, and when he returned his attention to Julie she had vanished. Mary cut a steaming slice of pie for Jack, who had returned with her, and then – Sandy had the impression she already knew everything that had taken place between himself and Julie – she sidled up to him, very close, and looking very nervous.

"I suppose," she watched him swallow a spoonful of black peas, "it's hard not to take your kind of work seriously?"

"Personally – is that what you're asking me, Mary?"

"Seriously and personally?" In the light of the fire he could see the muscles of her left eye twitching in a circle.

35

Fireworks again, the cheap stuff you put in the middle: rose, jasmine, cadmium yellow fountains.

He could hardly believe it was happening like this, that it could be so confusing and yet so damned ordinary – he would remember the smell of the potato pie mixed with acrid woodsmoke. "What the hell are you really up to, Mary?"

"Can't you stop all this, Sandy? For God's sake!"

Sandy Woodings realised he was more than professionally involved with the Stephens boy's kidnapping. He already suspected it at the bonfire and he knew it for certain some three weeks later.

In that time the door-to-door squads had collected over a thousand statements, taken from relatives and neighbours, local shopkeepers and postmen – even from drivers who used the road at the bottom of the slope to go to and from work.

Sandy gazed at the latest batch of one hundred, all placed in an even pile; he had brought the edge of the pile into line with the edge of his desk, with a thoughtful expression. He would not give up and when colleagues asked him why, he explained that if this character had got away with it once he would do it again, but that wasn't the real reason. The real reason was that he believed in spite of everything that the boy was still alive. That had been his gut feeling right from the beginning. Something in the reaction of those two small boys, in the way Bobby Stephens had gone with him. So who was this character? What kind of a man was he?

The image in his mind was that of a spectre, vague, a man skeletally camouflaged against the black wintry foliage. No matter how hard he thought about it, the man remained vague, out of reach. If only one of these statements could give him the slightest clue, the tiniest increment of knowledge from which he would begin to build . . .

Calling his secretary, Mrs Parks, over the intercom and

telling her he wasn't to be disturbed unless absolutely urgent, he opened the top statement and started reading . . .

A Constable Williams had taken a statement from a newspaper boy who had seen a man answering some vaguely similar description, only he was bald on top and wore an obvious wig, together with a mark across the bridge of his nose that implied he usually wore spectacles. Next in his pile was a letter sent into headquarters and addressed to himself personally from an elderly spinster, suspicious of her new neighbour, a young man whose crime appeared to be the lack of common politeness. Squeezing the bridge of his nose between his eyes, Sandy Woodings waded further into the pile, already regretting that he had insisted on reading it himself instead of the usual method, which was to allow the detectives under him to screen the pile before him.

His mind exhausted with statements, he drove back out to the Redmond district, along streets which were now achingly familiar and it seemed that the weather had taken on the role of magician because the dark afternoon had caused the streetlights to come on prematurely and now they glowed soft and buttercup yellow against the black-blue foliage and the sky was now as light as a summer morning, a pale turquoise with diaphanous puffs of wispy lead-blue breathing up out of the horizon.

Their total lack of progress was deeply worrying: he felt the skin of his scalp contract and refuse to relax again. Stepping out of his car at the spot below the slope where he judged the kidnapper had scrambled down with the boy, he felt increasingly excited by this charged air of stillness.

Here innocence had confronted evil. A man with such an intensity of emotion, his face had gone fanatically blank. So intriguingly blank that two small boys had drawn something too grotesque to be credible . . . unless the identikit picture had been an accurate portrait after all? The patina of madness, thin-faced, unemotionally staring, pale blue eyes . . .

Sandy Woodings prided himself on logic – yet now he was forced to abandon that attractive discipline. He returned to his car but he couldn't sit in it. He continued to stand by the open door and to gaze towards the curious stillness that invested the lights and the trees. Perhaps he had missed something in that first vital twenty-four hours? Eerie and beautiful at the same time: something about this scene mattered. A sexual pervert was driven by a simple if disgusting need. If that was all there was to it he need think no further . . .

But what if it really was something more unusual, more complex?

What possible motive existed, could or might exist . . . ? Something had to make sense here. God almighty! Sandy Woodings clamped his teeth in frustration, staring up into the latticework of twigs, as if they contained the message which, stupidly, he could not read.

His temples tightened so hard, it felt as if his head were gripped by a huge claw, as he imagined Mrs Stephens' face; he couldn't avoid seeing Mrs Stephens' face, the expression in her eyes when the news eventually came through – a heartbreaking discovery made by chance in some remote spot, some dog nosing in a ditch, or one of the ponds that had not as yet been searched by police frogmen.

When the car radio beeped, he appeared not to register it. He was standing absolutely still, staring up that slope, his eyes unfocused.

Then, with a sudden awakening, he had picked up the radio receiver, was bending through the car door to answer it.

"Woodings!"

"I have Sergeant Williams for you, Chief Inspector – "

He was furious with himself for daydreaming. Now he waited, faintly flushed, for Tom's voice . . .

"Something really weird, Chief."

"What on earth are you talking about, Tom?"

"It's a parcel. A parcel has been sent to Mrs Stephens."

5

She wondered if Pete had come to thinking the same about herself. This strange silence – silence she now realised must be the ultimate hallmark of strangers. Yet he did seem a stranger to her, this man she had been married to for eleven years, to whom she had borne a son. Of course Margaret Stephens was well aware that her mind was labouring under the most intense distortion of stress. Yet what she was seeing was true. His face had acquired a tense pallor, the skin appeared to have thickened, to have wrinkled into folds which hitherto had only been hinted at in a smile or a frown, and his eyes were red-rimmed, the lids thickened and heavy and the eyeballs themselves draped in pink veins. She had found herself noticing all this with a curious flat interest, Margaret Stephens, keeper of secrets, while inside herself a large part was irretrievably lost, while pain had over three weeks contracted and condensed like a black cinder at the core of her and then started to ignite, to burn and glow, as anger.

"We have to pull ourselves together," his voice said. "Here we are, Maggie, love – " Holding her overcoat, lifting it about the shoulders, so she could stand and be robed for the waiting police car, not as royalty but as a child.

It had affected them very differently. Obsessional attention to detail, to the breaking of a single crust for the birds in the morning, to the sewing on of his own buttons on even his oldest gardening shirts, to the making of the smokeless fuel fire in the turn-of-century grate they had thought so fashionable and cosy, the ash packed into plastic bags and carted off at seven each morning to the dustbin, the hearth raked and then swept spotlessly clean. And then, in the evenings, his constant pacing about the downstairs of the house.

Stop it, Pete! Will you stop following me about! As if he were expecting her to faint or have a fit or worse, until she indicated that he was driving her mad with it.

Fussing impotently about her and about the house. Insisting after the first week that he went back to the school, where they were absolutely astonished to see him, because he felt that order must be maintained, or that he must show them, these colleagues who regarded him as a nice man, a man who would always remain a deputy head because of what a nice man he was, or possibly – she only now realised this possibility – because he had to separate himself from his wife, Maggie. To separate himself from Maggie, who was reacting strangely and aggressively, and hardly talked to him for hours on end, but insisted on staring at the bedraggled runner beans on their cane skeleton through the back window, or who tramped for hours outside the house in the damp and miserable weather.

"Please – please, don't fuss me."

So it was, with the baffled rage of recollection, that her right index finger palpated her lower lip, as with her head rigidly inclined towards the car window, away from Pete, that she awoke into another dream, or nightmare, or reality, in which the police driver swung the car round the great roundabout and onto the parkway, which would take them to the M1 motorway.

The doctor had given her 10 milligram capsules but they hadn't been strong enough and now she took two capsules together, which was twenty milligrams, and if that wasn't enough, she had learnt the trick of biting into the capsules and swallowing them quickly, which was what she did now when that thought was yawning to devour her. That was the forbidden thought, the thought she would not think, that horrible, unbelievable, vicious cruel thought . . .

"Mrs Stephens. It's Bobby. Bobby is missing, Mrs Stephens." That memory of little Christopher, with his serious face, and the slight stammer, as he stood at her door and he refused even to come in. Little Christopher, with his blond hair so neatly parted, and that small frowning red face, with the mental effort of finding the right words, of finding the words which terrified him and made him stammer even as his mouth pronounced them completely out of character. Big words, forbidden words for him, unbelievable words for him too. "A man took Bobby, Mrs Stephens."

And all that waiting. Three weeks of waiting. And nothing. Nothing at all. Absolutely nothing. But now there was something –

Even the policeman somehow seemed different. Even he seemed to exude a different kind of aura. The police too had been humiliated by this wall of silence, this unbearable emptiness. Curiously she saw the trees, the trees with their last few leaves, the elder with its branches bare and only the fading arrowheads of bindweed alive in the wind-blown branches.

She dreaded this journey. She dreaded this sitting in a confined space for perhaps an hour and a quarter unable to move, just the monotony of a motorway journey, with a clear blue winter's sky and the overnight frost now only just melting about the grass and the remaining straggly leaves. At home she would have been able to do small jobs. Get up in the morning, pick up the post and papers after the police had checked them. Open the curtains throughout the downstairs house. Put the kettle on. Thinking of course. Always thinking. Like why had she never gone out and found even a part-time job, this woman who had three grade As at A-level and the first year, if without exams, at Birmingham University.

Why had she never even attempted to find a job?

She, Margaret Stephens, such a keeper of secrets that her own heart was a tangled skein that she herself had no hope of understanding. Sort out the washing – Pete's washing – and ironing. Some days pluck up the courage to try some shopping and counter the stares of sympathy and curiosity. Glad it wasn't them. So why did it have to be her? Why did it have to be her Bobby?

The violent start of emotion in her caused her eyes to moisten and she jerked her head round to stare through the window. Steel mills and industrial waste had given way to black stone farmhouses and new villages in pale yellow brick. Why wasn't anybody talking?

So why had she never tried to get a job?

Why – when she was hardly stretched with just Bobby and Pete to look after? And Pete, to grant him his due, had rarely pressed the subject. Why, when she had even considered it the aching weakness would resurrect itself in her bones and cause her to put her coat on and go for a walk. It was a feeling the opposite of claustrophobia, the sudden intense desire to breathe open air, to inhale deeply for several minutes while the electric shocks ran down her arms into the very tips of her fingers and the jellyfish neuralgia invaded her thighs.

She had not been able to face a job. That she now admitted while at the same time she could hardly claim it was an explanation.

But now she realised with a terrible dread how similar that feeling was to the mind numbing floating anxiety she felt when she handled Bobby's clothes. When, as every day, the need grew in her – a need she would resist for as long as possible – and then she climbed the stairs with leaden legs and pushed closed the door to his bedroom, and then she knelt down on the carpet by his bed and placed her head on its side on the blankets and her fingers touched and fondled the karate style pyjamas, black with red collars and piping, neatly folded under the pillow. Smelling his little boy smell from his clothes. Willing him life. And always that same question then, in his bedroom decorated with a hundred colour pictures, mainly of Sheffield Wednesday, but also Liverpool, Spurs, and England. Would he ever wear those pyjamas again? Would he?

A parcel – they had intercepted something important and that something had been a parcel.

Had she suffered all the horror there was to be suffered yet? Her breath shuddered as it left her open mouth. This nervous debility, once started, was impossible to shake off. Staring out once more through the side window – how bitterly cold it looked, the frost staying all day now on the northernmost inclines of fields, behind walls, in the shadows of houses.

Wouldn't it be better just to know? A horrible whisper – a whisper from the darkest reaches of her mind that nauseated her: *but you will have to face it. Better to know now. A deliverance* . . .

They were moving through town traffic, pleasant sandstone or maybe limestone two-storey streets. There was a security guard on the gates of the laboratory and the director himself stood at the entrance to meet them.

And then there was Chief Inspector Woodings inside, coming to touch her shoulder, as Pete had once again put his arm about her, shepherding her along a modern corridor with plate glass partitioning behind which she could see men and women working with starchily clean white coats.

There was coffee now on a table in front of her but she hardly heard the director's kind reassurances because a ticking in both her ears had become a low-pitched roaring. She mustn't faint. Oh, how stupid if she were to faint now.

The parcel had to be real because they were talking about it, in earnest voices, their words carefully enunciated, as if she were some legal expert and they must get their meaning absolutely and perfectly clear. A parcel – yes, yes, she knew all about that. She knew that was what all this was about. Something they wanted Pete and Maggie to look at first: something *first*. So they had more than one thing. But her eyes merely found those of the director, and in the background, Mr Woodings watched her, she was aware of his watching her with absolute concentration.

And then it seemed so simple and yet completely and utterly heartbreaking. It was just an ordinary brown bag which a man wearing a white coat had placed on the table in front of them. The man, with careful long fingers, was reaching into the bag and sliding out something wrapped in polythene, explaining all the while that the polythene was so that she could touch it, examine it, without interfering with the tests that remained to be performed on it.

The roaring was back in her ears and she could hear a child's voice, which was probably Christopher's, but she took no notice. For a moment she was no longer aware of anything, not of the men who were observing her, not of Pete, whose arm had tightened about her shoulders, not of the little piping voice inside her which proclaimed, "A man took Bobby, Mrs Stephens," not caring a jot about the sweeping restless burning electricity which had invaded her entire being from the head downwards, which had taken hold of her chest and was clenching her heart and lungs in a clamp that was powerful enough to destroy her.

Her voice came from her numbed lips as if she were ordering it to do so from some remote distance. It was only a little shaky, an extraordinarily calm voice, perhaps a little lower than her usual voice.

"It's Bobby's trainer."

6

"What makes you so sure it's Bobby's trainer, Mrs Stephens?"

"I know it."

"Let's talk about the make of trainer. We must think very specifically, make, colour – "

"Don't you think I know my own child's trainer, Mr Woodings?"

"Under these circumstances, the mind can play tricks."

"My mind is perfectly clear – rational."

For an instant anger flooded her, anger directed towards this tall man with dark hair, steady blue eyes. She resented how he felt empowered to hold her eyes directly. She resented, in that sudden furious instant, the very fact that evil to this man was not incarnate but somehow mundane and human. Evil was to be trapped by its very human frailty: a clue in a word, a carelessly dropped button, a fingerprint.

Then she looked from Woodings to the window, and from the window to the sergeant, Williams, in whose more gentle eyes, right now, the light, as clear as a summer's day only seventy degrees colder, fell onto the irises. They seemed reddish and yellowish at the same time, so that the overall effect was a very delicate orange.

"We would like to know where the trainers were purchased. If you still have a receipt for the purchase."

"I don't know." She jerked her gaze towards Pete, who shook his head.

"My mother bought them."

"This question is important, Mrs Stephens. And I would address it to you too, Mr Stephens. There may be something personal, a link, a personal link, to the kidnapping. In the three and a half weeks since then, you must have gone over it many times – discussed it between you. Has anything come of this? Have you any more idea now than you had at the time?"

She observed Woodings again, he had become as much an object for close scrutiny as she felt herself in his eyes. He interested her – for the first time as a person rather than the policeman he undoubtedly prided himself on being – in a curious sense of loneliness. Here she saw him for the first time amongst his colleagues and that toughness she had half noticed earlier now that of a man jostling with his own peers in what must be a perpetual power struggle. If he was alone, maybe he was also on her side?

"There was something else in the parcel. That's why you're asking me these questions."

He was polite but insistent. "You haven't answered."

"We'd have told you if we had come up with even the slightest idea."

"There has been nothing, no contact with a friend. The slightest suspicion from anybody – perhaps somebody even giving you his theory . . ."

"What else was in that parcel, Mr Woodings?" Peter demanded.

"A note, Mr Stephens."

"Then for God's sake, let us see the thing."

"The note was written out by hand and then torn into fragments."

She was staring at him now: Margaret Stephens was staring into his blue eyes, while all the time he continued to hold hers, his head slightly tilted, his hands at ease lying in front of him on the white Formica top of the table that separated them. They knew something. For God's sake what did they know that they were not telling her?

47

"A note," she uttered huskily. "You've received a note from Bobby's kidnapper?"

"We're putting the fragments together, Mrs Stephens. It must be done carefully to preserve whatever forensic information we can glean from it."

"Words? You mean he has written a message in words? To whom? I mean, to whom was this note addressed?"

"It was addressed, to you, Mrs Stephens."

She saw, as if under a magnifying glass, the broken veins in Peter's cheek as he called for the woman and ordered teacakes and a pot of tea for two. *Tea for two!* She was both amazed and revolted by the ordinariness of the event. Midday tea and scones in a small, spotless and colourful café in the centre of the small town, in a side street at right angles to the cheerful main street of shops built of pink sandstone decorated with festive lights and Christmas decorations.

Tea at thirty pence. Teacake, toasted, at precisely the same. Twice sixty pence: one pound twenty pence. Her mind worked in isolation to her heart. Her mind showed itself for the computer it was, gazing at other plates, seeing the food in front of excessively fat faces, the food those faces should be denying themselves, yet were the least likely to deny themselves. She hated them.

She hated the certainty in their hearts with regard to their children. Why had it been her child, why her Bobby?

"They know something," she whispered, and instantly she saw his eyes recoil with the hope in her whisper.

"They'll discuss it with us when we get back. They're piecing the note together, Maggie. You heard what Woodings said about it."

"He said nothing. Do you think they haven't already put the pieces at least loosely together. Woodings has already read the note. He already knows what it says. So why hasn't he just told us?"

"It probably doesn't say much. We shouldn't build up our hopes."

"Don't be stupid. That note is a message. It was addressed to me. They intercepted the parcel and it was on its way to me."

He was still frightened perhaps. This morning, at five thirty, Peter had woken up in a nightmare. Describing a large petrol-driven Qualcast lawnmower tearing up a small estate road, crashing into cars, he had declared in a horrified and shaky voice that when he, in his dream, had taken the mower into the house, he had realised instantly that the machine was possessed. Then he found the room full of friends and neighbours and he had exorcised the demon in their presence, which had emerged from the mower in a stream of navy powdery smoke, in which three very tiny but brilliant points of light moved sinuously round and about.

Peter had always been prone to nightmares. He dreamt in technicolour and saw everything with a fantastically de-tailed eye. He should have been an artist instead of a mathematician.

She was thinking how Bobby's loss had brought out all that had been papered over between them. She tried to think about those tensions but she couldn't concentrate above the smell of toasting teacakes. A surge of aggressive-ness had to be controlled or she might have said something she would have regretted. Yet, it seemed to her, there were cracks you could paper over for a hundred years by employing kindness and consideration. Silence spoke vo-lumes and she did not respect herself at this moment in time for her use of silence.

"Our love will count in the long time ahead for us both, Maggie." He spoke the words quietly, calmly, and they were all the more astonishing for their being totally unexpected.

Yet she realised that he must have read something of

what lay in her mind and she was swamped by her sense of shame.

She was certain now that she had been right all along. Oh, she felt its weight about her heart now as she held onto Pete's arm, walking along that same calm and lightly furnished corridor, with its internal windows into the laboratories filled with white-coated scientists. It expanded to fill her chest, this fearful dread, as she read it in every eye, in the restrained gestures, in the single warning from Chief Inspector Woodings, that what she was about to read would shock her. Even at her first sight of it, what should be ordinary, a single sheet of paper written over in black felt tip pen, seemed very far from ordinary. Invested between two transparent sheets of Perspex, it had the entire table top all to itself. And in her throat the palpitations reached a crescendo as her feet, which no longer registered the floor under her, gave way and she sat down before it. Yet for a moment she could not read it. A single sheet of paper, it appeared transformed by a diversity of interlacing cracks into something beyond the ordinary. The hand in writing it had emphasised its points so hard the pen had transfixed the thick cheap paper and the effort of having to be pieced together added greatly to its strangeness, the craquelured whole radiated an altogether deeper thrill of terror to the dark emptiness behind her eyes.

She read it agonisingly slowly, the words not at all registering, and then she read again, and then again, for the third time, as the roaring established itself in her ears and the room and the gathered people in it, Pete, who stood by her right shoulder, the two detectives Woodings and Williams, the director of the laboratory, who above all appeared to gaze on her with kindness: all now were curiously whisked away, to some distant cube of night outside this time and dimension. As she read it now for the fourth time . . .

I'VE GOT HIM, MAGGIE!
I'VE GOT BABY BLUE
HE'S MINE NOW, YOU'LL
    NEVER FIND HIM

        NEVER!

LOOK BACK, MAGGIE
STUDY THE EDGE OF DARKNESS

    LEARN FROM IT

HOW PAIN CLEANSES

ARTFUL JACK KILLS TITANS

. . . "Well, Mrs Stephens?"

She was making struggling noises in her throat so that he waited perhaps fifteen seconds and then repeated his question.

"I . . . I don't know. I don't understand."

Chief Inspector Woodings was insistent. "He knows you, Mrs Stephens."

"I don't know how he is. I don't know who or what he is."

"Think, Mrs Stephens. Think very hard. Read it through again, take your time, but think about it."

"I don't know who he is. I don't . . ." Her head was slowly shaking from side to side.

"Read what he has to say."

She was reading it again anyway. She wasn't so much reading the words as devouring them.

"What's going on, Mrs Stephens?"

"I understand what he is saying. I understand that perfectly well. What he is deliberately . . ."

"What *is* he intending, Mrs Stephens?" There were tears in her eyes now, tears blocking out the shock wave of that terrible communication, which nevertheless in its fragmented shimmering malice continued to expand inside, to swell out and tear apart her entire universe.

"He's telling me . . . telling me . . . he's alive. That's what he's saying, don't you see? He's saying that my Bobby is still alive. He is. He's telling me my Bobby is still alive."

7

The first Bobby saw of him earlier that morning was a huge shape, dragging noisily across one of the windows. One of those windows on the front: big windows, with round tops. That was when he knew that today would be different.

He had arrived when it was still dark, waking Bobby up when he dragged something heavy into the room. And then he had lit the paraffin stove so that a glow came out of the old fireplace, lighting up the big room like a small light at one end of a massive cave. In the dark Bobby actually screamed. Then when the oil lamp came on, he saw the reason for the heavy sound of dragging. He had brought a red bottle full of gas and attached it with a piece of black rubber tube to two gas rings.

Now, Bobby realises, as his mind starts to work through the terror, he can cook things up: beans and soup and a frying pan and things like that, instead of just hot coffee and Cuppasoup. And that's only the beginning of what frightens Bobby. But he didn't see that right away because it was pitch dark. All he saw was the shape when it moved across one of the windows. And the flame from the cigarette lighter, followed by the coughing sound of the paraffin in the stove when he lit it.

He's coming here to stay! Oh, cripes, he's coming to stay!

He has hardly slept all night long. It was so cold and there was rain tapping against the roof and against the window panes, like a nightmare trying to get in. Squatting on the floor in front of a brand new frying pan, tiny, silvery gleaming in the half light of dawn, this new fear is worse than any of the million others which have clawed at his heart since he was brought here. Outside now that same rain, that rain of nightmares, is drumming steadily and in his mind it troubles him as he performs his job, with shaky fingers – to watch the two eggs which are frying in the pan. It's the first time they have had anything as fantastic as fried eggs in all of the time he has been here, and he has no idea at all of how long that has been.

He feels sick from hunger for one of those two eggs frying. Just the smell of the frying oil and the sizzling of the frying and he almost pukes from slavering down the front of his yukky-smelling clothes.

Behind him, the man who calls himself Mag the Magician, is standing with his legs apart and stripped to the waist in the air which, outside the circle of the oil stove, is so cold you can see your breath and your skin goes straight into goose bumps as you take anything off. Yet that strange creepy man is already started on his exercises. He has those big heavy clubs made of blue plastic with a yellow circle about the top of the handle, and he is doing exercises by swinging them about his head, one hand in front and one hand behind, and then slowly moving the wrists, the elbows, the shoulders, and so on, so that his muscles are standing out hideously strong.

Those hands! He's got really weird fingers!

Awful hands. Like a ghoul's fingers. Long and thicker at the ends, like drumsticks, and really battered with horrible thick and crinkly nails. The closest thing Bobby can think of about those nails is that they are like the cockle shells you pick up on the beach at Filey. Now he darts his eyes, just for a moment, to signal to the man that the eggs are ready. And he picks up the glance instantly. Those eyes gaze back at him, silvery grey, they pierce right through his skin, those awful grey eyes, which must be the most horrible and cruel eyes in all the world.

"Time for breakfast, Humpty Dumpty." The man comes across so he is standing right over him. The music from the cassette player is still playing, "Come all without, come all within, you'll not see nothing like the mighty Quinn." That big bony face is sweating so much there are big drops hanging from his wet beard. He takes the burst egg, leaving Bobby the good one, both cooked hard as stones, and he puts his egg between two slices of brown bread without butter, showing Bobby what he is expected to do with his own. Bobby takes all the courage he has in the world and even refuses to bite into his sandwich because he has to ask:

"What about my mum and dad?"

His voice is like a quavery reed, coming out queer and high from the top of his head. The man's eyes continue to watch Bobby, angry with him for not eating his sandwich.

"What about her – what about my mum?"

"Your mam knows I've got you." The man cracks another two eggs on the edge of the frying pan and drops them into it, swirling it about with his eyes hardly leaving Bobby's.

"You . . . you told her?"

"That's right. I told her."

"You told her I was all right?"

"I told her you were okay and I've got you."

Tears just jump up into Bobby's eyes and he can't help them just at the mention of his mum. But he's not really crying, which is to say he's trying hard not to cry. And he takes a slow trembly bite out of his sandwich. "How did you tell her?"

"I wrote her a note."

"What kind of note?"

"A note."

"How do I know you're telling me the truth?"

All of a sudden the rain has stopped: there is an awesome silence, during which the man is staring wildly. The man has come up so close that Bobby can smell the soured-butter smell of his sweat. In a welter of panic, Bobby tries to turn to the eggs in the pan, he touches the handle of the pan with his fingers, but his hands are shaking so bad, he can't even hold it.

The man pulls back slightly. His voice is icy cold and very deep. "Today, we're going to have a look outside."

"Outside?" His thoughts veer frantically to this new danger. "We're going outside? Why are we going outside?" His hand jerks down and rubs unthinkingly where his skin was sore from his ankles being tied.

"Stop picking at it. Go on. Gobble your sandwich. You're going to need your strength, as we both are."

He brought clothes about a week ago. Brown tweedy old trousers, which he cut the lower legs off and now he makes Bobby put them on, tucking in the six inches where they overlap about the waist and holding it with a big safety in. Next comes a crumpled navy full-grown man's shirt, a green and grey pullover and the jacket Bobby was wearing when he was kidnapped. Finally the black Wellingtons, which are only about two sizes too big, and inside which Bobby has to put on two pairs of socks.

Descending the stairs, two tall storeys and across two landings, they emerge from the building, and then he takes him round the left side where there is a small place alongside the main building. And it is only then, only after he has been outside for several minutes, that Bobby's panting lungs believe it. Out of the cave! His heart is turning over and over and over. He feels so jittery, he couldn't run even if he got the chance. And he thinks of his mum and dad's warnings . . .

Never talk with strange men. Never go with strange men. Because strange men . . . because strange men . . . Terror brings up a small vomit that tastes of egg. Never talk to strange men. Never . . . never . . . Oh, God! Help me, Dad. Please, help me!

So his eyes are all bubbling up with tears again even though this is the first time he has ever looked round. That day, when they left the house, there was a lot of driving round and round and Bobby was brought here in the middle of the night. And that's how it feels – free. Just to let him see it. Just to let him walk on grass where it has just rained. And then . . . He doesn't even dare look up at this man with the silver eyes. Mad silver eyes . . . staring, always staring . . . In that moment he doesn't know what he is doing. There is a darkness that suddenly rises up from the wet ground to the top of his head and his mouth opens all by itself, his mouth opens wide in a long quavering moan.

"That's enough of that. Stop that!" The man grabs his shoulder with a firm rough hand and guides him into the yard behind the back of the building. Here are the woods, the land sloping upwards into them, and through two gateposts they walk, almost immediately, over what must be a bridge although it is nearly flat, under which a busy stream scuttles. Through the gateposts a drystone wall, made of big rough stones, covered in slimy green fungus, carries on for a while and then becomes tumbled down and up ahead he feels rather than sees that it must just disappear away altogether. The way a small boy can disappear. The path is ankle deep in brown oak leaves and the ferns over the tumbled down wall are a brilliant golden, in the middle of which splashes the bright liveliness of bramble leaves, still as fresh and green as summer. Through eyes stinging with tears, Bobby gazes on the cold beauty of a sea of ferns and brambles, he stares wistfully and hopelessly. *They take away kids . . . and . . .* Without thinking, he puts his fingers, red and slightly burning with cold, into the moist brilliant moss in the cracks between the top stones, where freezing water oozes out, and it is like the condemned man's last treat, the way the cracks between the stones glitter like lodes of diamonds.

"What do they tell you at school? What sort of things do they tell you that would mean anything here?" Mag the Magician asks him softly.

And Bobby feels that awful soft fluttery weakening of his guts, he feels that faint thrilling weakening from his leaking bowel jump right up into his heart, as the man takes his hand in his, forces his unwilling hand into that huge deformed paw. The man makes him walk along next to him, holding his hand.

His voice is the anguished howl of his protesting soul. "Why did you do it? Why did you pick me?"

"A solid and sensible lad, like you – you wouldn't believe me even if I told you."

Trudging on, walking into eternity . . . tearing his feet up out of the mud, letting them slurp back, his tongue licking nervously against his drawn lips. Horses must come along here because he can see a horseshoe sticking up out of the ground, just under his foot. They are just coming down to some big stones, across where the stream is a lot wider but not as deep. It is a weedy lake, and the stones are covered with a snotty green scum so that, wearing his clown's boots and big ballooned trousers, he has to totter across with his hands held wide out like a tightrope walker.

"Why did you pick on me?" his voice is querulous, missing his mum and close to tears, as he stares down into the water.

"To cheat time, Little Boy Blue."

Those eyes also stare down with a mad glaring intensity into the water, beyond the rounded chestnut-coloured stones on the bottom, the smooth, filmy grey surface. Bobby would never have thought that water could be dusty on its surface, yet now he sees it, and he would never have thought that, not without staring at it for several minutes. But there he sees dust, like a very old, constantly changing, mirror; and he sees the reflection of himself against the huge shadow of the man who will murder him here in this wood and Bobby feels roasting all over the skin of his face and there is a sweat forming on the hot skin which trickles in big salty globules into the corners of his eyes and his mouth.

"Why do you want to kill me?"

The magician is looking down at him with those strange too-kind eyes. Big grey eyes, so Bobby can hardly bear it. So he turns and grits his teeth and finds somehow he has picked up a decaying branch. It breaks under the crush of his clenching fingers. The bark squirms under his grip, a mummy's skin, ungluing from the underlying bones and tendons. He feels the scraps of bark unpeel into the palm of his hand, he feels the skin of his palm burn from something . . . something revolting it has left behind . . .

The man stares down at the fainted boy. Only for a moment does the man's voice remain so icy cold. In that moment, his words appear to come from somewhere deeper than human lungs. "Life is a straight thread, with a beginning and an end. That's what they want us to believe, Bobby lad." Suddenly he is shouting. He is roaring, turning round and round, crushing the mud into a circle with his boots. "That's what you bastards tell us. That's what you want us to believe. But I'll prove you wrong. I'll bend your needle!"

8

There was a sour foretaste of adrenalin in his mouth when, newly arrived at headquarters, Sandy took the stairs rather than the lift and as usual two at a time. Tom was waiting for him on the second floor landing, leaning backwards against a windowledge.

As they walked, slowly, along the corridor towards Superintendent Barker's office, Tom told him about a message taken by switchboard during the lunch hour.

"It might be nothing at all," he cleared his throat confidingly, "but Georgy already knows about it and you know how Georgy likes to play games. Something happened about a year ago in Bolton, when the Stephens lad was staying with his grandmother. It's all very vague but the grandmother thinks an approach may have been made."

"What do you mean, an approach?"

"Some man may have tried to grab Bobby Stephens when he was with some pal of his own age."

"An attempt at kidnapping!" Sandy stopped walking altogether a moment to digest this new information. "And Bolton – did you say this happened in Bolton in Lancashire?"

"That's right."

"And Mrs Stephens herself came from there? She was born there, wasn't she?"

"I think so – " Tom looked puzzled. "I mean, yes, I think she was."

Sandy had suddenly taken hold of Tom's arm. It was beginning all right. His gambler's heart was telling him that now it really was beginning. "So what have we done? Was there any report at the time?"

"Nothing at all, as far as I can make out. Something the grandmother just remembered in the light of the kidnapping."

"Have you contacted the local force?"

"We've only just got the information. We haven't as yet done anything."

Sandy had started to walk again, much faster. "Thanks, Tom."

They entered the office, single file, Sandy taking the chair to the right of the window, Tom sitting close to the door, warily. Georgy was wearing his early morning face, complete with lower eyelids swollen enough to push them away from the bulbous eyeballs so that the space in between was forced to fill up with a thick film that resembled a mucousy saliva.

"Did our Jack-in-the-box lick the adhesive paper on the wrappings?" Georgy asked him, accepting a huge mug of unsweetened tea from his secretary and placing it next to his pipe on the tobacco-scorched surface of his desk.

Sandy felt his debt of gratitude to Tom as he murmured, "There was no trace of saliva."

"So we have sweet fanny adams really."

"Except for oil smudges on the wrapping paper, a thumbprint on the note, and of course the words – not to mention the fact that he found it necessary in the first place to send the parcel."

"Words!" Georgy put power into the expletive grunt. "We can't even be sure about the galoshes."

"The trainer, Georgy. The mother recognised it."

"But we circulated the details. We showed pictures on television."

We told him her name: we told him in the papers and on

the television news. He said, softly, "The right size. Everything about it. We matched the make and fibres at the shop where she bought the trainers. And a mother's certainty. Georgy."

Looking like the older Orson Welles in his seediest of roles, Georgy made a soft grinding noise with the unlit pipe in his mouth, that orang-utan's jaw chewing on more than the ebony handle, and then he clattered it down onto the surface of the desk.

"A thumbprint is useless. The oil could be misleading because the wrapping isn't new. The words could have been deliberately designed to make fools of us." He inhaled, like a vacuum cleaner, then added an uncounted number of sweeteners before taking a connoisseur's swig from his tea.

Sandy Woodings saw Margaret Stephens sitting opposite him, across the corner of the spotless Formica-topped surface at the forensic science laboratory. His eyes were holding hers directly. Her eyes were curiously light-toned eyes for brown, as a result of the direct light falling on them. They appeared strangely yellow, almost golden, subtle and intricate, like the most precious antique gold filigree.

We must have told him: anybody could have guessed that Margaret would become Maggie.

He spoke thoughtfully. "He referred to Mrs Stephens by name."

"So?" Georgy had different eyes entirely from Margaret Stephens. Dwarf's suspicious eyes in a giant's heavily jowelled and double-chinned, red face.

Again Sandy paused. He saw the woman shaking her head. As she did so, he discovered in her face a sense of inner stubbornness – an iron strength? Now that was surprising, wasn't it? It had certainly baffled him at the time. A bird-like alertness in that delicate pointed chin, the big alert eyes, the pursed widish mouth, the hair, with strands much lighter than the overall brown, curling impishly under the right hand angle of her jaw.

Withholding something perhaps? Perhaps not even realising that she was withholding? "Perhaps he knows – or knew – her personally."

Georgy pounced. "Does she say that?"

"She denies it."

"A mother whose only child has been kidnapped – you'd think she'd open her own jugular to help us."

"She seems capable – an intelligent woman. But there is something about her, Georgy. I'm not sure. Maybe there is somebody and she doesn't realise who it is. It might still be someone she knows."

"Too bloody vague by half."

"There's something odd about this kidnapping, from the very start. A man kidnaps a child. He deliberately shows himself. He leaves us two witnesses." Sandy had made a fist and was bringing it down with precise deliberation on the opposite side of the desk to Georgy. "That's what I'm getting at. Showing himself – and then the note. Something odd. Personal. That's what I wonder, Georgy. I see it as something personal. As if he knew the boy, knew the family."

"But according to the other kids, Bobby Stephens treated the man as a stranger."

"Maybe he looked different. Perhaps he hadn't seen him in a long time? He went with him, Georgy. Why the hell – "

Georgy inched suspiciously closer and Sandy knew what he was thinking. He was thinking exactly what he himself was thinking. *Whatever we say, he called her Maggie. In the note he called her Maggie.* Georgy growled, "I'm not buying that. What about the parcel? He posted it here in the city?"

"He must live here in the city. He knows his way around. He must know the neighbourhood of the kidnapping like the back of his hand."

Turning his mug through ninety degrees on the desk surface, Georgy then suddenly walloped the desk with his pipe. "No. It's ludicrous. Out of all sense of proportion."

"Now listen to me. Let's make a supposition. We know that he really did mean the parcel to reach Mrs Stephens. Now he knows that the parcel was intercepted by us. It's been on the news and in the papers. Two weeks ago, more than two weeks ago. I feel some kind of pattern emerging, Georgy. There *is* a pattern and he realises that the pattern isn't quite working out as he wants it. He's feeling baulked. Yet, suppose that the pattern means something important to him. I feel something instinctive, Georgy: something from inside him, something vital, something that must be ongoing. Maybe it's so important to him it seems a matter of life-and-death to him. The right change must occur at the right time. He's taken great risks – it means everything to him. He feels he must get his message through to Mrs Stephens."

"Since when have you become a psychoanalyst, Sandy?"

"Since I had a word with Professor Lipmann."

"So – what did that old fart have to say – laugh that mad cackle of his and say it's the police who need the treatment?"

"I'm telling you what he said."

"Forget it. It's not nearly enough."

"I've just organised a twenty-four hour watch on the Stephens' house, which will cover the scene of crime too."

"You're very generous with my manpower."

"I need your support, Georgy."

Georgy's face looked at its most cunning, or at least he allowed cunning to show, for the briefest of moments, before realisation hit him. Sandy had no idea how he realised, but Georgy had the best instinct for wickedness that Sandy had ever encountered. The superintendent's voice was couched in a whisper. "So – you know about the call from the grandmother in Bolton."

"I've just heard. It may be nothing but we'll look into it."

"Well get on with it then. Let's see a bit of proper investigation instead of all this instinct and hunches."

9

Peter Stephens was increasingly worried about his wife, Margaret. At first it had been understandable. Shock had been the term for that. Shock, profound depression – and outrage. Yes, even outrage. But there had suddenly been this change in her. Quite suddenly. And it had left him feeling bewildered. That coming on top of his own state of shock over the loss of his son. So bewildering, so incomprehensible, that it all boiled over when they arrived in Bolton.

"So what the hell are they up to?"

"They're going over what happened again. I don't know. The police must know what they're doing, Pete." Margaret Stephens knew exactly how her husband felt and she also understood perfectly why he felt that way. But she couldn't help him. She couldn't even help herself.

"I mean to say, a year ago. If it happened a year ago, why on earth didn't your mother tell us about it?"

She was staring down the enormously wide boulevard which had evolved from Crook Street. The old houses on the corner were gone, the railway bridge, the British Queen pub.

He persisted. "She never said a word about it. What did she think she was doing?"

"She didn't understand, Pete. Please don't go upsetting her. Who knows what garbled story she received. She probably didn't believe a word of what the kids must have said about it."

Margaret Stephens, keeper of secrets. Secrets which had become so immense, so ponderously heavy, they were crushing the marrow in her bones.

Because, you see, Pete, it all began here. Yes – yes! Here in Bolton. Isn't that laughable, so very unlikely? Secrets, Pete – such terrible secrets that I must become my own mistress. Because so much depends on it, you see.

LOOK BACK, MAGGIE. Well, she was here now. She was looking back. She was noticing how little by little it had happened: that was the way the changes had taken place in the town. Changes that had once been important to her. They had been important, very important, hadn't they? Small haemorrhages. Oh, for God's sake, who cared? Nobody. Nobody cared. On the contrary, most people were in favour of it all. Who wouldn't swap an old terrace for a nice new house with central heating and a bathroom? And the new market hall – that looked very promising indeed. *But it once mattered to you, didn't it, Maggie?* Yes, yes – oh, damn you, yes! She had brought a hand up to cup her mouth with a growing mortification.

"What's the matter?" he sighed, standing and waiting for her to recover.

"They're doing their best, aren't they? Trying to improve things for everybody?"

"What are you talking about, Maggie, love?"

"If you destroy something, if you really go out of your way to wipe it all out, then there must be . . . be hate, mustn't there? We all hated the old mill-town image, at the very least subconsciously."

"Hate? Hated what exactly?"

"Bolton. The real old Bolton."

"Oh, come on now, love. We're talking about a town. A place where people live and go to work."

If only it were that simple! If only . . . She was haunted by the note, that crazy, fissured note, as she had been haunted by it every waking hour of the day since she had first set eyes on it. LOOK BACK, MAGGIE. STUDY THE EDGE OF DARKNESS. The panic that had frozen her to her chair on that occasion had never really left her. It surged back, time and time again, in monstrous waves. She wanted to keep moving because walking helped. They had walked the length of the new Crook Street and were facing Trinity Church. There was talk of converting it into flats for old people. Nobody to go to church any more. They had knocked down all of the old houses that surrounded it.

A street or two, a mill, a church. *All right. I can see it. I am looking. What do you expect me to do about it?* And the answering echo chuckled maliciously as it spoke what she already knew. *Save Your Son. Look, Maggie. Go Back And Look. And save your son.*

And explain? Oh, but just give me the chance to talk . . . to explain.

"Just look at what's really happening, Pete. Just look and tell me that we haven't gone right over the top."

"I don't understand you, Maggie. We've come here because somebody may have tried to take Bobby from a park here and all you want to do is ramble on about old Bolton."

She refused the proffered arm and walked on alone. Past Trinity Street Station, which was in the process of becoming another casualty, and she was aware that she resented him now. It wasn't a fair resentment, not fair at all and yet she could no longer bear the slightly protuberant hay-feverish eyes, the rounded shoulders, a Yuppie failure, his hands in his pockets. And yes, because he seemed so typical now of them all over these past twenty years: so prepared to stand in judgment, too ready to force the changes.

"I can't explain, Pete, but I know there is a connection."

"A connection?"

"With Bobby." Her lips then turned in, just controlled. Her left hand clenched to hide it from him, as she tried hard to find a suitable evasion, something less than an outright lie. "Once I was part of a group of people who cared about what was happening here. There was a lot about this old town that was unique. When you live in it, when you're so surrounded by it, it's difficult perhaps to appreciate just how unique it all is. And the destruction has been so widespread . . . so total. As if we were somehow ashamed . . ."

"What possible connection could there be with Bobby?"

She shook her head violently. "I'm fed up with being reasonable. You get nowhere being reasonable. This is what you get from being reasonable, Pete. I feel the same sense of loss, of death – it's as if my grandmother had died." She inhaled deeply, closed her eyes and stopped walking for a moment.

"I don't want to talk about it, Maggie. I don't care a bloody jot. Just the demolition of a dirty legacy of the Industrial Revolution," he spoke too calmly, altogether too dispassionately. He held her arm, crossing at the traffic lights at the junction of Trinity Street and the lower end of Bradshawgate. "People had been let down by the mills. The mills were a legacy of the past. Part of the dirty old town image. People wanted the place to look clean. They wanted a clean sweep, Maggie." They walked on, past what had once been furniture shops. He kept hold of her arm now, but his voice wasn't like Pete at all. His voice was quite insistent, suspicious. "You've changed. Ever since you read that . . . that crazy letter. If you know something – if you even so much as suspect something – for God's sake, woman – !"

Her voice rose, her voice shook. "I'm telling you that a war was lost here."

"Now you're being ridiculous."

"A dirty war, worse than any other in two hundred years. Don't you even begin to understand? This whole town was history. We should have put a preservation order on all of it." Oh, but she was talking carelessly. He already suspected and now she was allowing something – something lost, something buried – to resurrect itself. But she needn't have worried. Pete's white face was wearing that sweaty stubborn look.

"People felt let down. The mills were no longer competitive. People didn't want to be reminded of failure. Giants fall heavily, Maggie."

Giants! Yes, he was right and they had been giants. And each silent demolished square was the grave of a titan. *Oh, God – oh my God!* ARTFUL JACK KILLS TITANS. A sudden tidal wave hurled itself upon her. In that moment she was overwhelmed by a suffocating pressure. She needed sanity. She had to force sanity back. She had to grasp this tiny straw of objectivity, find strength from her depths of loss . . .

She forced herself to think Pete's view. But it was an immense struggle: for instance, maybe he was right too in suggesting that there had been some negative reaction. An emotional ring to it, the opposite of love for an old grandmother who had lost her usefulness and looked like becoming an embarrassment. God help an old grandmother who had allowed herself to become an embarrassment. And thinking this, having reached the Technical College, the repository of so many warm memories.

Let it come, let it flood my senses.

She didn't want to think about that. She wished those words away with every fibre of her mind – but those words were there, they were there still. ARTFUL JACK – ARTFUL JACK KILLS TITANS. *Oh, God help me! God give me the strength to make my legs move – don't let them go now!*

They were shaking. How she felt that shivering wave, one shivering wave after another, rising like the fury, from the ground upwards, a nauseating assault of waves, screaming up the skin of her legs, making jelly of the muscles, the joints, the tendons. She knew – *she knew!* Yes, she was absolutely sure now: there was a link growing – a link between her loss of Bobby and the bulldozing of her childhood playground. A link between the warmth of so much red brick and his small firm presence, the down of his skin and the leanness of his young growing limbs. Her throat tightened. A pain had registered in her chest, constricting like lightning, swelling up into the back of her throat. The back of her throat felt impaled on a rigid agonising iron spike.

"Somehow it all went wrong here," she squeezed the words out manically now, huskily, with her eyes liquidly shining. *So here is where I start, don't you see?*

"Every dirty town in the industrial north was that same community, Maggie. The whole of South Lancashire was one big filthy unhealthy community."

"All you say is true but it was more. It was rare, Pete. Distinct and different and warm. A different kind of warm." A community, she thought, where a stranger was addressed as "love". She was hurrying now and maybe a week ago there would have been tears washing the focus from her eyes. But she would never cry again. Crying achieved nothing.

"You didn't seem to miss it so very much when you left."

"Didn't I?"

But then maybe he was right and she hadn't. But that had been the confusion. Nobody had realised that it was all such a confusion. A family thing, introverted. A family vindictiveness, as a family's home might be pulverised by a big lead weight on a crane. All right, if perhaps they had been so lost in their own seas of troubles they hadn't realised the enormity of what was happening to Bolton.

They had never moved from the Technical College. They were still standing, arms linked, in front of the steps before the entrance.

"You know I'm not one for these bloody pilgrimages, Maggie."

"Then you take the bus. I'll meet you at my mother's."

"And how many hours later?"

"I suppose I loved it . . . the way a small child loves a parent. I loved it so much I only recognised it as a need. I loved every dirty brick that made it."

He was disturbed by the renewed vehemence with which she expressed herself, this middle-aged woman, with the tired face, and the damp hair, unwashed for four days, staring at a gloomy building of bricks and mortar.

"Why did you love it so much?"

She hesitated because she was unsure. She spoke softly, as much to herself as to him. "For the first time in my life I felt at home, I, one of the oddballs. The rebel who had failed her eleven plus. I was lucky. For the first time in my life I was lucky, Pete, because a tough old headmistress saw a little talent through the awkward skin and she went to some lengths to arrange it for me. She had me transferred – can you credit that – she had me transferred here to Bolton Tech, to join a class of similar oddballs. Passed-over mathematical geniuses, future writers and artists, all of whom had bucked the system or been sick in the heart or the body at the age of eleven."

He looked entirely unimpressed. He didn't want, per-haps, to understand.

"I went along with it, I the rebel, and do you know why? I believed her. I sensed the real interest in her. For the first time the child had been accepted as a human being."

"So what went wrong?"

"You can be such a bastard!"

"Me – I spoiled it? Is that where all of this is leading?"

She had watched them from her bedroom window, the young women's hair prematurely grey with their cotton haloes as they screeched cheerfully to each other pouring out from Pike Mill, where the noise of the warp knitting machines had made them temporarily deaf.

She was clutching at his arm with a sudden and startling

conviction. The Bolton link: why it was all deliberate. Of course it was. *Of course it was!*

"Don't upset yourself again."

"I was once a member of a writers' workshop here. At the A-level stage. I wrote short stories, even the occasional poem. You didn't know that, did you? We wrote about what was happening here. I wrote, Pete. I wrote poetry about it, for all the good it did. And do you know why I never told you before? I never told you because you would have made me feel small – incompetent."

"Well done, Maggie."

They met up with the police at 8.30 the following morning, Detective Chief Inspector Woodings, with his Scottish inspector, Andrews, and his sergeant with the broken nose, Williams. There was also a detective chief inspector from the Greater Manchester force, who spoke with a strong Bolton accent and who was called Farnworth. And she tried to tell them what she knew, her discovery, not with the forbidden words but with her eyes: here – it all started here.

They first of all walked Maggie and Pete round the perimeter of Heywood Park, which took them thirty-five minutes. And even in the dignity of her too calm voice, she confided it. Maggie, keeper of secrets, when she wanted to scream all she knew. The intimacy, could they not see, in the very names of the condemned? Marsden's mill on Fletcher Street, Tommy Taylor's on Lever Street, St Mark's Church. Could they possibly conceive what it meant to have to explain to strangers that she was christened in this small black ruin, that her parents were married here, that she attended Sunday school in this boarded up church hall. It must have started here. With dignity, calm tearless dignity, walking with these tall silent men further on to where they were demolishing perfectly beautiful terraces on Bridgeman Street, with her eyes and her voice and the utmost draw on her reserves of courage, with this ridiculous desire on her part to throw her arms round the surviving tiny oblong of old Bolton, nestling into the northwest perimeter of the park, she proclaimed it to them if they only cared to notice.

Here. Here was where it had begun. Here in this deliberate annihilation of memories, caring, respect. *Here!*

And the man in charge, Chief Inspector Woodings, just seemed to accept it all with a studious patience, hardly asking her questions at all, quite content to let her talk on in this white cold outrage: words, words, issuing from her mouth, words without thinking, as if it were the heart of her at last having its long-suppressed say.

But she could see how he wished to establish the location, how familiar Bobby would be with it, and it was a bonus for him to discover just how these bits of rubbish, this area of slum clearance, wrapped round a square flat park, was on the contrary her childish fairy tale. And he would stare, stare at another hole in the townscape: church and terraced row – the rows here with pitch-black painted gables – all equally and democratically condemned to liquidation. They would have been here, these houses and these mills and this one church, stone built and in perfect order, with its red-velvet upholstered pews. They would have been whole and intact then, almost a year ago, when Bobby aged seven had run round or through the park with his friend, David Bray, David who looked so like him he might have been his brother, also aged seven.

They would have seen the church, and the red brick terraced rows, and the red brick school on Bridgeman Street, which had been her school, and that was important. What was gone was important. This athletic man with the blue eyes looked first at herself, and then at the demolition in progress, and then that prolonged blink, so that for the first time she wondered if he might even begin to understand. She asked herself if there was even a chance that she was not alone. But then it was even worse for her in a way because his empathy made her realise that she might perhaps be right after all, which made it all so vitally important, which made it a matter of life and death.

Sandy Woodings turned, his calm face concealing a gathering excitement, as he left Detective Chief Inspector Farnworth outside the park gates, the Bolton man with his hand reassuringly on the shoulder of the boy, David Bray. As soon as they were standing inside the park gates, between leafless horse chestnut trees, coated a bright green with winter algae, he performed a prolonged blink. That walk about the park had been extraordinary.

Something about Mrs Stephens – there was something a little too excited about her, something she recognised, something she *knew*.

Jock mistook his silence for a question. He said, "You may recall, Chief, that the two lads left the Bray house at 3.45 p.m., which was much as they had done for the past three days. Bobby Stephens and the Bray lad walked as far as the park gates together – he may even have come just inside the gates here, left the Bray lad at about this spot, and David Bray remembers they talked about who would run outside and who would run through the park."

This dark-haired lad was certainly interesting. The clear resemblance between him and Bobby Stephens . . .

All three men did a three hundred and sixty degree turn. Sandy's heart was thrusting a little too forcibly with what was already feeling somewhat familiar: the wrought-iron railings, painted the muddy ochre of old fireplaces, the gap where the gate had long since disappeared – he could even see part of the red brick school over the partly demolished slate roofs of Bridgeman Street.

All this demolition – it was the demolition which seemed to upset her.

He brushed his upper lip with a nervous impatience. "Why did they separate, Jock?"

"Just a game, as far as I can make out."

"They didn't argue?"

"Apparently not. A sort of race, with frills."

"Because whoever ran round the perimeter of the park would lose?"

"That's right – it's a lot further that way." Jock scratched at his head, performed the opposite of nodding, with his head jerking upwards. "Like a question of timing. At the side gate, one would sort of pounce on the other."

"So they wouldn't have been running fast?"

"Not to begin with. David Bray says he was taking his time, moving in anything but a straight line."

Like Jock, Sandy had his hands in his pockets because it was freezing cold. He nodded, turning slowly so that he could follow the indicated direction across ruined turf, stubby filaments of grass and crinkled dandelion leaves that were silvered along their edges with frost.

"Bobby Stephens then walked along outside the railings. And David made a play of watching him, at least while he was still visible. What he said was that Bobby seemed to be deliberately taking his time, delaying for some reason."

"Possibly waiting for someone?"

"I couldn't say. Not in any one spot, that's for sure. Then David starts walking – walking or trotting – he's doing sorts of figures of eight," Jock took a hand out of his pocket to perform the manoeuvre with flat palm and flipper fingers.

"But Bobby didn't say anything to David about meeting anyone?"

"Nothing. As far as his pal is concerned, it was a whim of the moment. Up to that day, on each of the three previous days, during which they seemed to have worked out the rules of this game, it was Bobby Stephens who went through the park. I think it must have been a race to start with but it was too biased and so they invented more and more rules. He'd carry on through the park, walking, twirling about, hiding, the idea being he'll run for the last leg when running looks necessary, to time it so that he comes out of the side gate at just about the same moment David arrives there. If it makes any kind of sense, they plan to surprise one another."

Start right from the beginning: Sandy Woodings lit a cigarette for Tom and then for himself – Jock didn't smoke. Something ongoing, with all the compulsive force of instinct!

He inhaled smoke, in no particular hurry, continuing to search about him with his eyes.

"And his friend lost sight of him when he – Bobby that is – got as far as those houses on the path outside the railings?" There was a small square block, two short terraced runs in parallel, with a cobbled back street between them, cutting into the park at the northwest corner. His eyes followed the line of the railings: perhaps a hundred yards, then they ended abruptly, set into a stone pillar, and this directly abutted on the wall of the end house.

"You must have done a calculation of the time, Jock?"

"Minutes – no more."

"Playing a game," added Jock emphatically. "That's what he was doing – he was playing a game. A game he always won. A game he'd won three times already. Hence the discussion inside the gates. David was fed up with Bobby always winning. David insisted it was his turn to run through the park. His turn to take the short course. Ready to spring out on Bobby when he arrived . . ."

He continued to smoke: to his right, and at a right angle to the main entrance on Bridgeman Street, he stared again at a chaos of short rows of red brick houses, privately owned since they had been coated with pitch on their gable ends, and nestling snugly in the organic centre, with its four-beaded corner pinnacles, the smoke-blackened steeple of the small condemned church. *She looked so strange. What does all this mean to her?*

"We'll have to measure it out, but let's say a few minutes.

Three minutes, four at the most – walking round the park, by the long way, as the pal walked – "

His eyes followed the course the boy must have taken: across the grass, ignoring the path, at a diagonal, which led alongside the toddlers' play area – a play area where Margaret Stephens would have played as a child, brought Bobby along for the next generation of childish pleasures: two different kinds of swing, a broken roundabout, a slide with its polished brass gleaming from a million small gasps of pleasure, the ornamental garden – !

The ornamental garden abutted onto the railings at the south-west corner of the park; the railings rose high above the toddlers' play area, a height impossible to climb over, then gradually fell back towards the ground again, arriving at a normal level somewhere in the concealment of the shrubbery.

They were already walking.

"Say four minutes, allowing for the ritual of the game. Let's suppose that as soon as his friend reached the level of the houses – when he disappeared from view – David Bray started running."

They had started running themselves, cigarettes discarded, Tom puffing and lagging behind. Sandy's eyes had taken in the time on his watch and he kept glancing at it at intervals: one minute, one minute thirty, two minutes . . . They had reached the ornamental gardens, flower beds, a small defunct stone fountain, the impression of a hilly landscape somewhere in Kashmir, which had been conjured from completely flat terrain by hillocky flower beds and masses of rhododendrons.

At least four minutes by the outside route, which was still being followed by Farnworth and David Bray at that moment, only two minutes forty-five seconds on the route followed by David Bray on that day in late October a year ago: a day during the half-term holidays, a boy waiting, chuckling to himself, his little ambush all prepared and a good minute in which to choose a hiding place, to build up that delicious blend of tension and amusement that is the heart of all pleasure.

Tom, panting, had caught up with them. Even now, with the sounds of feet running along the pavement but still thirty seconds away, they had reached the small side gate almost concealed in the massive post-mature evergreen jungle. Only somebody who knew the area would have realised there was a gate there. Bobby Stephens would have known, since his grandmother lived only thirty yards away, it would have been his natural entrance to the park.

"All our man had to do was to park his vehicle outside the gate. He'd have been screened off from everybody's eyes except for that single moment when he crossed from the gate to the vehicle. Nobody would have been likely to see him."

Sandy Woodings nodded. He emerged from the side gate to glance across the High Street to where Margaret Stephens, together with her husband, was standing and watching, under the shadow of a small church.

She wouldn't need him to explain this. She would understand as well as he did, the man waiting – waiting for that childish body to come hurtling along, anticipating that loss of all care except the sense of glee. And in Sandy Woodings himself the realisation was a blue flame licking away at the core of the darkness that had been this case until now.

"That same calculation, Tom. I've got that same feeling."

"Me too," replied Tom, pausing with a handkerchief cupped before blowing his running nose.

The enormity of it was only still spreading, diffusing, into Sandy's consciousness as he stared for a moment, like a daydreaming poet, into the quietly impressive sky. A real winter's sky, overall a heavy mucous grey, but in places brilliant and oily silver like fishskin.

They sat in the back of a regulation police car, a Rover, for quite a while, probably a full five minutes, in silence. Keeping Pete outside – he was being led across the park by Sergeant Williams – was of course quite deliberate. Yet oddly she was glad of it. Just as she was glad now of the silence on the senior detective's, Woodings', part.

What she would say, her first words, would be important.

He didn't stare at her, although he must have a vision of her exactly as she sat there, eyes to the side, head fallen back against the seat, too heavy for her shoulders: *was she still on sedatives?*

And during the silence Margaret Stephens watched a tiny bird in the lower branches of a small leafless tree. Small enough to be a wren, perhaps a very young robin, it flitted from branch to lower branch in a clumsy erratic manner, like a July butterfly. Now he did look at her for a moment, her answering glance was furtive, embarrassed almost: his blue eyes, not unfriendly, not even unemotional. But there was a calm there too that frightened her a good deal because there was no place in that calm for any sympathy with dark places, of personal secrets, the growing awareness that you did not, could not, share with others.

And there perhaps lay the reason she was pleased that he had sent Pete away. Pete who would have sensed this about her instantly. Pete, whom she could see now, his sloping back, hanging shoulders, walking slowly past the light tan single-storey building, the toilet complex in the centre of the park, with the graffiti, white sprayed on the light tan brick, PIKE MILL GANG RULES OK. Then, as if waking from a dream, she sighed, as if asking what she must now understand of him, or perhaps she was begging it of him. Begging him not to question her just now.

She said, "I'm confused, Mr Woodings. I'm very, very confused."

He still did not speak. He was thinking about the sudden shakiness in her voice. She had seemed much more assured when they had been outside, walking. She was wringing her hands together as if the skin was burning or perhaps it was pins and needles and the fingers looked a mottled blue and white.

"You were born here, Mrs Stephens?"

"Here. Just round the corner."

"And you lived here – until your marriage?"

"I left Bolton to study English in Birmingham."

"How old were you when you left?"

"I was nineteen."

"You wanted to be a teacher?"

"Dropped out – at the end of the first year."

She could read him, she could tell that these were all intended as gentle questioning. Now she waited, with her heart tapping erratically, like a learner's typewriter, gazing across at the pillar between two wrought-iron arched gates, before the small church with its foundation stone laid by AKKEY BAMBER in 1893 and the figure of Jesus, with Sacred Heart exposed, in a niche between the twin church doors.

"So you returned to Bolton, when you were twenty?"

"I returned to live in my parents' house, where Bobby came, when he stayed for a week at half term with my mother."

Facts, a steady accumulation of small facts: here she had given him several more interesting little facts for that calmly gathering brain of his, as with one or two seconds' silence, he appeared to register these.

How could he remain so calm, his voice so even, when he must be suspicious now of what she had realised.

She blurted it out then. "It wasn't a random kidnapping at all, was it?"

"I don't think it was, Mrs Stephens."

Across the road the Bray youngster was having a lift home – to his new home, since Bridgeman Street had been condemned. Inspector Farnworth, with a wave to Woodings, allowed him into the passenger side of his car. And then, as Woodings looked at his wristwatch, her gaze fell vacantly onto the small curling wisps of hair on the backs of his fingers.

Here: a full year ago. A year ago, next to where she had grown up, where Bobby would have felt safe and secure next to his granny's, a man had tried to kidnap him. The kidnap had not worked because he had caught the wrong boy. He had been waiting for the boy to come across the park, the boy running, the boy winning the game – only it was David Bray, dark-haired David, who had fallen into his trap. And he had grabbed hold of David from behind. A tall man with dark hair had grabbed David from behind. And then let him go. He had let him go because when he called him Bobby, David had said he wasn't Bobby. And then he had turned him round and looked at him and he had let him go.

"It was him, wasn't it? It was him, the one who took Bobby?"

"I don't know for certain, Mrs Stephens."

"But you think so. Really, deep down, you do know, don't you?"

81

10

In a house that has lain empty for a month you do not expect to find condensation on a windowpane. It is so startling that he suddenly hugs the wall outside the house, he stares at it for a very long time, just that one window, the downstairs window of the living room. For several minutes he is lost in that horrified realisation. A man who has not slept in perhaps thirty-six hours, a man who has been very busy ferrying materials through every back street and minor road across the north of England, yet he has been wary enough to park at St Chad's Church, eight hundred yards away. It is such a fierce concentration that he doesn't even blink with the rattle of noise from the lane immediately behind him, a narrow little lane which runs parallel to the red brick street and against the junction of which he is now leaning.

A fox! Father and mother of all creation, it's a fox here, deep in the heart of Liverpool.

They are close enough to look each other defiantly eye to eye and he notices that the commotion was the noise of dustbins being ransacked. He finds a source of cool amusement in the gaze of this sharp-faced old grandfather, with his black burglar's eyes above his old man's white cheeks, his fur, a lurid orange in the street light, jauntily disarrayed and whiskers tousled from rooting. *No, you don't find condensation – because condensation comes from human lungs.* He laughs now, hearing every desul-

tory pad of the departing fox's feet on the frozen tarmac.
You most certainly do not expect to find condensation on
that windowpane when it is your own house you are
looking at!

So why don't you come on into my parlour – come on in!

His eyes sweep along the other side of the street on his
left, which is towards the house, then he turns and coolly
gazes to his right, towards the major road. Nothing comes to
mind from this perusal. He turns to look behind him, to
where a gable window with smashed glass points to a
property which is evidently on the market. An empty
property. In his eventful life, nothing has ever been quite
so fruitful as an infinite patience.

Sandy Woodings lay in Josie's bed and allowed her to curl
round him while he turned on his back and squinted at the
illuminated numbers of the digital alarm. The time was 6.30
a.m. – two hours to daylight.

Josie was awake really, after a restless night. He had
communicated his own restlessness to her. That restlessness
had never left him. With a smooth slide, he disengaged his
body from her clinging hands, slipped from a sitting posture
for a few seconds' revival to walking across the deep pile
carpet, dressed only in boxer shorts.

"Next time you sleep in the spare room," she moaned
half-seriously.

Sandy was thinking ahead to the divisional meeting later
this morning. He would have to make a case for twenty-four
hours' observation of the Stephens' home. But there was
something else, another idea now in his mind, and that was
to involve Professor Lipmann's psychiatric expertise.
Downstairs, pondering now on how this might help him,
Sandy poured orange squash which, with added hot water,
was Josie's morning tipple because coffee gave her heartburn. He put instant coffee into a mug for himself, intending
to drink it black. Whistling "Whad d'ya wanna make those

eyes at me for", he thought, as the kettle promised never to boil: *alive – is it possible after all this time?*

In Josie's softly lit kitchen, he poured water onto the brown dust of coffee. Then, grinning at Josie, he passed her the hot orange and a slice of toasted brown bread, with marmalade.

They had made love twice since 2.00 a.m. and regarding her now, ignoring the words she was hissing at him with marvellous vehemence, he felt like it again.

He bent to kiss her averted cheek, while she didn't pause in munching her toast and regarding him with lukewarm eyes about which the midnight mascara had organically expanded.

Thursday, December 8th: he was still half tumescent from fancying her here and now, but he ignored it. He felt no capacity for cruelty, only the human certainty that punishment lurked behind every corner and it was one of life's lessons that one had to learn how to avoid that punishment. He ate his own two slices of that same thin toast with a vague ache in his chest which might have been in sympathy with her heartburn, but which was not heartburn at all but a mixture of excitement and agitation. That same uncomfortable fervour had come back over the Pennines with him yesterday. It had begun during the interview with Mrs Stephens in the car, had grown more complex – by turns a torpor, a faint nausea, an excited restlessness – while discussing the events of the day with the police force in Bolton. He had mistaken it for hunger as they travelled back over the Snake Pass in the dark, under an extravagantly starry sky, and he had tried to cure himself with a pint of beer and beef sandwiches with mustard at the Snake Inn. This morning he recognised it as a gambler's anticipation. An anticipation where time mattered, where precise time was vital in a day where there would never be quite enough of it. For today, in addition to the high-powered early morning conference, was his son's, Gerry's, birthday, and Sandy was determined that he would not be too busy to forget that.

For the man with the grey eyes, sitting patiently in front of his window in Liverpool, precise time was also vital. But here the similarity ended.

Time to this man is something so monstrous and yet so familiar, its passage is a true sixth sense. Time is the dark of the deserted bedroom in which he patiently sits. Time is the freezing damp air that rushes constantly through the hole in the window, to buffet his half-lidded eyes. And he sees himself again in the dining kitchen of his mother's house, watching the battle take place within the boy. The boy, weeping, struggling to control the overwhelming sense of terror. He marvels once again how the spirit can overcome such a huge debility, at how hunger, a thing of the flesh, will always overcome the constraints of the spirit. But who better than he understands, in this bewildering sharp focus of time, how it is the body which really registers change, as it is the body which registers the terrible weight of shadows.

Only minutes before he broke a pane of glass in the door at the back of the unoccupied house to gain entry. Now he has discovered a decrepit office chair, upholstered in worn leather. In moving the chair, his large hand almost covers the backrest, which has long ago burst and is affected by a rash of paint spots which he can palpate under the pulps of his fingers. You see, Bobby lad – he thinks now, while in the act of converting this chair into his observation perch in front of the window – in this murderous grip of time, it isn't trees or houses that change but those darkening shadows. The shadows grow and thicken, they darken and deepen. While we are awake they pretend to falter, only to speed up, to swell like mushrooms, while we rest, if we so much as close our eyes and sleep. It is hard to explain what is essentially instinct, a terrible sense of foreboding: that shadows do time's work for it. As if, when a house or a tree falls, a part of its shadow remains. You see, Bobby lad, what we are talking about, what we really care about, is not houses or trees but people. That's what I'm really trying to explain.

Sandy picked up Gerry at 4.00 p.m. and took him to a snooker parlour where he presented him with his birthday present, a shining two-piece and man-size cue. Mary had been accurate when she had remarked Gerry's similarity to the missing Stephens lad, since he was close in age and had those same calm brown eyes. The remarkable thing about Gerry was that he was so fine-boned – nothing like the rough and ready creature that Sandy had been at the same age – and yet he shared the same love of sport. In the car they talked about football.

"Guess who's in the first team, Dad?"

"Get away – when did it happen?"

"Saturday. Goalie, that's all though."

He laughed as they dodged across a busy main road after parking the car. Gerry held his hand like a much younger child and the simple closeness of the act touched him. How much younger than his nine years he really seemed, more like an eight-year-old with that delicate round head topped by thick blond curls. Sandy Woodings imagined how he would feel if Gerry had been kidnapped in place of Robert Stephens and the sense of horror stopped him dead as Gerry bounded energetically up the lavatory-green staircase in front of him.

"How are the girls, Gerry?"

"Okay, Dad!" Gerry pocketed his first red and his father groaned at the prominence of a blue, which had somehow lined itself up over the middle pocket.

"Did the twins pass the fourth grade piano?"

"The twins got a credit each. They always do, you know that. I'm going to use backspin – watch me."

He watched, just sparing enough in showing his admiration. "And Mum – how is she keeping these days?"

"She's keeping just all right, I suppose," Gerry coughed as he pocketed the blue: it was his nervous cough.

"You will still see me. We'll see a lot of each other still. It won't be so bad. You wait and see."

His son coughed again, that jerky little movement of his head. "Your shot, Dad – I missed the red."

"You believe me now, don't you? You, me, the three girls, we're going to see a great deal of each other."

"Hey, Dad!"

It was a moment of extraordinary intimacy, of that strangely awkward boyish tenderness that exists between father and all too quickly maturing son. Sandy would remember it, he would be haunted by it, gazing into the eyes of their two small witnesses in the wintry landscape the following morning. Right now, he felt a flush of intense emotion sweep over him as he brushed his hand through the blond curls, playfully tapped the small tensed shoulder.

Gerry had those same brown eyes as Julie. It was Julie's eyes that all of a sudden relaxed into a shy delighted smile.

11

Like, she imagined, a lot of other women, Jacky felt herself
unfairly influenced by hormones. In particular, the ups and
down of her monthly horrors and the routines of twelve
hours' surveillance work did not easily come together. And
loath as she was to admit it even to herself, Jacky was a
once-a-month girl. Nothing quite so simple, of course. Was
anything ever quite so simple? She was eminently capable
of a bit of canoodling more or less any old time, vagaries of
a demanding job permitting, but there was no getting away
from the fact that there was this one day, the third day after
the end of her period, when she was hot.

She supposed it wasn't all so very unusual, not really, not
when you saw gardeners on the box at the time of the
Chelsea Flower Show who swore they could predict a
bloom not just to the day, but the hour and the very
minute . . .

So blow worry and all that. Weren't we all victims of
sodding old nature in the end?

Then of course winter's depressing dank depths, not to
mention the city of Liverpool and the fact she had been
given the midday to midnight shift, didn't help one little bit.
That plus the fact that this was her third night in this creepy
house. And of course she felt like it as usual. That was the
reason she had brought Nicholas Salaman's book, *The
Frights*, along with her. It lay at her feet now, the panting
half-naked woman on the cover – good old Julia, whom she

was already identifying with in both lust and carefree wickedness – Julia frolicking with a soldier, who was trying to get seven or eight arms out of his uniform, while the lower half of him was rooting in the embrace of widely straddled gartered thighs.

Jacky had been unable to read a line of it since four o'clock because she was sitting in the armchair, two thick rugs covering the lower half of her body, in the dark. Even the cover of the book was just barely recognisable, because of the streetlight directly outside the window with its open curtains. It lay almost half-read, opened on the floor, concealing the gun.

Sitting in complete silence through the almost closed door into the dining kitchen, her partner, Roger, was a six foot twenty-three-year-old barely past the agony of pimples. Roger was sulking, passing the time drinking whisky-laced coffee from a flask which he kept under the dining table. She felt so lonely and horny and desperate, she was close to making it up with Roger, close even to inviting young Roger to do her a favour. I mean, for pity's sake, what lunatic was going to turn up now after three days of nothing happening and all for the sake of two packets of frozen peas and a few assorted ready-made curries?

Of course she did nothing – nothing so crazy, nothing that would inevitably mean impossible expectations on the part of the immature Roger from now to eternity. She was, after all, the senior officer and thirty-two years old – and midnight, no matter how distant, would eventually come round. Instead she pulled the rugs a little higher, finding comfort with daydreams which, coloured by Salaman's book, were a delicious blend of racy and comic, while with her right ear she listened through one half of a set of earphones to a pocket radio small enough to smuggle through in her bag without Gill noticing at the change-over. And while, all the time, with a professional competence, her left ear listened for strange sounds in the dark.

Probably, given any other night of the month, she would have heard those sounds. Very likely, if she had not strayed into Radio 3 and somehow, for Handel wasn't exactly her cup of tea, found a strange attractiveness in a performance of the *Jephtha* oratorio.

What this performance of father's sacrificial promise to God had to do with her state of mild intoxication with lust, boredom and the cold, Jacky would have been the last person in the world to know, only that time drifted as she was listening. She was carried out of herself, lost for a time in a dreamy wandering – when hands covered her eyes from behind and the voice asked,

"Guess who?"

She was aware of the fact that she was dreaming, she had to be dreaming because that voice was not Roger's – Roger would never have come out of the sulks with a prank like this – and those hands covering her eyes were very firm and as cold as marble . . .

I'm dreaming. I've fallen asleep on the job and I bloody well know I'm dreaming.

Because nothing and nobody had come in through that bolted front door. Not a pipsqueak of sound. Nothing. And, through that partly opened door behind her, young and immature Roger was sitting with his elbows up on the dining table, pouring himself another out of that big one-litre flask. The ear-phone had pulled from her ear but she could still hear the church music, if tinny with distance. That was uncannily real, the way her imagination could think up a thing like that tinny music, the way nightmares so parody reality . . . Only those freezing cold hands had suddenly shifted, from playfulness to murderous reality. One of those hands was crushing her nose into the plane of her face, that hand was choking off her nose and her mouth and she was suddenly fighting for her life.

She jabbed with her elbow, back hard, struggling at the same time to try to get onto her feet. Her elbow clunked against a rib cage, covered with cold outdoor clothing. Her right hand was flailing backwards, trying to get hold of something – it felt thick and rough like a denim collar – she tried to pull down hard but there was no leverage because of her sitting position. In the space of two or three seconds, her trousers were twisted halfway down her goose-pimpled buttocks and pain was swamping her face from her blocked airways. *Roger is dead.* Stabbing her fingernails into the hand over her nose and rocking her head from side to side, she managed to clear one nostril. Blood was gushing from her nose into the back of her throat. She was coughing on her own blood, trying to cough it out of her throat against the pressure of that hand, trying to swallow it rather than inhale it. But blood was going down into her lungs and causing her to panic even more. Her clawing right hand encountered a face, the angle of a mouth, a bearded cheek . . . Her fingernails gouged flesh, her nails raked the flesh under that light beard, hunting for something better, hunting for an eye . . .

He's dead. Oh merciful Christ – Roger's dead!

She had wriggled and gouged her way into a half-kneeling position, with her left foot on the floor. Manoeuvring her weight over that left foot firmly planted on the floor, she took hold of the overcoat somewhere about the lapels, she took a second to gauge what appeared to be a huge and monstrous weight, and then she threw him. The sheer effort and the size and weight of him crushed her, even as he tumbled, and she fell gasping onto her outstretched hands, blowing blood out of her ruptured nostrils, spitting blood out of her throat, while at the same time she registered his body crashing through furniture. The gun . . . she must get hold of the gun.

Her armchair had crashed against the wall behind her and she was nowhere near where the book had been lying, opened and facing upwards. In the struggle, she had moved – she had been carried – halfway across the room and away from the window with its pale orange streetlight. On her hands and knees she scrambled in what she imagined to be the right direction, feeling desperately with splayed fingers . . . Extraordinarily she could hear his grunting breathing. Even with her mind on the search of the carpet, she realised that he must be standing nearby – he was standing and watching her search the carpet. He was standing and watching . . .

In that instant of realisation, he had changed. He was suddenly looming over her, attacking her again. Even as she remained crouched down on the floor, she felt his mass descending through space onto her back. But he wasn't attacking her. All she had sensed was his shadow blotting out the streetlight coming through the window. The side of her head clumped against the door into the dining kitchen. She could see . . . *No – search! Don't even think! Search!*

But why wasn't he attacking her? He was looking out of the window. Looking up and down the street, checking the bleeding coast was clear. Checking . . .

"How much do you know?"

When she heard the question put so calmly, when she heard the deep-throated voice, all the hairs on her skin stood erect like a nutmeg grater. She continued her scuttling about the floor. Searching . . . searching . . . until her fingers found it like ten desperate eyes. Her fingers were sliding over the shiny cover of the book. Nicholas Salaman's paperback was closed. It was closed because he had picked up the gun while she was carelessly dozing, even before he put his hands over her eyes.

This was when time started to change, when her awareness of time began to veer drunkenly to one side. *I'm going to die. He has killed Roger so he has to kill me.* Panic was causing her ears to pop. Huge, mind-destroying surges of panic . . . That was also when her hand touched the heavy metal weight of the gun.

The gun – oh, thank God! The gun, the gun – the gun!

Her hand, slippery with sweat, was desperately trying to turn it round so she could snatch it up. Only the muscles of her arm were bizarrely wooden and stiff and it seemed to take eternity. She had slid it round with her forefinger, she was picking the gun up off the floor with two hands which felt encased in iron. Tears were mixing with the blood running from her nose. In that veering, mad dimension of time, he was reaching out like a giant from next to the window and his hand had closed round her right wrist, his strength had pulled her two cradling arms apart, so the gun was suspended high in the air from her right thumb and forefinger. His other hand had taken her about the breasts and was dragging her backwards. There was a crash against the door into the dining room, a momentary vision in the murky light, Roger's shape, Roger's head fallen down onto the table with a dark blot high up on the back of his neck, at the hairline.

They were half in and half out of the dining room, she was pulled up hard against his curving body. Her back scraped against his breastbone as he lifted her, her spine locking arcs with his, and he was pressing his thumb into the fleshy part of her right wrist.

"What's your name, she-devil?"

His voice was strained now. He was breathless from the effort of lifting her violently struggling torso off the floor. Her hand tried to tighten over the gun. She was holding onto the gun for life itself, retaining a grip somehow between her thumb and flesh of her palm, but her forefinger had disappeared. A whole half of her hand had disappeared, there was an agonising neuralgic numbness in the half of her hand that included her trigger finger. The gun crashed onto the floor under the table, where Roger kept his flask.

He was dragging her still struggling body back into the sitting room, until they were once again close to the window.

93

"You're damned right to be worried," she gasped. "My boss is out there right now. He's waiting for you to come out."

He was watching the street even now as he changed his grip so his forearm was across her throat. He was squeezing her throat so she couldn't breathe.

"Your name?"

She tried kicking backwards. By a marvel her left shoe was still on her foot. It had a good two-inch heel and now she lashed back at his legs with it. But the grip on her throat only tightened and she was being lifted again. That huge strength in him had her dangling, only touching the floor with the toes of her right foot.

"Jacky!" Her voice was a gurgling, choking. "My name is Jacky."

"They're not out there, Jacky. I watched them leave. The early shift. Two men, one in a light grey mackintosh, Gill in a sheepskin." His arm was still strangling her but the grip had loosened just enough to allow her to talk. Her feet were completely off the ground.

Against an ordinary human being, she would have had a chance. But not only was he physically huge, but there was something else about him. Some frightful sense of power and purpose.

And Jacky was dying. If her situation didn't warn her, the awful shivers that were racking her body must do so, the sense that whatever pours out the adrenalin was exhausted.

"Tell me, Jacky – how much do you know?"

Her voice was hoarse, a husky whisper, cracked with tears and clots of blood. "We brought you back to life, didn't we? We know everything."

And in that instant she really did feel that she knew everything. There was a wonderful, magical, awareness of time as if it were a thousand veils over some inner eye, she could see those veils falling, they were tumbling and swirling with a diabolic beauty, they were falling with the speed of light and yet she could pick out each individual veil, she could follow it like the erratic downward spiral of a butterfly into an all-consuming flame.

"You're lying to me, Jacky. You know nothing."

She spoke painfully slowly, through a throat that was being crushed away, a last desperate note of defiance. "Fuck you!"

12

The scene of the kidnapping was fixed by winter as if in a spell. Hoar frost grainily encrusted the soil, creeping over the dead leaves, like a crystalline rigor mortis. Christopher Taylor and Andrew Totley, seven and eight years old respectively, were not small for their ages, but there was a chilly grandeur to their surroundings, to the tall unmoving canopy of trees, that diminished them, that caused them to seem very small indeed, vulnerable little manikins. Christopher, with the blond hair, was wearing that same blue parka as when Sandy had last seen him, with the brown furry hood thrown back, a closely zipped-up front against the cold, and thickly bulging pockets above his jeans and moon boots. Andrew, with the sulky face, wore a red and blue ski jacket, which must have been handed down from an older brother, over similar blue jeans to Christopher's, and trainers.

At the moment, in regarding the grandfatherly face of Professor Lipmann, who was just starting to ask them questions, the younger of the two, Christopher, fiddled anxiously with a spray of fine twigs, pulling the encrusted beads of frost, like white frozen glass, into the burning red palm of his right hand. Christopher's face was rather more expressive than Andrew's. It was Christopher now who was nodding his head with a desperate seriousness in reply to the latest question.

"He was stood here," his eyes moved from the professor

to Sandy, a bright quick movement, which compensated for his hesitant speech.

"Just as I am standing right now?"

When he nodded, without speaking, his big front teeth showed together with an equal amount of gum.

The professor was a gnome-like man, only about five feet four inches tall, with an impressively coarse and sensual face. He had a shiny olive head, completely bald on top with lateral fins of white wool encroaching over his large fleshy ears. This morning he had covered his head with a midnight blue homburg, which matched his heavy wool overcoat, so there was a certain resemblance to a Mafia godfather, which wasn't dispelled by the sparkling vitality of his deep-set black eyes.

"You're not too cold for a few minutes are you?"

The two boys shook their heads.

Sandy Woodings could see that the boys were terrified. Their pupils were glistening marbles. Repeatedly, they threw their eyes wistfully in the direction of their waiting parents, fifty yards back up the slope.

In bending, the professor's large and rounded face was only inches from the faces of the two boys and he studied their faces with his head in that posture of his, the moon on a slant.

"You see, I want all of us to just wait here for a short while. Is that okay with you two? No talking, just for a moment. I want you two young men to think right back inside your heads. Fine – now, I'm the man who took your pal. Here I am. Now you see me, don't you? Lovely big bright sparklers. Now, what am I doing? I am coming towards you and I have a sparkler which I hold out in my hand to you."

They had got over the novelty of the professor's Ukrainian accent. Now Christopher became agitated. His face flushed and he started stammering so much it was virtually impossible to tell what he was saying.

"You remember, don't you? You remember exactly what I am saying. Here I am. My hand is out to you. Here is a bright sparkler. What am I saying to you? What are the words in your head as I hand you the sparkler?"

"You're saying hello!" It was Andrew who replied, talking clearly. "Hello! Hello! And then you're saying as we wasn't to be afraid of it."

"Aha! I thought you might be afraid of me, is that what I thought?"

"Yeah! You're saying as we wasn't to be afraid."

"Is that the way I say it? As now – listen carefully. Now then – there's no need to be afraid of me – okay?"

"No! You didn't say it like that."

"Aha! Now will you tell me the way I did say it. We shall play a little game."

"You said it different – softer like."

"Then I must try again. Ready – I'll whisper. Come on now, boys. Both of you. Here I am. I have a sparkler in my hand. Here you are. Here's a sparkler for you. Don't be afraid. There's no need to be afraid."

"No!" Suddenly they were both highly excited. Little Christopher was laughing, but it was a jittery false humour. "That wasn't it. You said, *freightened*."

"Freightened? I didn't say afraid, I said freightened? Okay – now let me see, let me try again – now then, boys, there's no need to be freightened."

The professor felt Sandy Woodings' hand on his shoulder firmly but politely, as he was ushered out of his place and the detective took it. Sandy didn't bend in the fatherly way of the professor but stood erect in his grey herringbone overcoat, his hand outstretched, face taut and earnest. He held out his right hand, the fist full of imaginary sparklers.

"There's nay need to feel frieghtened on't – "

"That's a bit like it. That's the way as he said it. Only a big different and he said it softer. He said it softer like – and he didn't have such a fat face like yours. I mean, not like you've got a fat face, but his face was thin. And he didn't have your kind of hair neither. His hair was black sort of, only sort of greasy."

"Dialect!"

"Chief Inspector?"

"He spoke dialect, Prof. I didn't quite realise – "

"Does it tell you something you don't already know?"

"I'm not sure yet what it tells me." Sandy turned his attention once more onto the two children. "How do you mean it wasn't just as I said it?"

"Can you say it again, Mister?" It was Christopher, his big dilated pupils, which Sandy focused on.

He said, "There's no need to feel freightened on it."

"It was like that but he didn't say freightened exactly. He said it more like frittened or something like that."

"Frittened?"

"Yeah!" Both boys were nodding in deadly earnest.

"You both seem very certain?"

"It sounded kind of . . . kind of funny."

Sandy waved towards Tom, who was waiting with the boys' parents. Tom waved back and began to approach them. "What does it all mean, Chief Inspector?" the professor stood by his right shoulder, ruffling the hair of Andrew.

"Freightened is Yorkshire. Frittened in Lancashire. Lancashire dialect, Professor."

Tom had joined them but the professor had not finished questioning the boys. His tone was still calm, still the grandfather, but now his eyes had taken on that more serious look, the look a child receives when his parent is insisting this time on what must really be the truth. "I want you to look back – see this man as he was when he talked to you. How did he seem to you? Did he seem angry?"

Sandy Woodings too had tautened. He had read what the professor was after and it was important.

Neither boy answered.

"Did he seem unfriendly? Did you feel frightened of him?"

"I was frightened," said Christopher.

Sandy Woodings studied those two frightened faces. They seemed considerably more afraid today than on the actual night of the kidnapping. In the cold their faces should have looked shiny: instead they looked white, overwhite, floury, downy white. It seemed so horribly wrong to him that two more innocents should be tainted with their first intimation of great loss. He felt an impotent grief that the ripples of evil should continue to spread and spread.

The parents, standing where Tom Williams had been keeping them, were looking restless.

It was Sandy himself who repeated the question. "Did he seem angry?"

It was Andrew now who spoke, Andrew, who was seven and would in four months be eight, the same age as Bobby. "He was sort of laughing. That's what I thought when he walked away with Bobby. I thought he was laughing."

The reply disturbed Sandy Woodings more than he could possibly explain.

Not facing one another, they stood in silence for perhaps thirty seconds, before Sandy Woodings recovered his composure and exhaled, then asked the professor bluntly what he made of it.

"You can't seriously expect me to provide you with a worthwhile opinion on so very little?"

"That's as much as we know."

The professor sighed, nodded his head, while gazing with an old man's envy at the lively pace of the disappearing children, now being shepherded by Tom towards the road in the wake of their parents. He shifted his stance slightly: ice crackled underfoot.

"Do you know the meaning of psychotic?"

"It means mad – criminally insane?"

"Oh, our science may not be a science at all – certainly not in the eyes of some of our other medical colleagues – but we're not quite as nebulous in our definitions as that. Psychotic is not psychopathic. The Victorians were familiar with what we now refer to as psychopathic. They defined your moral insanity. Do you mind if I diverge slightly – to make an illustration?"

Sandy said nothing, regarding that plump, slightly ridiculous figure, who seemed as fascinated by the frost in the sprays of twigs as the children.

"I came to Britain as a refugee during the war. When I arrived, barely qualified in my chosen field, I was sent to work in one of your big old-fashioned mental institutions. There was a woman in this institution who was committed there two decades earlier for having had two illegitimate babies. Moral insanity! Do you know how she had been treated? Do you wonder how our wonderful profession, as yet in its infancy, saw fit to improve her? They had severed the connection between her frontal lobes and the remainder of her brain. It was then the fashion, you understand – the operation of frontal lobotomy." The professor, whom Sandy had known for at least ten years and who had survived enforced retirement from his university post in his sixty-fifth year by continuing in his honorary appointment with the police force, was gripped by the most violent of emotions. His face had wiped itself clean of its almost permanent smile as he spoke now, in the too gentle voice of furious restraint. "After this operation, she offered herself to visitors in the hospitals grounds for a cigarette."

Sandy had started to walk, for no other reason than he felt unbearably restless.

The professor had quickly controlled himself. His voice, but not his wrinkle-enwrapped eyes, had adopted neutrality. "Is this the route he took with the boy? Where you've marked it out with coloured string?"

"As far as we can make out, yes."

"Do you mind if we walk along the actual route as we talk?"

"Provided it doesn't prolong things overmuch, Professor. I'm due for another press conference."

They manoeuvred their way through the scrub and followed only an approximate path, silent for many minutes, with Sandy taking the rear so that the corpulent figure in the navy woollen overcoat could interpret direction. They hadn't gone twenty yards before the professor's coat was beaded with white whiplashes.

"So tell me what you mean by psychotic."

"Policemen and their definitions! Let me say that the important thing, if you must have your definition . . . the fundamental thing is a lack of self awareness. If your man is psychotic, he will not be aware that his behaviour is in any respect abnormal."

"A simple question, Prof – "

"Is he mad or isn't he? I have already answered your question, Chief Inspector."

"Then a different slant – "

"Whether mad or sane, what exactly is going through his mind? What do you think – I can answer that? I can't answer. I think you must ask yourself what information you have on him up to the present. He kidnaps a boy. He seems strange to our two boy witnesses but I'm not sure if they sensed hostility. I think they're more frightened of us – of the whole ballyhoo of the manhunt – than they were of your kidnapper. Unless the act of tearing the note asunder is hostility. Yet he seems to have attempted to kidnap this same boy a year earlier and in a different town and county. Therefore a personal act, a personal motive. I'VE GOT HIM, MAGGIE. I'VE GOT BABY BLUE. HE'S MINE NOW. Oh, yes. Personal. But then you have realised all of this already. You have been putting Mrs Stephens up to talking to the television news people. Poor Mrs Stephens – and not even once but twice I see."

During this sudden outburst, Sandy had stopped walking. He had not put Mrs Stephens up to speaking to the television news people. She had thought of that, of appealing to the kidnapper, all by herself. But it was true he had not prevented her. He doubted that he could have prevented her. Now he hurried and caught up with the professor and walked along behind him, within touching distance. The old man spoke tersely, over his shoulder as they negotiated a somewhat slippery bend. "Whether sane or not, I can assure you that your man is intelligent. More than intelligent, he's calculating, cunning – and he's cruel."

"Then you don't really believe he is mad?"

"And you will persist in asking me that same impossible question."

The professor kept his hands high in his pockets when he wasn't waving or gesticulating with his words or pulling at a frosted twig, and they walked in slow motion because of the slippery nature of the ground and because any faster and the old man would be breathless.

Abruptly Sandy took a grip on the professor's arm. They had arrived unexpectedly on the embankment and below them was a sheer drop onto the main road, a good ten feet.

"Can I emphasise, Chief Inspector, very firmly, as firmly as I possibly can, that mental illness rarely leads to violence, or indeed any form of crime."

"If you say so."

The note loomed suddenly large in Sandy's mind, huge and sinister: an invitation to some terrible and desperate game – *and we're playing right into his hands, we're playing his game at this very moment.*

"Tell me something, Prof – why are you avoiding the Maggie angle?"

"The Maggie angle, as you put it, is too much like a red rag before my psychiatric eyes."

"Mrs Stephens denies any understand of it."

"Were you convinced she was telling the truth?"

"Would she keep anything from us that might have a significant bearing on our hunt for the man who kidnapped her child?"

"Human behaviour has never ceased to amaze me, Chief Inspector."

Sandy might equally have stated the opposite. That nothing any more would ever surprise him. "It seems very important to me."

"Let me ask you a blunt question – you are still thinking sex offender, am I right?"

"I don't know."

"Think sex offender and you will be mistaken."

A car passed them by on the bottom road: the sloping sides seemed so very steep . . .

"I'd need a good deal more convincing."

"I take things too quickly perhaps. What can I say? You know the story of the art connoisseur – he looks at something and decides immediately. This one is genuine, this one a fake. Then he takes a month to explain his decision."

"Try putting it into plain words, for my sake."

"First we have the unusual business of sending the boy's mother the shoe. You must have wondered why bother at all. You – please forgive me for saying this – are not hot on the trail, as the saying goes. Why render you any kind of favour? Again, you may recall the precise intonation, not the words, but the intonation, of the letter. I have taken Bobby from you, Maggie, and now he is mine. And now what? LOOK BACK, MAGGIE. STUDY THE EDGE OF DARKNESS. He is causing pain. He is in the business of inflicting pain. Again, what does he say? He says the truth. *I've got him. Learn from it.* It is indeed awesome.

Possessiveness, then the infliction of pain, and finally a curious warning. The last line of a letter is always important. ARTFUL JACK KILLS TITANS. What does that warning mean, Chief Inspector?"

13

Margaret Stephens was wearing a heavy floral print dress, with elbow length sleeves and buttoned under the neck, with a floppy collar. He had never seen her wear this dress before. The top button was undone exposing a vee of pink bare throat. On entering her home, Sandy had noticed that the end of her nose was also slightly pinked and swollen, as if she had been crying, but he had also noticed the green raincoat thrown over an armchair in the lounge, glimpsed in a matter of seconds before she closed the door on it and led them into the dining area, so that he realised her nose was not swollen from crying but from walking out of doors in the bitter cold.

"Are you often alone like this, Mrs Stephens?"

"Peter works weekdays," she inclined her head slightly, as if in an unsuccessful attempt to shift the front-curled wisps of unruly, dark hair that had encroached beyond the floppy dress collar and which appeared to touch her skin, like delicate consoling fingers.

Sandy Woodings hesitated long enough for Tom, sitting at the end of the table, to notice the pause. He spoke softly, while studying her reaction closely.

"You've had a little more time to think about things now, Mrs Stephens. Firstly about the note – " he allowed several seconds to rest on that – "and then what happened previously in the park. Have you thought of anything else, no matter how trivial, that you should tell us?"

"If I had thought of anything, I would have called you immediately."

Would she? A tiny shocking doubt had entered his mind. It was totally irrational. Sandy's eyes took stock of this modest room of about five yards square, the view onto the small front garden, Tom's car conspicuous outside the garden wall, which was built simply of three eight-inch courses of stone, below the triangular sectioned coping stones. The dining suite was beech Ercol ware and there were amateur oil landscapes on two of the four walls.

"There are questions of a rather intimate, even embarrassing nature – questions which I must ask you." He raised his eyebrows. "They may upset you." He hesitated only a moment. "About Bobby – "

She sat silently. Her forearms twitched nervously on the table's surface, her eyes darting fleetingly to meet his. But there was more to her than just nervousness. He was conscious of an interesting thinking alertness.

His voice was suddenly very insistent. "How long exactly have you been married, Mrs Stephens?"

"Eleven years."

"Since you were married, has a man shown a particular interest in you? Pestered you perhaps?"

"My husband, Peter." There was even a trace of a smile.

"My enquiry is a serious one. You're an attractive woman."

"Friends, occasionally colleagues of Pete's – "

Sandy was imagining her differently. He was imagining her sexual attractiveness. She was curiously attractive. She would have been almost obsessively attractive, twelve years younger? He was struck once as before how coquettishly elfin her face might look.

"I apologise for this question but I must ask it. Could there have been another father?"

She looked dumbstruck for several seconds and then she exploded. "You mean, could Bobby not be Pete's son?"

"That's what I mean, yes." He continued to gaze at her evenly.

"Bobby is Pete's son. For God's sake, he even looks like Pete when he was a boy."

"It's a very personal question but also a vital one. You must answer me honestly, Mrs Stephens."

She had flushed a beetroot red, shaking her head madly at the impossibility of it.

But Sandy felt increasingly puzzled. He was sensing something – something was disturbing him behind the nervousness. "In the note there was – well, it was a sense of intimacy."

"Then let me answer you once and finally on the subject so that you need never ever bring this question up again. Believe me, Mr Woodings, Bobby is Pete's son."

He was looking at her, silently, assessingly, when she gazed up suddenly. There was a fever now in her gaze as she held his eyes for longer than at any time during this interview. Yet her gaze was unflinching.

Outside, the temperature had fallen precipitously, although the sky was still blue. Tom drove Sandy back to headquarters so he could pick up his car to go and see Harry Dunn about the divorce.

Sandy wasn't looking forward to talking to Harry Dunn and he hung about in the car for several minutes at headquarters, restlessly silent, watching the change from dusk to nightfall in the townscape across the main road.

"She seemed different, Tom."

"Different?"

"How different – how did she seem to you?"

"Stubborn," Tom lit a cigarette and nodded.

"As if she knew something we didn't, wouldn't you say?"

"I just don't know," Tom said thinkingly.

In Harry Dunn's office, fifteen minutes later, he was still puzzled about Margaret Stephens, about this new change in her, about the way she had looked in that moment of – it seemed ridiculous yet that is how it had seemed – an inner determination. Harry had made the appointment especially late to suit him and as he sat for what seemed a very long time, listening to the legal pros and cons of the divorced state, he was haunted by something below consciousness, something close and ominous.

The divorce seemed unreal: this very conversation with an old rugby opponent, now balding where Sandy could recall a luxurious wilderness of brown hair, could not be taken seriously.

Something's on the move: I know it. I sense it!

He could just make out the reflections of some street-lights now on the copper canopies of the new town hall extension: which meant bad weather, rapidly freezing weather. He spoke again, touching a spot on Harry's desk, gazing fleetingly at the secretary who brought them coffee in china cups.

"No pretence on my part, Harry. Julie doesn't care any more. Partly my own fault. Not all my own fault. But I want it all sorted out. I want to be reasonable."

"Let's not get too carried away, Sandy." Harry spooned brown sugar into his own cup after Sandy had declined it.

What was it the professor had been talking about? Mrs Stephens appearing on television. *Twice.* Sandy had seen that first interview. He hadn't even known about the second interview.

Harry was studying him for a moment in silence, but the rogue was half smiling. Something about that second interview had caught the professor's attention.

Employing that same professional silence, Harry shifted in his chair, studying his cup of coffee for a moment. "So you're agreeable to its being mutual. Irreconcilable break-down – "

"It seems wrong to me that there's no way of saying – saying I damn well care."

Sandy noticed that Harry was brushing with a thick bony thumb at the droplets of coffee that trickled down the outside of his cup, like mistakes.

Two television interviews! So there would be tapes, wouldn't there?

Over time there have come a lot of changes. The man comes and goes all the time and every time he comes he brings new things with him, so that by now there are lots of things lying about the floor in the big room.

Often these days he brings Bobby little presents. A Lion bar, a Yorkie, a Mars, peanuts, packets of crisps. He doesn't seem to have any special sort of present he brings, more like he walks into the shop and picks up the first thing he sees in front of him. Bobby can tell this because there is a vagueness in the man's eyes – the man he has now come to call Mag – that is the single most disturbing thing about him. That and something about Bobby's mother. Something funny happens inside Mag's head whenever Bobby mentions his mother.

At first he refused to eat these things because he certainly didn't want presents from the magician. What he wants more than anything else in the world is to let Mag know just how much he hates him. He absolutely hates his face, which is growing a dirty beard, he hates that too calm and deep gravelly voice, and he hates his sticking out ears and his hair, which is never properly combed, and most of all he hates those vague grey eyes. You never know what he is thinking behind those eyes. Those eyes have a nasty habit of staring . . .

And how he has had time to think, it's no good saying no to the presents anyway. Not when you're starving hungry. And every day Bobby feels hungry. He feels hungry and he feels cold and thin and often there is a kind of darkness now, which isn't just the crying darkness of the room at night when he is alone. Mag leaves a nightlight high up on the black mantelpiece over the fireplace, with its flowers made of black iron. He leaves it up there because he's smart and he knows that Bobby has already thought of burning through the tights that always hold his hands and feet when Mag is not here. And what if Bobby just starved to death? Mag wouldn't care. Mag wouldn't care a jot anyway. It even occurs to Bobby that maybe that's what Mag wants to happen.

Because he now feels weak in his legs and how is he ever going to escape if he stays weak in his legs like this? Now he is eating the crisps and chocolates, now there is a little sort of – well, a sort of agreement, although nothing is really talked about – but Bobby is still as scared of Mag as the first day. And maybe – maybe with how Mag goes real quiet when Bobby's mum is mentioned! Worse still, worst of all – Bobby has seen the guns!

Mag has two guns!

These are two of the things he brought here into the big room, only a few days ago. One is a shotgun and the other is a rifle. The guns are the most worrying thing yet although Bobby guesses now that Mag has had these all the time, hidden away in one of the other dusty old rooms in the building. But he has hidden them away for reasons of his own and for reasons of his own he has brought them out now.

So why had he brought them out now?

Oh, God – he hates my mum!

The day he brought in the guns, all taken apart in that old brown bag of his, was the day he brought Bobby the football. Only it had been a trick really because Mag, when he brought him the ball, kept asking about that stupid car.

"Did you hear something, Bobby lad? Like a car's engine?"

"No – no, I didn't."

Of course it was the calm voice but Mag was sweating.

111

And when he saw Mag sweating like that, Bobby started to sweat too.

"Now you understand that you must tell old Mag the truth. No porky pies, eh. I know there's been a car, Bobby. I saw the tracks down there on the drive. Maybe you heard tyres? Maybe tyres just going by down there outside the window?"

That's when he brought in the ball. A small red plastic ball, half the size of a real football. He was staring at Bobby real hard, smiling with his lips, pretending they were pals. He was down on his haunches, rolling the ball backwards and forwards under one hand.

"Maybe I heard something. I – I don't know."

"When did you hear something?"

"I don't know." Bobby was sweating more now, panicking just a little with how serious Mag looked. Mag had hold of his shoulder and was kneading him very gently. Any minute now those eyes would change. Any minute now . . . "Maybe when it was dark. I was dreaming – I – I keep dreaming . . ." He had been about to add, dreaming that same scary dream. But Mag didn't want to hear about his dream.

"You heard what?"

"Maybe I heard the engine . . . and tyres. Maybe I thought it was you."

Mag was heaving a great sigh. Mag was shuddering and his hand was still opening and closing on Bobby's shoulder. That hand could rip Bobby off the dusty floor and smash him to shreds against the filthy cracked and peeling wall. "And old Mag didn't come?"

Bobby was shaking his head violently . . . Now Bobby can remember the quivery clutching in his guts when Mag's eyes closed with that long long sigh, and that same tingle of fear when Mag questioned him every day afterwards.

Mag wants to know badly about the car. And Bobby even thinks he did hear some engine or tyres some nights when

Mag didn't come. All Bobby knows is that since then Mag brought in the guns. Since then, Mag has those guns on his brain.

Every day he comes now, he takes the guns out. He pours oil into bits of them with a spiky very thin spoon which unscrews from a tube like a fat brass pencil. And that same question over and over – *did you hear the car again last night?*

And then today, only hours ago, when he asked that same question again, and Bobby just asked him, "What is it about that old car anyway?" He pointed the rifle at Bobby's head. Bobby hadn't seen him put any ammunition into it but he felt ice-cold horror all the same, and it didn't stop him crying his eyes out – the fact that Mag was chuckling in that crazy way of his after he pulled the trigger and it only clicked.

Maybe Mag thought there was a bullet in the rifle?

Now Bobby stands up from where he has been sitting close to the oil lamp and he rolls the ball across the floor with his right foot. He rolls it along, walking slowly, swishing softly on the bare floorboards, as he takes the ball right along to the wall at the end which has just a single window, round-topped, like the others, set about the top of Bobby's head, so he can't see out. He's doing his best not to annoy Mag today.

These last three days, what with all that about hearing a car, Mag has been too quiet and . . . and dangerous. Mag looks as dangerous today as on that walk in the woods. Today the most Bobby has got out of him is a grunt and earlier when he came he didn't bring any sweets or chocolate.

His mum – Mag hates his mum!

Thwack, thwack. *Your mam knows I've got you.* He begins to kick the ball against the wall under the window. It's hard, bouncy and comes back at him too fast. *You told her? That's right, I told her.* He can't move his leg fast enough to keep on kicking the ball. Just twice and then a rest. Thwack, Thwack. He twists his head back very very carefully, to glimpse the man sitting with his legs wide out, with the pieces of rifle in front of him. *I told her . . . told her you were okay . . .*

Bobby suddenly feels a chill invade him. It hits him like a blow over his thighs and wallows up over his belly.

It's because of his mum. He's suddenly howling, tears filling up in his eyes. "Makes you feel good, that rifle. Stupid rifle! *Stupid rifle!*"

It all means something, doesn't it? Mag taking him. Mag telling his mum. Mag . . . and his mum.

Mag didn't bring him here to this weird dark and drippy castle for no reason. Mag isn't the sort of person who did anything at all for no reason. There was something about that reason, Bobby now realises, in that soft chuckle of his when he played games aiming the rifle and pulling the trigger. The reason Bobby now knows this is that when Mag's mouth was smiling his eyes were not smiling. No, Mag didn't go to all that trouble to keep him here for all this horrible long time, playing that old music and stuff – bringing all those hundreds of things here and spending money on Mars bars and crisps and chocolates – without having some very good reason for all that.

And suddenly, like a baby bird out of its nest for the first time, the world is full of snapping jaws. There's a reason all right. There's a whole world of reasons. He doesn't want to become a crybaby again, but he knows . . . Mag getting the rifle ready . . . All of a sudden he is more terrified than at any time since he heard those footsteps climbing the stairs in that smelly house and all he could see was that wallpaper with the brown stains over the flower pattern.

Now Bobby's jittering legs tell him he knows the reason Mag has been a different man for three days. Right now, without daring to look, he knows that Mag has finished whatever he was doing, that he has broken the rifle down again and has put it back into that brown bag. Oh, yes, the tears are here. Now he stands, with tears filling up his eyes, without resisting as Mag's footsteps approach him, he allows Mag to pick him up and carry him back to the blankets where he will be tied down as usual for the night. "Don't hurt my mum," he hears his own tear-crackly words as Mag first ties his ankles and then his hands, and he takes more than the usual trouble to cover him over really heavy.

Which means that Mag is going to be away for a long time. He's going away some distance and he's taking the rifle with him. And he's going to punish Bobby. That's why, after snuffing the oil lamp, he crosses to the mantelpiece and blows out the nightlight, throwing Bobby into pitch darkness.

Cubes of hail rattled the bonnet of his car as Sandy left headquarters just after eight in the evening. Tom had been sent to Leeds immediately after their shared canteen tea some hour and forty minutes earlier, where he had an appointment with the regional television news team. Sandy was becoming increasingly curious about those two television interviews with Mrs Stephens. By the time he had arrived at the neighbour's house where they had installed their twenty-four hours' surveillance of the Stephens' home, it had worsened to sleet.

What the hell was happening? He felt jerkily tense – since that interview with Margaret Stephens.

Sitting for a while in the company of the two detectives already in position there, a sense of danger cut right through his worry about Harry and the divorce. Then Tom burst in out of the blizzard, huffing and puffing and banging his hands together.

"One pint of piping hot tea, landlord!" he wisecracked, with his calculating face set into a hangdog look, even as Sandy put a firm arm round his soaked shoulders and sat him down forcibly on the edge of the single bed.

"Did you get a copy of the interviews?"

"I got copies of both."

Sandy shook his head because there was no video recorder here in this house. "Did you watch it – the second tape?"

"Yeah, I watched the tapes."

"So – ?"

"I couldn't make out much that was of interest." Tom sighed, more than a little resentful at having had to make the journey to Leeds in this weather. "What about the lads here – have they seen anything?"

"Nothing much." It was Palmer, an experienced detective constable. The other man, Huntley, was a uniformed man just going through the motions of his mandatory six months with CID. Palmer handed Tom his mug of Yorkshire brew. "Just Mrs Stephens in and out like a yoyo, as usual."

"Just like the tape – " grumbled Tom, sipping and wincing with the piping hot temperature of his tea.

"How do you mean, Tom? Just like the tape?" Sandy turned from where he had moved, opposite the window.

"Well, you saw the first interview. We set the first interview up down at headquarters. It was the second interview."

Sandy felt like shouting with a tense exasperation. "What about this second tape?"

"They must have filmed it on location here. About twenty or twenty-five minutes, that's all. I recognised it was somewhere on the slope, at the top of the slope where the lad was kidnapped," Tom misunderstood Sandy's snatch of his cigarette, lifting another from the case and placing it in his mouth, but Sandy again interrupted him, just as he was about to apply the lighter.

"Tom – I'm warning you!"

"Keep your hair on. Just that she said something like Palmer here just said. You know – how she couldn't rest.

116

They asked a question or two and she said she couldn't rest. She kept coming out and walking about on the slope. She couldn't stop herself, anytime, sometimes even in the early hours of the morning – "

Sandy would have given a lot to have seen that interview himself.

"What kind of questions did they ask her?"

"The usual. Just how she felt. If there was anything she wanted to say – that kind of thing."

"Anything she wanted to say to whom?"

"To the viewers, I suppose."

Frowning, Sandy shook his head. "What did she say, exactly, Tom? Try to give it to me, word for word. Where was she when she was speaking? What exactly was she doing?"

"I told you where she was and what she was doing. Just like Palmer here said – "

"She was walking? They filmed her walking just down there – on the slope in front of her house?"

"I told you," Tom muttered aggressively. "Right there – top of the slope. Stretching her legs."

"So – what exactly did she reply to that question?"

Tom winced, cleared his throat. He had the cigarette perched on his bottom slip as he pressed at his temples, with his eyes shut. "For God's sake – something along the lines of – I'll do anything. I'll see anyone. I'll go to the ends of the earth if he'll just tell us what he wants. Or maybe why he did it. Or what he's after. And Uncle Tom Cobley . . ."

Sandy tore himself back to the observation window, with the curtains slightly drawn back in the almost dark room. Now he understood why that interview had interested the professor. "She wasn't talking to any viewers, Tom, you idiot."

"I don't get it," Tom came across to the window to stare out into the dark next to Sandy.

117

But Sandy had turned his attention now on the other two officers. "What time did you see her walk out?"

"About half an hour ago."

"I can't see her now."

"I was telling you," Palmer too had come over to the window now. He joined Tom and Sandy, with a pair of binoculars held loosely in his right hand. "She does it most of the time. Leaves the house. Walks the streets about here. She often stands right there outside, where Sergeant Williams was talking about, at the top of the slope. She just stands there and looks down the slope."

"Even in the dark?"

"Dark, light, it makes not a jot of difference."

"So where is she now?"

"I haven't seen her go back into the house – unless she did it like lightning, while you two were talking. But I don't think so. I think she's probably just walked a little distance down there. Down the slope."

"What – do you mean to tell me she's down there, in the dark, alone?"

"Tonight, like every single other night since we've had her and her house under observation."

"Tom. Get over to her house and see if her husband is in."

"He's in all right."

"Get over there and talk to him. Find out if she is back. Find out where he thinks she is – as far as possible, don't let him know we're watching."

"Oh, no!" groaned Tom, taking a last fond swig from the mug of still piping hot tea.

"Here – let me have the binoculars," Sandy spoke urgently. Palmer stood next to him as he scanned the streets and the top of the slope. But all he could see was a night as opaque as charcoal, with islands here and there illuminated by neon headlights.

Over the space of five or six minutes, he watched the

occasional passing car, a couple scurrying through the sleet with a common umbrella. A man knocking at a door, a teenager dragging her disgruntled puppy by its leash and with its bottom making a wave through the slush, two middle-aged women with cagoules pulled down over their heads waiting at a bus stop in the company of a workman heading for the nightshift. The trio obtained what shelter they could from a cluster of half-grown beech trees, through which a roadlight made beams and forays.

The gathering excitement in him brought on heartburn but he accepted a mug of instant coffee, swilling it round in his mouth anyway, inspecting two parents ushering their children from an orange-glowing car, another couple under an orange umbrella, then the sound of the bus, which led him back to his trio at the bus stop.

The women boarded, the man stayed on the pavement. He just stood there looking lost, his pale oblong of tool-kit at armslength by his side. Huntley said something to Palmer behind Sandy's back; Sandy registered the voice only, his concentration so intense he did not register whatever was said in a soft and confidential tone. The door downstairs slammed shut – Tom back already – he ignored it, he ignored Tom's footsteps ascending the stairs to the first floor bedroom where they were standing; he watched the bus move away, he watched the tail end of it disappear round a bend, and then he returned his attention to the hatless workman only to find that he had vanished.

"Bring me the street map, will you," he said, without turning to look at Huntley.

Scanning the streets to the left of the bus stop, he saw houses – but they were too close. What would he have been doing out in this weather if he lived only across the road! Another mouthful of bitter oversugared coffee, and he moved the binoculars in the direction of the dark that was all he could see to the right of the bus stop. The darkness was very near to the slope, the darkness nibbled away at

119

that slope where Mrs Stephens must be standing – standing, maybe lost in some nightmare of formless, timeless worry.

Or, infinitely worse, infinitely more dangerous, a nightmare of expectation . . .

"Quickly!" he shouted to Huntley. Tracing the road with his fingers, discovering the location of the bus stop, he confirmed it; the darkness fell away below the road, from where it would have been simple to walk in a circle, completely out of view of this room, and enter the wooded slope. Suddenly his heart had risen into his throat and was throbbing with appalling vigour.

He spilled coffee on Huntley, swivelling round so violently. Looking through the window again . . . two hundred yards. The workman's build had been tall and slim. Now, with the light out again, using his binoculars, he focused on that yawn of darkness, he persuaded himself – no, he was certain – that something, a blur of light, was moving – something pale and oblong – the workman's holdall!

He was through the door when the sleet reminded him that he had forgotten his hat. He could hear Tom behind him, Tom who wouldn't be able to keep up with him because he was lunging ahead like a madman. Carrying on running, across the road, he bounded over a low brick wall, grabbing at a sapling to stop himself sliding as he searched for some short cut. His hat no longer mattered but the lack of a torch did. He cursed his own haste but continued to swerve and trample blindly. The roadlights behind him were his only guide as to direction, his feet were awash in rotting vegetation, which soaked his trousers, and the ooze from the branches attacked his arms, saturating his coat as high as the elbows. He ignored the top of the slope – Palmer would make for where Mrs Stephens had entered the slope. He rushed downwards, two hundred yards of abandoned mad trampling through freezing saturated undergrowth. Jumping into a void, he landed within feet of the site of abduction, then suddenly stopped, crouched on his haunches, his fist pushed against his lower lip, his ears finely prickling. He could hear what must be Palmer, further down than he anticipated, and very likely Tom behind him. They seemed a long distance away. He could make out the gloom of trees, silhouetted against the distant roadlights, the patter of sleet hitting branches and the splat of water on the squelchy ground.

Where was she? Where was this crazy misguided woman?

The way he had come was directly to his back, so he gauged that the man must approach from his left. Taking a chance, he advanced in that direction, his right elbow pushed out in front of his face and one foot placed squarely in front of the other, so as to keep his balance on the treacherous sloping ground. Suddenly he was aware of a shape against the dark bronze sky above him. There wasn't a sound, not even breathing, but he guessed it had to be Mrs Stephens.

"Get back. Get out of here!" he cried out, his voice tremulous, hoarse with breathlessness.

Within seconds he felt an almighty blow to his extended arm, which felt as if it must have penetrated bone immediately above the level of his elbow.

He dived in the direction of the blow and got a kick in the centre of his forehead that sent him rolling through ten feet of undergrowth. There were other noises now. Violent scuffling. A terrible drawn-out moan. Then he could hear running feet and he clawed his way back up and took after him.

They covered the distance to the main road at the bottom of the slope in a matter of minutes. They must surely have heard that awful moan, Tom and Palmer. They must search lower down the slope and find her. It was all he could do to stop himself falling headlong at the point where he had restrained the professor, and now, slithering down the embankment on the seat of his trousers, landing with his feet in a good eight inches of smelly rubbish, he caught a glimpse of the navy-coloured donkey jacket, blue jeans, the hand holding a canvas bag, pale yellow in the roadlight, all three disappearing over a vicious-looking barbed wire fence as in the distance he heard the first wail of approaching sirens.

Vaulting the barbed wire, he fell into a crouch again in the long undergrowth on the far side. This character was fit all right, he was making better progress than himself despite the holdall. The sounds of crashing steps about fifty yards ahead of him made him realise there was nothing for it but to forget caution and make a run at full speed. He made good time and then slid heavily onto his side, stopped where he lay and listened intently – baffling and unexpected silence . . .

God! he implored. *Don't let me lose him.*

Testing the solid-looking murk below him, he jabbed air with his foot – the edge of the railway cut, which itself formed the southern perimeter of the Redmond district.

Staying where he was for the moment, he groped for a stone or a piece of wood – anything that might have been useful as a weapon . . . but found nothing. Then, sliding carefully, a yard at a time, into what seemed an interminable descent, he landed eventually in real water, about a foot deep, ice-cold and numbing. He stood in it and spat dirt and wondered which way to go. To his left was a railway line that had once carried passengers into open country and the Pennines, to his right a long tunnel which opened a good mile distant in canal-land and at the outer fringe of the industrial guts of the city. It was such an obvious trap, the tunnel, he was inclined to go left. But then this man had proved himself just a little too smart in the past – smart enough for Sandy to splash right, breathing like a traction engine, the eighty yards' distance to another major road crossing, under which lay the mouth of the tunnel.

If there were a hundred shades of darkness, then the

tunnel was the hundredth percentile. He shouted out, standing at the entrance.

"Listen to me, you mad bugger. I know you're in there. So you haven't got a cat-in-hell's chance."

The answering silence forced him to step into the mouth of darkness where there was a dank prickling hush over all sounds of the outside world: each step echoed like a firecracker so he was forced to pause at intervals and to strain his senses beyond the slime-dripping and feculent-smelling corruption and the scuttling of what he presumed to be rats, into the silence.

"We only have to block the two entrances. Wait for daylight." He shouted again. "The only chance you have is to make a run for it. So why not? Go ahead – try it."

Maybe he should have felt some satisfaction on hearing the abrupt cackle of laughter than came in reply. He was too busy realising that it was no more than feet from him. Swearing loudly, and diving into the air with sweeping arms, he clutched with the fingers of his left hand a wrist that was encircled by two straps. For a second he felt the texture of the holdall as it swung against him and then clunked against the arched stone, then another almighty blow, better aimed this time, caught him on the side of the neck and confused his senses so he crashed spreadeagled against the unyielding stone wall. But his hand was more awkward than the rest of him and it refused to let go.

He swung himself round and did his best to bite the wrist that was holding the straps but another of those bone-jarring blows found its target in the region of his left shoulder, which must have caught a nerve because his hand fell uselessly by his side. Kicking out with all of his strength, he met with a satisfying resistance. There was a gasp and then he heard the other body take a tumble, but before he had time to follow up, there was another disturbing cackle of laughter, which worried him all the more because he would have expected his kick to have demolished a sixteen stone quarter-back on the rugby field.

He tried diving with flailing arms again and his fingers encountered wet curly hair. Swinging with all his strength in the direction of the wall, he managed to smash all ten of his own knuckles. This was followed by the nauseating pain of a kick in his groin and he let go of the hair. Another of those powerful blows caught him just above the neck, on the back of his head, and he tumbled, retching, onto his knees, with just sufficient sense left to try crawling out of the way of what he expected would be the murderous blow.

The final blow never fell.

It could have been the thundering overhead that saved him, in which case he was grateful for one of the coaches ferrying in men for the hunt. This was followed by the continuous caterwauling of police sirens. Then suddenly Sandy was aware of exactly where the man was standing. He was standing very close to him, close enough to hear his breathing: and then the words, a gravelly deep voice, and icily calm. "The fun is just beginning, Mister Detective!" The man didn't find much difficulty in getting past him and Sandy heard his footsteps receding from him in the direction of the mouth of the tunnel, hardly hurried, just a careful and light padding, like those of a cat which has exhausted its purpose.

Taking some time to prise himself to his feet, he made painful progress, leaning against the slime-oozing wall. He was at the entrance before he registered blood in his mouth and it took an exploration with his fingers to discover a torn right ear.

Inhaling for a bit, his immediate instinct was to stand and shout, but that would have cost time and, now that he was recovering his senses, he had no intention of letting his man escape.

He clambered up the one in three incline with a single functioning arm and two frozen feet, reached the top, then fell sprawling over a low stone wall and tumbled into the glare of a coach's headlights. He was picked up by two burly constables wearing yellow overmacs, who, in his blurred vision, looked like giant lemons on matchsticks.

"Get me Inspector Earnshaw," he mumbled, as they half carried him back to the vehicle and the radio.

"Dogs, Charlie! For the love of Pete! The old railway bridge across Nelson Street!"

Tom arrived with the forgotten hat, chewing a mint and looking at him with a face that was at once furtive and incredulous. "You look as if you've just done ten rounds with old Nick himself!"

"If that's who it was, he was carrying a knuckleduster." He sipped ruefully at a flask of brandy, brushed down antheaps of mud still clinging to his coat and he confirmed from Tom, who was massaging Sandy's neck and left shoulder and causing white hot pokers of pain to flash down his arm, that they had got Mrs Stephens out safely. The groan had been Palmer's. Palmer had been knocked on the head.

"Can't we cut down that racket with the sirens, Tom? Concord could take off fifty yards away and we wouldn't know it."

There wasn't even time to do anything about it. They were on their way again, down into the railway ditch, which was about thirty feet below road level, searching the edge with hand-lamps, until they came upon some railway sleepers which were rammed into the ground along the perimeter of some allotments, like a palisade of giant rotten teeth.

The allotments . . . !

Sandy shouted ahead to the dog-handlers to let them have their head. The dogs quickly found a gap in the sleepers and they all poured through. On the flat ground, just inside the fence, the sleet seemed to find its vocation. It sprayed them fiercely and with a tendency suddenly to change direction so that no matter which way you turned it was impossible to keep it out of your face. The only dry piece of clothing he had left was his hat, which he now pulled down hard over his eyes, as he closed the top button of his overcoat.

"Go on," he shouted. "Let the dogs loose."

They had run into another steep embankment, a slope which divided the allotment into two levels. Sandy borrowed somebody's master cane from their bean patch to drag himself up in the wake of the slithering excited dogs, ripping at the ground, at anything that gave him a grip, because he knew they had found something, he could hear the dogs up ahead barking themselves hoarse. He lost a shoe in the mud but continued to climb over the top and then to run, ignoring the pains in every muscle, and with Tom taking the Lord's name in vain, following on with the lost shoe in his hand.

Sheds, greenhouses, vague impressions of boundaries, skeletal hawthorns. The night was a lost void outside the cones of lamplight through which the sleet gusted in big sloppy globs like cuckoo-spit. Up ahead he could make out Jock's accent, Jock's voice calling. Pushing his way through a circle of fluorescent overmacs, he joined up with Jock in staring despairingly . . .

"We've lost him. We had him and we've lost him." Sandy's voice was husky, barely above a whisper. There was a ferocious roaring in both his ears. His pulse was hammering against the back of his neck and his teeth were clenched so bitterly, he was in danger of shattering them.

On the ground lay one boy's trainer, torn apart, the sole ripped completely from the upper, the canvas mauled and sundered into five or six fragments. From it led a set of tyre tracks, so crisp and pristine in the mud they could have been etched out with a sculptor's chisel.

14

"An encounter with the devil," one of Georgy's eyes was opened wider than the other, "and he didn't even make you an offer?"

Sandy replied curtly, his face pallid. "He's got my number already."

Georgy nodded: he appeared to give this his serious consideration, while Sandy just stood there, dripping water on the carpet. At two in the morning, Georgy exuded an overwhelming animal malice. Hardly animal at all, something at once more brutal and sweaty, a corpulent lividity mixed with human halitosis. Both men were standing, Sandy before the desk, Georgy by the uncurtained window.

In a monotone of animosity, Georgy added. "Palmer has a fractured skull. He's in hospital intensive care right now. The man could have died." He inhaled a furious indignation which sounded like a sob. "So what was in the bag?"

"What bag?"

"The bag he tried to knock your brains out with."

"Something hard and heavy. More than one thing. Tools maybe."

"Tools? What kind of tools?"

"Breaking and entering – I don't know."

"Breaking and entering? So our man is a burglar – is that what you think?"

Then suddenly realisation flooded Sandy. Realisation froze him for a moment, paralysed him from scalp to toes.

His voice had fallen to a husky whisper. "No. That's not what I think."

"What else then?"

"A weapon – it must have been a weapon."

"A gun?"

"He was carrying a gun. A gun – that was what he was carrying in the holdall."

"A handgun?"

"No, it wasn't a handgun. Maybe a shotgun. Even a rifle, maybe. A rifle or a shotgun. He disassembled it. That was why he went into the tunnel. Time to disassemble it."

"So that's what broke Palmer's head – a rifle or a shotgun! So what was he up to? Our man down the slope with a bag that might have contained a gun?"

Sandy was remembering that first huge kick delivered to his forehead. Not a kick at all – the butt of a rifle or a shotgun! He had been that close . . . A faint sweat beaded his brow as he realised how close to death he himself must have been. And now he heard that curiously deep voice with a frightening clarity, that voice so calm under those crazy circumstances that it was hair-prickling now even to think about it. *The fun is just beginning* . . . A challenge? Yes, that was the way he saw it. Opening up something directly and deeply personal between himself and the kidnapper. Something personal – something he wouldn't tell Georgy, he wouldn't even tell Tom, about. He whispered his thoughts aloud, "Mrs Stephens – "

"You think he was after Mrs Stephens?"

"I'm sure of it."

Georgy just couldn't control himself. He was shouting at the top of his voice. "After her? How after her?"

Sandy didn't shout. His voice was if anything softer, barely above a whisper. "To talk to her. Frighten her. Injure her. I wonder Georgy, I really do wonder, if maybe he meant to kill her."

Georgy now held several seconds of silence, looking out at the sleet languorously drifting onto the city centre streets.

"You can come off this case if you want to. Right now."

Sandy was startled. He gazed in open-mouthed amazement at the powerful rounded outline of Georgy's suited back.

"I don't want to."

Georgy gazed flatly towards the soft buttery lights in streets utterly devoid of people. "Think about it."

What was it, for God's sake? Then suddenly Sandy had a glimmer of understanding. It wasn't losing the man in the chase tonight. It was his marriage. Georgy was trying to tell Sandy something about his marriage. Sandy felt a white-hot ball of anger explode behind his eyes.

"I don't want to jack it in. I don't need to think about it."

How was it possible that in the space of those few seconds, Georgy's silent contemplation of the view through the window, his offer, the rejection of his offer, that Sandy felt deep down at the core of his being that their relationship, never easy but at least workmanlike, professional, had irrevocably changed?

"He went down the slope," Georgy's voice had squatted into that monotone again, his back held stiffly, his head bowed at a curiously broken angle as if under some dreadful burden of virulence, "in order to kill Mrs Stephens?"

"That's one possibility. Maybe the most likely possibility."

"He came back. Took an almighty chance. Right under our noses. So how the hell did he know she would be there waiting for him?"

"I don't know." He lied easily. He needed an edge at that moment, even the slenderest edge, over Georgy's paranoia.

"Everything he does, then, is aimed somehow at Mrs Stephens? The note with the shoe, tonight's escapade, the kidnapping itself?"

"So it would seem."

"Don't give me that kind of vague crap. It's what you think?"

"Yes. It's what I think."

"Because he – our man – has some kind of hang-up about her?"

"An obsession. Possibly."

Georgy did not turn. Georgy didn't look at him. His tone was locked in that same monotone. "Tomorrow. Go and get some sleep. We'll talk again tomorrow."

Sandy turned with his hat in his hand, walked out of Georgy's office, making his way to the small canteen which was kept open throughout the night. It was almost two thirty and Tom was waiting for him at a small square table.

For several minutes his mind was a witch's brew of too many conflicting priorities: Palmer badly hurt . . . an attempt to kill Mrs Stephens? Mrs Stephens would have to keep until tomorrow because her doctor had been called out by her husband so that when Sandy had returned to the house after losing his man, she had been asleep, under heavy sedation.

Curiously, in spite of everything, Sandy did not feel depressed. He felt more excited, restless.

They would be able to identify the type of tyre and from that get a shortlist of possible vehicles involved. For what use that would be, since with no description of the vehicle, the job of tracking it down would be a non-starter.

He took another bite at his sandwich, fell almost immediately deep into thought. "That video – I want to go over it myself but it will have to keep until tomorrow. I must go over it – that and the crazy letter again."

"Not a lot to go on."

"Maybe more than we realise, Tom. Vibrations."

Tom drank from his cup, cradling its edge parsimoniously with that great lower lip. Tom wasn't as generous as solicitor Harry Dunn. He would not allow droplets to escape. "The way I see it," Tom interrupted his coffee drinking to rub noisily with the cupped fingers of his right hand on his stubbled chin, "is he came up deliberately early. He parked on the far side of the allotments because he reckoned nobody would see him. Then he took his time approaching the spare ground, and you saw him when he was sizing up the house – "

"He could certainly see the house from the bus stop."

"All right. So what was he up to? He wants to leave the second trainer – and that's what he does – he leaves us the second trainer as a present."

Sandy told Tom about the gun.

"You're a bloody madman, with all due respect. A rifle – Christ! You could have got yourself killed."

Sandy ignored that because he didn't want to think about it. "No note this time, Tom. Not unless that too was torn to pieces. He might have torn it up in that same frenzy. It might have all blown away. Blown to the elements in that neuralgic wind."

"All that, just to tear up one boy's trainer. He must like tearing things up, this character."

"Okay – what we have to consider, Tom, is that this vehicle, this car or van or whatever, must have been parked at that spot for quite a while. Maybe longer than an hour."

"That's exactly the point I was coming to – I'm saying, maybe he wasn't as clever as he thought he was."

Sandy gazed at Tom: he really did wonder why Tom had never married. Tom was playing some ace up his sleeve, looking pleased with himself, while Sandy, consumed with restlessness, could do nothing but wait patiently for the play.

It was because of Julie, her lack of sympathy with the job, that he had taken to spending nights like this hanging about headquarters.

"All right, Tom – I give up. Let's have your theory."

"It's only that he might have made a mistake thinking the allotments would be deserted this time of year."

Sandy nodded: he felt a sudden lancinating reminder of that series of murderous blows. Not a brass knuckleduster but the butt end of a shotgun or a rifle! He didn't want to think about it but it kept on coming back to mind. And maybe he didn't want to think too hard about more than the gun. There was a good deal that was beginning to puzzle him about that slithering chase and the final one-sided hand to hand combat in the claustrophobic murk of the railway tunnel.

The fun is just beginning, Mister Detective!

"Go on, Tom. Tell me the reason you never married?"

"You'd give your right arm to know, wouldn't you?"

"I'd treat you to a second cup of coffee."

At 8.30 a.m. he drove to Mary's place but she wasn't at home, in spite of the fact that he knew it wasn't one of her working days. Maybe it wasn't such a good time to call on her but then maybe that made it the best time in the world to call on her.

He recognised her car outside the local supermarket and he caught up with her as she wheeled her trolley through the doors. Walking side by side, neither of them said anything. Then, after he had helped her load the shopping into the boot of her car, she stood and confronted him in the rain.

"I blame you, Sandy. I blame you for everything that has happened."

"So why are you and Julie still seeing one another. I want to understand what is still going on between you."

"Do you think I'm just going to give him up? Maybe that's what Julie thinks."

"It's no good asking me what Julie thinks, Mary."

"I'm going to fight. I've got my own way of fighting. From the inside – I'm still hanging around because that's the only way I know how."

"Innocents are getting hurt, Mary."

In the silence of her fury, he heard the radio beeping in

his car twenty yards away. But he ignored it. She climbed into her car and he leaned against it so she was forced to open her window. She said, "Don't give me that about the children. Look at yourself in a mirror, Sandy."

He smiled and meant it. For some reason he couldn't quite understand, he actually cared about this dark-haired feminist, even if she was as naive as hell about her continuing relationship with both Julie and her husband. "I know she still talks to you about things, Mary."

"Like how often she and Jack manage it, which position – according to the moon and the prevailing winds?"

Leaning against the door jamb, he laughed at her struggle with her own notion of modern woman. She was wearing her Little Red Riding Hood face, the social worker determined to apply jargon and principle to her own unhappiness.

As she switched on the ignition, he could hear his car radio beeping again: he put his hand over the glass – she would have to cut off his fingers to close the window.

"Forget the blame and the guilt, Mary. That's dangerous. All we have left is the children."

She left the window open, but the car had started to move. "I blame you – I'll always blame you for it, Sandy." She had completed a small reversing arc, had started to pull away before emotion ground her back. "You knew what was going on. You never had enough time for your own children."

15

Through driving rain, he ran to his car, yanked the door open and reached through for the receiver.

"Woodings!"

"I have Inspector Earnshaw – can you hold on a moment, Chief Inspector."

By now he was sitting in the driver's seat, watching individual drops of rain splatter the glass as he listened to Charlie's down-to-earth voice.

"We found an old character at the allotments. Says he saw a van parked yesterday. Do you want me to take him into headquarters?"

Woodings forced his over-heated mind back into concentration, while Charlie hawked over the radio to show his impatience. A witness? He couldn't believe they could actually have a witness.

He said, "Stay there with him, Charlie. I'll come out to the allotments to meet you."

"Just how long are you going to be?"

"Twenty – maybe thirty minutes at the most."

"Well, can you make it as snappy as you can, Chief. It's brass monkeys weather here."

His eyes were on the video tape which was tucked against the back of the passenger seat, the tape Tom had brought back from the television news studio. He desperately wanted to look through that tape. But a witness! His heart would not stop fluttering. His heart had been fluttering ever since that grotesque vision of disappointment last night. He could feel a disturbing sweat oozing from his neck onto his collar, reminding him he had had no sleep.

He spoke abruptly, "I'll be there as fast as I can," then slammed the receiver down, lay back for a moment against his seat and tried to control the excited pattering against his rib cage. The incident centre was on his way: he would just have to find that extra five minutes.

Rain was stringing itself together like beads outside the Portakabin window as he hunched anxiously over the telephone, waiting for Henry Bancroft to answer.

"How's the family situation?" asked the solicitous Henry.

"Give over joking and tell me what you've been able to make out on the tyre tracks."

Henry tutted, while Sandy refused a mug of coffee, tattooing like a machine gun with his finger tips on the table. Henry said they had made casts of the tyre tracks, pretty decent really considering how hard it was sleeting and raining and the delay, as usual, in the police calling out the technician on emergency call, and Sandy, who had been trying to give up smoking, accepted a cigarette and he fretted over a mental image of the stout scientist, with his reddish wispy hair and the inevitable spatula in his hand. Right now the spatula would be gesticulating, a delicate pointing in the direction of the casts which, to judge from what he was saying, lay on the bench in front of him. Henry was now remarking with annoying calmness some tiny nipple-like excrescences that were poking out of the cast.

"Remoulds?"

"Yes, remoulds. Standard size, thirteen inches, 155 millimetres across the tread."

"Which would fit at least half the vehicles in the city."

"Unless you manage to pare the list down a little with your witness."

His witness! Sandy had consumed his cigarette in one minute flat with his hunger to meet that witness.

"What about the torn-up trainer?"

"Give us a chance."

"How soon then?"

"Later on today, if you're lucky. Are you feeling lucky?"

Sandy had already put the phone down and was dashing into the rain. He felt vibrations all right but he was far from feeling lucky.

Their witness was an old man called Templeton, who was hopping from one foot to another while waiting for him at the entrance to the allotments. Charlie Earnshaw made no secret of the fact that he too felt frozen to the marrow. Sandy took the old man by the arm and questioned him, as they walked back through the gate.

"You come here every day? Even this time of year?"

"That's me – unpaid caretaker."

"Seven days a week?"

"More or less."

"And you were here yesterday?" Sandy glanced away from the old man's bald head and long anteater's nose, to inspect the place by daylight. The slope up which they had scrambled last night, and which divided the allotments into two, was shades of green rather than black, more messy and a good deal more homely than he remembered.

"Yesterday I arrived at maybe eight in t'morning. Stayed until after me snap last thing."

Screwing his head restlessly about, Sandy saw a hedge of bright orange berberis surrounding the allotments on the three sides other than the railway sleepers: in front of them a dilapidated greenhouse and garden shed, whose owner was following his gaze with predatory eyes. This man was their only chance. Sandy gazed very deeply into Mr Templeton's eyes: at the constricted black spots in the centre of blue steel circles. What he saw gave him hope. A character who would split a gnat if there were a halfpenny in it.

"Exactly what time did you leave?"

"Happen half past four. Thereabouts. Reckon it up for yourself since it were going dark."

"Yesterday it went dark at what – say four thirtyish?" He was turning again, sharply observant, studying the higgledy-piggledy greenhouses, ramshackle sheds, scattered about and all seemingly painted decades ago with that same olive green paint: "So you were here, Mr Templeton, when the van arrived?"

"That's right. Right here in me shed and I heard it. So I come out to see who it were, like."

"Because you know them all?"

Mr Templeton lifted his nose in the air, to have a good look at Sandy's ruptured ear. "More or less."

"Did you get a good look at the driver?"

"I saw him."

Sandy's heartbeat missed, became regular again. "Was it somebody you recognised?"

"I never clapped eyes on him before in me life."

"But you saw him clearly? You realised he wasn't one of the usual people here on the allotments?" A big drop of rain spattered the back of Sandy's hand, and he wiped it dry against the side of his overcoat.

"The trouble is, you never know. Sometimes they change hands, you see. I asked meself – maybe it were someone new or something like that. Winter's a time for handing over."

"Did you try to speak to him?"

"He were too far away."

"Damn!" he murmured softly. "Just how far away from him were you, Mr Templeton?"

"I reckon," said the old man, wiping something closer to a taloned claw than a hand across his nose, and displaying a copper bangle round the wrist, which, to judge by the state of his fingers, had failed in its design to ward off arthritis, "it might be a lot easier on us both if I was to show you."

They made a careful way along a beaten path oozing slime under a big freezing yellow headlight: the headlight was the sun, shining through a grey smog of rain. Mr Templeton led him through an incandescent gloss which haloed everything but cast no shadows until he could point from a much closer distance.

"Maybe sixty yards," Sandy estimated aloud, the distance from Mr Templeton's greenhouse to the spot where the van had been parked. "Get us closer, will you, Mr Templeton."

Zig-zagging then round the remains of vegetables, trampling the rangy cabbages and frost-whitened beanpoles, it was – dammit it was – Tom's silhouette he could make out for a moment against the sun, high up on the scarp of the slope. And suddenly Sandy felt that same mad urgency as that chase over this same ground yesterday. It was so powerful he was physically breathless and he had to force himself to think now – to think distances and angles, reasoning that in the evening the sun had to be shining from almost precisely the opposite direction, from his side onto the slope above him, which meant that the parking spot must lie immediately due east of Mr Templeton's position. And that meant a decent view of things. Provided the man's eyesight was sound and making due allowance for the showers of hail and sleet which had been such a plague throughout yesterday afternoon and evening.

"Did you try to get up onto the top level to have a good look at the van?"

"You must be joking."

"Did you get any closer than we're standing now?"

"I came a slightly different way. You see that stump of an ash yonder," he pointed to a spot which was a little to the right of them, but hardly nearer to the top. "Wonderin' about t'beanpoles – whether I'd better have 'em up or whether I might get away with it for next year. The ash marks the end of my territory. And besides – if it's someone as knows me, they generally come round and I puts teapot on t'boil."

So near! God in heaven, of only the man had been a little more curious. Sandy found himself drumming frantically with his nails on a galvanised barrel, full to the brim with cold black water.

Just how had the van been positioned? From his memory of the tracks . . . "Point, will you, to precisely where the van was parked."

"The'er!" He indicated exactly the centre of the present activity above.

Sandy's throat felt dry as he spoke softly. "Did you see the registration number?"

The old man shook his head.

"Not even part of it? To say if it was a local number?"

"No. I don't reckon it were visible at all. He browt it in side on."

Just their luck! Sandy sighed very deeply. "What time do you think it arrived?"

"If we was to say that it went proper dark at half four, then I'd say maybe four. Wouldn't be more than five minutes out."

"But you saw the van clearly. A grey van – !"

"Something close to the colour of the barrel. Grey. Couldn't say the make though, only you see lots of 'em all look the same."

"Anything else? Did you notice anything else at all? Anything?" They were making their way back through those beanpoles, scattered last night, so they stood at rakish angles. Thoughtfully, Mr Templeton turned to gaze in the direction of the slope. "I noticed another thing, Mr Woodings. Half noticed, more like. Only I think there were writing on t'side o'th' van. Yes, there were definitely writing there."

Sandy stared at the man, with those disturbing palpitations back, and many times more powerful. He clutched at that thin but wiry arm.

"Writing – you mean there was some kind of lettering on the side facing you?"

"It could have been a name or something. Maybe like a works' name. Or maybe a telephone number or something!"

He had forgotten it was raining: no, he knew very well it was raining, but he didn't care, he could have hugged Mr Templeton.

"Don't rush it. Take your time. Try hard to remember – what kind of writing? A row of letters? Two rows?"

"One row definitely. Had to be because they were big letters. Big white letters, all in one line."

"Think hard, Mr Templeton. What did those letters say?"

"Now you're asking. I wish I could – nay, it's no good, I'm sorry. I haven't a clue."

At 11.30 that same morning, in Liverpool, a man called Gill, wearing a permanently open sheepskin coat, knocked on the door before being called into the presence of the chief constable, called Emersyn, together with Chief Superintendent Pauling, who was in charge of the Merseyside CID.

There was scant allowance for courtesy. No handshakes, a hand indicating the preferred chair in which Gill should take his seat. It was made abundantly clear that he was here on sufferance.

Pauling, who had come here today despite a mild dose of flu, took the offensive. "Let's cut through all of the nonsense from the outset. Let's dispense with that cock and bull story you people have fed us. We don't believe a word of it. Added to that, we've come under almighty pressure from London. We're not used to this type of pressure here." Pauling coughed from deep within his chest something unpleasant into a large soiled handkerchief. "We bloody well resent that pressure."

The answering expression on Gill's face was pained but controlled. He spoke with a surprising passion. "We have told you the truth, in so far as we are free to divulge information."

Pauling was entirely unimpressed by this. "Five days ago, a man and a woman were murdered here in Liverpool. Maybe it surprises you to hear that we take murder very seriously. In a case of murder – double murder – there's only one way of dealing with it. You go in hard. Pull out every stop."

"With respect, sir, there is always another way."

It had been clear from the start that there would be confrontation at this meeting. And more would be learnt from intuition than words. The chief constable was now studying Gill's solid features, the square heavy face, thick head of greying straw-coloured hair with the strikingly reddish moustache. Both policemen were studying Gill with a pooled experience of greater than fifty years of disbelieving precisely this expression of maligned innocence.

"Stanley Park!" the chief constable directed their attentions with a judicious pursing of his lips.

Gill seemed to understand perfectly the concern behind this direction, which he acknowledged with a smile that held not a molecule of humour. "We know they weren't killed in the park."

"Dumped under the trees, all a little too neatly and tidily," interjected Pauling. "So damned neat and tidy – was it your people who dumped them there, Gill?"

"That's an outrageous suggestion, sir."

"What sort of work were they engaged in?"

"Routine."

"Routine what?"

"I regret that I'm not at liberty to say."

"Safety of the nation depends on it, does it?"

Gill's broad head was very slightly lowered so that the

141

thinning crown was exposed, sprinkled with flakes of dandruff. During the silence, his florid cheeks had pinked a little more, immediately to the sides of his fleshy nose. There was ample time to notice the prominent dimples of hair follicles in that noise, the darkening of the grey in his hair caused by a liberal palming of oil or cream, the thickish pale eyelashes fluttering contemplatively during this time over eyes of a medium blue.

"I suppose what we are asking for – and offering – is mutual cooperation."

"Which is what when it's at home? We all graduate to the university of liars?"

"We are also under our own pressures from that same source . . ."

"You know who killed them. Let's not take this tally-ho a second further."

"I assure you we do not know who killed them. Nor do we know why."

"Maybe you people are trained to lie. But you don't fool us. You're not even good at it."

"Believe me, we do not know who killed them or why. We do not know why their bodies were taken from wherever the murders took place and dumped in Stanley Park. But we are pulling out the stops in our own way and we're working on it. What we desperately need is your help, your cooperation. But we move in totally different worlds. What would be embarrassing to you would prove a devastating scandal for us."

While Pauling was racked by another fit of coughing, the scene remained as it had begun, one of open confrontation. But signals had been sent, signals were being exchanged. And it was clear that all that could be expected was this mutual acknowledgement of anxieties. Gill had no doubt that his salvation here lay with the more politically astute chief constable than his bulldog chief superintendent. And it was to the chief constable now that such nuances were being directed. There were two courts sitting and it was the unspoken, the very private, that really mattered. Such was the significance of the green, military style tie. The heavy fixed cast of his head. The continuing bruised gaze of his eyes under lids which were permanently raised, explaining the deeply wrinkled forehead. There had been a premonitary warning from the start in the down-to-earth thrown open sheepskin.

"They were expertly put away. The man with a single stab through the top of his spinal cord, the woman throttled."

"Yes."

"Which means that whoever killed them, this mystery killer still at large in the community, is very dangerous?"

"Extremely dangerous – indeed."

"And the victims' occupations – your role here in this room today – would imply that there was a political motive in their killings?"

"We must assume so, yes."

"Five days – in those five days we haven't a clue as to the who or the why or the wherefore. Still you claim you know nothing?"

"I have no concrete knowledge as yet. And that's the truth, sir."

"Not only do you know nothing but you want us to keep the media misinformed about the political aspects of the murders. You want us to do your cover-up, thereby inevitably interfering with the normal channels and guidelines we would follow in a case of murder."

Another silence, but important as silences are always important. What had to be communicated had been communicated. That Gill, like Woodings, was essentially a hunter. His face wore the hunter's essential endurance.

Outside the office window, at Sheffield Police headquarters, it was sleeting again: Sandy had had to scrape sludge from

143

his car windows with the wipers just before pulling into the car park. He was thinking about the fact that they should be able to narrow their search down to four types of van: Mr Templeton might not have recognised their suspect from the rogues' gallery, but had proved more helpful when it came to the van. They knew now it was a Ford Escort, a Morris 1300, an old Thames or a Bedford. In Sandy's mind a clearer picture was crystallising. In Liverpool, and at that precise moment, Gill had an almost identical vision. A very tall man – Gill could accurately have stated six feet four inches, two hundred and ten lean pounds. A large bony face with eyes, not pale blue as was Sandy's impression, but, as Gill knew perfectly well, of a uniform ash grey.

16

Was it possible? Something familiar in that crazy note – something so obvious? Sandy was interested now in what the professor had deliberately avoided. He was very interested indeed in what the professor had called the Maggie angle . . .

Something personal. Something so deeply personal that Sandy felt a queer tingling of excitement in addition to a more mundane sense of guilt. Josie was out for the evening, having dinner with some new friends who were into the Open University and adult education. But there was no mileage in pretence here. He had known exactly what he intended to do when he had taken the tape from Tom during the hours of darkness as much as when, a little earlier, he had made certain that Georgy knew nothing at all about it. And here he was, quite alone in Josie's apartment . . .

The note and the tape – instinct warned him that they were linked. Understand one and he would understand the other. Yet what he was thinking was so ridiculous he had to shake his head, to sip abstemiously at a cup of coffee, to close his eyes with a controlled patience while sleet pattered against the double glazed aluminium-framed patio doors. Part of this exercise lay in seeing through fresh cycs. To perceive not through the eyes of a policeman, aged thirty-nine years, marriage in ruins, a recently acquired mistress of somewhat nervous and uncertain affection for him, four highly emotional and frightened children . . . but to see it through the eyes of a woman, perhaps not quite the mother . . . I'VE GOT BABY BLUE!

In its very enigma lay a vital clue. What was the note all about? Communication? Then how to communicate if there was nothing here but riddles. LOOK BACK, MAGGIE . . . HOW PAIN CLEANSES . . . First riddle, then intimacy.

Intimacy? What had old Mr Templeton remarked, towards the end of the second interview, that very frustrating continuation of interview back in Sandy's office at headquarters?

"Oh, I reckon he saw me reight enough."

"You mean he gave you some kind of indication?"

"Waved his hand at me, cool as you like."

"He waved at you?"

"The stupid daft 'aperth! I'm just looking up at him and the'er he is, looking down on me." Mr Templeton did an imitation of a confident wave.

Sandy remembered frowning. "But he didn't speak?"

"Not a breath." Mr Templeton was grinning. "Casual as you like." Mr Templeton laughed at the impertinence of it. His voice was unconsciously rising. "A wave, nice and friendly like. I didn't even have to tell him about putting t'owd horseshoe back on t'gate."

Thinking back now, Sandy thought about a second conversation from this afternoon. Little things were beginning to loom greater in importance. He heard Tom's voice, Tom who had taken the late message from Henry Bancroft in forensics. "The torn-up trainer matches the other one perfectly. Size, make, right foot, degree of wear, foot imprint patterns, fibres, dyes . . ." Which certainly meant that the man he had chased down the slope and fought with in the railway tunnel was also the kidnapper. But it meant something else too, didn't it? It confirmed a pattern in which this character deliberately and scientifically furnished them with proof of who he was.

So Sandy tried a simple assumption. What if Margaret Stephens understood the real meaning of the note?

He watched the first of the two short video recordings with relative equanimity, just the occasional sip from his coffee. It was a normal interview, the sort of thing the police customarily arranged when somebody was missing. That left him all the less prepared for a second.

It began abruptly, just a few seconds of snowstorm on the screen, and there she was: Margaret Stephens. She had allowed them to film her as she left the path to her house, crossing the road, then just as she approached the camera-man, her feet trampling the red mud which had once been fallen leaves, Sandy Woodings was alerted by the strange-ness of her. Something he had barely sensed before, a property about her that seemed totally out of keeping here. Her pale face glowed in an unearthly fashion under the watery light of what he presumed was late afternoon. The tape was longer than anything that would have been transmitted. This was the full recording, perhaps half an hour of recording, and Sandy forgot his coffee, which he had placed on the table to the side of him without taking his eyes off her. And this again was additionally intriguing: they had filmed her for such a long time before speaking to her.

Surely this television crew didn't give a hang if they never asked her questions. They had come back to speak to her again for some reason other than asking her questions. It was the cameraman – it must be the camera-man – who had introduced a deliberate quality to this recording, because the trees appeared to be placed like stage sets, the distances were somehow perfect for some thing, the sky was just changing, as if this were a much later time, a late evening dusk instead of maybe 3.45 in the afternoon. And all the time Margaret Stephens held the camera in those liquid-black pupils. She held the camera so obsessively that some light from in front of her seemed to illuminate her face; that light glowed in her face so that the brown of the irises faded like the fading of pigment in a precious illuminated manuscript, so that he could only see the black centres surrounded by pale exquisitely fine amber circles that marked the junction of the irises and the whites of her eyes. There was a haunted radiance about Margaret Stephens in this film which Sandy would never have anticipated.

Abruptly he reached out and turned the video off. He needed to think clearly. He walked across once more to the window and stared out into the garden, ravaged by winter.

What the hell am I seeing here?

A girl born into that small red brick terraced house, now demolished, in a street in industrial Bolton, at the top of which stood the mill where her father had worked. *PIKE MILL GANG RULES OK*. A closely knit community. Closer than anyone who did not know these Lancashire streets of thirty years ago would ever have imagined. A community in which a young girl born there and growing up there would know everybody else. She would have as intimate a knowledge of the boys in the streets about as a villager in a farming community in Dorset. Her first contact with boys would have occurred in those streets. But she was brighter, took A-levels, went on to Birmingham University . . .

Now he knew he was excited. Thinking about the younger Margaret Stephens had caused him to feel a tremulous inner agitation. But he was only halfway there. He didn't fully understand this excitement.

With a forced exhalation, he switched on the video once more, turned it back five minutes and watched that same movement of the woman through space and time . . .

Her eyes constantly changed, moving out of shade, moving always it seemed in the wake of, and usually approaching nearer to, the camera. There was a sudden movement of the neck, the head turned downwards, as if summoning up courage: *she's afraid, of course she's afraid, she has been terrified from the beginning.* But there was more, wasn't there? What kind of young man would have been attracted to that young girl back then? And what kind of man would that girl, brought up in those red brick streets, fancy?

With a flush of guilt at his own invasion of intimacy, he understood perfectly well what he had intended all along. But embarrassment was irrelevant. He would undress this woman in his mind if it would help him to understand her. Love. There it was: love was the word – more than the word, more than the idea. Sexual love, the only kind of love that would matter to a young woman aged about twenty. Sandy Woodings imagined himself drawn now to that younger version of the face in front of him, a face even more delicate than it appeared here, with its bird-sharp wary eyes and pointed chin. That sexual attraction could only feel strange, curious. Maybe that was him now, the circumstances? Surely this whole exercise was condemned to the ridiculous?

The sky was bronze, perhaps 3.55 in the afternoon. In the twilight she would soon fade into the near distance, she would become a ghost. *What else?*

Then she was there, right in front of the camera. Her eyes looked astonished, a startled gaze of haunting uncertainty. A man's voice asking if she had had any communication from the kidnapper.

Yes. Yes, a communication. A note. And it was all left unsaid, what the man was really after. If she believed her son was really still alive or not. A communication which took place all the same with the very conviction now that seemed to seize her.

"What was the content of this note, Mrs Stephens?"

"I think he is saying my son is still alive."

"Do you believe that, Mrs Stephens?" The question

directly asked. He had forced her to answer, in front of millions of viewers.

"Yes." A very nervous if defiant confirmation.

Good for you, Maggie Stephens! She had guts all right. But what was the idea behind it? Here, in front of millions of viewers, she had been asked and she didn't know. She didn't know what to say. But she would go anywhere, do anything, if it would achieve anything.

There it was, exactly as Tom had reported. This was the part that had certainly been transmitted. And Sandy knew now that he had been absolutely right in his presumption the evening before. This was a message, pure and simple. This was intended to be a communication, directed at the kidnapper. Those words and her gaze, which must be towards the slope off to her right, which even indicated a possible meeting place. If the words had not been clear, the look in her eyes now spoke volumes. He had thought it haunted but now he saw beyond that and realised it was something vastly more complex, more delicate and simultaneously more primitive.

Sandy switched off the video again. His essentially logical nature rebelled against what he was thinking.

LOOK BACK, MAGGIE. STUDY THE EDGE OF DARKNESS. LOOK BACK, MAGGIE!

Look back – why look back? Back to what? And that was an interesting word, wasn't it – STUDY.

Childhood was the world of magic. Yet it was easy for the middle-aged adult to underestimate the true stresses, the pressure of school, peer pressure of friends and enemies, of terrible rushes of love and hate. And childhood was ultimately bound up with this kidnapping. He felt certain of it. That lost world of childhood. And the mother in Margaret Stephens would have recognised this. She had sensed it. All this plus the words contained in that note – that was what had been going through her mind that day as they filmed her. Indeed every day as she walked through that nightmare landscape where her son had been taken. She must have gone over those words a thousand times in her head. The pain those words must have inflicted on her. And all the time she had understood . . . Just as she had understood all along for one simple and overwhelmingly obvious reason.

And that reason was that Margaret Stephens knew who had sent her that note.

Was it possible, he wondered, watching the whole thing through again from the beginning, that this pre-pubertal, or pubertal, sexuality might be the finished product in certain women? He even thought about Josie – Josie, who had preserved that inner child in many ways. For instance, she laughed at the most silly things like a child. She loved physical comforting, loving for the sake of loving, even food, the most simple of physical pleasures. She would spend all day playing games if she could, and she was addicted to chat shows and competitions on the television. Yet she wasn't unintelligent. Josie was close to brilliant when it came to instantly sizing people up. All the same, inside the adult Josie, the child was bubbling through.

If however, the same were to apply to Margaret Stephens, what a different child altogether must she have been.

The clue must lie with that girl, as he now understood it. Yet still he found it impossibly difficult to see that child, the adolescent girl, to envisage how that girl might still hide herself in the mature Margaret Stephens – because that was what we all were, wasn't it – the child dissolved into the adult, watchful, thoughtful from the inside, a spirit frozen in that tremulous tentative discovery, a spirit that had never quite grown up?

Sandy switched off the tape for the last time. He rubbed at the inner corners of his eyes, hardly crediting this last hour's work, wondering if he would think differently about it tomorrow. He had had no sleep last night, he had found himself in a ridiculous mood when confronting Mary, maybe he was high on fatigue. He even laughed mildly because the idea that was coming to him was so unlikely, so grotesque . . .

17

In our minds, Maggie, we are all of us rats in the maze. Now and then we catch a glimpse of the universe that lies beyond the glass, only to withdraw our whiskers. Because knowledge is terror, Maggie.

Tuesday, December 13th: he gazes up into a moonlit sky. Hunger has tormented him all day. He hasn't eaten anything solid since yesterday, thirty-six hours, and he senses its prickling in his gut with foreboding. A high old sky, Maggie. Have you noticed how different you feel when the sky is high or low? High or low, Maggie, or a thousand variations in between. But high all day today, opaque and scumbled with browns and greys like the skin of burnt milk and with a big diffuse silver sun shining through. But it is night which brings the real excitement. It is tonight, with a three-quarter moon and cloud thrown across it like a fine infinitely distant ivory dust, through which the stars are nearly all visible and a halo round the moon which makes it ten times as big with crenellated edges all the colours of the rainbow. How could you hate on a night like this, Maggie? How can you hate when the savage pangs of hunger are salved by a lightness in your head and a trembling fluttering about your fingers and that pleasurable weakness in your thighs, as if you were making love . . .

And the van – the van, Maggie. You see, I've seen it.

Twice before I've discovered just their tracks. Once I only just missed them. I could still see their exhaust smoke

153

hanging in the air. Tonight I've caught them at last. It's blue, an old blue Morris Minor, and I can still smell them, her cheap scent and his tobacco-fouled breath, through the open window.

The excitement has become a sudden drumming across the taut skin of his temples. Kerouac, Sartre, the Beatles – those bastards have all let us down. All that shit has taken him through the very gates of hell. He has roasted in its heat until his eyeballs baked. *You never escape. They have me still, Maggie. It's only a parole, you see. Only out on sufferance.*

The thrill of memory, of communication, of confession, of the fact he could kill in this careless lively humour, elevates him, courses like a billion corpuscles of ice through the pumping stations of his heart and out along the great arteries, stabbing, stimulating, until they expand like an exploding nebula in his universe, in an ecstasy of singing light. Her hard little brown eyes in her hard little girl face: she loved him then. As his eyes roved the cherished skin, perfect and goose-pimpled, with the haunting impossible beauty of coffin lilies. You were my coffin, sweetheart. His coffin, all right: now the feel of the two breasts, a perfect handful each, the smallish vulnerably pink nipples, a breast in each hand, still eye to eye contact. We're dancing, little Maggie. Quick looks. Stabs of delight. We're in the honey and we're dancing, Maggie. Eyes like a fox's fur in the light reflected from his own eyes. As he entered and she held. She just held him there as she held him in her eyes. As she held him crucified then between those three nails of exquisite torment. *I want to come. No. Not yet. I want to come like crazy, Maggie. No – no, no, no . . .*

He could see them even now from where he has been standing amongst the winter trees. He can see the blue of the van body, turned cheesy by the moonlight. But he fancies a better position. He wants to see them clearly.

So he walks about them in a third of a circle until he is standing in the shade of the little hawthorn tree, about twenty yards back from the lemon yellow stone of the chapel. They could hear him approach if they had their ears working. But it isn't their ears that are working right now. He chuckles softly, then more loudly. He could kill the pair of them right now.

I'm a murderer, Maggie. I've killed two human beings.

The fact is he has never killed anyone in his life before those two in Liverpool, even if there were a couple of hundred thousand he would have liked to. Now it's easy. He could start with the woman, put a rose amongst her dyed platinum hair, a rose the colour of her bright red skintight plastic boots, which dig in so hard he can see the flesh on the back of her thighs bulge out above the top of them. He could do it just to see the expression on that silly fat man's face, that greasy moon, which only wants a fag hanging out of one corner of the slavering mouth. The moon above a second moon belly, it's droopy exposure between the splayed tails of shirt. He eyes that grey obscene expanse through the telescopic sight, he moves the crossed lines over the coarse piggy hairs that droop wetly, close to her working mouth. He focuses on the stump of paleness that is clearly visible, the stump that grows and recedes, grow and recedes, gobbled up by her nodding mouth. Could he do it? He could, he could give this customer with the tobacco mouth the erotic surprise of his life. He can't stop himself from a fit of the giggles. I have you now, fat old piggy. *I'm going to chop off your pecker, you sweaty old grunter, and she'll be so surprised she'll swallow the whole thing right down her slavering throat.*

The universe presses upon him. The stars, the white-dust midnight sky, the unmoving whispering forms of the trees, the shadow of the building beyond. *Go on!* they murmur and the murmur grows with a furious rapidity and intensity. *Go on!*

But they're not who he expected. They're not the right people.

He has long since squeezed the trigger but there is no round in the magazine. The rounds are in his pocket. He can feel the rounds weigh against his skin from his left hip pocket. They could be white hot, they radiate their presence to him and his hand turns, his hand lifts from the barrel of the directed rifle, as the noise enters his ears like a whiplash, a lash with each surge of blood to his temples.

How have the millennia treated you, Maggie? Have you been happy? Contented? Did you realise what was coming? Did you somehow sense it all even back then?

Memory comes urgently, the tone of skin against cold papered walls, the paper itself with pores much the same size and texture as female skin. He can smell her now, lilac maybe, as if deodorant comes through woollen top garments, cardigan over cotton dress, like sweet-scented perspiration. Sometimes she wears a pullover over her nightgown. The bedroom was always cold and damp. In winter the walls perspire freely and there is a crack in the top corner where on a sunny morning a dazzling rapier of light falls into the pupil of his eye. Her breasts feel pointed and elfin under all this wool and cotton. She wears all of this but no bra and her breasts feel strangely intimate yet still distant as she insists he holds and does not grope, while all the time she is understanding maybe that it is finite. That she could even consider then that this is finite . . .

When I think about you, Maggie, you appear powdery, like the sky. Your skin is heavy and yet fragile and dry as if I can only remember you through my fingertips. I feel your voice rather than hear it, I feel it the mellow way it comes out of the back of your throat, and the nervous way you always talked to me, with your head a little sideways and your eyes too widely opened. There were times, Maggie, when I really saw the diabolical in those sideways wide-opened eyes. There's the fanatic behind them somewhere.

The fact is I just want to touch you, to feel the touch of your skin, to feel your breath on my cheek as you lie next to me. I want your love still, Maggie. I couldn't change even now. That was all I ever wanted from you, Maggie. Just ordinary physical love. The contrast of your shining eyes against the white damp mat of your face. I could have examined your cells under the microscope and I'd have wanted them. The physical thing, Maggie, love. You saw me too intelligently, you should have aimed your sights altogether lower.

The night of loss is longer than the night of death. He can feel this now, objectively, as he watches them as he would two innocents. Like squirrels under the cold eye of a gamekeeper, he watches them now and he feels the dark that will be their death touch him, like a cloak brush against his chest. Death after all is timeless. He cannot believe the religious afterlife. Death, if quick, carries no greater suffering than a needle prick in the arm, considerably less than a common cold. The pain of death is to those left, not to the departed. And he will not make them suffer. He bears them no malice.

Go on. You're the wrong people. Get the hell out of here. Get out now and save yourselves.

It is as if the moment has become special, a whispering of the wind turns him, he pivots on the heel of his right foot and he gazes up towards the gable end of the building. He is speechless, unaware of the need to breathe. He is spellbound. The light of a single nightlight in that cavernous room has reached out and illuminated a single gable window. How can they fail to see it for it is directly facing them. He ignores them and simply gazes up, while the world murmurs like a low-pitched chanting about him.

Come on! Come then to the window!

He wills the small face with its dark eyes to the glass, he wills that careful, broody gaze down here, where he has only now fully realised the true nature of the act that is being performed here. He turns very slowly, his eyes have found the face of the woman, slightly dissolved even at this small distance, and it seems that there is a recognition there, a casual movement of the features, maybe a gesture about the full lips that suggests both the sensual and the cruel. She is resting now. His eyes follow the cigarette that she lifts and holds at her lips, allows to fall again into a position of cradling under the bulge of her breasts, and it is in the very act of studying her that he has found himself nearer still, so that the acrid smell of cigarette smoke seems brutishly foreign to his nostrils, and he can actually hear the indrawing of her breath, as like the man, she exhibits that interesting total concentration on the cycles of inhalation. Now he can hear their voices.

"Everything's a lot tougher now," it is the man's voice, higher pitched than he might have imagined, "than maybe ten years ago. I used to change my car every three years, now I'm thinking of a good two-year-old."

"You don't look so bad on it," her voice is husky, sexily cajoling. And so leisurely, excited all right but also relaxed with it. *See how they're in no hurry!*

He could join them at this moment. He could accept a cigarette from that workman's hand, he could join in and his voice would be Lancashire, like theirs, he would enjoy that, talking Lancashire with these two strangers, while knowing that the excitement was still there. Oh, the excitement was never going to go away now, the excitement would grow like some exotic winter flower.

She is amusing, this gypsy woman, with her red boots, now with her right leg flexed, the female-smooth skin of a strong supple leg alternately flexing and extending, in a dance-like rhythm, with her sole against the chapel wall. She *is* dancing. For suddenly he is aware of the music. He has only just become aware of the music that is coming from the open van window, the music of a pop show from the radio.

Go on then – dance for me then.

He can see now that dancing is in her blood, the way it seems closer to the female blood than the male. There is an urge in his belly to dance with her now, something obscurely religious, but sexual too as the stirring of his prick tells him, to dance together, not apart, to dance holding one another, to feel the hold of those hands about him, to grasp her waist, to draw her towards him and feel the weight of her breasts against him, to find abandonment in this dance with a strange woman he did not and could never have loved.

With this coming together of everything, he senses an utter stillness. The sky, the stars, the moon, the ice-brilliant wind that thrusts onto his unmoving face and stings his unblinking eyes.

The woman had finished her cigarette and makes a vague gesture, coquettishly obscene, and the man, still smoking, still leaning against the wall, flicks his cigarette away with a smile. It is preordained. Time is fractured. Time is merely an interruption of the world that is full of agreement.

They are shifting but not moving as yet. In this terrible moment, this moment of purity, there is a stillness, suddenly a serenity under the green-purple sky, the stars, the moon, the trees. The watcher has slipped off his shoes and now his stockings and he stands there with his feet in powdered snow, in continuity with the blue purity of a world without time. In yet another little act of obscenity, the fat man relieves himself against the chapel wall and she fondles him, she draws him inexorably towards the chapel door, even as the watching man fumbles with fingers that have grown clumsy with cold, takes the bullets warm from his pocket, inserts them, one at a time. It is proper that obscenity becomes poetry. How sweetly comes the darkness.

HIS BOY BLUE. BABY BLUE LIES IN HIS MOTHER'S RED HALO.

The darkness floods his senses, from all sides, from the five dimensions of his mind. He is almost beside her as she leads the man through the doorway, the pale-waxed oak door which is open, has been open for past violations, and there is a profanity in the moonlight about her face and her ivory ball of hair, the sparkling lust of sacrilege on the fleshy moistness of her lips and in the unreflecting mats of her eyes.

He is now one with the darkness, blackly transparent, liquidly motionless. He is by the van now, gazing into the old-fashioned interior, smelling her scent in a dozen years of human smell, touching an unopened twenty park of Park Drive, one of those old-fashioned skeletons suspended from a spring attached to the windscreen, a tax disc one month out of date, her professional purse, containing nothing of monetary value, on the passenger seat. The radio is playing and his hand reaches out then stops. He does not switch it off. Instead he turns the volume up.

He is aware of a movement out of the dark masses of trees that encircle him as he leaves the vehicle with its window still open: it is as if a cloud of ravens had arisen from the high masses of the branches. In his feet the intense cold that has risen numbingly to mid-calf is reassuring, a cutting punishment. It urges him on now, the surging gathering darkness.

The woman was not so preoccupied as the man: she noticed the sudden increase in volume of the Flying Pickets singing "Only You". Her name was Ruth Spencer. Now Ruth felt, in that single moment, the worst chill of fear that had ever danced in the aching emptiness of her chest.

Now she watched and listened even as the fat man continued to root into her, and almost immediately her heightened senses picked up the faint groaning which was the doors being prised open, no more than a foot wide, and then her eyes, her staring eyes, straining with a careening panic out of her skull, picked out the vaguest shape, a huge bearded shape, which might have been the devil himself, for the effect it had on Ruth's howling brain. Ruth had suddenly lost all knowledge of time, of the seconds, minutes and hours. The time had become now. Terror was beating at her face with hideous suffocating wings.

Terror was the price for entering this strange time world in which Ruth's heart was crazily yammering at the roof of her mind, as her mouth opened wide in a circular scream, as she emptied her bladder in single agonised contraction onto the cold marble floor under her weighted limbs.

The fat man knew nothing until he heard the voice, the words which seemed to reflect a prayer yet were spoken with a gravelly mocking humour:

"The' shall see him face to face and bear his name on thy foreheads."

The fat man noticed his danger only for a moment. Time only for that sudden wide gaping of eyes and mouth, time for the slow stiff movement which was the involuntary reflex of absolute terror, as the muzzle of the rifle paralleled the slow elevation of his mouth, with lips drawn hugely back from bared teeth, from a distance of inches. As the gun blazed and the bullet smashed through the man's mouth, Ruth was sprayed over her cheeks by fragments of shattered teeth.

Now the gun was rising again. The gun was pointing at Ruth, straight into the tortured cavern of her mouth. As if terror must be swallowed physically. Ruth had abandoned her senses to an infinite paroxysm of screaming. She was sitting on her legs, one hand on the urine and blood-soiled marble floor supporting where she had been partly unbalanced by the man's dead weight, and her screaming mouth was so thrown open that her jaw was locked in agony, below the ovals of watery gravity that were her eyes. The huge bearded man spoke again, that same icy gravity, that same mordant humour:

"When the devil visited Eve he was looking for tips!"

18

"You understood the note, didn't you, Mrs Stephens?"

"Not at first. I . . . I wasn't sure . . . not until Bolton."

Your voice is a part of yourself, not really a sound at all, but a projection of what it is your mind is thinking, your tongue does the work automatically so you are not even aware of the act of saying it. This morning Margaret Stephens felt she had lost this knack. This morning, when they had brought her into police headquarters because it was no longer interview but interrogation, in the presence of these two detectives.

Chief Inspector Woodings repeated his question. "Let's be clear about this, Mrs Stephens. Let's be absolutely and perfectly clear. This man – "

"His name is Bamford. James Bamford . . ."

"This is the man you believe has taken your son?"

"Yes."

"Just how sure of this are you?"

"How sure?" her voice appeared to turn inwards, she swallowed the question deep into some inner realm of darkness, penetrated now by an unbearable army of lances. "I'm sure."

"You know it?"

She was nodding, her whole body nodding.

"Why – how do you know it?"

"Because of the note."

"So you did understand the torn-up note?"

162

"In Bolton. I understood when I went to Bolton." She could have explained that they would do that, they would tear up little messages to each other, in each other's presence, messages of love, of wanting, of violent need, poetry.

"Because of the words of the note?"

"Because of the words. And the description of the man."

"Artful Jack kills titans?"

"Yes."

"You lied to us. You deliberately misled us. I don't know why – but you *must* explain now, Mrs Stephens."

"Explain the words? Yes, I can explain the words. You see I wrote them. Once upon a time, I wrote them. I wrote those words, ARTFUL JACK KILLS TITANS."

Was he surprised? Perhaps not as surprised as she might have anticipated. But then she had already worked out the fact that this man, this detective, was intelligent enough after that business down the slope to have put two and two together.

She added, "They were the opening lines of a poem I once wrote . . . started . . . never finished."

"Nobody else could have known those words?"

"Nobody."

"So – what are you telling us? That you and this James Bamford had some sort of . . . relationship?"

"Yes."

"You were lovers?"

"Yes."

"When did you last see him?"

"Eighteen – perhaps nineteen years ago."

"Come on now, Mrs Stephens!"

"That was the last time I saw him."

"And now your ex-lover has turned up, just like that . . . out of the blue, out of the dead?"

"Yes."

Sandy Woodings studied this woman now. He assessed

the straggling locks of hair, never properly brushed this morning and almost meeting in the middle under her chin, the shine on her cold pink nose, lips dry from tension, the lower lip with a central sore-looking fissure, and the voice piped into the air in front of her, as if with all her courage, with all of her desperate small might, a voice from that same darkness.

"How did you meet him?"

"I was studying English at Birmingham University. He was a postgraduate in philosophy. We met at protest committees . . ."

Sandy ignored the "protest committees" for the moment, but a prickling sensation had begun in his scalp and was running down his back, like a crawling hand with pointed nails.

"Were you engaged? Thinking of marriage?"

"Nothing so conventional."

Sandy's eyes met those of Tom Williams, who was the silent observer of this interrogation.

"What does that mean, Mrs Stephens? Nothing so conventional?"

Margaret Stephens was silent.

"How unconventional, Mrs Stephens?"

Still she maintained her silence.

"I don't need to remind you. Your son has been kidnapped by this man."

"I can't explain. Something out of the ordinary. We're talking about the late sixties. Do you remember the late sixties, Mr Woodings?'

"Obsession – is that the kind of love you're talking about, Mrs Stephens?"

"We were lovers. In deep. Very deep – over our heads. More to it even than that. More than hearts, more than hearts and minds even – although a meeting of minds was probably the way it started. I don't know what I'm trying to say. I've said it already. It was the sixties . . ."

"Nineteen years! I find it incredible, Mrs Stephens."

"You don't know *him*."

"But why – why on earth should he come back? Why kidnap your son?"

"Because he hates me."

"Why should he hate you?"

"I let him down. I deserted him."

"People let each other down all the time. Come on Mrs Stephens. We're talking about a man you haven't met for all those years."

"I don't know why after all this time."

"I don't believe you."

"I'm confused. I haven't been sleeping. My mind is confused . . ."

"He was going to kill you."

"No. No!" She was shaking her head with her eyes closed.

"I'm trying to understand you, Mrs Stephens. I'm trying very hard. Your only son. Kidnapped. He may have been murdered. I'm sorry, but we most look it square in the face. You know who did it. You knew and you didn't tell us. You made a crazy arrangement to meet that man. Why, in God's name?"

"The words . . ." She was rocking her body slightly from side to side.

"The words in the note?"

"I've got him, Maggie. You'll never find him . . ."

"If you had cooperated with us, we'd have caught him."

"No."

"What else do you know about him? Do you know where he lives? What sort of work he does?"

Her head was shaking violently.

"What kind of man are we dealing with, for God's sake?"

"You'll never catch him. Knowing who he is, just knowing his name, will make no difference. You'll never find him – just as you haven't found my son."

"Why?"

"He's too clever for you. That's why I had to do it my way. I thought if I could only talk to him. I . . . yes – I could have saved Bobby. But you ruined it. You stopped me."

"You must have some idea where to look, Mrs Stephens? Have you a photograph?"

"He never permitted a photograph."

"It's crazy. You must have some idea."

"Will you never believe me? I'm telling you the truth. I have no idea where he lives. I haven't seen him for all these years."

"Where was he living nineteen years ago?"

"He lived nowhere. He moved about. You didn't even know which country. Britain. France. Germany. The United States. From one protest to another. Why do you think I had to meet him? I know James Bamford. I know him well enough to realise your search is hopeless. He could be anywhere."

Sandy Woodings was trapped in a dream. In that curious way one knows it is a dream and it makes no difference, he heard the sound and knew the sound was not really part of this dream, but for a long time he could not respond to it. The sound was a loud ringing, interspersed with brief intervals of nightmarish calm. The ringing had been incorporated into the fabric of his dream, a background music to a macabre sequence involving ghouls in a ruined church. Julie was a succubus who made love to him with a loud whinnying and her orange hair at the moment of climax flared into a terrifying sunburst. It was several more minutes before he awoke in a sweat to find the ringing was his telephone. Glancing at the digital alarm by his bed, he saw it was surprisingly late, five minutes past eight.

It was Chief Inspector Alan Farnworth, the Bolton detective, on the telephone and his voice sounded strained.

"We've had a message from your kidnapper."

"What are you talking about, Alan?" Sandy hadn't got to bed until 6.00 a.m. And there had been a little too much celebrating last night. He and Tom had sunk a bottle of whisky between them celebrating the discovery of Bamford's name. Now he hardly felt he had had any sleep at all.

"We've got two bodies," Farnworth announced peremptorily.

"Two bodies?"

"Here – in the churchyard."

"Let me just wake up and then tell me again, Alan."

"You can't believe it – I know. I can't believe it myself. Bolton Parish churchyard. Two bodies – and one of those crazy notes. You'd better get on your bike, Sandy."

Why hadn't he trusted his instincts? After that interview with Mrs Stephens yesterday, it had seemed a little too easy. Only an hour and a half after his telephone conversation with Alan Farnworth, he stood in the churchyard of Bolton Parish Church and gazed down directly at the proof. A rising gush of fury shook Sandy as a detective constable lifted the tarpaulin and Sandy stood rigidly and stared without blinking, still unshaven at 9.45 a.m. and with his chin matted by the drizzle of sleet. Two victims but it was the woman he stared at now. She was wrapped in her red plastic coat, redder than a cardinal's cloak, like a futuristic funeral shroud, and with her red plastic boots poking out from the rectangular space between two black stone buttresses – so small in death, so pathetic, it was a miracle that anybody had noticed her, even in broad daylight.

"Shot through the mouth," Alan Farnworth informed him, wheezing huskily. "Same as the man – pair of them shot through the mouth. Powerful gun – exit wound took the backs off their skulls."

"Shit!" he murmured to Farnworth, or to anyone else who cared to listen, to the wetly huddled forensic men, the impatient pathologist's chief technician – who must have

167

been waiting hours because they wanted Sandy to see this personally – to the gravestones poking determinedly out of the hard snow-encrusted mud, even to one obstinately surviving dandelion which looked up at him from between his two widely spaced feet.

He felt dizzy. The sight of the shattered teeth, of dried coagulated blood matting the lips and pooling down one side of the woman's face, nauseated him. A voice inside his head said: you've had no breakfast so your blood sugar is low. So take it easy. Move and think slowly.

And yet at the same time there was a powerful inner conviction: something important, some realisation subconsciously made now, gazing down at the murdered body of this woman.

She was a prostitute – who else would wear that coat, the miniskirt in late December, and those skintight thigh-length red boots? Her age must be approximately thirty. There was a great deal of guesswork going on because her purse, which had been deposited here with her, contained nothing except the murderer's note. *But a church: this is deliberate. There is some meaning to placing the bodies here. He chose this church, this parish church of Bolton, deliberately.*

"Thanks for saving them for me," he turned to Chief Inspector Farnworth. "I very much appreciate that."

"I couldn't have held the mortuary off much longer."

"I take it they've checked the bodies over, taken temperatures . . . ?"

"Pointed out the holes in the backs of the heads – yes!"

Sandy Woodings drew his hands down over his eyes and turned his attention to the dead man.

A heavily built – fat was the description – man of about mid-forties: he had a round florid face, dark brown hair slicked straight back and long at the back, a little redolent of the teddy boy era, and nondescript blue eyes, half open. If there were a look on his face it was mild surprise. He was wearing a brown herringbone suit, ill-fitting, cheaply and obtrusively stitched along the collar and edges. His pockets were empty. Indeed they had found no money on either body.

He found himself looking up at the church: a towering imposing edifice built out of a light beige sandstone. They had recently recreated the surrounding graveyard, shifting most of the gravestones and landscaping the undulating area – he could see lawn under the light fall of slushy snow. The very grave of Crompton was only yards from where he was standing. A raised tomb, he could read the inscription with a perfect clarity: SAMUEL CROMPTON . . . OF HALL I'TH WOOD . . . INVENTOR OF THE MULE . . .

When we've got his name. We've got his description, a description of his van – He was staring at his feet under which he saw a most curious gravestone – it looked really ancient, the writing made difficult because of trampled slush and mud. He whirled suddenly about himself without reading it, in a mixture of rage and naked fear. Fear that his man had now killed. The boy's life, if indeed he was still alive at all, was in terrible danger. So why hadn't they found even the slightest trace of Bamford with their searches last night? Was there a clue here? In Bolton, in the church, the churchyard, at the end of the medieval boundary wall that had given rise to the modern street name of Churchgate, and not least – oh, no, not least at all – was this feeling that it all linked in with the late sixties.

"Why would he choose to dump them here? What's so special about this part of Bolton?"

Farnworth had been standing next to Sandy throughout, his hat drawn down tight to protect his face from the sleet.

"The only thing that's special, at least so far as I know, is it's the parish church."

Only beginning, Mister Detective . . . Sandy turned abruptly from the bodies, took a couple of steps to close up to Farnworth. "Let's walk a little and talk – all right?"

"Fine by me."

"You'll take over here?" They had reached the gates and turned into Churchgate, towards the town centre.

"We'll keep in touch, don't worry."

"You saw the note before it was sent to forensics?"

"Yes, I saw it. I'd say it was definitely from the same character as the other you received in the parcel."

"What exactly did it say?"

"I couldn't give you the exact words. But I can assure you they were right along those same lines. That same kind of flowery nonsense. God knows what it was all about. You'll have to see it for yourself."

"Did it mention Mrs Stephens again by name?"

"It mentioned Maggie – yes it did."

Sandy paused to read the inscription over an old pub called the Man and Scythe. The date over the door read an unbelievable 1251. He read the inscription, *In this ancient hostelry James Stanley, 7th Earl of Derby, passed his last few hours prior to his execution, Wed 15th October 1651.*

Another challenge? Or was he being stupidly fanciful? He had to remind himself that only thirty yards behind him, the bodies of a man and woman lay with holes in their heads under a stained-glass window of the parish church.

"What's the local history, Alan?" he stopped in front of a monument that looked like a war memorial.

"You must be joking?"

"Humour me just a moment."

"Can't say I know very much myself. Bolton sided with the Roundheads. It was besieged and sacked by old Prince Rupert. The seventh earl was in charge when they came through, raping – or then again maybe not raping but sacking and knocking babies' heads against the paving stones. That's why he lost his head, the old earl. When Cromwell won, he was brought back here and given a taste of his own medicine."

"Bamford's playing games with us again. I know it."

The gravestone next to the bodies – why hadn't he taken the trouble to read it!

A plain-clothes sergeant came hurrying down from the church to tell Farnworth that they had a possible identification of the man. A butcher of precisely his description had been reported missing on Tuesday the thirteenth from the town of Radcliffe.

"Anything else on this butcher?" Farnworth addressed the sergeant.

"His van is missing too."

"Description?"

"An old blue Morris."

"We've had a look round the church?"

"We're still looking but no sign of any blue Morris."

"Anything in the van? Food? Meat?"

"We don't know."

"Find out. And money – find out if he was carrying much money. Got that? Get hold of somebody who has some information, wife, relative. Get a description of the van and its registration circulated. Make it top priority – have you got all of that?"

"Right, boss."

After the man had gone back to the incident van outside the church, Farnworth looked very thoughtful. He plucked his hat from his head, beat slush off it against the side of his coat and then placed it back very firmly again. "Why do you want to know all about this local history?"

"I don't know yet." Sandy shook his head and felt a hard ball of nausea press against his throat.

"So the churchyard is a clue?"

"I don't know. I may be indulging in the fanciful. But something is driving this character."

"Looks like he's got the butcher's van."

"You think he was just after food?"

"It's possible. He might be desperate enough."

171

"Why the woman?" Sandy Woodings had started to walk back with Farnworth in the direction of the parish church. They walked in thoughtful silence until they came to the doors, which were firmly bolted, with wrought-iron gates padlocked in front of them. Sandy didn't need to ask Farnworth if they had checked the interior. He had formed a very healthy respect for the quiet Boltonian. Yet, as Farnworth had intimated, kill for money, even for food? Somehow he doubted it would prove that simple. No – he felt all the more convinced now that this church was a much more important clue as to motive. There were easier and less conspicuous places to deposit bodies. Yes! He was certain there was calculation behind it, calculation in the very deliberate and specific act of moving both the bodies here from wherever else they had been killed – for he was certain from their position and the complete lack of surrounding blood that they had not been killed here – moving them, carrying them out from a vehicle one by one, not to mention the extraordinary purpose in the deposition, if it proved to be what Alan Farnworth believed it to be, of another of those bewildering notes. The constant goose flesh about his skin since his first arrival, everything, his whole instinct was stronger now, as painstakingly he brushed the surface of the old gravestone with his shoe until the inscription appeared, in a lacy seventeenth-century script, legible only with difficulty.

John Key, servant of God,
born in London 1629, Married
Mary Crompton of Breightmet
and had 4 sons and 6 daughters.
In his time were many great changes
and terrible alterations. The
Crown of Command of England changed
8 times. Died 1684.
Come Lord Jesus O Come Quickly.

Gazing up from the gravestone to the stained-glass window that overlooked it, Sandy felt a sweat break out on his brow; a dizzy sensation, perhaps the low blood sugar, gripped him for a few seconds. He willed the dizziness away, continuing to stand there, in a grey light like the interior of black ice, convinced that whatever clue that had been intended should now be clear to him.

Was it history that was important here?

His head was shaking involuntarily. No, it wasn't history. *We met at a protest meeting* . . . Not history but something very closely related. He felt a big step closer now to this progression, to that notion of challenge, a sickening reminder of those blows he had received in that tunnel. Not history. *Politics!*

Was politics what Margaret Stephens had really become involved in back in the late sixties?

It would explain so much. Yet even allowing for politics, what on earth was the connection between this large mill town, pulling itself painfully back into economic viability after the collapse of its world famous cotton industry?

Hard politics?

Tension has a way of concealing itself deep within you, of insidiously tightening its grip until suddenly, you can't go on.

Sandy Woodings pulled the car into the service station on the M62 motorway, causing Tom to glance at him questioningly. Tom, who had only just arrived in Bolton as Sandy was about to leave. Now Sandy sat in silence and closed his eyes for several seconds and Tom understood enough to allow him that privacy of thought. He had left Jock Andrews, who had arrived in Bolton with Tom, in charge of liaison there. Jock would stay to collect whatever further facts were discovered about the woman's identity and the questioning of the presumed butcher's relatives and acquaintances. Jock would also attend the postmortems . . .

They arrived at forensics at 12.40, were vetted by the guard on the gates and then pulled into the car park opposite the entrance, where Henry Bancroft, senior scientist, was standing inside the glass doors apparently waiting for them. It was very unusual for Henry to show such impatience yet Sandy was even more surprised when Henry, with his practised equanimity, took a pincer grip on Sandy's arm, steering him past the jumble of bags and pieces of glass and metal arriving from some major road disaster, down the left hand corridor towards the avenues of laboratories.

"Got something, have we, Henry?"

Henry led them into his laboratory, smelling of complex alcohols, where he picked up something wrapped in cellophane, then hesitated, as if reluctant to let him see a prize possession. Sandy, in the act of taking the note from Henry's reluctant grasp, realised suddenly the real cause of his wave of panic while driving on the motorway. He had allowed it to become personal. But how did you stop it becoming personal when it was an eight-year-old child? He prayed that whatever crazy game might have kept the boy alive this long, it might continue to amuse Bamford just that little bit longer . . .

"Not much doubt about it, Henry,' his voice was strained, hoarsely weighted.

"Same paper, same hand – not had time yet to test if it is the same ink."

Sandy shook his head. No, he needed no refined chemical corroboration. There was no doubt at all about it. Here was the proof he needed to link these two murders with the kidnapping, to draw them inexorably together – in what? One of the most bizarre and incomprehensible sequences he had ever encountered. The man with grey eyes – grey, not blue, as Margaret Stephens had now corrected them – who had spoken softly and in a Lancashire dialect, had

INNOCENCE IS AN ACT OF FAITH

MAGGIE

BURNS US UP ALIVE
LET ME SHARE YOUR

PAIN !

LET ME KISS THE TEARS
FROM YOUR EYES
BROWN EYED DARK ANGEL CHILD
LET'S ALL THINK HARD TO GET

RID OF IT ——

NO PAIN! NO PAIN !! NO PAIN
NO PAIN !!

squeezed the trigger on a butcher and a prostitute who wore red boots. That same man, James Bamford, a philosophy graduate, had kidnapped Bobby Stephens.

"That's it then."

"Oh, I don't think that's the full shape of it."

"What are you getting at, Henry?"

"Didn't I tell you it was your lucky day?" Henry waved in a mysterious fashion with that favourite spatula of his towards the laboratory door. Henry played that same favourite little game with him, leading him into the adjacent laboratory where a microscope was placed on the spotlessly clean working surface, a microscope with double eyepieces and two bench chairs, so whatever was placed under the objective lens could be viewed by two people simultaneously.

Tom stood back and allowed Sandy first look as Sandy remarked warily, "You'll have to spell it out for me – just precisely what it is I'm supposed to see."

"Hair, Chief Inspector. Hair which was included in the same envelope that contained the note."

"Careless of him."

"Not at all. Not careless – quite deliberate, I assure you. Two finely cut little locks of hair. Cut cleanly and accurately – most certainly thoughtfully – using what I must presume was a sharp knife blade."

"Cuttings of hair – why in God's name . . .?"

"You're the detective – your job to tell me." Henry fiddled with the illumination under the microscope and continued softly. "We nearly missed something vital, I confess. Because one of the locks was really so very delicate and fine . . . But here you are, I've managed to mount a sample from each of the two locks side by side. Now have a glance and tell me what it is you see."

"They look different."

"Exactly. Two dissimilar types of hair. But definitely human hair – animal hair looks entirely different. Two different types of human hair – ipso facto, he informs us with delightful scientific accuracy, from two different human heads.''

19

"I shall need samples – "

"We know what you need, Henry," Sandy was already standing, whirling towards the door.

" – from the lad's parents." Henry inhaled, then yawned, with his sharp little teeth widely bared. Henry had been out of his bed very early this morning. "While you're at it, if you could possibly find a few examples from the head of the lad himself – you know the sort of thing, comb, hairbrush, pullovers, nightclothes, sink drainer if he had his own sink – "

"Get your skates on, Tom, or I'll leave you here."

Henry's voice followed the hurrying pair down the corridor. "Hair from the parents, that would be decent ale. The lad himself – that would be bucks fizz."

Driving southwards with speed, Sandy knew exactly what he wanted. Under a thunderous black sky which promised more snow, he reread the two notes in his mind's eye, put them together, as they needed to be put together. I'VE GOT HIM, MAGGIE. I'VE GOT BABY BLUE. LET ME SHARE YOUR PAIN. Bloody sadist! How he loathed child crime. But the second note had not been torn up. The second note had been delivered pristine and intact inside the handbag of a murdered prostitute. And that sickly poetic rhetoric was more marked in the second note. As if he had had time to think about it, time to mature his intentions?

Anger boiled up in him: anger so destructive that he could have killed the man now with his bare hands.

ARTFUL JACK KILLS TITANS. What about the remainder of that poem? He would have liked to have read the rest of that poem written by the younger and seemingly very different Margaret Stephens. When he had asked her she had claimed it was never finished. The Jack referred to the steeplejack who had played his part in the destruction of the once proud forest of red brick chimneys that was the industrial heritage of old Bolton. Bolton – *Old Bolton!* So many connections here with Bolton. Now the two killings. And the enclosure of hair, two different locks of hair!

Then, suddenly, sweat erupted onto his forehead and he could feel the hairs prickling along the line of his spine and even at the nape of his neck. A small voice, a whispering voice, quite awesome in its portent, seemed to speak into his ear.

Look, Mr Smart Alec Detective! Look you too, Mrs Smart Alec Margaret Stephens! Look everybody! Look at the simple lesson I have taught you. I have killed. I have given you the corpses. I can kill anybody – it's really easy for me. Now do you see how simple the message is? Could I possibly make it any simpler for you dumbos?

He took Tom, ordered to his silent role, with him when he called at the Stephens' home and when it was Peter Stephens who showed them into the hallway, he made no attempt to conceal the urgency in his face, his tone of voice.

Seated about the dining table, his voice was deliberately grave as he addressed Margaret Stephens once again. "Since yesterday we have mounted one of the biggest manhunts ever for this man, Bamford. We haven't found him. We haven't found a trace of him, Mrs Stephens. You told us that would happen. I want to know what is really going on. Why haven't we found him?"

Margaret Stephens felt her skin lose its colour now, under the pointed gaze of the two detectives. "I have already explained to you – but you never believed me."

"A broken love affair! Do you expect us to believe that all of this – nineteen years later – has resulted from a broken love affair?"

"I'll tell you what *is* happening, Mr Woodings," it was Peter – poor Pete – who interjected on her behalf. "He wants to wreck what we have – he, Bamford, wants to destroy Maggie and wreck our marriage. That bastard has taken our son. He's consumed by envy, that's the reason he has taken our son. Envy. Simple explanations, Mr Woodings. Envy – *malice*. That's why he has taken my boy . . . taken him . . . taken him and . . ."

Poor dear Pete, with tears close to his eyes: her head inclined briefly, her own eyes momentarily closed. Yet she said nothing. She hugged silence.

The detective, Woodings, drew a deep breath, exhaled noisily. "Is that what you think, Mrs Stephens?"

What do I think? What does it matter any more whatever I think? Her eyes sought the sanctuary of the window: snow – snowing again. She gazed out of the window at the whirling menace of snow, dry and as aerially insubstantial as smoke. It would land for certain. It would obscure branches. By tomorrow morning the branches would look as if they had been sculpted from polystyrene.

"Two people have been murdered, Mrs Stephens. Shot brutally, from close range. A man and a woman. Two people he probably didn't even know. Two entirely innocent people."

Pete, whose voice wasn't really his own, spoke with uncharacteristic sarcasm. "I'll tell you what she told me, Mr Woodings. Do you know what my wife of twelve years marriage told me this morning? She informed me that when I married her, she was incomplete. She had to force herself to tell me that."

"Would you please explain that to me, Mrs Stephens."

Explanations. How do you begin to explain instinct, feelings, emotions – that sometimes you just *did* something. Was that insane, just to *do* something? The words were not there. The words were not at the tip of her tongue, not even at the back of her tongue, they simply did not exist in her. Yet she suffered poignantly with Peter, she felt his pain. Pete had suffered terribly since this morning.

"Here is a copy of the note. It's addressed to you again. Go ahead – read it, Mrs Stephens."

She read the note in a mental state that was not quite intelligent. As she read it, waves of weakness rolled over her in a debilitating tide. She spoke evenly, in a voice that appeared to control an inner welter of senses. "I don't know why he killed two people."

"To show us he was capable of killing, Mrs Stephens."

"That's insane. Utterly meaningless."

"You can't believe it – because you once knew him? Because you feel you understand him?"

She froze momentarily. She sighed very deeply and then forced herself to talk again, her voice cracking, her mind sickly calm.

"He took Bobby. But I think he would have taken me. He would have exchanged Bobby for me. But you stopped him. If Bobby dies now, you stopped me."

"He would have killed you, Mrs Stephens."

"I would have gone with him. Talked to him. Maybe that's all he ever really wanted."

"He has killed two people."

"He wouldn't have killed me."

"The day you tried to meet him he was carrying a gun. The same rifle that he used to blow out the brains of two perfectly innocent people."

Her eyes were glazed, fixed onto the table surface.

"Help me, Mrs Stephens. Help me to find your son."

Did he realise what he was doing to her inside? He asked

181

for explanations. Understanding? She would try to explain. Try, even if the words could never be adequate. She coughed, touched her fingertips to her forehead, with her head bowed. "Nobody could really understand . . ."

"Oh, I understand all right, Mrs Stephens. I understand that what we're really talking is politics!"

"No – not politics."

"For heaven's sake, woman! You practically admitted it to me. You met him at a student protest committee – "

"Everybody was into protests then."

"Don't insult my intelligence. I know it was more than that."

She was shaking her head again. Tears now in Pete's eyes: she saw them, felt their wetness on her fingers, tasted them, like the taste of blood, in her mouth.

"Will you for once tell us the plain unvarnished truth, Mrs Stephens?"

A blank wall, a great blank wall: she had hidden in the circle of that wall for nineteen years. Now she could feel it crack, every sentence she uttered was a new crack in that wall.

"Kids. We were only slightly older kids . . ."

"Kids playing dangerous games?"

"We thought we saw through to the rules. It's frightening – it's actually terrifying – when you see through to the rules."

"You – Bamford and yourself – got mixed up in the big protest movements?"

"Try to understand. I – it's hard to imagine myself, eighteen, nineteen years ago, younger. Very young really. Nineteen, twenty. I saw the rules, Mr Woodings. I saw the restraining wires. Can you begin to understand what an effect that had upon me? When you see those wires and you realise what they are, what they will do to you over a lifetime, and you're still only young, you believe anything is possible . . . You are consumed by a desire to destroy them.

You want to tear them apart with your bare hands, until your hands bleed, you ache to snap them off with your teeth . . ."

Sandy Woodings gazed in astonishment, something close to wonder, at this woman. Was she desperate enough at last to be telling him the truth? Did she realise what she was saying – how important all of this was?

"So – we *are* talking politics, aren't we?"

"You're exaggerating the importance of how groups of youngsters felt. Everybody felt that way at the time. Everybody . . ."

His voice was very calm now, deceptively gentle. "Are you saying you understand him, Mrs Stephens?"

"I don't know."

"I'm not talking in terms of subtlety. I'm talking bluntly. I think we both know what stark raving mad means."

She shook her head.

"Answer me, Mrs Stephens."

She inhaled deeply. "The man I knew would never have killed anyone. He cared . . . perhaps he cared too much."

"What about his family? Did he talk about his family?"

"He may have talked. Nothing much. He rarely mentioned any family."

"Just what family did he talk about?"

"His mother. She was religious. Devout. He could quote chapter and verse of the Bible."

"No father? No sisters, brothers, aunts, cousins?"

"If he had, he never talked about them."

Sandy shook his head disbelievingly. "Where did his mother live?"

"Somewhere in Lancashire. I'm not certain."

"But in Lancashire, you remember that?"

"We were both from Lancashire. That was what we first discovered we had in common. He used to speak . . ."

"What about his speech?"

She had flushed, was biting her lip so hard it was in danger of bleeding.

"Dialect? Was it dialect, Mrs Stephens?"

"Sometimes – when he was playful."

"His mother – she was definitely alive then? His mother was alive in the late sixties?"

"Yes."

"In Bolton, perhaps?"

"No. Not in Bolton. Somewhere further north. Burnley, I think."

"You must remember. You came from Lancashire yourself. If he told you, you would remember."

"He never took me to see her. He was . . . secretive."

"Secretive?"

"He seemed very reluctant to talk about her. I never met her."

"What did he tell you about his origins? Was he working class, middle class? What sort of work did his father do?"

"You don't understand the way we lived, the very air we breathed. Things like origins were . . . were irrelevant."

"Your relationship would appear strange to the point of the ridiculous, Mrs Stephens."

"Things were so different then. Now it seems like a different world."

"You despised society? You rebelled against it?"

"That's an exaggeration."

"You shared attitudes?"

"We felt the same."

"But he was older than you were. A great deal more experienced – already a graduate. You were in your first year."

"He was studying for his PhD."

"Studying – or dropping out? In fact you both dropped out, didn't you?"

"We broke free."

184

"You broke free. And the year was what – 1969? The attraction of the hippy life? Flower power. Free love."

"Love is never free."

"No." Sandy Woodings paused for a speculative moment. He found himself on his feet – he had risen to his feet in what he now realised must have been emotion – and he was standing with his left side facing the window which appeared to fascinate her so much. For the first time in this interview, they had hit the bedrock of absolute common agreement. Love was not free: love was never free.

"I'm not exaggerating, am I, Mrs Stephens? On the contrary. We're not talking about putting up posters outside the students' union. We're talking extreme politics."

"No!"

"Yes, Mrs Stephens."

"We reacted in a way that students are always reacting. We might have been naïve, expecting a better world today and not waiting for the next century."

Sandy Woodings turned, abruptly slapped his two hands on the table. "You understand his note, his second note, don't you, Mrs Stephens?"

"I'm not sure – "

"Because Bobby is not his brown-eyed angel child, is he?"

"I don't think – "

"Not Bobby – but you, am I not right, Mrs Stephens?"

"You couldn't be more wrong."

"Correct me then."

"He identified with the pain of others. The child referred to was a little girl on a news film. A Vietnamese girl badly burned with napalm."

"Pull the other leg, Mrs Stephens."

"It was what finally made the break for him. A small girl, when she was filmed her skin was . . . was still smouldering . . ."

185

"So he decided to do something about it?"

"Yes." She nodded. "*Yes!*"

"And you went along with him? But you weren't even studying philosophy. You were supposed to be studying literature."

"He was so intelligent. You wouldn't believe how intelligent he is, Mr Woodings. I saw . . . I saw genius in him. I felt . . . what was right in him. Right. Good. Caring. I was only beginning to understand. Call them rules, wires, strings – he showed me what I had instinctively already realised. He had the intelligence to put things into words for me. I had felt the trap since I was a child. I was aware of the trap but it took Jimmy to show me that you didn't have to sit back and allow it to envelop you. He made me believe in myself, in me, Maggie Helliwell, one little person, that one little person mattered in all this, that you couldn't force me to dangle from the strings, that I really did have free will."

Didn't we all rebel a little? We all recognised the rules. We rebelled against them in our own ways – by snipping away just a bit at a time.

Accepting a mug of tea from Peter Stephens, Sandy sat down once again at the dining table, spoke more gently:

"Those words at the bottom of the note? NO PAIN, NO PAIN . . ."

"Woodstock."

"Woodstock – the big hippy thing – you were there, Mrs Stephens?"

She barely nodded.

Sandy sighed again, placed his mug down hard in its saucer. "Half a million students were involved in the protest movements in the way you claim. So what was different about Bamford?"

"He was a good organiser."

"I can believe that."

186

"For a time . . . the world seemed to promise something new and wonderful. That was all we really wanted. Nothing bad. No violence."

"Naïve hardly covers it, does it, Mrs Stephens?" He spoke with that same quiet, but he felt excited.

Her eyes, not amorphously brown, but spiked through, like concentric corollas of petals, with a delicate, paler hazel, now liquid with held-back tears, regarded him with a pitying fierceness.

"How long did your relationship last?"

"A little more than a year. Perhaps fourteen months."

"What happened? Why the bust-up?"

"We discovered differences."

"What does that mean? Did he beat you up? Sexual violence? Unfaithful? Move onto hard drugs?"

He was still studying her and she continued to return his gaze with that same curious directness.

"I found I no longer loved him."

Sandy stared at her. He stared at her and refused to believe her. "What then? You kept in touch? You must have met him again, if only by chance?"

"I never met him again."

The liquid eyes, the pink now suffusing out beyond the wings of flesh either side of her nose, proclaimed this to be the bone-hard truth.

"How soon afterwards did you meet Mr Stephens?"

"I don't know. Many years."

Sandy inhaled deeply, exhaled very slowly, his fingers fluttering on the table top to either side of his tea.

"It just doesn't make sense, does it, Mrs Stephens?"

She was silent again, breathing deeply and quite flushed.

"I mean, nineteen years, no contact whatsoever. You must have thought this over."

The flush appeared rapidly to deepen, to extend down the sides of her face and wash, like a diffusing pink dye, into the web of her neck and the front of her chest.

"How could it possibly make sense? It doesn't answer the one critical question. Why in God's name did he come back and kidnap your son? Why, after nineteen years?"

20

Hunger screws up like a big fat spasm in his gut. It's been like that for two days, settling down between spasms into a gnawing ulcerous ache. Even worse than hunger is its mental twin, a debilitating nausea. He has begun to think hunger.

When he stops to listen there is the sound of his own noisy breathing, here, where he has long been standing in front of the big window.

"Come on over, Bobby. Come over here and look at the snow."

Bobby moves slowly but careful to make it just slow enough and not too slow. He comes across from where he was sitting with spreadeagled legs on the front of the fireplace and now he has to stand up on a box so his face can be as high as the man staring down through the window. And in looking out with him, that same fearful thought – which he is even more careful to hide from Mag – just keeps on crawling around in his mind.

Maybe out there it looks pretty good, the snow on the trees and the very white light sort of misty, because the sun is just about flat through the trees.

Mag stands there, with his hand on Bobby's shoulder. That's all he does: he just stands there so they can look out of the dusty windows together.

Mag looks relaxed, just looking out like that, but Bobby is not fooled. Bobby knows for certain, that if he were Mag –

If I was Mag, today is when I'd get rid of the boy! Over
minutes there is a crazy flashing about of lights, like you see
in discos, with beams moving about through holes in the
trees, but Bobby isn't interested in the lights. *Mag kills!*
That's the thought that interests Bobby. Mag kills people.
Mag can kill somebody with a gun and then take money
from their pockets and buy sausages with it and he can just
stand here and look out at the snow.

"In the very old days, the smart alecs – the really smart
alecs who think it is their right to tell everybody what they
must think and how they must see the whole world out there
– those smart alecs believed that all of us, every man and
woman and every boy and girl, were made up out of four
ingredients, which they called humours."

Bobby listens to him as he has to listen, trying to guess
what the words really mean – only that thought, that
terrible thought, goes crawling and creeping around in his
brain.

"Aye – four humours, Bobby, like the ingredients in your
mam's pudding mix. All rubbish – except for one thing.
They never underestimated the powers of darkness."

Bobby doesn't underestimate the powers of darkness.
Bobby knows now that Mag is deliberately telling him
what is in his mind. *Today is the day I have to kill thee,
Bobby lad!*

Bobby's eyes fall mournfully down to see the van still
there, with the picture of a grinning pig on its side. Mag
has moved the van right up until it's under the trees but
it's still not much of a hide-out because you can see its
blue colour, covered on the top, like the icing on a cake,
by snow.

The man has caught that fretful glance, but his expression is unchanged. For a moment he is back there loading
the bodies into the back of the old Morris, sliding them
along the wooden runners which were designed for a
different kind of meat. Then it had been the woman he

had felt pity for. He sees her again now: that look frozen on her face, the slightly backward-arched neck trailing the rose-stained, white-dyed hair over his left shoulder – almost an embrace then – and as in that moment he had seen broken humanity, his heart had filled with foreboding and a weakness had afflicted his arms so he was forced to drop her more roughly into the van than respect demanded.

He knows. Of course the boy knows. But he will not ask about that, no more than he will volunteer information. Instead he will continue to humour him, pretending interest in the landscape which is so white and ethereal in the misty light, where the horizon is now becoming brilliantly visible, fold after fold, like overlapping angel's feathers, or the scales of a gargantuan pure white fish. In this moment the man gazes languorously to where the horizon is subtly suggesting the curvature of the earth and in the metamorphosing cloud, in its delicately paced, slow-motion minuet, he feels the spirits glide, he can sense the rolling of the universe about its axis.

Then abruptly, "Sausages later, Bobby. First we get rid of the van!'

And now they are dressing in that careful way you move when you're really hungry. The man is pulling down the pullover over Bobby's thinning arms – how white and pale they look and how soft and flabby the muscle is becoming – and he jokes him softly yet sternly. "You niff a bit – more than a bit if I were to be honest, Bobby lad."

"You smell like a pig's fart yourself." Those words just come from his mouth before he can stop them, but Mag just goes on pulling on the pullover over his other arm and laughing. And Bobby, while he is being followed down the stairs, where the dust always comes up like sandstorms in the Sahara Desert, is thinking that Mag could laugh just like that when he was killing people.

Last night he couldn't sleep at all because of those

shots and the screaming. Last night he kept hearing those shots ring out inside his head. Haunting him. One shot, just like he remembered, a loud clap, or like a door banging shut only it wasn't any door. And then he was awake even if he had been half-asleep at first and he jumped up from where he had been lying with his heart thumping in his throat – he remembered his heart thumping so hard in his throat it lifted his chin up in a jerk every time it thumped – and he knew things were very very bad because he could hear that bloodcurdling screaming. He didn't want to but he just had to stand up on the box there at the end window, paralysed with that terrible thumping in his throat, and the screaming just went on and on, a woman screaming, and he knew there would be a second shot. He just knew it. And then when it happened, just when he knew it would happen, there was a real yukky feeling in his stomach. He vomited then, like when he suddenly jacked forward and puked all over his dad when they were driving to Truro.

"Well then – art' going to keep us tongue hangin' out?"

Mag is standing there with the van door open. It is the door on the driver's side, which is the door that was left open all the time the night before last, which Bobby noticed because there was a light on inside the van when he looked out of the window. He had been staring down at that opened door all the time during the terrible screaming. That open van door was the last thing he saw before he heard that second shot. That shot made him jump right off the box onto the floor under the small end window. Just as he knew then for certain it really was a shot and he knew the other had also been a shot and he knew that it was Mag that had the gun. And so the sick came up into his mouth then, because he was certain that if Mag was shooting at people, he wouldn't miss. He knew that much for certain just as he was figuring out in his brain where all this must be happening – in that church with a cross over it like the

Methodist church he passed on his way to the rec when he was going to play football and Danny Weatherill told him that his grandmother had been left in there in a coffin with the lid open all night.

And even though he knows Dicky Dee would think up all sorts of arguments about food, all the same Dicky was right that if you did without food you would surely croak. And if you croak you don't escape, never ever. And if you don't escape and you are lying there and Mag just put you down into a hole in the ground under all that snow, then nobody'll even know you're down there. You'll be croaked anyway and then Mag will really have won, won't he?

The ride is grotesque for Bobby, who has never driven more than a dodgem before – the ride is the most totally mad thing in this world.

Branches whip and thump across the metal of the van and bang into the windows. Mag carries on just laughing his head off all the time because he doesn't care anyway. He doesn't even care when, after only thirty yards, they smash deadeningly into a tree. Bobby is shouting and screaming and the engine makes a horrible strangling noise and the snow thumps down onto the glass so they can't see a thing. But Mag just keeps on laughing fit to burst, with his eyes closed. All he does is to make a crazy grab for the gear stick, nearly breaking Bobby's fingers, and starts the engine up again. He makes Bobby drive it back, with his hand over Bobby's on the stick, back out of the tree, which has a great big white piece where the trunk has split from the bang, and with snow stuck all over the glass and the wipers smashing themselves to pieces trying to clear the hard bits, he makes it go forwards again, so they're bumping and lurching all the time down a tunnel of trees all hanging down and swatting the van with their branches heavy with snow. And the tyres keep slipping this way and sliding that way, with Bobby totally lost on the edge of his seat and with his eyes big circles of panic.

Mag's eyes are shining, really shining!

Bobby groans in his stomach and his tongue is huge and dry and pounding like dynamite and his lungs are going in and out and his neck is swelling like a balloon and there's spiders crawling all over his head and he knows it is a blood van and he knows at the end of this journey . . . oh, God, but at the end of this mad crazy journey!

There! You see – *you see!* Look at that – there's a drop all the way to Australia now on the left and he has to learn how to turn right fast. The trees lurch up in front of him, they seem to rear up, howling about and hurtling from side to side, bursting heavily against the van and roaring buckets of snow at them so as to stop them dead all the time. And then, suddenly, there is nothing at all. Suddenly he is looking out and he is looking straight down, because the van has dropped down a bit at the front, and Mag doesn't say a single word but they're staring down the big drop near the place where they walked once, and down there now are treetops, covered white with snow. And Mag, the madman, still laughing his insides out, screams out, "Okay, driver. This is it, the end of the line!" And Mag's voice, the promise at last, is total screaming terror on the inside of Bobby's skull.

Help me, God! Help me!

Mag lumbers out on his side, holding onto the open door because there is only a tiny ledge of ground, and Bobby stares at him, with his hands frozen numb and clinging for his life to the steering wheel. His eyes are glued to the big letter "M" in gold letters on ruby red, like blood, in the middle of the wheel. He can hear his mouth and nose making noises like Jenny Ashworth who takes a puffer thing for asthma.

Help me, Mum – Mum and Dad. Why didn't you help me! All this time . . . all this time!

But they will not be able to help him. Nobody can help him. His whole head is swooning, like he was stuck down, gripped in a terrible death grip, by weeds under water. His own voice sounds shrill, a screeching seagull in his ears.

"You're going to push me over in the van. You're going to push me over because then you won't even have to look at me. You can just push and you won't even see me."

"Lead us not into temptation," Mag's bearded face grins down at him, those horrible blank grey eyes in a bearded mask that looks queerly green, now poking right in through the big hole in the door where a freezing wind hurls itself into the van, blasting snow.

"Because if you kill me you can have all of the sausages to yourself."

Mag has suddenly appeared outside Bobby's door and has wrenched it open. His awful hand has taken a firm hold of Bobby's shoulder. He is still staring with those devil's eyes, staring from real close for the longest time ever imaginable. Then suddenly he is prancing about, throwing up his arms, picking up handfuls of snow and slapping it into his face, so it clings to his hair and beard like an abominable snowman.

"So I can have all the sausages!"

He is yanking Bobby out of the driver's seat, even as with only a touch on the handbrake lever, he sends the van bounding into the open air. The van makes a car-ummmmmppphhh noise as it bursts through some bushes covered in snow and then it falls a bit and then bounces and rolls madly down faster and faster. Mag is hopping and skipping from side to side, then diving himself down in the snow, howling like a baboon.

"So I can have all the sausages, can I?"

He showers snow into Bobby's face, grabs him, lifts him up in a bear-hug and then rolls him over amongst the ferns covered in snow. There is snow on his tongue, on his eyelashes, and still he tries to see where the van is going, because it has gone really strangely quiet, now it is really rolling. Even when it crashes into a big tree, there is only a sickly crunch, lost in a mini snowstorm, maybe the van has torn the tree right up out of the ground, maybe that's roots and all he can see, the stuff the van drags on down with it, and gently just disappears – it really disappears completely – as Bobby stands all wrapped in snow like a small snow-man. He stares down to where the storm of disturbed snow is quickly settling in to fill in the tracks from either side. There will be no sign, no sign at all . . .

Now Mag's grey eyes are watching him so closely. Those silver metal eyes in a ghost's mask of white know and see everything. Those eyes penetrate to the back of his brain and he knows now, as if he hadn't known all along, what Bobby has worked out for himself.

You killed them like you were going to kill me. Because you were going to kill me, weren't you? Bobby knows now that he saw death, like a horrible awareness in Mag's eyes, that day crouching over the water.

In the way understanding dawns, in the way you feel things even when you don't understand them all the way, Bobby senses that for Mag the Magician there is a special time. Like the night-time is a special time or in the little church, and right then by the dusty water. There is a right time when Mag decides he wants to kill people. Bobby is quite sure about this now. Mag nearly did croak him then. Mag took him out that day and death was what he was thinking about when he took him out and they crossed the stepping stones.

Croaking people comes out of Mag's brain like a genie came out of Aladdin's lamp.

Escape is a frantic hope which floods Bobby's soul. The thought that in all of that journey along there in the van, in the excitement of all that, Mag didn't notice that he had found a Stanley knife blade. He had found a Stanley knife blade, like his dad used and always warned him about touching, on the shelf in front of the steering wheel.

Looking down now to where the trail of the van has already almost disappeared, he feels the blade, pricking against his skin inside his sock.

21

Sandy Woodings felt excited, bewildered, frustrated. All along he had sensed that he was somehow close to this man. They already knew a great deal. Yet there was also the nagging worry they were in a blind alley of their own making. He had difficulty sleeping. He was suffering from palpitations. He would find himself lost in thought and a sweat would begin to prickle under his arms, at the hairline of his brow, in the palms of his hands.

He was looking for something new. Just the slenderest lead . . . Then Henry called his secretary and left the message he might have something for him.

Sandy and Tom arrived at the forensic science laboratory at 3.35 p.m., on Monday December 19th, just as it was falling dark. Henry Bancroft came down to meet them at reception and then, with a pinkish flush of excitement extending up into his balding sandy-red-haired scalp, he led them down the corridor between rows of tidy laboratories.

"You said you had found something – something important," Sandy addressed the man's back, without concealing his impatience.

"Human hair," Henry remarked with an annoying bright humour, "is a fascinating study quite in itself. Given a single hair plucked violently from the head, we can tell the sex of the individual – there is a thing called the sex chromatin which we can determine from the living cells at the hair root." He held a door open for them, continuing to proclaim didactically as they walked along a new corridor at right angles to the previous. "For instance negro hair is easily distinguishable from Caucasian. The hair from your eyebrow tapers to a point, while that from down below is only bluntly pointed. If the young lady in the act of being raped does us the favour of pulling hard enough on her assailant's Mexican moustache, then we know that too, because moustache hair is triangular as opposed to oval or rounded in section."

They passed through the main laboratory into a darkroom, where Henry had connected an expensive-looking metallic-grey microscope to an overhead screen. "Look for yourself, gentlemen."

Projected onto the two foot screen were various strands of human hair, magnified to a hundred times their normal size. Henry, who had taken the familiar metal spatula from the pen pocket of his white coat, slipped onto a stool and began to explain. "The one on the left – let's call it hair type A – is a sample of one of the two different cuttings which we found in the envelope. The two hairs on the right of it are those of Peter and Margaret Stephens."

"They'e different?"

The spatula reached out, hovered over all three hairs. "Watch again – those same fibres under polarised light."

Henry did something to the background so the hairs resembled the trunks of saplings constructed from a translucent silver.

"Definitely different."

"No doubt about it – hair type A could not be from the natural son of Mr and Mrs Stephens. Although the study of hair is interesting, it is at its most accurate when the hair fibres do *not* match." Henry tapped twice on the palm of his hand with the spatula before projecting, in similar fashion, a fibre from type B, the second variety of hair found in the envelope, against the samples found from the continental

199

quilt on Robert Stephens' bed and also from an imperfectly cleaned hairbrush.

"They match?"

"Perfectly."

"So we can identify hair type B as from Bobby Stephens' head."

"Yes."

"Is there any doubt about it, Henry? We have to be absolutely certain on this."

"We can say that the hair, type B in the envelope, and the boy's own hair are identical. That is all we can say."

"But under the circumstances . . ." Sandy Woodings nodded with a bitter satisfaction. It was good enough for him: quite vital in fact. This was absolute confirmation that the kidnapper and the murderer were one and the same man.

"Here, I'm afraid, we dispense with such attractive simplicity," Henry wheeled away from facing the detectives to attending to the microscope again. "We must remember that what we are now looking for is not a perfect match. Look again at the hairs of both parents. Notice that Peter Stephens has quite different hair from that of his wife, Margaret. The lady has thick strands, darkly pigmented and barely curling. The father has much more curly hair, thinner in cortical thickness and lightly pigmented."

"We're looking for something in between?"

"Step two, exactly correct, gentlemen." Henry, with that constant glint of excitement in his eyes, now projected two slides side by side. "On the left now we have types A and B from the envelope. On the right, the two parents."

Sandy and Tom stared wordlessly for at least two minutes. Then Sandy nodded urgently. "I think I follow . . ."

Henry tapped at the screen with his spatula. "The hair from the envelope, type A, is very thin in cortical thickness, yet very deeply pigmented. Which is very odd – curiouser and curiouser."

"From what you were saying earlier, Henry, about failure to match being significant, Robert Stephens is unquestionably Peter Stephens' son. His hair falls intermediate between both parents."

"A little closer to his father's, perhaps, but yes. Was there ever uncertainty in your mind about that, Chief Inspector?"

Sandy did not answer that question. "So where did hair type A come from?"

"Fine hair – very, very fine . . ."

"He sent us a sample of his own hair?"

"This man, Bamford, has been described as having a full head of dark curly hair. I would expect his hair to show curling – and to be much thicker."

"But why on earth! When we know he positively isn't the boy's father . . ."

"You're the detectives."

"Come on now, Henry!"

"Are you suggesting that I, a man of science, should make a somewhat unscientific guess?"

"An educated guess."

"A baby's head."

"A baby!"

"And a very young baby at that. A very young baby – with very dark straight hair."

"Good Lord almighty!"

"Don't get overwrought – we haven't finished yet – quite. Henry has one more slide to reveal to you. This one is all down to Henry."

A slide quite different in its layout, Henry projected a much lower power, with dozens of hair fibres, teased apart so that they lay scattered randomly about the field, like the remains of a spaghetti meal. He pointed with his spatula to what might have otherwise seemed specks of debris included by accident.

"Dirt!" said Tom in disgust.

"Perfectly correct. Dirt, glorious dirt," intoned Henry.

"Did you know, gentlemen, that I wrote my doctorate on the glorious subject of dirt?" He made a sucking sound between his small perfectly even teeth, as if savouring the moment. "Dirt is never quite as it seems, " Henry continued enthusiastically, turning up the illumination so that the particles, which were now seen to be firmly adherent to the hairs themselves and not just part of the background rubbish, glowed like brilliant moons.

"White dust?" Henry enquired.

"Wrong on both counts," Henry's tongue curled playfully into the corner of his mouth. "What I asked myself was the question going through your minds right now. Let's accept that hair type B does indeed come from the head of the kidnapped youngster – then what else can we learn from it? Does it mean the child is alive or dead? Well, I'm sorry to say I can't answer that. Human hair, above the root, is a dead structure, rather like fingernails, and has remarkable powers of survival long after death and even against the assault of all types of weather, burial, and so on."

"Burial!" exclaimed Tom gloomily, with his fingers walking over his pocket.

"Precisely what I asked myself. If the lad had been killed six or seven weeks ago, surely the body would have been discovered before now, unless it was hidden, say by burial. In order to obtain the hair for his head, our man – allowing that this hair was recently cut from the boy's head – would have had to dig up the mortal remains."

"In which case the particles would represent soil?"

"You have the general idea, Chief Inspector. So – over to Henry's thesis –"

"Watch again," he arched his corpulent frame to tease carefully at the delicate controls, altering the brightness of illumination, slowly dimming the screen, so that the brilliance of the particles was reduced to a glow, a mere shadow, until they had practically disappeared into the midnight background.

"They're blue?"

"Half marks," said Henry, "because you took your time about it. Blue indeed, because dirt is never dirt. Dirt is displaced matter, you might even say a jewel dislocated from its proper setting, and the setting here proves to be a wall coated in a particular variety of old emulsion. Perhaps it will strike the right chord if I were to remind you that it was the cheerful decoration chosen by a generation of mothers for the outside privies – powdery cerulean blue."

"Which does not prove that the child is still alive?"

"I don't claim it proves the child is still alive."

"What you are saying is that, alive or dead, he or his mortal remains lie above ground, in a building which has walls decorated with an old-fashioned blue emulsion."

"Just a minor little observation – nothing more."

Sandy Woodings was very impressed. It meant something. He felt it deep in his bones that it meant something very important. But exactly what? He felt overwhelmed by an anguished ignorance. He gazed with absolute concentration on those tiny specks of pastel blue: *Why send us any hair at all? Why send us that second lock of hair? Black hair from a baby's head!*

Detective Inspector Jock Andrews was every bit as puzzled. A day later, in the lunch hour of Tuesday, December 20th, Jock needed to speak urgently to Sandy Woodings. He found him watching a film in the briefing room, with the lights switched off and sitting towards the front, entirely alone, a solitary shadow in the dark. The circumstances were such that the Scottish detective pondered what was happening, watching several minutes of film during which a young man wearing a bemused expression and speaking with an American accent, said, "People are very lost, I think." Or something like that. Jock Andrews had difficulty working out just exactly what because the young man's voice was shaky and slurred. His eyes glittered a little too brightly from where he was sitting in dappled shade, and sitting next to him was a girl who looked drugged out of her mind.

As Jock made his way forward, having to duck under the cone of projected light in order to get close to the chief inspector, a part of his mind still listened to that tremulous young American. "It's like everybody is looking for some kind of answer, you know . . . It's not where they are at . . . so they think it's where we are at . . . here." Then he took the chair next to Woodings and spoke softly, in a forceful whisper, as if reluctantly interrupting some pleasant entertainment in order to point out a painful truth.

"We've tried it. The Redmond Estate. Grey registered vans. Nothing. We've drawn a complete blank."

Sandy Woodings sighed and he performed a long blink, looking thoughtful. "I keep going over it in my mind. Over and over, Jock. I know there's a pattern. I can feel an acceleration in that pattern. But I don't understand it. I don't understand what I'm actually feeling." He patted the chair next to him. "Take a look at this, Jock. Tell me what you think."

Twisting his mouth to the side, Jock glanced askance at the screen, where an old farmer, with an incredulous smile, talked about living on cornflakes for two days. "I'm telling you – we've drawn a blank."

"Very well, Jock – so we've drawn a blank. So we move on to the next phase – grey vans, the whole city – right." Sandy continued to watch the film with a bright hard intensity.

Jock didn't bother to hide his dismay. His face, turned flat towards the screen, was a mask of exhaustion.

In the film, the old farmer was talking about something that was big, too big . . . too big for the world. Was it possible that something, whatever had shattered the love affair between Margaret Stephens and James Bamford, was here, right here in this very film?

Jock murmured in reluctant interest. "What's it supposed to be?"

"Woodstock. We managed to dig it up from somewhere. They made a film of it."

Why kdinap the boy in the first place? For heaven's sake, why do it? Everything really hinged on that first mad act!

Was the boy still alive? What had really gone on all those years ago between a philosophy graduate and a first year literature student, in that same year when the Rolling Stones gave a free concert to half a million people in Hyde Park, London, and when an uncounted number of people, perhaps as many as a million, had gathered here in this farmer's field outside New York to welter in a philosophy of music and words that promised . . . a new dawn?

A baby with black hair!

The note which had accompanied the hair had not been torn. What baby? Whose baby? Did it imply some closeness, some intimacy, other than the blood tie of paternity? *You don't understand the way we lived, the very air we breathed . . .*

For a longer time, perhaps a good ten or fifteen minutes, they watched the film in silence. They saw a farmer reap in his corn and on that same field, outside New York, they watched the organisers arrive on motorcycles, men with hippy-style beards, young women who looked like angels, with liberated hair almost to their waists. They stared at colourful scenes of wigwams, dancers with legs completely bare from the crutch down, psychedelically painted single-decker coaches blocking a country road.

"What's the point of it all?" asked Jock.

"I don't know, Jock. I wish I did know."

They were listening to a journalist interviewing the handful of men who appeared to be organising it. Organising what? Something bigger certainly than any of them realised in those preparatory days. A dream perhaps. There were interviews with local villagers, farmers, shopkeepers, next the arriving young, those young who had come from all over America, creating a crisis in their very numbers. A dream, certainly. A monument to whatever the sixties represented. And here it was, all duly recorded: the unpredicted crowds, totally unprepared for, blocking all roads, numbers of people so enormous that all notion of ticket sales had been abandoned, fences dropped, fleets of portaloos brought in, the singers having to be flown in by helicopter.

Jock was not possessed of Sandy's patience. He sighed, looked down into the pool of darkness beneath his feet. "The boss is very sceptical . . ."

"I know that Georgy is sceptical, Jock."

"But maybe he's right. I mean, what if we come up with no man answering the right description, no suspicious white lettering, no occupational links or fingerprints – nothing?"

Sandy said nothing. He thought about what Jock had indicated while listening to Joan Baez sing her protest about a murdered union organiser. In her preamble she had drawn attention to her own husband's being imprisoned for avoiding the Vietnam draft. Something jerked in his gut. Something important because it was his gut and not his brain that was saying so. Jock was a fidgeting presence, who no longer gave a damn about this film they were watching. And he knew that what was worrying Jock, who was a sound and steady detective, was real. It was tangible as compared to this nebulous philosophising from the past. He also knew that van existed. That van existed somewhere here in this city. They just had to find it. They just had to . . .

He continued to watch a group of young people, squatting on the grass, who were performing yoga exercises to the direction of a man with his blond hair crimped and tied into a ponytail at the back. Peaceful. There was such a sense of peace, of non-violence, about them. The man talked about a nerve of awareness. He talked on in a jokey comforting voice as they all hyperventilated together in order to reach some common astral plain. The camera flipped through twelve hours, a bearded guru was explaining how America must help the world not only materially but spiritually. A dark-haired teenage girl, wearing a navy T-shirt and torn-off denim skirt with bare feet, lay curled on her side fast asleep. All of a sudden there was a huge change in atmosphere in the film. Even Jock was now gazing up once again at the screen. Rain! Suddenly it was pouring with rain.

The change was so unexpected that the huge crowd was thrown into confusion. The organisers were shouting instructions to people to head away from the giant light towers. Wind was hurling rain with great force, whipping the big tarpaulin sheets into horizontal sails. The crowd milled about, discovering flimsy shelters of polythene, hopelessly porous blankets. One of the scuttling figures desperately attempting to cover up the electrical equipment on stage suddenly screamed into a microphone.

"Hey – if you think really hard, maybe we can get rid of this rain!"

Sandy had suddenly taken a grip on Jock's arm.

"This is it, Jock. Listen to this, for God's sake."

Twenty years ago Margaret Stephens had been amongst those million, squatting on the ground in that muddy field, her mind filled with what . . . that dream? And sitting next to her on the grass, with shoulder-length hair, shoulder-length dark curly hair and those eyes . . .

Three men on the stage, their hair, beards, moustaches all plastered to their faces with the rain. Who were they? Organisers? Maybe part of a band? They were suddenly commanding the crowd, screaming above the roar of the wind in the microphones, against a long rumbling discharge of thunder.

"LET'S ALL THINK HARD TO GET RID OF IT . . . NO RAIN! NO RAIN! NO RAIN! NO RAIN! . . ."

22

Taking the stairs at a clatter, Sandy had descended to the landing of the second floor when he heard the familiar huffing and puffing from a flight below him and he waited, while the throbbing in his temples established itself in earnest. Georgy gasped a little, he seemed to find a need to interrupt his progress for pained breath. When he came into view on the turn below the landing, his enormous head was momentarily bowed, he appeared to be snoring through the concertinaed folds of neck, and he was clearing his felt hat of snow by banging it against the stair rail. The physical rigour of the climb was such that he registered Sandy's presence without troubling to look up directly at him.

"What are you up to – read that interview with Mrs Stephens – my opinion – load of hogwash!" Georgy's tirade was interrupted by deep breaths as he climbed again, a phrase thrown up at alternate steps.

Pressing a finger against the bloated artery in his right temple, Sandy waited restlessly as the stout man made his laborious progress. "That's coming on a bit strong, isn't it."

But Georgy, now only two steps away from him, jerked his eyebrows upwards, those bulbous eyes swivelling chameleon-like under their own volition in a plum-coloured hopelessly battered and pockmarked face. "So what about the search for the van?"

"You know we haven't found the van."

Pretending to brush something from his ballooned trousers, Georgy had one of his little pauses. He caught his breath or maybe waited for his angina to settle down now, on the landing, and with Sandy standing with his back holding the fire door open. "What do you think? Do you think the news exactly surprises me?" Georgy was staring furiously.

Sandy spoke with ill-suppressed husky emotion as they proceeded down the corridor towards Georgy's office.

"We've covered the Redmond district for all four kinds of van and we've covered the city for grey vans only. The next step has to be the whole city for all four kinds of van, irrespective of colour. That's not on with only twelve men."

They had entered the office, the door of which had been standing open, and now Tom, who had been waiting there for them, stood up to greet them. Georgy ignored the greeting, making his limping way round to the chair on the far side of the desk. He collapsed into his chair and inspected the reports which had been newly placed on the desk by Tom.

"I thought you were dependable, Sandy."

"So now I'm not dependable?"

"I did – I looked on you as . . . as a son!"

"Don't be bloody ridiculous!"

"Something salutary, don't you think, Sandy, about the pathologist's reports in a case of murder. All that grisly detail. Brings those poppy-flights of fancy right down to the seat of pants level – don't you think?"

Sandy could see the drawings now, upside down, the methodical working through of the vital areas of interest. Page 5 – marks of violence. Only one in each case. No defence wounds on hands. It was all down to the single horrible head wounds. And the pathologist's report very quickly moved on to that. Under Georgy's roving fingers, he watched the pages turn. Drawings of the head to show the entry wound through the mouth, photographs of shattered teeth, photographs of the inside of the mouth to show the holes – in the butcher's case in the soft palate and the back of the throat, with a white probe poking through the hole; in the woman's case, a hole more directed upwards, the bullet cutting a deep gouge along the hard palate, shattering bone here, before entering the head at the back of the nasal cavity. All a preliminary to the silkily scarlet inside of the skull. At moments like this he sometimes wondered if the obscenity of the murder were not mirrored by the prurient poking about in these hidden places by pathologists and by policemen such as himself. He wondered perhaps for the thousandth time just what made a reasonably intelligent and apparently rational young man choose a career such as his own. Then, when Georgy handed him the two reports, it was with particular reference to the preliminary pages that he first studied them, sniffing the formalin of the mortuary about them.

Thomas (Tommy) Chatwin. Age: 47 (d.o.b. 21:1:42). Sex: male. Occupation: butcher. Body identified by: Leonard Chatwin (brother) . . .

Georgy said: "You and Julie – I like Julie. If I'm to be honest about it, I prefer Julie to you. Any day!"

Sandy, with his face white, turned to Tom and spoke in little above a whisper. "Anything from the brother?"

"Nothing really useful. His brother last saw Thomas Chatwin alive the afternoon of the day he was murdered. Saw him at Bury. Thomas Chatwin's movements have been traced to London's Smithfield market. He drove down in his old Morris 1000 van – "

"The van we haven't been able to find?"

"That's right. He set out in that van onto the M6 at 3.30 in the morning. Dropped off the meat he bought at roughly 12.30. Told his wife he was tired and had two hours in bed. After tea, maybe 7.15 p.m., he left home to go drinking with the boys – "

"But so far we haven't found any boys who saw him drinking?"

"Right again. We've confirmed the times, that's all. Wife and brother know nothing more."

"Because Chatwin covered his own tracks." Sandy was wondering about Chatwin living in Bury, Lancashire, which was only a few miles from Bolton. *Bolton*. He had turned over the page; he gazed down under the headings, Clothing Removed and Specimens Taken And Handed To. Presumably Chatwin had, early in that evening, met the woman and fellow victim, Ruth Spencer, a known prostitute. Where had they met up? Where had one led the other? Those questions remained unanswered. The Greater Manchester police were working hard at those questions still. But a sudden huge wave of restlessness told Sandy they would discover nothing working backwards from the victims. That same agitation in his gut made him certain that their only hope lay in analysing the man who had killed them.

NO RAIN! NO RAIN! NO RAIN! NO RAIN! How that desperate litany reverberated in his mind. A way of thinking?

"Semen stains?"

"On trousers, yes," Tom acknowledged.

"Fresh?"

"As a daisy," Tom could not suppress the crinkle of a smile. "Clothing on both man and woman had been disturbed. We think the murderer did that."

"Why?"

"Farnworth thinks he actually put their clothes back on. To cover up the fact they were killed during the act."

Sandy's gaze moved on: height – 1.73 metres: weight – 13 st 11 lbs: race – Caucasian: hair – fair, balding: eyes – blue: mouth – damaged. He turned over the page and gazed on that damage again, the damage he had seen at the church, the same photograph he had seen upside down as Georgy inspected it minutes ago on his desk. He moved the pages briskly: stared now at the photographs of ravaged brain, the photographs of the inside of the skull, the top lifted completely off, the brain taken out. Next to the photographs were the pathologist's drawings, intended as an aid to understanding the path of the bullet. One bullet – bullet not found.

Sandy remembered a case of strangulation. The victim had not died immediately but remained alive on a ventilator in a hospital intensive care unit for two whole months. There had been a lot of discussion in court about the part of the brain called the brain stem. This was the bulge in what was virtually the continuation of the spinal cord after it entered the skull through the foramen magnum. It was rather a vital bulge. The brain stem controlled your breathing. There was a part of it which determined if you were awake or asleep – or as far as his previous case was concerned, whether you were in a coma, and therefore, whether you ever woke up again or not. His case had not woken up. The brain stem controlled the heartbeat . . . A heartbeat, in the case of Thomas, known as Tommy, Chatwin, which had stopped the instant a .303 calibre rifle bullet had smashed its way through it and blown it to pulp.

"What chance do you think you have of making Superintendent?" Georgy growled, his face scarlet. "Or do you want me to spell it all the way for you?"

"Save your blood pressure, Georgy."

"Here!" Georgy slammed the other report down on the desk surface. "Go ahead. Take a close look at the woman's report."

Politics! That was what was upsetting Georgy. So, let him stew in it! Sandy forced himself to work through the postmortem report on the woman just as he had the man. Ruth, also known as Stella, Spencer. Aged: 32 (d.o.b. 11:6:57). Occupation: prostitute. Last seen alive: circa 6.25 p.m. on day of murder. He read that she lived in a high-rise council flat in Denton, Greater Manchester. Dyed blonde hair, dark brown at the roots. Brown eyes. Clothing removed: etc . . . Semen traces on front of her imitation silk blouse . . .

He glanced at Tom.

"Semen traces recovered from her mouth," Tom made a yawning movement, which hideously stretched his jaws.

"The vagina?"

"Nothing recent."

"So what the hell do you make of that?" Georgy's eyes had something of a leer.

"It could mean anything. Condoms. Maybe. Alan Farnworth is right – interrupted before they could finish?"

Georgy considered this for a moment. "I'll tell you what it tells me. A well-known and popular prostitute. She was seen to leave her flat at 6.15. Estimated time of death was 10.00 p.m. to 2.00 a.m. the following morning."

"It corroborates what her friend said about her. She was having a night off – or at least a night out alone."

"A night out with one favoured client, namely Tommy Chatwin, who had just returned from a bulk-buying order in London." Georgy's face was almost black as he performed the manoeuvre with the pipe and now filling the bowl with powerfully scented St Bruno. "And I'll tell you what that means to me. That means money, quite a lot, in Tommy's back pocket. Enough to pay Ruthie for a whole night. And, if I guess right, Ruthie doesn't come cheap for a whole evening."

"I can go along with that,' Sandy spoke icily, then exhaled. "But not as the whole story."

"Is that so!"

"The shootings were very accurate. Almost pinpoint accurate. This was no ordinary robbery, Georgy."

"So tell me what I don't know. I taught you all you know, Sandy." Suddenly Georgy was roaring. "I own you, Sandy."

"Nobody owns me, Georgy."

Sandy's eyes glittered with a false calm. Was Georgy

more than just irritated? Sandy suspected it was more than just Georgy's total hatred of anything political. Maybe Georgy was feeling it too. A sense of progression: *a sense of time!* The fun is just beginning, Mr Detective. What fun exactly?

Tom spoke his thoughts aloud: "Why go to so much trouble placing the bodies under the church window?"

Sandy felt provocative. Georgy just couldn't go on avoiding it. "Politics!" he muttered hoarsely.

"Don't you bring politics into this case!" Georgy's eyes watered with fury.

Tom intercepted Sandy's reply, very quickly. "I wondered about something else altogether. I wondered about the fact that we're looking for one type of van and the Greater Manchester force are looking for a different sort altogether. I wondered if we should all be looking for the same van. A 1975 Morris 1000, chalk blue."

A way of thinking. That's what we are dealing with? Sandy's tormented vision turned inwards. He thought back to that last conversation with Margaret Stephens. She had described Bamford as what – a good organiser! Sandy was suddenly staring wildly towards Tom, who thought he was admiring his double-breasted suit with stripes that were at least half an inch wide. Tom's tie was about fifty per cent wider than it should be also but at least he had toned down the colours.

"The brother – Leonard – do we believe him when he says he doesn't know where Tommy might have gone with this woman?"

Georgy answered this question. "Why should he lie? We've got to believe him."

Sandy murmured quietly, "So – if we credit the evidence that is in front of our eyes – if they were interrupted . . ."

"How often did he go down to Smithfield market?"

"Maybe once a fortnight."

"And on the evenings?"

"His wife said he often went out for a drink with the boys on those evenings."

"Surely, Tom, we can check if Ruth Spencer took those same evenings off – as special?"

"Not so easy. Not when her chum is dead vague about that. I'll tell you now that her chum is not reliable."

"We're not asking for references. This is too damned important, Tom. Go back and talk to her. Talk to her again. Get Farnworth to help you. I'll bet my month's salary there was some regular or favourite haunt."

"Thanks a lot. Only don't forget what I've been saying about the van," urged Tom. "That's important. The fact we haven't found the butcher's van, my nose tells me that's important."

Sandy was struggling to concentrate with his eyes screwed shut. He was rubbing in groaning bewilderment at his forehead with the tips of his fingers. Yes, Tom had made a very relevant point. "Murdered . . ." he said thoughtfully, "because they were somehow a risk to him? Which generates two vital questions: when exactly and where?"

Georgy had started to pull so hard at his pipe that his bowl glowed and billowed smoke.

"Don't let's forget that all this started with the kidnapping of the boy," Georgy grated, unable to bear his own growing excitement.

But he was perfectly right. The boy had to be the key. Sandy restrained his own inner agitation with an effort at enforced calm. "Let's assume that there was more to it than just robbery. The fact of their murders – and the still missing Morris van – suggests very strongly to me that there is more to it. So let's take things a little further. He kills them somewhere, possibly he interrupts them at their business. That makes their rendezvous very important. It would also explain dropping the bodies off elsewhere. A false trail. Deliberately set up to baffle us. Even so, why not dump the van elsewhere as well? I think I know the answer to that one. Why – because he's aware of how important forensic evidence gleaned from that van might be? Which makes him very smart."

Georgy didn't like something about this but he made no immediate comment. Exhaling hard with the pipe still gripped between his brown teeth, and permeating the office with suffocating smoke, he glowered at Tom's suit.

"When was the projected time of death again?"

"Between 10.00 p.m. Tuesday the 13th and 2.00 a.m. Wednesday the 14th."

You could hear Georgy sucking on that damned pipe. "That's two days between the murders and the bodies being found. Which would give him time to drive from here to Turkey and take in the sights in the meantime."

"He delayed to cover himself. And the only possible explanation for that delay is that it was somewhere local."

Georgy guffawed. "Local to Yorkshire, Lancashire? Even below Manchester, into Cheshire or Derbyshire? Use your head, Sandy. Don't put your eggs in one basket." Georgy's eyes glittered. He made a play of fighting smoke with a cutting left fist, he used a pearl-handled penknife to empty a deluge of sparks into his metal wastepaper basket.

"Figured something out, have you, Georgy?"

"Politics! Don't make me sick. What we're dealing with is a sense of humour."

"A sense of humour?"

"Placing the bodies next to Bolton Parish Church. He put them there, Sandy, so they wouldn't have far to go to find grace."

Sandy felt shocked. He felt a sudden goose flesh of shock run over his body. Because he believed Georgy. The explanation, implausible as it sounded, seemed ridiculously appropriate.

So why, even as he asked it, did he sense that grotesque sense of wrong? They were still missing something, some-

216

thing really and absolutely vital. *Love is never free. No – dear God, No!* "I need thirty men, minimum," he spoke calmly, but his heart was anything but calm.

23

By midnight, Christmas Eve, Sandy had the evidence he had both anticipated and dreaded: the full-scale search of the city for all sorts of vans had drawn a blank.

Christmas morning, leaving his flat early, he drove through streets that were almost deserted, yet the nature of the problem was apparent even today since he encountered several vans between home and the Redmond district which might have fitted their more general description. A very bright red Ford Escort van seemed to follow him for half a mile before turning off in some other direction. He drove slowly, watching it disappear in his rear-view mirror, but it only increased the frightening restlessness that now consumed him.

Parking his car below the slope where Bobby Stephens had been abducted and near to where Bamford had crossed the main road when he had been chasing him, he sat there for about fifteen minutes, just staring at the not unpleasant view of winter trees, the snow-covered ground. Then he climbed out and found a way up the embankment, picking his way along the barely familiar path. The wind howled. His hands were in his pockets because of the freezing cold. Arriving at the spot, he discovered that the little pile of tinder was quite invisible, under a few inches of snow which had partially melted, then frozen again into a porous white ice. Otherwise things were much the same. Inhaling deeply, he looked all about him, at the wilting grasses and weeds poking through the white surface, everything in hibernation, wet-brown trunks of trees sweating winter's thick glairy mucus, in the distance the purple halo of fine twigs on more trees.

He didn't want to smoke: he didn't want to do anything except just stand and reason. So many unconnected pieces of spaghetti were spiralling in his mind, a myriad of data, conversations rememberd, the professor's tone of voice, those black eyes fixed on his, as if pivoted on gyroscopic fulcrums, while that queer-shaped head nodded with the inexpressible first glimmerings of understanding.

A man aged much the same as himself, a tall lean figure, patiently waiting. Schizophrenia – the professor had mentioned it only to pour doubt on it. Now he could see what the professor had been getting at. Don't think madness. Madness is just too convenient a label. But if not madness . . .

Think human. Didn't it always come down to human in the end?

Sweating openly with a gathering inspiration, Sandy pitted himself against that merciless wind, set himself once more into the position in which the man had waited. Waited for maybe half an hour in that cold. Waited while some inner furnace drove him. Certain of himself. Certain of the purpose of his waiting.

Bobby! Bobby!

A bright flash of phosphorescent light: the boys are taken completely by surprise. He walks out from where he has been hiding. Their eyes, wide open, simply stare at his hand holding the sparklers.

All right – so why don't they run? Why do they wait and listen to him? Something in the way he looks and talks. Something Mrs Stephens had intimated? A man with some special facility for communication? A calculated soft way of speaking. That use of dialect? Has he some special and childish level of communication which might approximate obsession and the fantasy world of childhood?

Here! He hands a sparkler to the smallest of them, with the big teeth. *The's not fritten'd on't, eh?*

Little Christopher's head is shaking.

Aye – and here! Another fear calmed with another sparkler. *And one for Bobby!*

The man smiling: those pale eyes in his face glittering. A face that seems younger at this moment than any chronological age. The face of childhood, smiling, his breath bathing him, warm and moist, he blows air from pouted lips in a spasm of amusement. A man who doesn't care. But it isn't a criminal sweating in the act, no more than there is any sense or element of daring. A man whose purpose is so overriding, so essential, that it wouldn't occur to him to care.

Thee mates aren't frittened on a couple o' sparklers!

Sandy had followed the movements of the man with the boys. Now he followed the path down the slope. Probably he had carried the boy down the sheer embankment. Just how quickly had Bobby realised that the man was not friendly? Sandy felt so much closer, warmer.

There was a progression all right – he palpated again the thrill of that progression. A man who didn't care about the police. He didn't send messages to the police at all but to the mother of the missing boy. The mother of the missing boy who was his ex-lover, and who had let him down all those years ago. Then did he equate Margaret Stephens with her child, Bobby, or was it really mundane jealousy as Peter Stephens had surmised? Something sordid, a malicious envy? *Go for understanding . . . play his game . . .*

There was a fidgety drumming in Sandy's chest.

He had arrived out at the sheer slope. Below him was his car. He noticed, perhaps a hundred and twenty yards further along on the same side of the road, what looked very much like that same red Ford Escort van, the van that had followed him earlier for half a mile . . .

Slithering awkwardly down the slope – the van was still there. He found his balance agian, started to edge towards it, crossing to the same side of the road as it was parked. Was it deliberate that the number plate was unreadable? Caked with something like mud. Suddenly the van's engines erupted and it gunned into action, lurching in his direction. He stopped, turned abruptly back towards his car, took one look over his shoulder and started running.

His hat flew off as he took a second look over his shoulder, but he registered two things: the van was not trying for the open road but was actually hunting him. *Hunting him* – and it was closing rapidly. He changed his gallop into an abandoned sprint, his heart pounding, his ears tortured by the screaming of the van's engine. There was no escape to either side, with the steep embankments, so his only chance lay with reaching his car before the van smashed into him, and he didn't think much of his own chances. Any second he expected the bone-grinding jar against the back of his legs, any second, any second – and his car was still a hopeless five feet distant. He dived from where he stood, spiralling onto his right shoulder, thudding across the bonnet, feeling the shockwave of impact beneath him.

The fury of the van battering the bonnet of his car dislodged him into the space between the car and the embankment. At a spreadeagled angle, he caught sight of the van backing from the car, but he could only see reflections in the van's windscreen, because of the oblique angle. It screeched past in a swerve, then forwards again, grinding past him and the car and in the opposite direction to which his car was pointing. He jerked open the passenger door to his car and fell in.

"Damn!" he muttered. "Damn it to hell!"

The dashboard was a mess of dangling wire, where his radio had been ripped out. He twisted his ignition key in the slot and was gratified to hear his engine start. Now, glancing back over his shoulder, he was startled to see the van idling only a hundred yards away, provocatively waiting, and he could even hear the taunting revving of its engine.

"Right!" he shouted, skidding his car into a U-turn, and crashing through the gears. The red van set off with a roar of acceleration, along the main road which led them out of the Redmond district and into a hilly area of council estates, for perhaps five or six hundred yards, before swinging abruptly right into a maze of narrow and densely populated streets lined by council houses.

"You think you know this place better than I do!" Sandy was actually laughing to himself, shoving his right foot to the floor.

They raced along a circuitous route, through tree-lined crescents, one-car roads and bicycle tracks. The red van twisted and turned at whim, screeching round bends without braking, always that thirty yards or so in front of him and seemingly able just to rip away whenever he managed to close the gap. He guessed the van's engine must have been souped-up. No van could turn acceleration on like that. Still he kept on its tail and hoped and waited.

They came to part of the estates where some big renovation programme was taking place, with council workmen's huts, warning signs and holes in the ground next to hillocks of soil and building materials. The van driver treated this as some kind of obstacle race. He was enjoying himself, skimming between trees and the neighbouring houses, more often than not with two wheels on the footpath or off the road altogether, and scattering workmen's signs and tackle like skittles. Sandy thought he could guess where this was all leading – eventually the van would pull onto a major road on the northern perimeter of the city. There was a junction up ahead where the road had to bear left at ninety degrees. The chance he was waiting for – he turned left early.

Powering along one of those crescents euphemistically named after a flower – there was a whole horticultural collection of crescents, and they all came out onto one single road – he cut across a grass playing area, skating on a patch of ice under the filthy snow and walloping the side of his car into a tree; but he saved a good thirty yards and was now back on target, the crescent coming out onto the same road as the van, but with the van on the main limb of a T-junction. That limb couldn't be more than a car in width, so that if he charged at it full pelt, and blocked the road immediately in front of it . . .

His speed was almost fifty as he aimed the car straight at the junction, putting his foot right down and bracing with all his strength with his arms against the padded dash and with his eyes closed. The thunder of the van's engine was suddenly in the car with him, his eyes tearing themselves open, a flash of red and the van was broadside across his path. There was a horrible grinding of metal on metal, almost immediately a dull sickening thud as the two vehicles rammed into the gable end of a house in front of him . . . And then a floating unreal calm in which he could hear the echoing tinkle of falling glass.

He felt utterly bewildered. He couldn't see. His eyes were open – *and he couldn't see!*

He could hear and he couldn't see. No more could he move. Not so much as a finger or a toe, never mind attempting to lift his head where it felt embedded in shredded glass over the junction of dashboard and what had been windscreen. *I've been knocked out. Dammit, I've knocked myself out!*

He could feel his strength returning. It had seemed much longer but it must all have been just seconds. He was beginning to see also. A face, a very large face, large and long, a bearded face, with two huge ears protruding from an unkempt mass of hair. And a voice . . . a too calm, deep-throated voice . . .

"Just when you thought hell went out with the dino-saurs, Mr Policeman!" His face rocked with a slap. Some-thing was slapping his face . . . a large and spatulate hand was slapping his face. A man as huge as a bear was laughing and slapping his face, from one side to the other. "Just when you thought Jack Hell was extinct, Mag had to go and find him for you." That huge gnarled hand was walloping his face so hard, it was rocking his whole body . . . and the pain – his entire body wilted with each agonising jolt from his neck. "No expense spared, across the cruel and briny ocean, to bring Jack Hell all the way back for your amusement." Those eyes, two large pearls, two perfectly round and shining grey pearls, punctured by two central black pits . . .

Oh my God!

Sandy could move one leg now, first his right leg and then his left. But the searing torment when he tried to straighten that right knee! He had to make himself move. He had to will himself into moving. That crazy giant was doing some-thing to the vehicles. He was rocking the car in great bouncing waves . . . disentangling them. He was disentan-gling the two vehicles. Dammit, the bastard was thinking he would get away!

Sandy could hear himself groaning but he took no notice of it. He was shaking his head, baffled momentarily by the opaque glass that still filled most of the windscreen, opaque glass full of millions of tiny cracks. He jabbed cautiously with his elbow – more pain, an agony in his left shoulder – and it took more effort than he could ever have imagined just to knock a bigger hole through the fractured wind-screen. And now he saw that the van was revving up again, finishing the job of disentangling its tail end from the wreck of his car and the livid wound of red masonry. His door on the driver's side was mangled, it had been through the passenger door that Bamford had leaned to torment him: now he turned himself round across the seats, pushed down the handbrake, pushed with his stiff legs against the crumpled driver's door so he was sliding across the seat. He fell out of the open door and landed on the frozen ground, cursing the pain that seemed to welter out from every sinew of his body, aware also of the reek of spilled petrol. The van was about fifty yards up the street but moving awkwardly, with a buckled back wheel and a tremendous clanking and groaning.

Run – run after it, you blockhead!

He tried running after it, but his right knee buckled and he fell face down onto an agonising trap of rubble. There was a call box further up the street in the same direction, so he stumbled towards that, only to find on reaching it that it was hopelessly vandalised. Ignoring pain, loosening up through a virtual wall of pain, he limped from house to house, only to discover the nature of the council's operation – the houses here were empty and gutted internally, so it was useless . . . damn and blast it.

And only then he heard it – he couldn't believe what he was hearing but he was hearing it all right.

That crazy man had been whistling in between slapping him and tormenting him about hell. Sandy had heard that whistling only it hadn't registered then. The reason it registered now was because he could still hear the man whistling. Or maybe it was the fact that he had, just now, recalled the actual tune, he recognised the tune he was whistling out of his open van window. From a position in the centre of the road, Sandy could only stand in the snow and listen as the creaking van turned right at the major junction. It was a tune he hadn't heard in years but he would have recognised it after a hundred years because it reminded him of his favourite film, *Zorba The*

Greek, starring Anthony of the same name. What Bamford was whistling was the Bob Dylan song, "The Mighty Quinn".

24

His head ached. His neck did not ache but it pained him, a gouging pain that ran through his left shoulder and went down his arm, as if a six inch nail had been hammered into the top of the shoulder joint, and then pinned there in the marrow of the bone. The pain flared out in a nauseating cuff about the shoulder and halfway down his arm all at the same time, also into the left hand side of his chest, gripping the pectoral muscles there like a big square wood vice. But the pain was nothing. Not compared to the fury. Sandy Woodings was only aware of that fury, as he limped through bedraggled streets, peering into broken houses, with his right knee poking out through a rent in his trousers. Minutes were passing. Desperate and vital minutes. Another vandalised telephone box: Lord almighty! His man was getting away. But surely he wouldn't get far, not with a rear wheel damaged like that. A spare wheel – he would change the wheel. He was stopped somewhere only a few miles away, down some back street, and he was changing that wheel right now. The fury rose in a monstrous swell in Sandy Woodings.

Bamford must know who Sandy was. He had followed him in that red van. *Followed him.* Sandy kicked another door open, only to find the house empty. Recognised his face? Did he just know Sandy's car, which was a black 2-litre Capri? He knew where he lived. That had to be it. Bamford actually knew where Sandy lived. My God! What else did he know?

Sandy stopped on the street again and listened. Nothing. He could hear nothing. Why would a car come down these gutted streets? Sandy had given television conferences. His face would be known from those television conferences. Only a matter of watching the car park at headquarters . . . Watching . . . following. Bloody hell! While he had been hunting Bamford, Bamford had been hunting him. And doing a better job of it too. A car? No, he couldn't believe it. Yet there was a car: he could definitely hear a car's engines. Maybe it wouldn't come down this street. Maybe . . . So what else did Bamford know? Had he followed him to Josie's place?

He had started running. Now he couldn't miss his shoulder. The pain with every jolting step was agonising and he had to put his right hand under his clothes and try to keep the weight of those clothes off the joint and off the left hand side of his neck, which was just about impossible. The car was rolling down a side street at right angles to the one he had been standing in. From the sound of its passage it was moving reasonably quickly. He had to try and catch it before it zipped past at a small crossroads. That bastard, Bamford – Sandy could imagine him now, that same calm predatory patience. The wheel changed now. No more than a few miles away. Driving off again. Where? North perhaps? Or back into the city to lie low until nightfall. And nightfall came very early these days. Added to which, most of the traffic patrol teams would be off work, enjoying their Christmas dinners.

It was a white Ford Escort, with a front spoiler. It was only twenty yards from him, approaching the junction. He stood in the gutter and threw out his hand, almost fainting from the shock of pain produced by the impulsive manoeuvre. But it worked. It had the effect of an emergency stop on the car driver. A young man, a young Pakistani, no more than twenty-one or twenty-two years old, stared at him with wide eyes, then seemed to be wrestling with the gear stick. He was frightened. The youngster was trying to reverse out and get away from him. Sandy wrenched open the door and thrust his card fleetingly before the youngster's terrified eyes. "Police! And I don't have time to explain. Now I want you to get me first to a telephone that works and after that police headquarters. And don't worry about picking up a speeding ticket."

Two hours later he arrived back at his apartment and Julie was waiting in her car outside the entrance, together with all four children. Sandy thanked his driver, who climbed into the second headquarters car, leaving him temporary use of the green Ford Sierra he had arrived home in. Then he opened his door and allowed Julie and the kids into the apartment, while he felt stupid and sheepish and a good deal of bewilderment, as if a part of him were somehow resentful at this intrusion of what was normality.

"We —" she began, confused by his appearance. "We all wanted to wish you a happy Christmas," she said obstinately, as he stood aside to allow the tribe to rush in past him.

He regarded her in silence a moment, feeling his shoulder settle into a nauseating throb, and realising it had been that same camel overcoat she had worn the last time they had walked out along Porter Clough as a family.

"What on earth has happened to you — look at your clothes!"

But he had already limped past her into the bedroom. He spoke to her through the partly open bedroom door, where he was trying to get his injured right leg out of the ruined trousers. "Nothing serious! Nothing broken!" But even the clockwork of his voice sounded out of condition.

She had located his medicine cupboard, which was a biscuit tin containing Panadols and Elastoplasts. She had also put on the kettle and now, when he joined them, she forced him to take two Panadols, while waiting for the kettle to boil. She spoke almost fondly. "We're doing it all rather stupidly, aren't we?"

Sandy thought she was doing rather well, considering her initial shock at his appearance. He saw her now in his mind's eye, as she had looked only minutes before, appearing to hold back in the doorway before entering.

He hadn't concealed his wince of pain as he pulled the bedroom door shut with his damaged left arm. My God – and he had had time to see his face in the bedroom mirror! And then his fury returned, a prompting thrust, and he couldn't believe it. He couldn't believe that they had put out every car they had and they hadn't found a sign of that damaged red van. He found himself shaking his head at that and being misunderstood by Julie, who stood her ground, studying his black and blue face, his pain-racked movements and his furious eyes.

"I suppose I couldn't expect you to make it easy for me, Sandy?" She was pottering in the kitchenette, had found a mug, a tea bag, was pouring hot water into just the one mug.

"You have it all worked out, haven't you? The reasonable couple arriving at our very amicable relationship." He waved her towards a chair, too preoccupied to restrain the kids, who were already scattered on four voyages of discovery. But she refused to sit, still regarding him, playing whipsy with the wrapover belt of her coat. "I called in to see Mr Barker, you know."

"Comparing notes, were you?" But he only spoke mildly, falling down with a painstaking delicacy into one of the ridiculous chairs, and letting her make her own mind up if she wanted to sit or not.

"You and he are not hitting it off, are you?" She had taken the tea bag out with a spoon, poured the milk and now she passed him the tea.

He couldn't help but notice how her eyes had darted

about during this operation: the cooking utensils sprawled over any convenient horizontal surface, the second-hand furniture – he really did wish now he had allowed Josie her way and let her buy him some really expensive three-piece suite.

"Is that what he said to you – Georgy?"

"When you refused to take my calls," she said in that same resignedly reasonable voice. "He told me he wasn't too well from the health point of view. I got the impression you weren't making him any allowances."

Sandy winced, only now swallowing the Panadols, followed by a swig of scalding tea. "Did he tell you he writes things down about me in his little black book?"

"What kinds of things?"

"Not very nice things, I have to presume."

"What's going on, Sandy? You look dreadful. You look as if you've been in some awful accident."

Out there was a man driving a damaged red Ford Escort van. That man had killed two people without mercy and had kidnapped a boy. That same man must know this address: was he very close right now? Did he now know that Sandy had four children?

Sandy performed a long blink: she must have noticed his sweat – since that car chase the sweat had never dried on his forehead.

Julie was sitting, although only on the edge of the settee. A ridiculous notion of lizard-like patience struck him and he laughed drily. If Julie had not forced the separation he would never have discovered Josie. He was so damned lucky with Josie. An hour from now he would have a real Christmas dinner with Josie.

He spoke softly. "Do you know what's my most stupid thought ever? There's a part of me that still says, forgive you. That's really stupid. I want to forgive you, Julie. I want to be able to just put it all away into a compartment labelled the past."

"It's insecurity, that's what it is, Sandy. I'm the same. We're all frightened of change really. Really. I'm so frightened myself, I'm a nervous wreck." She hesitated, as if suddenly aware of, suddenly embarrassed by, the revealing posture of her pressed-together legs.

"We'll be friends. Maybe in time we really will be friends. That's what you want?"

She made one of her little gestures, the globular head and the hand together, while her brown eyes just went on gazing, embarrassedly uxoriously still, in his direction.

"You haven't made yourself a cup."

"No, thanks all the same. I have to go. My mother is on her own . . ."

He doubted very much that it really was her mother who was alone but he sensed it would be a mistake to mention Jack. But then it seemed to gush up, like a foolish self-righteousness anyway.

"Mary is pretty cut up. Mary will take it very badly."

"Yes. I know."

"I tried to talk to her. Maybe I didn't make a good job of it. I want to help . . . you could tell her . . . if you're speaking to one another."

"Everybody has such a dreadful impression of me. I know they all have. I've treated Mary very shabbily."

He sounded a little like Harry Dunn, saying, "I understand, love. You were only trying to claw your way out."

"I'm behaving selfishly – but it's for the first time in my life, Sandy."

"You're determined to marry Jack, then?"

"Please, Sandy –"

"It's no good wishing these things away. We have to talk about it. What are you thinking? That we'll both have to sell out, sell both homes, pool resources? Don't tell me you haven't thought about it."

"I have to think of the children."

Even without looking at her directly now, he knew

exactly how she was sitting: her hands limp in her lap, her head erect and her eyes staring.

"Don't sell the house."

He heard just a rustle of surprise, but she didn't reply.

"For the kids' sake, that's all."

"You're hurt. You're not yourself. I'm not going to argue, Sandy."

"That's what I've been trying to say, Julie." He spoke reasonably, almost lightly, because the problem seemed clearer to him now than it had ever seemed before. "I'm saying two families. The families stay put."

He looked at her face now, at her cheeks which had flushed a delicate rose. She murmured, "I can't bear the thought that you hate me."

"I don't hate you. I feel sorry for Mary. Maybe I feel better. Maybe the worst of the pain is over. I don't know what I feel. I accept that my job caused a lot of the trouble between us. I accept that. And I feel a little bit sorry for you, Julie. I know what it was between Jack and Mary and I suspect you know all that too. You probably know it a lot better than I do. Maybe I'm wrong. Maybe you really are under the impression that between you and Jack it's something out of the ordinary, a meeting of hearts and minds. I hope that's so. I want you to be happy. But Mary used to talk about it, didn't she? Mary used to talk to you just like Jack talked to me. And there's a little nagging doubt that maybe Mary knows Jack a sight better than you do. I even think that Mary was mainly at fault with Jack because Mary never went in for the physical side. I've been thinking – that's why she is still talking to you. Mary can't afford to grumble about the physical side. Poor Jack – is that what you're thinking? Poor Jack – she's starved him all of his married life. What worries me, Julie, is that you're his reacton to all of that starvation."

"You're not yourself. It doesn't even sound like you, Sandy," she spoke with that same dangerous equanimity, but he could see how her lips were everting, that pouting look about the upper mouth which showed to perfection her baby-fine blonde moustache.

"You're going to need the house as security for the kids. For when Jack lets you down. That's the reason I know that the clever little Julie deep down will agree to my proposal. Because that clever little Julie will have weighed up the pros and cons – and as you say, you're frightened. We're all a little frightened, Julie, love."

At the door the kids all lined up to kiss him. Marty, aged ten, with Victory-V cough lozenges dangling from her ears and a crinkled thatch over her eyes as she gave him a second hug – for the Swiss cottage inside which a platinum-haired ballerina pirouetted to the *Blue Danube*.

An oasis of normality? How could he possibly believe now that this little glimpse of normality was real? He waited until the car had vanished with its waving hands and then he stood thoughtfully for a moment by his telephone.

Three quarters of his body lancinated mercilessly: outside, about the road, painting out the houses opposite, a sleety snow whirled and buffeted.

He checked Professor Lipmann's number, dialled it.

When he put his weight on his right knee, it locked in a partly bent position. Yet that fury was there, that fury was just as obstinate as Julie's reasonableness.

He spoke urgently into the telephone. "I need your help, Professor. A very special favour . . ."

Mr Templeton wasn't at the allotments because it was Boxing Day, but they found him at home, a small pebble dash and red brick terraced house. When they called on him, he was trying to sprinkle table salt from a can onto black ice which covered the path between his back door and the outside loo. A limping Sandy, wearing an air-flow collar fitted only an hour previously by a hospital casualty department, gave him a hand with it. They supported one another along the way. Sandy mentioned, through the partially closed door of the loo, what they had in mind.

"Hypnotise me!" There was a jerky interruption to the old man's having his pee.

"It won't cause any lasting injury, Mr Templeton – so the professor has assured me."

"That's as maybe,' he muttered suspiciously, as he corrected his trousers, but he agreed to give it a try, taking his place in the back of Sandy's car with a fierce expression under his cap as if attending a funeral.

The professor hypnotised him in the hut on the allotment, with his pyjamas poking out below his trouser turn-ups and enthroned on a bag of peat compost. It was all surprisingly painless, without the aid of mesmeric eyes or even the silver watch on the fob chain.

A few minutes, nothing more alarming than quiet words of persuasion, and the professor suggested that Chief Inspector Woodings would be putting some questions to him and that all he had to do was to think carefully and answer to the best of his ability.

Outside the hut the wind moaned piteously and it was sleeting with a steady determination. Sandy took Mr Templeton's arm as he led him into the elements, taking it step by step because Sandy couldn't easily look down because of the collar and the ground was covered with that same treacherous black ice.

"It's about four in the afternoon, Mr Templeton. You've come out of the shed because you hear the sound of an engine. You see the van up on the higher level. I want you just to describe the van to me."

"It's grey – like the old battleships."

"Grey? You're sure?"

"It's grey all right."

"All right. It's a grey van. The man gets out of the van. He's facing you. He sees you down the hill and he waves at you. You wave back at him. Can you see that happening, Mr Templeton?"

Mr Templeton, with eyes that could have been squinting at dream or reality, waved his right hand.

"How would you describe the man?"

About their hunched-down forms, leaden grey mists swirled and buffeted through the ravaged landscape of winter.

"Youngish, I'd say. Like as not, middle forties."

"Is he bearded or close-shaven?"

"In between. Like he's in need of a bit of a shave right now."

For some reason Mr Templeton took a step backwards and Sandy had to dance to his lead.

"The man is leaving the allotments, Mr Templeton. You see him walking away from you. He has walked out through the gate and you find yourself studying his van. The grey van. Tell me what you see."

"I can't say as I'm all that bothered."

"Can you make out the writing on the side of the van?"

"Aye! I reckon as the'ers numbers."

Sandy dashed sleet from his sodden hat, startling a bedraggled robin, which hopped dejectedly away on one foot.

"Tell me about the numbers. What do you make of them?"

"I can't see them close enough as to read them."

The professor's toby jug face was making signals, but Sandy pretended he didn't notice, edging Mr Templeton in that same direction.

"What colour are the numbers?"

"White. Just ordinary white. Sort of rough-painted, like he put them on himself. Black along one edge, to give them a touch of the fancy."

The professor was waving at them, and Sandy glanced, only to find he was waving them on. Excitement burned like hunger in the pit of his stomach. Excitement thinking about the importance of the van – the van which had been resprayed a bright and noticeable red. But there was something more to his excitement. He had felt a sparkling restless excitement. A strange sort of excitement, disturbing and a little debilitating. *Some reason – some overwhelming reason!* He had to force his concentration onto that souped-up van.

"You decide to get closer, Mr Templeton. Here we are – we're walking up the path and you can see a bit clearer." Guiding the old man past the worst of the ice traps, he held his arms to either side of him like a wicket-keeper, moving him along in this ridiculous tandem, zig-zagging towards the sloping ground that separated the two levels, while the professor leaned on whatever he could find to follow on behind them.

"How does it look from here?"

"The'ers a funny kind of wrinkle in front of the numbers." He painted it with his index finger.

"A wrinkle? Like a sign for lightning?"

"Could be. Something like that."

"And then the numbers. Okay now – how many numbers?"

"I don't know. Five or six numbers and then some writing. The writing is a deal smaller than the numbers."

Sandy could have murdered a cigarette. He could tell he was still sweating even though his chin and his nose were iced over with sleet. And four soluble Panadols had barely touched the pain. It took will-power not to rush things.

"Never mind the writing for the moment. Concentrate on those numbers. Let's take the first of the numbers. What do you make of it?"

"It's a mite bigger than the second."

"What else – try to draw it with your finger."

"The'ers a curved bit in it – maybe a three or a two."

"Which – a three or a two?"

"A two – I reckon it's a two."

"A two – that's good. That's excellent." He blew a miniburst of snowflakes out of his eyes, scattering them with his steamy breath like a swarm of gnats. "Now I want you to forget the first number and concentrate on the second number. You're doing well. You're doing wonderful."

"Happen it's an eight."

"You can make out two circles, one above the other?"

"I don't know as what I can make of it."

In the space of seconds it had really started to snow. The top of Mr Templeton's cap was already whited over, like cake icing, with a rise in the middle.

"A sign for electrical and then two numbers. The first number – it's a two, Mr Templeton. Now let's take a good hard look at that second –"

"Happen it could be a four. It could be a four as much as it could be an eight. I can see a four and then it seems to change all by itsen to an eight."

Sandy took a large white handkerchief from his pocket and he dabbed his frozen nose with it, then mopped his brow, his cheeks, hlding it like a towel, taking it in cupped hands, he just wiped himself down systematically, patting his entire perspiring face.

"Wake him up, Professor. I want to buy him a gallon of beer."

25

Boxing Day – or what was left of it – and he was sitting in the briefing room at headquarters, next to the big window. It was twenty minutes past one in the afternoon, just two and a half hours after he had dropped off Mr Templeton. There were eleven officers already present. Even Georgy Barker didn't seem to mind his having been called in: in fact Georgy appeared dangerously exuberant, cracking jokes and sitting back in his chair, all two hundredweight of fat and gone to seed muscle wobbling and heaving with his display of good humour.

The telephone rang and none of them made a move to answer it. It rang for a full half minute before Georgy, with a sheen to his face like dead fish, picked up the receiver and handed it to him. "Your gamble, I believe, Chief Inspector."

Sandy listened to the voice of a detective constable: his party of two had found nothing. Should they come back to headquarters?

"Yes. Just come straight to the briefing room."

Sandy gazed at the others a moment in silence: the first team to report failure. He tore open the Velcro sealing the surgical collar. He ripped the collar from his neck and slammed it down onto the table surface. "Bamford was an apostle of that – that naïve hope. Naïve beyond anything that we could possibly conceive now in our cynical eighties."

Georgy's reaction was instantaneous. "So now the devil has become an apostle?"

"No, Georgy. The *apostle* has become the *devil*."

When the telephone rang again, he listened, nodded, gave the same instructions. Another group reporting failure.

And so it continued. A telephone call or the men themselves reporting up from the reception downstairs. This waiting was the hardest thing to bear. Sandy took a deep breath, found himself glancing at his own reflection in the window: he saw the bruises and swellings, ripening since yesterday. He saw his own periwinkle ears, the eyes Julie said were his best feature, the colour she once described as Welsh blue. By degrees his squad of men were coming in to join him, filling some of the empty chairs, all only too perfectly aware of the shrinking shortlist, that same shortlist drawn up over two painful months, the hundred and eight vans they had failed to locate in the city-side search. They had ruled out the forty-eight which weren't Ford Escorts, leaving them sixty names, sixty addresses, which they had visited, where they had first talked to neighbours, asking about a man with his own van who did some kind of electrical repairs job. And another half of his group of detectives had visited every known owner of a Ford Escort van who had a telephone number beginning with the numbers 24 or 28.

An electrician? A motor mechanic? A washing machine repairs man? It had to be something like that. *Just when you thought hell went out with the dinosaurs*.

Sandy whiled away the waiting by remembering the saddest picture of all from that newspaper research. The picture of a father at his daughter's graveside – that headline from an American newspaper featuring yet another closed university in Ohio – *Death of a Campus Bum!* Had Bamford been there too? Just how big a part had Bamford played here in England, in Europe, even in the United

States? And there was a bigger question still – a question that had been growing in his mind until it now assumed gigantic proportions . . .

More men coming in. Jock's voice: "Shit, Chief – there can't be many more men left out there!"

Sandy didn't answer and when he did not, when he just sat by the window, his battered face pale and drawn, Georgy answered for him.

"The chief inspector isn't worried by our local failure. No! He isn't worried because he no longer expects us to find Bamford here in South Yorkshire."

Jock was staring at him, staring at the two dully glowing blue eyes at the heart of the bruises and swellings.

"The chief inspector is waiting for a call from Greater Manchester, if I'm not mistaken. Because while we've been undertaking our exercise here, he's had them undertake an identical exercise. Am I right?"

The telephone was ringing. Sandy's hand in reaching out for it felt as bloodless and stiff as marble. The telephone appeared to weigh a hundredweight as he lifted it from its receiver, as he held it to his ear and heard the voice of Chief Inspector Alan Farnworth, that Bolton accent he now both dreaded and anticipated.

"We have an address for you, Chief Inspector. A different name. See if you can believe this. Deane, with an 'e'. James Deane. But it's your Charlie all right. We haven't moved in yet but we've talked to some of the neighbours. He fits your description. Ford Escort van. How do you like something else – the house used to belong to an elderly woman who died four or five years ago. According to the neighbours, she was called Deane too. Only guess what! Never claimed any old age or widow's pension. Not at least that anybody noticed. I'll bet you that officially she never existed. Yet, judging from her description, she looks so much like him she has to be his mother. Seems the house remained empty for a long time. Toing and froing of parties unknown. A nephew abroad said to be next of kin. House meanwhile becomes a bit of a wreck, supplies cut off and so on. Neighbours complaining about the state of it to the council. Council says nothing they can do legally. Then he just appears out of the blue about twenty months ago. Had papers to prove he was her nephew. Just moved in one day and seemed sure enough of himself to take it over. Tall man, dark-haired, well spoken."

"The electrical sign, Alan?"

"Set up only in the last three months. New telephone number – not yet found its way to the directory. How do you make any sense of this? Car emergency electrical service. Tuning and how's-your-father. Only if you ask me, the only thing this Deane, or Bamford, or whatever his name is, ever tuned was his radio."

There was a silence. Sandy's hand was squeezing the telephone to his ear beyond the threshold of pain.

"You still with me, Sandy?"

"I'm listening."

"That's the name he calls himself – James Deane. Home address – Bolton – 43 Tompkins Crescent."

In Bolton, Sandy had a hurried conversation with Chief Inspector Farnworth, while six rifle marksmen took up positions covering the front and back doors of Bamford's house. Tom had driven Sandy across the Snake Pass, skidding dangerously on corners under six inches of snow and under a sky rolling tumultuously in the opposite direction, laden with murderous black cloud.

They had parked several hundred yards from the house and surrounded it on foot. Now the Bolton chief inspector, with a Smith and Wesson concealed under a newspaper, tried knocking on the front door. Nothing happened.

Standing opposite in the trampled snow, Sandy watched as Farnworth's men broke through the front and back doors simultaneously. A detective sergeant called Mellors was supervising round the back while Tom shouldered the door at the front, together with its retaining frame and a good deal of dislocated rubble, into the hallway. Six men clattered over the fallen door while Sandy hurried round the back of the house so he could have a good look at the backyard, which had been made hard standing, presumably for the van.

The forced entry took place at 7.27 p.m. precisely. Five minutes later Farnworth was back with him, letting him know in four-letter language that the bird had flown.

"The telephone?"

"Phone's there right enough. The number we were after. New job. On the windowsill in the sitting room."

A fluttery empty burning excitement had been with Sandy since he left Sheffield. Now he acknowledged that they had been expecting this to be too easy. Nothing was going to be that easy. "Take a look in there," he pointed his torch inside the backyard dustbin.

Farnworth pulled out several pieces of newspaper, cut to size and shape to fit a van's windows and scalloped along their edges with fresh red paint.

"So we're sure we got the right place. He did the respray here in this yard."

"Could mean he came back just to do it in the last few days, which takes some nerve." Sandy exhaled forcefully.

Farnworth nodded to his sergeant. "Put the lid back on and tie a pink ribbon round the bin for forensics. Then let's go and lift the door we knocked in and see if there are any newspapers or letters under it."

Walking back through the house itself, Sandy wanted to get the feel of it. He stalked past the fallen door under the naked bulb in the small front hall, out of the front entrance, through the tiny front garden and across to that same vantage point, on the other side of the narrow street. He took his time, having a good look at the house and its neighbours under a lurid orange streetlight, until Farnworth, with the expression of a co-conspirator, came across and joined him, with a clutch of letters in his hand.

Together they regarded the state of the house, with weeds higher than the windowsills. There was a hole in one pane blocked off by a rain-soiled sheet of hardboard.

"He gave us that telephone number, didn't he?" Farnworth nodded in sympathy.

"So – you've figured it out for yourself. It's a political game, Alan."

"Don't I know it."

Tom joined them, taking advantage of the mood to light a cigarette, while Sandy continued to assess this small red brick semi-detached house, roofed solidly in blue slate and built along with half the town at a time of peak prosperity for the cotton mills, about the turn of the nineteenth century.

"What exactly do you know, Alan?"

"I know there were two murders in Liverpool with a very similar MO. When I tried to get full details, I got my head chewed off by the ACC. But I've got my contacts. The murdered couple were a man in his twenties and a woman in her thirties. Both of them intelligence agents."

Sandy blew out his cheeks in anger. Nobody had informed him. "When did these murders happen, Alan?"

"Thursday, December 8th."

"Bamford isn't the only one playing games." Sandy shook his head in stunned disbelief.

"I'll warn you about something else too, Sandy." Farnworth inclined his head conspiratorially. "Some character called Gill has been nosing about. I'll give you one guess which department."

Sandy chewed his lip thoughtfully, then clapped Farnworth's shoulder. "Thanks for the cooperation, Alan."

Tom, who recognised the danger signals, carefully docked his cigarette. Re-entering the front of the house,

Sandy said, "Your ball game, Alan – but would you agree that we should leave things without too much of a disturbance. Bring forensics in straight away – get an immediate check to see if they can find a match for the prints of the left thumb."

Then, while Farnworth was considering this, Sandy started a more meticulous tour of the living room and the kitchen. A superficial glance might have led you to think it was decrepit and filthy, but that wasn't really the case. Not dirty but old. It was a mistake to equate the two. There was a definite feeling and that feeling was the unchanging life and needs of an elderly woman.

There was little to the living room apart from a three-piece suite without any cushions. Evidence of stuff having been moved from here all right. And that made Sandy question if the kitchen were just a little bare on pans, cutlery. *He's taken what he needs away. He's had time to take stuff somewhere else!*

There was a cheap and relatively new rubber-backed carpet in the living-room, otherwise the floor was covered with patterned lino, worn to a matt brown on the stair treads, the excavated hollows under chairs and in the causeway between the doors at the two sides of the room. A turned drop-leaf table under the living room window was as solid as the oak tree it had been carved from. An ivory telephone, which looked brand new, decorated the sill over this table. The only form of heating in this room was an ancient gas fire.

Look for something so ordinary it is unusual. What had Alan Farnworth told him – that time when he had come through with the news over the telephone? Services disconnected for many years after the old lady's death . . . Toing and froing of parties unknown.

A constable, who was checking round the back, suddenly gave a shout:

"Here, Chief!"

Sandy had been inspecting the clean and perfectly functional Baby Belling oven in the kitchen, but now he stepped with a cautious limp into the alleyway leading from the back door. In the small unheated closet that was the next step up the evolutionary scale from Mr Templeton's bottom of the yard lavatory, was the corpse of a dog. It explained the odour of decay that permeated the entire downstairs of the house.

Ignoring the throbbing in his neck from bending, he inspected it with interest: a black and white mongrel, a cross between a sheepdog and something smaller, dead – he was guessing from the most recent dates on the post they had found under the door – about a fortnight.

"What does it mean?"

"At a guess I'd say it meant that our man knew when he was going that he was going for keeps."

He poked with his ballpoint pen at a length of twine that secured the neck of the unfortunate animal to the pedestal. The top of its head was missing, scattered over the floor and in an acute angle downwards, over the two walls that made up the white-emulsioned corner. White-emulsioned! He also noticed, as he leaned over the maggot-infested carcass and delicately poked with his pen in the litter of brick dust, something discrete and grey. This he placed in the centre of his handkerchief and, standing once more in the clean cool air of the backyard, he identified it.

"Shotgun pellet!" He passed it to the constable, who put it into one of the plastic bags for forensics.

"His own pet – the monster!" said Tom.

"Mercy killing," Sandy whispered thoughtfully, turning guardedly on his heel and then back into the living room to have another look at the previously opened mail.

"Margaret Stephens – " Tom muttered to him in a discreet voice, "said the mother didn't live in Bolton."

"Yes. Enlightening, isn't it, Tom?"

"She lied."

"So it would seem. And that's the least of what's puzzling me, Tom."

He read through the letters once more on the seat of a dining chair because the forensic technicians were already looking for prints on the excellent top surface of the table. He learnt little: bills, addressed to the fictitious James Deane, for electricity and gas, circulars, some firm trying it on with a brochure for winter sunshine holidays. Nothing new apart from the most recently dated postmark, which they knew already – a full fortnight. Probably that same visit during which he resprayed the van. Not only was Bamford two weeks ahead of them, but he had also had the nerve to come back here for a full two weeks after their struggle and chase in the dark.

The lavatory was sealed for a proper scraping down by forensics and Sandy had all he needed from the two downstairs rooms, so he encouraged Farnworth to get on with questioning the neighbours while he and Tom took themselves upstairs to the bedrooms.

"All that trouble. Setting up the van. When, Tom? Just three months ago. Three months. When we know he was planning the kidnapping for at least a year."

"So what's the game?"

"I don't know. Almost as if . . ." Sandy was thinking again of what Mr Templeton had remarked. Stupid daft 'aperth – waving . . . "I can't believe what I'm thinking. What's your gut feeling, Tom?"

"I've known closer to human warmth coming from those little pots they hand out at the crematorium."

Sandy's attention was arrested by a single picture. It was a black and white cutout from some magazine and it looked worn and creased, as if it had been folded over into eight and carried on Bamford's person, perhaps in a diary or wallet: a small oriental girl screaming, with mutilated hands over the lower half of her face.

"Look at the picture!"

247

"I'm looking – and I'd understand it maybe if I had your brains."

The big bedroom was the only one with lino on the floor, with furniture of the heavy oak variety, a solid wardrobe so big they must have carted it upstairs on horseback, a bed without linen or blankets, the dressing table another of those old fossils with its huge circular mirror backing onto the front upstairs window. Sandy gritted his teeth, gingerly worked his neck and shoulders a little looser, then took out one drawer after another and upended them systematically onto the bare mattress.

This revealed an anarchy of knick-knacks, pieces of old silver jewellery, a broken wristwatch, a flat stainless steel penknife, a good quality pocket-watch with Edwardian hallmarks – which astonishingly ticked away merrily when he gave it a wind and a shake. Tom made his own discovery from the lino under the bed. A small leather-bound Bible. This was well-used. On the opening page was a dedication to Clarissa Entwistle from her mother, Sara, on the joy of her confirmation. *Devout . . . his mother was devout . . .* Sandy registered the Bible. He registered the maiden name, Entwistle. From the central drawer tumbled a black leather vanity case, with a zip that ran round three of its four sides. With fingers that trembled with a fine uncontrollable shakiness, Sandy opened this and peered into its compartmentalised interior.

"This is more like it, Tom." Maybe his voice showed what he was thinking. That inner voice which was groaning aloud: too easy. It's all just too easy. Yet he couldn't keep a husky excitement out of his voice. Scooping all of the rest back into the drawers and replacing these in the dressing table, he now tipped out the contents of the vanity case onto the top of the bed and he sat on the edge and nodded, in a state of bemused shock, to Tom, who gazed wordlessly with him at a marriage certificate, fifty-two years old, two birth certificates, two death certificates, a small collection of photographs. On every certificate, in clear running script, the name, Bamford.

"Some people are born lucky," cracked Tom laconically, as Sandy placed each item back carefully in the vanity case, before sliding the case snugly into his overcoat pocket. Tom was watching him, prepared to ask him several questions, but Sandy looked away oddly and Tom hesitated. *Too easy – why? In heaven's name, why?* Suddenly Sandy was descending the stairs too quickly, being reminded of his knee just as quickly, grabbing Farnworth at the bottom and showing him the contents of the vanity case.

"The neighbours?" Sandy asked of the bemused Bolton man.

"They've seen nothing of him for weeks, maybe more than a month," Farnworth grumbled, but his eyes never left the vanity case, which Sandy was holding onto.

"Don't think you're taking that lot with you," said Farnworth, who was now infected with Tom's curiosity.

"I've got to have it. Let me have it just overnight. I'll have it back to you first thing tomorrow morning."

"Not on your nelly!"

But there was a grim certainty in Sandy's gaze. "I'm close and you know it. I'm a lot closer than you are, Alan. You know I have to take this stuff back with me."

"I don't give a monkey's. You're not taking it, Sandy."

"And you could do me one other favour," Sandy gripped Farnworth's arm and was gazing at him urgently. "Details of those two murders in Liverpool. I want anything you've got."

At forty minutes past midnight, Tom was tapping the mouth end of a cigarette against the most famous and delectable bottom in the world. Tom could no longer maintain his patience.

"Okay – so what's happening then?"

"Little things are vitally important." Sandy felt that as

certainly as he felt the sour bilious vapour that clung to his teeth from the adrenalin-charged heartburn of excitement. "That's him – the picture I want circulated."

Tom inclined his face, holding up to the light the coloured photograph of a young man, perhaps in his middle twenties. It was the only original Farnworth had allowed Sandy to take from the vanity case. In the photograph the man was wearing a beige duffel coat with drum-shaped buttons. He was unsmiling, dark-featured. They had confirmed that his thumbprint matched that left on the parcel addressed to Mrs Stephens. Tom studied the face which gazed back out of the picture, a tough face, with a heavyish brow and a large stubborn nose under hair brushed hard to his head to flatten the curls. Even at that young age, he bore a pronounced blue-beard.

A Siberian wind rattled the window frames behind him as Sandy huddled over his cup of coffee. He knew he was too excited to sleep tonight. He studied Tom exhaling smoke, as Tom placed the photograph between the sheets of his notebook, remarking, "So why don't you tell me what you know and I don't know?"

They were only thirty minutes arrived back in Sheffield, sitting at one of the square-topped tables in the head-quarters canteen. The air was wet and scented with pine from the mopping, hours earlier, of some disgruntled cleaner, who must have drawn the short straw over the Christmas holiday.

Little things – like that tune in his ears as his head was slapped from side to side on his agonised neck. "The Mighty Quinn". Sandy swallowed two bitter tasting Ibuprofen tablets. Like that same tune he had heard as he stood in the snow-encrusted road between gutted houses and watched the battered van groan round the corner.

Sandy explained. "Let's say you intend to do a bunk. You have plenty of time – two weeks is a lot of time. You know it's goodbye to the old place, never to return. You go to the trouble of removing the sheets, blankets, food, even the chair cushions. You do in the poor old dog, for God's sake. So would you leave all that personal stuff lying in the middle drawer of your one and only dressing table?"

"Maybe I'm not as smart as you," said Tom, smoking with an expression of jaded satisfaction.

"Then again, maybe you're smarter." Sandy had cleared the table top of crockery. Now he wiped it down with his handkerchief before laying out his clues in neat rows: photographs in the near column, certificates in the middle, in the outer layer all they knew about Bamford, including the two letters.

"How do you mean? He deliberately left all this stuff?"

Sandy didn't answer a moment, but rubbed distractedly at his injured shoulder, studying the conundrum laid out over the table.

"One death certificate, Tom, has got to be that of Bamford's father. His name was Robert, the same as on the marriage certificate. So we know that Bamford's father was called Robert, that he was a coal miner and he died in a colliery accident roughly thirty-eight years ago."

"Coal miners – last bastion of dialect," Tom narrowed his eyes, sucking deeply.

Sandy drew both his hands down over his face, as if throwing water over himself. He felt the need to cool down, to reassert the forces of rationality.

"It puts Bamford at about seven or eight. Seven – I've just totted it up." Sandy was tapping on the photocopies on the table surface in front of him. Farnworth had not allowed him to take the case but he couldn't object to photocopies. "Have a look at the second birth certificate and the death certificate that follows it, Tom."

Sandy continued to think hard while Tom peered under the light again: a boy dead at the age of eleven years. That boy was James Bamford's brother. The brother had died

251

only fourteen months after the accidental death of his father. Two brothers: there was no evidence of any other brothers or sisters.

"You mean about his name being Robert?"

"The elder brother was named after his father – Robert. Makes you wonder why Margaret Stephens called her son Robert, doesn't it? Bobby! Read the cause of death of the brother, Tom."

"I can't make it out in this light,' said Tom, struggling.

The writing was faded but legible with effort: written, Sandy recalled the originals perfectly, in that old blue-purple ink of thirty-three years ago. Sandy read it out for him. "Meningococcal meningitis – whatever that means. But there's something else, Tom. A secondary contributory factor. Imbecility – that's a cruel old word for it. Robert Bamford junior lived and died in an institution. He was mentally handicapped."

"Interesting!" Tom mused.

A photograph of the wedding of the parents, Robert and Clarissa. Two ordinary working people. The thrill of that first pregnancy, Robert Junior. Three and a half years later, James. Bobby and Jimmy. *Bobby* – the horror gradually dawning of that most serious of misfortunes. The dreadful realisation in the minds of these two stolid people . . .

Tom was nodding at a furious rate. "There's something else. Something even more important!" he exclaimed in rapturous excitement.

"What's that, Tom?"

"The same age. The same age, exactly. Bamford was eight years old when his brother died."

A death, and then a second death. First the father, then the elder son. *Just when you thought Jack Hell was extinct.* Two murders in Liverpool with the same MO! Sandy felt the crush of certainty about all this: it mattered. In that ordinary household, this had mattered greatly. Try taking it simply. When the father had died unexpectedly, thirty-five years ago, just how severe would have been the financial hardship left behind him? Clarissa faced with two sons, the elder of the two an increasing handful . . .

Yet his brain warned him to trust nothing. Trust nothing that Bamford was putting on a plate in front of him.

"So what is your impression then?" Tom asked.

"My impression is they were close. Very close. Mother and son."

"How the hell . . .? "

"He protected her. The house and the new name were her protection. That's why she never had to draw a widow's or old age pension."

"How? How did he do that? Come on then – tell me how?"

"Not personally. He didn't do it personally because he wasn't here, Tom. Those same persons who to'd and fro'd after the old lady died. The persons unknown did it for him."

INNOCENCE IS AN ACT OF FAITH, MAGGIE. He was staring now at the child's face in one of the oldest photographs. It wasn't such an unkind face, not a crazy face at all, that face a dozen or so years later looking so very different in the militant duffel coat. *He cared too much, Mr Woodings!* Non-violence had after all been the whole point of it. So what had changed? A screaming child, an innocent destroyed by napalm? Or had that just been – what? A trigger for some more complex moral outrage? Something a good deal more personal which had been building up in the soul of that human being between the pleasant boy in the first photograph and the hard-faced man in the duffel-coat?

"Answer me one question, Tom."

"What's that?"

Sandy's voice was almost drowned out by that furious wind, which rose again, scraping icy fingernails against the

253

window. "He breaks up with Margaret Stephens roughly nineteen years ago. Two years ago he reappears. So where has he been those seventeen years in between?"

26

Mag can change. Like the huge black clouds that wheel and scream across the wind-tormented sky through the window, boy can Mag change! Maybe it was getting rid of the van or maybe it's just that he gets some kick out of killing people. He laughs a lot more now. And he's told Bobby things, really weird things, about when it was very bad for a long time – like pulling out his fingernails, thinks Bobby – he used to think pop songs in his head. That's what he says anyway.

When he was inside what he called "those four walls" he kept his marbles by remembering the words of pop songs, like the Beatles and the Rolling Stones and the Beach Boys and those soppy girls' groups, he keeps on telling Bobby about, like the Ronnettes and the Crystals. Da Doo Ron Ron – yukkkk! He used to think of the words, he'd spend days on one song, just wiping everything else out of his brain except the words of that song. Only guess what songs were his really for-all-time favourites. Good old Bob Dylan.

As if Bobby believed all that!

But look at him burning fires now. You wonder if he doesn't care any more. People should see the smoke coming out of the fire. Why can't the police see that smoke coming right up the chimney out of that fire? And he has been burning fires for days, maybe almost a week. He's been burning fires ever since he got those sausages. And now they have no sausages left, they have nothing left except some tea and sugar and no milk, not even milk powder, and all Mag is doing is lighting fires and cutting those big old dirty sheets of plastic up, into long sorts of bandages.

"Come on over!" he looks up now, from next to the fire, from where the flame on his face makes him look like that picture of Abraham Lincoln in his dad's encyclopaedia, because his nose has got bigger as his face has got thinner.

"Here! Let's have a try at this. Take a lesson from the pig-shit military."

The man by the blazing fire is cheerfully businesslike despite the boy's guarded response.

"How would you fancy a spot of hunting, eh? Thee and me, we're going to hunt for our supper tonight."

Bobby slouches forward, from where he has been hugging the dirty stone wall between two of the windows. He falls onto his bottom sharply as the man tugs his right ankle and he allows his leg to be uplifted. Maybe he truly doesn't care if he lives or dies any more, since nobody loves him. Nobody wants him or else they would have come and taken him home, which is what he thinks as the man begins to wind a strip of polythene in a spiral about his toes, the ball of his foot, ascending past the ankle.

"God knows I'm here. God knows that you took me."

All day long it has been howling snow, maybe all of last night, just as it has for two days and two nights. The man is aware that the boy is irritable as a result of renewed hunger. Hunger is tormenting them both again. He gazes down into that lowering truculent face, the eyes welling up with tears.

"Why did you take me? I can't see why you did it at all."

"What dost' want of me as explanation, Humpty Dumpty? Does Little Boy Blue expect eloquent words?" He talks with a laugh in his voice as he winds the plastic. "I took thee to bring time into a fine sharp focus. Because the music stopped for me. Like the old song, you are my sunshine."

"That's only fatso snodgrass clever."

"I need you, Bobby, like Stanley Spencer needed his Hilda. You make eternity into reality. Fatso snodgrass words, they are. But sometimes fatso snodgrass may be close to the truth. Eternity isn't up there on the clouds, smelling of Chanel Number 5 and all the colours of the rainbow. Eternity is sweaty and smells like a fart. Eternity is all square days. When you finally see it, you know it will break your back."

"Look at my bones. If you keep me here, I'll die."

"There's food out there. Do you want to stay here and die hungry? Is that what you want to do? Let me tell you once I knew somebody I really admired. She was half an American Indian. She could smell food in a desert."

"You never knew no Indian squaw."

"She wasn't a squaw. She was a woman. Only five feet two inches tall with bandy legs. But all the same she was the bravest person, man or woman, I ever met in my life. She had brains and real guts only she didn't remind you all the time about that. That's another fatso snodgrass word called modesty. She used to just sit there knitting when we were working things out. A little half-Indian woman knitting, Baby Blue, while we were arguing out a master plan to save the world."

"I don't care about your Indian woman."

He has wound the plastic right up to the boy's knee and now he bites it to tear it off at the top. "She was pretty too. Very pretty, with gold earrings in the shape of sunflowers." He tucks the loose end in to secure it. His face is momentarily severe, then calm, his voice gentle.

"You see, Old Mag loved her. Old Mag loved everything about her, Little Jack Horner. Her jet black hair, parted down the middle, just like you see on the goggle box. She wore her hair in two pigtails. She was intelligent but they wouldn't let her get a proper education so she got her education from the streets, sweating in the cornfields when she was still only your age, and selling what she could sell to men who thought they were doing her a favour if they spat at her."

For a moment now those terrible flat grey areas are looking at Bobby so close and so straight, that Bobby feels a squeeze of terror in his bowels. Mag really looks out of this world, his lips slightly smiling, into the boy's disbelieving eyes.

For a long moment they gaze into each other's eyes, the man's eyes still shining, the boy's throat working hopelessly against that absolute gripe-panic in his bowels. "You can do it. It's only up to you and you can do it. You can let me go. Just let me go."

"You'd die for certain out there. It's starving cold. And you're too weak to walk far."

"I'll take my chances. Go on. You can do it. All you have to do is to let me go."

The tall man gazes down, the next strip of polythene in the fingers of his left hand. For a moment he appears to consider it. For a moment . . . but then that horrible cruel stare is back. He will never let Bobby go. Never – *never!*

"It isn't fair. What you did isn't fair."

"Life doesn't pretend to be fair. Fairness – that's the delusion of a Christian education."

When they are outside and standing by the little door, Bobby can hear the snow falling. The snow whispers as you hear sometimes just before a record really starts playing, like that musical box that Dicky's sister had when she was just a baby, that didn't play a tune at all and was supposed to sound like the arrival of Father Christmas' reindeer. And Mag has changed again . . .

Boy has Mag changed!

He is huge! His white face, which Bobby can see right clear when the moon isn't behind one of the clouds, is up there amongst the trees. Mag is like one of the giants in his stupid old fairy tales, tramping through the snow in his

258

Italian boots and getting his trousers all wet, with the rifle upside down over his shoulder.

"Breathe through thee mouth, lad," he whispers from up there, from where his voice sounds soft and far away, because Bobby has to keep stopping all the time. He has to keep stopping because his heart is whooshing jet fast in his ears and he can't breathe fast enough and his legs won't go on until the pumping gets a bit less whooshy.

Following the tracks in the snow. That's very clever of Mag, getting him to go first as scout. That way he can keep an eye on him all the time and it's so hard sometimes to see the tracks that Bobby can't stop and think proper. Because that's what he has to do right now, stop and try to breathe with his mouth up and open, the big soft snowflakes falling onto his eyes and his tongue, and the snow falling down in the blackness between the trees, freezing him right down through his mouth and making him cough in his chest.

What was all that stuff Mag was parroting on about – about eternity and all that?

Eternity – that's a thing you only see in the Bible maybe. Eternity and God. And as to Mag carrying on with a half-blood Indian squaw! Bobby touches the blade, which he has in his right hand inside his pocket. He finds its razor sharp edge, running his finger along it, turning it in his pocket until he is squeezing the covered part, where he has wrapped cooking foil round the other cutting bit.

"Supper's waiting," says that voice, from way, way high up.

Bobby, starting to trudge on again, tries pushing his foot through the snow, which is halfway up to his knees, but he finds it's better like before, lifting his foot up so it's mostly out of it. That's when his pal Dicky Dee decides to start off whispering again, whispering real soft as if Mag can even hear thought whispers. *You've got to kill him, Bobby. You've got to take the knife and stick it in him and kill him dead. That's what you've got to do, right now, as soon as you get the first chance.*

Oh God! Maybe Mag is not the sort of person who can be killed by any kind of knife. Oh God – what if he's a real black magician!

Just then his legs feel as if they don't belong to him. His legs would just fall down only they are stiff and tight from the plastic, like a knight in real armour. Dicky says, you know where you are now, don't you Bobby? And he knows all right, because right there, only just about visible in the darkness, is that twisted tree, where the van went down. And Dicky's voice is trembly . . .

What if there are no tracks at all really? What if this is all one of his tricks to get you out and to come down here so he can strangle you and roll you down there into that big black hole, just like the van?

That's when he realises it must have stopped snowing. There is a mist already over the trees, a mist which is creeping down out of the trees, along with the ploosh of falling lumps of snow, and the light isn't coming down from the moon any more. The light is much brighter and it's coming up out of the ground. And he knows that Mag is singing his all time favourite, he knows that from the way Mag's eyes are shining with the light coming up into them from the ground, and the way he is laughing really, moving his big wide mouth under his big thick nose with his big floppy ears standing out. Mag is singing, *Come all without. Come all within. You'll not see nothing like the mighty Quinn.*

Bobby can see it now at last. Mag creeping along here with his rifle, dressed in that big old brown coat over his blue denim shirt – the shirt with the brass buttons and the neck open and the collar all crinkled and worn white here and there and all round the edges – that he looks like he's wearing a whole heap of rags, like one of those warriors on video from another world or the world of the future next to

New York, after the bomb has been dropped or something like that.

And now Bobby realises that Mag isn't even standing behind him, following like always, and Bobby isn't even tied up. That's the way Mag has changed once again. It's talking like that that has changed him, talking about his Indian squaw and all that. And he's holding his finger to his lips now. Bobby can see the light shining off the whites in his eyes and the steam coming in snorts out of the holes in his Abraham Lincoln nose, and he's struck by the idea that maybe all this mist is really the breath out of everybody's noses, maybe everybody in the whole world. The idea swells in him, it's a huge excitement. Mag doesn't really care any more. Any minute now he'll turn his back on Bobby and . . .

His finger touches it again, touches the deadly sharp point of the foil-wrapped knife in his pocket.

Then he knows why Mag has stopped because he can hear the sheep baaing. A sheep that has lost its way, like the nursery rhyme. An injured sheep, Mag says. Cut itself probably on barbed wire. "Ssh!" Mag says again, sliding the rifle down and then moving it so he's holding it between his two hands. Even Mag is excited. The light isn't white at all, it's blue really. There's a blue light over Mag, curling up in the misty breath that's coming through his teeth now, while he still keeps on humming that crazy song to himself. The world is suddenly exploding with excitement.

Excitement flickers with the light over the white ground and the noise of the snow falling has gone or maybe really it's just changed, as if the snow even lying there on the ground is tinkling away, melting maybe.

And Bobby can see little holes where the puddles of sheep shit have melted down through the snow. He can smell the sheep shit and he can hear the sheep, which he can't see but Mag can see from where his eyes are up there in his giant head, only very near to them now. Bobby can see every line deep in Mag's forehead and the big heavy bags under his eyes in his long face, and the pinky blueness of his thick fat nose, as he looks for a moment, a trial run, down the barrel of the rifle. One-shot Mag . . .

"Ssh!" he warns again, because Bobby is moving around too much.

Bobby is turning round and round, making himself dizzy with the swirling of those really grotesque shaped branches. He is swirling round on his heel, buried under the snow, turning and turning, staring up, smelling the sheep shit, turning, listening to the snow melting. Well, he can't stop the noise of his bones shivering now, can he? Blue cold, like a blue fire. Blue burning cold, so he puts his frozen hands under his armpits and turns round and round like that. Mag has done something to the rifle now. He did that ever so slowly so as not to make a noise. Bobby is gasping little puffs in and out. The pumping is in the top of his head again and the whispering has become a gale force wind. He doesn't even bother when his left ear comes out of the Balaclava and feels instantly frozen. He boxes the ear and doesn't feel anything only that howl like a guided missile.

Bang! One shot. One-shot Mag has shot his sheep. Sheep kebabs tonight, while Mag plays Dylan songs on his comb in front of the fire.

Mag has grabbed Bobby's arm and he is running. They are running through the snow, both of them shrieking, over to where the sheep kicks away, lying on its side for the time they are running, a really crazy kicking, dead fast, throwing snow all over the place, with dark spots in the snow, which are the blood. Maybe he's hearing the mighty Quinn now in his head, as loud as big guns. Maybe he's hearing the whole lot, music and all. Mag is dancing about and shouting stupid things, like "What about that then!" And "Mutton chops!" and – Bobby knew it – "Mutton kebabs, Bobby lad. Mutton kebabs! Mutton kebabs!"

Then Bobby is really amazed because Mag doesn't seem

to care at all, *he doesn't care at all, any more*. He has turned his back on him and he is bending over the dead sheep, with the snow showering in over the tops of his boots. Where's the rifle? Where's the . . .

He sees it. Bobby sees it, where he has rammed it, butt downmost, into a one foot drift of snow. The rifle is just standing there, only three feet away, with its barrel pointing up into the sky and held up by the snow.

Bobby's heart is banging and banging. You could fall down dead from your heart banging like that. Mag doesn't give a hang. He's down there, next to the dead sheep, gutting it with his knife. And Bobby is touching it. Sick – oh, gobbins, but sick is coming up into his mouth. But still he is reaching out now, touching the barrel of the rifle with one finger, just to feel . . . just to . . .

Oh, God! Oh Jiminy faggot-face carambah! He has it now. His stomach is coming up his throat with the smell of the sheep's guts but he has the rifle. God but it's a ton. He's holding it in his two hands and he's turning it up into Mag's back. Sick is in his mouth, his nose is puky with the awful hot stench of sheep guts. His heart is thundering. His shoulders are stiff, like wood, and his finger on the trigger won't move.

"Go on!" says Dicky's voice. "Don't pull, just squeeze. Go on!"

Mag knows. It's the silence maybe, but anyway he knows. He slowly stops pulling out the sheep's guts. He seems ghastly calm, sort of taking his time, twisting round as he is standing up, the bloody knife still in his hand. Mag is standing there, only feet away, and he's watching him now. And Bobby can't believe it. Mag is smiling. He is, he's smiling. His chin is covered with water from the snow melting in his hair and his beard. A strange kind of smile, like a secret smile.

Go on! It's your chance. Go on, you blockhead! Ooooh . . .

263

Bobby is staring at him. And what goes through his mind is the fact that Mag sometimes is kind to him. Almost . . . almost as if . . . The barrel of the rifle is drooping under a huge weight and he struggles to pull it up again. He wrenches with numbed hands until he's aiming it shakily into Mag's belly.

"Go on then. Shoot, if the's going to shoot."

It's that funny voice. A Bolton voice. And Bobby is trembling all over. He's thinking that Mag has gone hungry too. Mag has given him maybe more than half of the sausages. His knees are shaking and his shoulders are made out of wood and his finger is all sweaty, slipping on the trigger.

"Let me help thee, Humpty Dumpty. This is the place. Right here!"

Mag has pulled open his coat, with the knife still in his hand. He has pulled open the old blue denim shirt, and the knife has smeared his chest with sheep's blood, cloggy in the black curly hairs where it brushed against them. He is pointing into the middle of his chest bone. Bobby can hear his big knuckly finger knocking like a drum on the bone. "Here's the spot. One shot right here!"

Bobby wants to vomit. That smell – bollicking hell! That smell of sheep's guts is going right down into his lungs and his bowels. He feels a faintness jump into his head and there's a prickling coming down like cold water, pins and needles in both his hands, those same pins and needles in both his legs. If he shoots Mag with this rifle, which feels as big and as heavy as an elephant gun, he'll kill him. If he shoots him he'll kill him stone dead . . .

He's going to take it off you now and he'll use it on you. He will . . . after this, if you even miss, if you even just wound him, he'll blow your head clean off!

It's all really happening fast, right fast. Only still he seems to have a year to think. And he *knows* that Mag had death in his eyes that day by the dusty water. And maybe that time with the van too. And yeah, what about those two people! What about that too!

His finger is trying to squeeze the trigger. As his finger goes white his eyes roll about and he can see the sheep's guts and blood all over the place. Mag isn't even trying to grab the gun. Mag is just standing there, with that secret smile, with his coat and his shirt open.

Bobby closes his eyes, really screws them up tight. He groans as he tries to pull at the trigger, as he tries to make his shoulder work, to make it pull all the way down his arm, which is welded into a big stiff paralysed lump.

An explosion . . . a gunshot!

He is screaming and the gunshot is echoing over and over in his head as he throws away the gun and then he runs. His legs are wobbly and stiff in the plastic armour, but he runs all the same. There is the explosion still happening over and over in his head and a loud high-pitched screaming, like a million sea gulls, and through all that he can hear Mag's running steps just behind him. Maybe he shot him and maybe he's dying right here and now, but Bobby can still feel Mag's arm reaching out all the time to grab the back of his coat or his hair. He runs into the gaping blackness, without looking, without seeing, without hearing anything except the clump clump clump of Mag's footsteps pounding the ground behind him.

Let him die. Let him be dead. His legs tear at his body, they rip away at his hips with every step. His heart is twisting itself into a ball inside his chest. His breath won't come, not even with his mouth wide open, not even with his teeth all chattering and his tongue bleeding onto his face where his teeth keep on biting it. *Let him be dead. Oh, God, let Mag be dead* . . .

He doesn't know how far he has run. He doesn't know where he has been running, only that there is the wood still, the wood goes on and it never will end, the snow is falling again, but there isn't even a proper wind and that mist is all over the place, he can't see where he's going in the mist, and the dark is closing in all over him. The dark is closing in, in waves of grey. The trees look so black and twisted and the blue-white coming up out of the ground is the colour of dead things on the beach at the seaside, the colour of old bones.

All the time he had been so afraid in the dark, when Mag left him alone in the big place, but it had walls round it and there was a fireplace, and Mag's stuff was all spread out, and there was food and the nightlight and milk powder. Always, when he had been afraid then, he knew Mag would come. He lay awake in the dark and he listened for the noise of the van and he could always tell if it was Mag's van and not the other one which had only come twice or three times, and then he heard the side door and the footsteps on the stairs. He didn't really feel afraid then of the footsteps because Mag was coming and he wouldn't be alone for a time, even if it was only Mag. Even when he was alone then he could close his eyes and often he would just fall into sleep. But this is a dark where he cannot just fall asleep.

This is a dark like that film on television called *The Fog*, where ghouls had come up out of the sea . . . Ghouls that were drowned sailors coming back to take revenge on the town. People died here. People died in the big building and probably out here too in these woods.

Mag said so and somehow he knows now that Mag always says the truth.

Tears suddenly burst into his eyes and feel freezing ice-cold running down his face into the corners of his mouth. In a frenzy of terror, he pulls back the Balaclava which Mag had made for him with his own horny fingers out of an old knitted pullover, and he jerks round and round in the mist and he tries to shout, but his lungs are clotted and they don't seem to have any wind in them. His lungs are turning solid like cooling wax. Panic grows so quickly and so suddenly, it is a crawling thing, freezing his booted feet to the snow, nipping the skin of his legs as it scrabbles up, shrivelling his balls and scraping with sharp talons at the skin of his belly.

I killed him! I killed Mag!

That wasn't Mag's limping footsteps hunting him, that was his own heart pounding. *Mag is dead. That's what you wanted isn't it?*

No! No, I didn't want to kill him.

You're out. You're free. Run, Bobby, run!

I can't. I can't run any more. Help me, Dicky. Tell me what to do.

It's as if he has become a statue. He can't feel much any more because his skin has become frozen. One of the plastic bandages has trailed away behind him, where it has become undone and the wet cold has penetrated his leg to the bone.

I'll die. I'm going to die.

A sighing wind has appeared, like a dank cold breath, enough to swirl the mist about over the ground, lifting it up into the trees, so Bobby can't see further than the next tree. He wants to just lie down and sleep but he doesn't dare lie down in the snow.

He is stumbling on again, falling forwards over his legs, tripping over and over from the plastic tied to his legs, so he tears it off one and then the other. He crashes into the snow, he is encased in snow, but still he is lurching on. He doesn't take any notice of his lungs. He doesn't feel the crushing squeezing pain in his heart. He just keeps blundering on. Try to Run . . . Try to Run . . . He can't even feel his legs moving under him. He doesn't even tell them to move. They just keep on crawling, picking him up every time he falls. His lips are screaming too. His lips are screaming into the snow and the dark and the cold. He doesn't know what his lips are screaming, only they just keep screaming as his legs keep running.

"Don't let me die! Don't let me freeze to death! I don't want Mag to be dead! I don't want him to be dead!"

267

He feels so alone.

He is back in that terrible world again, a whole world black as sin all to himself, and now there isn't even Mag. Now he is utterly alone in this sobbing darkness, with the snow falling stronger and stronger and the mist thinning but still rising and not a sound except the occasional slurp of falling snow from the twisty black branches, not a bird or a sound, not even the sound now of the running water. Dicky Dee is asleep in his bed with his Christmas presents. He just bets that Dicky had got a new football, a real Mitre-Delta football. And Dicky isn't all that good as a centre back, not as good as Bobby is a winger or even a centre forward. Running again . . . Somehow, somehow, running . . .

It seems a whole lifetime he has been running. How far has he gone? He can hardly remember why he is running any more. If he has gone closer to anywhere or if he has been running right round in a circle.

It's just what Mag was telling him. Something about time. Something he can't hardly imagine. Something about time passing slowly, or maybe it has stopped, or maybe all the time in the world has gone by and he is still running. Suddenly he is tumbling. He is tumbling over and over, rolling deeper and deeper under the snow, his arms and legs are flung out into the air only it isn't air any longer – it's just snow everywhere. He is lost. He is buried in it. It's what being dead must feel like, buried under the snow. He tries pushing with his hands to get back on his feet but he can't feel his fingers. He is breathing snow, like salt and vinegar past his nose now. It burns right down into the deepest bits of his lungs. His head is going round and round. He feels the darkness come and find him. The darkness suddenly clutches him, a tightening fist, smothering him.

"Help me, Mag! Help me!"

He won't run any more now. Not now. Not when he can't even feel his legs to put them back under him. He's dead anyway.

It is a nightmare of floating. He can see Dicky Dee, very sweaty in his judo pyjamas and he is reaching out his hand with the Mitre-Delta football on it. *I'm really sorry, Bobby*, he is saying. *Because we'll never be able to try it out, just you and me and Chris and Andrew on the rec. That's what I'm really sorry for.* And he knows it really is Dicky Dee, with his face deathly white and freckly, when he sees Mag standing over him. Mag's face has a black bruise over part of it, all grainy like soot, and his nose is scarlet and his nostrils are lunging in and out with his groaning breaths.

"Now dost' see – the' cannot escape me, Bobby lad!"

Oh, the thought turns over and over even as in his vision Mag's face darkens and floats, Mag has two bright holes for his eyes and the curls of his hair weave and spiral into a myriad ethereal horns. There is no fury. What is there is beyond fury. In the deep melancholy gaze of those bright circles of light, Bobby knows he is doomed. Nobody will ever find him. He will never escape again. In those eyes he sees a longing which is as pure as it is monstrous – and utterly insatiable. They will die here, maybe they will die soon, and even then they will stay here. Mag and Bobby. Their skins will rot from their dead bones and even then Mag will possess him.

27

It baffled Sandy Woodings to find Professor Lipmann angry. It was the first time he had known him to be angry in the ten years he had known him.

"You look tired, Chief Inspector."

"I'm not tired. I'm desperate."

"I can see you haven't been sleeping."

"I'm so very close. There must be something, some tiny further clue, that would help me."

At 9.15 a.m. Wednesday, December 28th, there was nobody else in the main university building except the entrance hall porter. Maybe the professor was embarrassed because the office in which Sandy was sitting was little bigger than a broom cupboard. Some pathetic grace and favour allowance from the authorities after the old man's retirement. Sandy had to remove psychiatric journals from a chair in order to sit down.

"To perceive we must use more than our eyes. More than our intelligence."

"Forget all that. I'm almost inside his head. It's absolutely vital for me to know – is he mad or isn't he?"

"I can't help you. I'm sorry."

Sandy felt an impatience so severe it was hardly bearable. His calves were hard balls of tension. He just couldn't sit still any more so he walked over the heaps of journals piled over the cramped floor until he stood by the window.

"We don't lack for clues. We have an entire house!" He

thought: a house steeped in the triumphs and the pains of one particular family, of which the only surviving son was their quarry. "I know we have all the information we need."

Snow was raging about the students' union buildings opposite. Yesterday he had been taken by Range Rover over the barely drivable Snake Pass to Bolton once again where a very cagey Alan Farnworth had allowed him just to look at a copy of the file on the Liverpool killings. It was all so secretive that Farnworth wouldn't even allow him to make a photocopy. But Sandy confirmed Farnworth's suspicion of a connection between the murders of the two intelligence agents, whose bodies had been dumped in Stanley Park and the subsequent murders of the butcher and the prostitute. The political aspects only further confirmed it.

Sandy insisted: "You said you needed to get inside this man's mind?"

The professor only shook his head, sitting back in his chair.

"I'm in an almighty rush, Professor. Is he mad or isn't he?"

"I'll tell you what I think. I think he knows what he is doing."

"So there has to be a reason. There just has to be. Something big. Something huge. Bigger than just Margaret Stephens leaving him. We've been putting too much emphasis on Margaret Stephens."

The telephone rang so unexpectedly, Sandy almost jumped, and then the professor handed him the receiver. He said, "Somebody called Gill – he wants to talk to you."

Gill! It was proving to be a day for surprises. Sandy thought rapidly before speaking into the mouthpiece. He guessed that Gill must have located him through headquarters switchboard. Now he frowned deeply, hearing this unfamiliar voice informing him that he had already spoken to ACC Meadows and was setting out by rail from Liverpool to come and talk to him. In the background, Sandy thought he could make out the announcer's voice at Lime Street Station.

The professor seemed uncharacteristically agitated as Sandy replaced the receiver.

"There's something else on your mind, Professor?"

"Human mystery, Chief Inspector."

"Don't bother. I don't want to hear it."

"No! You do not want to hear what it has taken me forty-five years of psychiatric practice to realise."

"Happy New Year to you, Professor!"

Gill's coming was quite enough to cause Sandy to hurry back to headquarters, where he called a crisis meeting with Jock Andrews, Georgy Barker and Tom Williams. They were agreed to a man that the killings in Liverpool must be connected – all the more certainly, given the intelligence service's imminent intervention. But what could they do? Nobody came up with a single new idea. Sandy asked Tom to pick up Gill from the Midland Station, while he rushed back out of headquarters for one final confrontation with Mrs Stephens.

At 11.45 a.m., he found her exactly where he anticipated he would find her, in her obsessional vigil at the top of the snow-covered slope.

A white sky had descended to little above tree level and it was so bitterly cold that the birds were silent in the trees.

"His mother lived in Bolton, Mrs Stephens. You must have known. It just isn't possible that you didn't know that." The densely falling snow obscured the view down the slope. She couldn't even see the spot that must be the focus for her eyes.

It was he who spoke again, insistently, urgently. He had been standing beside her, his hands in his pockets, but now he removed them, clenching his left fist and waving an admonishing finger down the slope. "You have lied to me.

Yes, lied. You have lied constantly from the start of this enquiry. For God's sake, will you at last tell me the truth."

"Lied?" How could she possibly invent that look of shock in the eyes, almond in colour, two sharp ovals in a face that was half-transparent with adrenalin?

"Woodstock was 1969. You claim you broke up with Bamford then, in 1969. But that wasn't the case at all. You were with him in 1970 – perhaps as late as 1971."

She was shaking her head. She appeared lost in some inner depths, even while shaking her head. Abruptly, her voice was hoarse. Her voice was wrung with feeling. "I don't even understand where this is leading. We didn't break up in a single day. There was no single terrible row." Now she was audibly sighing. Her hair seemed shot through with grey over just two months. Her face was honed right down to the skull. "If I have seemed vague – these things aren't easy to describe. Then as now – it was agony for me. At the time of Woodstock, Jimmy was already in the States. There were people . . . people who arranged things. His life was no longer his own."

Sandy laughed disbelievingly. "People who arranged things?"

"Somebody in London even bought my ticket."

More half-truths? He most certainly had to assume so. Yet there was that feeling again: that feeling about this man called Gill. Things Sandy didn't know.

Frustration lent a heated note to his voice. "Two murders – maybe more! The kidnapping of your son. It's personal. I won't believe otherwise. Personal." His voice had risen involuntarily. He was almost shouting but now he contained himself abruptly before continuing. "No more lies. I don't want to hear them. I want to know what is so desperately personal to him. I want to know where he disappeared to over those eighteen years. I want to know what makes him so dangerous. What makes him murderous, Mrs Stephens?"

"She didn't live in Bolton. I know she didn't live in Bolton."

"I don't believe you."

"What do you want from me? What do you all want from me?" Her hand came up and moved in a nervous flurry, rubbing at the waxy pallor of her right cheek, above the standing collar of her outmoded diagonal tweed green coat. Suddenly she was altogether too excited. She seemed quickened by something more complex than anger, an impassioned fury. "How dare you ask me to explain. How dare you. How can I possibly explain how I feel to you, a total stranger, when I can't even explain to my husband . . . ?"

"Explain what?"

"Explain! All one's life is spent explaining things to people who don't care for your explanations. My husband finds it hard to believe . . . to believe . . ."

"Your husband doesn't believe you – any more than I do."

"No! Of course you don't want to hear me. You don't want to believe me. You want to believe that the truth is just what lies in front of your eyes. Don't talk to me about logic, reality, cause and effect. Do you imagine – do you really imagine for one moment – that deep down, in the part of us that matters, we give a damn for logic?"

She had so surprised him with her outburst, he thought about it; he stopped walking and he considered it but what really interested him now was a different question altogether. Which was the real Margaret Stephens? Was it the seemingly very ordinary mother, the woman dazed out of her senses from two months ago . . . or was it this life-scoured and more impassioned stranger? He would have liked to believe . . . Maybe if he wasn't the cynical policeman? And then, abruptly, with that renewed neck-prickling suddenness, he was hearing that awful knocking. *What if she's telling me the truth? Is it just remotely possible that she has been telling me the truth all along?*

But that would imply something monstrous . . . some

fantastic conspiracy,. And yet . . . a man called Gill, a man from the intelligence services . . .

"What about your husband? Do you feel you have been fair to him?"

"My husband is what they call a good man. He's a very good human being. I . . . I love him. Do you know why I'm telling you this? I'm telling you because I'm ashamed. I love Peter. But I'm ashamed of my love for him."

The family was the clue. The family must be the real reason he came back. Back to the woman he once loved and who had let him down. *But it's more complex than that, and you know it*. Complex – that's what everything she was saying implied.

"You got involved over your head, didn't you, Mrs Stephens? In the student demonstrations. All that violence on the campuses. Bamford and you – you were involved in organising that violence."

"Things were going on I never really understood."

"Something went wrong – something bad. Something very bad – "

She had started to cry, walking on a few paces, over the edge of a small embankment so her boots were firmly planted in an inch or so of muddy snow. "Only women get agoraphobia. We choose the prisons of our own homes. Isn't that interesting? Revealing? We imprison the most vital part of ourselves inside the thousand and one household chores, the thinking of what to make for the next meal, the shopping routines, the washing, ironing, cleaning, hoovering." She cried quite openly, without wiping away the tears or attempting to control herself.

"What happened, Mrs Stephens?"

"I want . . . I want to know. Yes. I must know if Bobby . . . To grieve, you see." She drew herself erect, blinking, with her face barely flushed.

"They got to you, didn't they? The intelligence people? They debriefed you all those years ago?"

Her face was a ghastly pallid mask with livid scarlet eating into the angles of her jaw. "In real life it doesn't . . . does it? I mean it doesn't somehow come right, does it? Not all bright and good and beautiful?"

He listened to her: but it wasn't really to the words. *Things I never understand. Things I shall never really understand.* But she couldn't help him any more than the professor.

'Mr Woodings, I hurt so badly. I hurt so very badly. I pray all the time to a God I don't really believe in. Dear God, bring him back to me. Just in case. Dear God – bring him back to me!"

She was walking very slowly, in the snow parallel to the road. But he was no longer walking with her. He watched her closely, his eyes were upon her face. But his vision was suddenly and intensely inward.

He sat at his desk at headquarters and he was sweating as freely as Margaret Stephens had been weeping. He lifted the telephone . . . "Get me Bolton in Lancashire. Central Police Headquarters."

He would have confessed that he was a compulsive gambler. He had never backed a horse except in the occasional Grand National, but he knew he was a compulsive gambler – and now, only twenty minutes since he had left Margaret Stephens standing alone at the top of her slope, he sat with that gambler's weakness in his legs and that gambler's void in his stomach, as he held the telephone in a hand that felt numb and unreal.

"I want to speak to Chief Inspector Farnworth. It's urgent."

On the opposite side of his desk sat a fair-haired man with an untidy reddish moustache; a man with a floridly wrinkled face, aged perhaps late forties, with quite a lot of grey difficult to see at first glance in the thick straight hair. He heard Henry Bancroft's voice, good old Henry. *Half marks . . . because dirt is never dirt.*

The business tone of voice could not cover his breathless excitement. "Hello – Alan? Thank heaven you're in. A place called Woodside Grange – "

"Woodside Grange? Never heard of it."

"It's near Bolton. It's somewhere near Bolton. It just has to be."

"Woodside Grange?" Farnworth had caught the agitation in his voice. Suddenly there was a new tension on the other end of the telephone line. "What's so special about Woodside Grange?"

"Blue dust in the hair sample. Old blue emulsion. Bamford's brother died in Woodside Grange thirty-six years ago. An old institution, Alan. One of those places that have gone out of psychiatric fashion."

"Hold on the line. I'll look it up. You just hold the line . . ."

The man opposite him had permanently raised eyebrows and thick fair eyelashes. This man was speaking calmly and softly. "I doubt it will be close to Bolton, you know."

"What do you mean?" Sandy Woodings stared at him. He had almost forgotten his presence.

"I would suggest you look a little further north. Closer to Burnley would be my advice to you."

Sandy felt it again, that lurch of the heart, the sudden overwhelming patter of debilitating excitement: so Gill knew things he didn't know. He didn't ask any further questions. He was hammering with his fingernail against the mouthpiece until he had drawn somebody's attention so as to bring Farnworth back to the telephone.

"Try Burnley, Alan."

And then, after the sort of time that moves so infinitely slowly and yet has gone, after passing, in one twinkling dot of memory, Farnworth was back on the telephone, his voice jubilant.

"Got it. Has its own drive up to it. North of Burnley. How the hell did you know that?"

"Never mind that now. Check it out. See if there is anything suspicious. You know what we're looking for."

"I know what to look for all right!"

"Now listen to me, Alan. Listen and think just a moment. I'm not giving you any kind of unnecessary advice – just be very careful."

Sandy Woodings replaced the receiver and it felt as if a savage blow had reexcited the pain from his accident. Now he rubbed at his left shoulder unconsciously as he stared with unconcealed curiosity at this man, sitting opposite him, wearing an opened sheepskin coat.

"I'm going to Lancashire. If you want to talk, you'll have to come with me."

Sandy Woodings held his breath as the two Range Rovers screeched round a corner and then the sirens started up again. His heart was in his throat and it was reluctant to come back down into his chest. He was thinking: *why did you call your son Bobby, Mrs Stephens?* A question, like so many others, he hadn't got round to asking.

No good worrying any further. It was too late for worrying. Yet there was something else, wasn't there? There was something else, something twinkling in and out of consciousness . . . something very important . . .

"Why Burnley?"

His voice just had time to be heard before another caterwauling of sirens blotted out any attempt at response on Gill's part. The drivers were taking horrendous chances in the snow because they were in an almighty hurry, because he wanted to get across the Pennines close to the proverbial bolt of lightning – because of that return telephone call from Alan Farnworth no more than minutes ago. *Something going on . . . place is supposed to be derelict . . . due for demolition . . . smoke definitely coming from one chimney!*

"Why Burnley?" he repeated his question now, sharply,

irritated with the silence during which he could hear the tyres churning through the wet road surface.

"Because he was born there."

"I don't understand. On the birth certificates – "

"It's fairly easy to alter certificates, as you well know, Woodings. Burnley – Bolton! The trick is to keep it absolutely simple."

It was also easy to underestimate this greying blond intelligence man: Sandy had no intention of underestimating him. "So why all the secrecy?"

"To conceal the fact he moved his mother. He will have arranged a lot more than changing certificates."

"Moved his mother!" Sandy made no attempt to disguise incredulity.

"A Lancashire woman – she would have stood out a mile in a different part of the country. Bolton is a big town. Just another cotton-town widow."

"He couldn't have hoped to keep his mother's existence a secret."

"At the time he most certainly did. Who noticed? We believed she was dead. And she was dead. It gave him a bolt-hole we never suspected existed until you found it for us."

Sandy spoke softly, all the more enquiringly. "Personal for you, Gill, isn't it?"

Gill said nothing: which was answer enough for Sandy. So at least they knew where they stood now.

The irony was he felt like talking. He wished Tom was with him and not in the following vehicle. There was a part of his brain that wanted to talk over crazy notions. Notions such as time. Such as nineteen years, which was an awfully long time. And again he experienced that tantalising twinkling: that star burning and fading in the mist, which was something vital that was still missing.

Something else . . . a yawning, overwhelming, sense of purpose. Passionate. Something terribly vulnerably human. *Let's all think hard to get rid of it . . .*

When he spoke again, it was in a flat voice, a deliberately neutral tone. "What do you know about Bamford?"

"There's a limit to what I can tell you."

"Don't give me that nonsense, Gill. I've been behind this character for two months."

Gill's voice had a glittering softness. "And I've been behind him for nineteen years."

The leaving of the city was quite sudden: it ended in a scrabble of stone cottages, a garage built out of a redundant church with the windows blocked up with brick rubble, then no houses, no wall posters, back to nature. *Nineteen years!* The heavy fall of snow had made a more successful blanketing of the countryside than it had the city; here it was no longer the trampled cabbage of the city's streets, but pure virgin white, worn like hair on the hawthorns and clinging like a new skin to the upthrown vertical branches of the trees.

"Then it must be something big – I was right. I knew it had to be big. The forged documents at the house, the house in Bolton . . ."

"The tail end of something very much larger. Bamford is a much bigger fish than you could ever have realised. You find the simple forging of a birth certificate incredible. How about stone-age man, Woodings. The last of his kind. We've known him under many names. Weitel, O'Gorman, Vasares, Urquist – but Weitel for the vital years . . . He's quite a linguist, you know. I'll give you something totally unbelievable. He survived eight years in a very unpleasant prison with his jailors actually believing he really was German."

Sandy thought Gill was parting with a lot of information too easily. "Let's get this clear. You're admitting he was some kind of underground leader. Of what? Of something organised? There was an international organisation?"

"Of course."

Sandy shook his head violently. "Margaret Stephens was telling us the truth?"

"He would have concealed things from her – especially from her. We're talking about a dedicated professional of a very high intelligence. Much more than university intelligence. We're talking about cunning. Street intelligence. He avoided publicity. He was never there on the platform, or holding the banners in front of the marchers."

"But his mother did exist. The house, the death of his brother – the Grange – that's all genuine."

"That was our mistake. A very important mistake!"

Sandy's overheated mind struggled to come to terms with this confusing new information. Bamford born in Burnley. His mother moved to Bolton – by what forces? *There were people . . . people who arranged things*. This was all a bit much to take in at this stage in the hunt. When did things become so organised? Even before he had met Margaret Stephens? And why move his mother to Bolton? Because Bolton meant something to him then? Or was Gill confabulating a fable?

"I can't believe it. English revolutionaries! We're more green-belt activists. I can see it as far as the women at Greenham Common . . ."

"You just go on believing that, Woodings."

For an instant a totally unexpected anger gripped Sandy: perhaps a product of tiredness, of overexcitement – yet it was so powerful, such a crimson searing anger, he had to take a breath and douse it with deliberate cold logic.

"Those missing years, Gill. I want you to give me an exact breakdown of those missing years."

"Latin America. I can't say which country. For the first eight years in military custody."

"God almighty!"

"I told you. An extinct breed nowadays. How he survived those eight years! He was the only one to survive from his group. They still believed he was German, for God's sake. What was left of him, they wrapped it up and passed it on to

Germany. The Germans realised he was ours. They gave him to us."

Gill was doing it again, harping too much on this German angle. Sandy felt more angry than ever. He was still baffled. He was not so bwildered by all this as to forget to ask himself why Gill, without even the usual accompanying officer, had turned up in such a desperate hurry on his doorstep.

But his voice retained its cloak of calmness. "When? When did they pass him on to you?"

"Seven years ago."

All a little too plausible. He was offering Gill a cigarette, knowing he would refuse, before lighting his own. "Is that where it all ended up then? All the hopes of those kids? Eight years in some tin-pot dictator's torture chamber?"

The vehemence took Gill by surprise. For a moment the bluff moustachioed exterior appeared shaken. He shook his head a little too sharply, then decided he would after all accept that proffered cigarette.

"A physical and mental wreck. What is left of a man after eight years of that, Woodings? We put him together again, piece by piece."

Sandy passed him the packet, watched him apply a match to a cigarette. "You took him because he was still useful to you."

Gill smoked without replying. Turning away to the side window, Sandy saw alder seed-cones caked over, like conical buns capped with icing.

"It's pathetic, Gill. Do you know what? It disgusts me."

"I didn't expect a sermon from a policeman." Gill smiled cynically.

"Do you know what I think, Gill? I think you're afraid of him."

"You bloody fool! Don't you realise anything about Bamford? He was always dangerous. That was what attracted your nice Mrs Stephens to him in the first place."

Sandy reflected for a short time in silence, while the car idled at a widening of the road at the junction before the A629 turn-off to Huddersfield. In the hedgerow he saw icicles beading cobwebs, little black stalactites where the snow had melted in the few warmer hours at midday, then frozen again, as it dripped to escape. From horizon to horizon, ranged black trees, black scrub, black drystone walls encircling the multipatterned white quiltwork.

"Released into your custody. He was to be your puppet?"

"Dirty washing now – come on, Woodings,' Gill pulled down his window to dispose of half a cigarette of ash. "This world favours the short-term memory. Give me forgetting and you can keep forgiving. Any day."

He's lying.

Sandy reappraised Gill's averted face, upon which a faint beading had appeared over the flushed and lined brow, like the sweat on refrigerated butter.

"What else happened?"

"Nothing else happened."

"You took a human wreck and rehabilitated him. Set him up with a roof over his head. Two years ago, brought him up North – home. He should be grateful to you."

Gill merely shrugged.

"So why all this? Why the kidnapping? Why the murders?"

"Madness. You've already worked that out for yourself."

He's lying through his teeth. And I know why.

For a long time they did not speak. Sandy no longer smoked. The two cars screamed up the M1 until they could turn towards Lancashire along the M62 motorway. There was an ominous silence over the car radio during this time, which continued into the twenty miles or so before they took the slip road towards Burnley. Then very quickly it seemed they were negotiating the smaller roads of North Lancashire.

While you thought you were attaching strings, Bamford was resurrecting himself.

Suddenly he was tapping his driver to stop because they had come to the first of several roadblocks, two Land-Rovers parked astraddle with their blue lights flashing. Climbing from the heat of the car, he had a word with the uniformed inspector in charge, who told him that Chief Inspector Farnworth, in charge of a combined force from Greater Manchester and North Lancashire, was about ten minutes ahead of him. They had seen no sign of Bamford's van. The man pointed ahead, northwards, in the direction from which the snow was blowing. Squinting in the direction of the inspector's gloved hand, he couldn't make out very much because the cold seemed to paralyse his eyes. After another four miles, they would come to the turn-off, which was an end road. Sandy climbed back into the car and settled himself down for those final few minutes of thinking patience.

When he spoke, he spoke softly, as a man does after he has made some important decisions. "What kind of man are we really dealing with, Gill? What can we expect him to do when cornered?"

"He'll kill. As he has killed already – "

"Like the two agents in Liverpool, you mean? Pals of yours, Gill?"

Gill's eyes were glittering like a man who has thrown into the air not a fistful of peas but diamonds. He refused to reply, but for a single unguarded instant they reflected their dangerous brilliance in his eyes.

Sandy's voice was if anything softer still. "If the boy is still alive – "

"If!"

"How will he react? Will he kill the boy?"

"I have no crystal ball."

It was Tom's expression, and said so often it twisted in Sandy's heart like a remorseful smile. If Gill had not come,

Tom would have been chain-smoking next to him. Complaining about time, because under tension, Tom was surprisingly impatient.

He's lying to cover Margaret Stephens. Sandy struggled desperately to hold that twinkling star of intuition. Nineteen years ago she had broken the relationship with Bamford. Nineteen years ago Gill had started to hunt Bamford. It just couldn't be a coincidence. They got to her. Interrogated her. Maybe Gill himself – ?

That had somehow resulted in the arrest and torture of Bamford nineteen years ago. And later still to his being handed over, like the remains of yesterday's dinner, seven years ago . . .

Gill, sweaty-faced, wiped a knuckle in the condensation of his window. He had, it seemed, reached the limit of what he was prepared to say. Sandy sat back again, sensing with growing foreboding how abruptly the afternoon was changing. The scenery was becoming flat, two-dimensional, as a result of the waning light and the ground reflection. Trees appeared only as silhouettes against the vertical slate of sky and there was the beginning of a ground mist, blurring out hard detail.

Then, for the briefest of moments, the star shone brilliantly. He glimpsed the truth.

"There was another woman. There had to be another woman?"

Gill was wearing that smile which wasn't a smile.

"Who was she, Gill?"

"He had his floosies, like any man."

"Damn you, Gill. You're lying. Tell me the truth."

"A peasant. Just one of his floosies. She got in the way during the altercation when they came to arrest him. We *are* talking about Latin America, Woodings. They don't run around in ballet slippers, these people."

As his vehicle swerved round yet another bend, Sandy's

eyes picked out a horizontal, which must be the line of a roof. The Grange looked black, positively frightful, like the waking realisation of a real life nightmare.

But his mind was distracted by this new information. Two hammer blows: that Margaret Stephens must have been debriefed by the intelligence people nineteen years ago; and now this other woman . . . *a peasant* . . . *just one of his floosies* . . .

Less than a mile from the gates, they came upon four cars and a van which were stopped and waiting. Sandy recognised the tall figure of Alan Farnworth, clambering from one of the cars as he alighted from his own halted convoy to go and confer with him.

Farnworth's face was pallid and oily with sweat and Sandy thought he looked exactly as he himself felt. Time for a brief discussion on territorial responsibilities. Farnworth had already cleared it so he was in overall charge. The Lancashire men were armed with revolvers and they included those same six rifle marksmen who had covered the entry to Clarissa Bamford's house.

"We've talked it over. Best to go on foot from here."

Sandy nodded: he thought it sensible.

"The van's armour plated. So we thought we'd take that into the grounds with us for cover – "

Walking through virgin snow, they talked in whispers, and when they were two hundred yards from the gates, they allowed the van carrying the marksmen to go in front. Without further discussion, they walked close behind the slow-moving vehicle, Sandy automatically buttoning the top of his coat under the collar. *She got in the way during the altercation* . . . They had covered about two thirds of the distance before Farnworth lifted an arm and Sandy took advantage of the pause to step onto the slight slope to the right of the road to take a closer look.

Three, no – it had four storeys, the lowermost concealed by a high stone wall encircling the grounds. Built out of the shaggily dressed grey gritstone popular at about the turn of the century, it was perched on the side of the hill so that on a fine summer's day it would have enjoyed a pleasant prospect through those tall Victorian windows.

Altercation – or are we really talking death squad?

"If we can see it now, then its odds on the mad bugger can see us too."

It was Tom's voice – Sandy had heard his steps on the snow-clad slope, approaching him from behind.

"Watch out for Gill, Tom – he's a bastard." He spoke softly, realising that Tom was right, that even in the poor visibility, their figures must stand out against the snow and the ground mist.

"Aren't we all?" replied Tom in a husky voice. Although neither spoke his thoughts aloud, it was apparent that each of them had the same feeling.

28

Against a panicky awareness of exposure, they clambered over the snow-capped wall, sprinting towards the gable end of the main building, where they pressed their backs against its walls. After too short a pause for breath, they split into two groups of three, one inching frontwards and the other rearwards, round the main building.

Sandy and Tom went round the front. As they rubbed their backs against the dripping wall, the van was noisily crushing snow along the short curve of the main drive, flanked by overgrown rose bushes. From the shelter of a big protruding window, which was, like all the others, curtained by a hoary lace of dust, they waited for the van to halt in the snow over what must be a gravelled courtyard, directly in front of the two heavy and weather-blackened oak doors.

No shots. A complete and utter silence from the main building.

This silence was almost as frightening as an attack from above. But now, under the protection of the front porch, they had a whispered conference with Farnworth, who had made his way all the way round from the back.

This established that all the doors and ground floor windows were securely bolted. There wasn't a print in the snow to indicate which entrance had most recently been in use. Farnworth's three men had quickly searched the out-buildings, which had once been stables and had later been converted to garages, workshops and a hospital laundry.

There was a small empty church, with its doors firmly locked. In one of the garages they found tyre impressions, but no van. Farnworth now called in the rest of the men, with the rifle marksmen already taking up whatever positions they could in the grounds and covering the grimy windows.

They gathered in the two safe areas, behind the van and under the lee of the porch.

While Farnworth was organising his men, Sandy tried to organise his own thoughts, leaning back against the big water-soaked doors.

Bamford was just the other side of this wall, behind one of those windows. Sandy was certain of it. Yet things had not become simpler: things had become progressively more complex.

"There's a master plan, Tom. And we don't know it."

"We know enough to watch our step," wheezed Tom, who was already showing signs of the familiar impatience on his lined face and the restless tapping of his hands against the pockets of his coat.

A picture put together from many fragments . . . The elder brother placed here. Yet Bamford would have been no more than a child then. So why the familiarity? Had Bamford himself been incarcerated here? A crisis following the father's death . . . had the authorities placed both boys here? Other fragments: the murders: the kidnapping: one much earlier killing: and now this building . . .

Tom was accepting a Smith and Wesson revolver from a sergeant, who broke it first to establish the full barrel. Sandy accepted one for himself, grimacing down on the flat brass-coloured caps of the bullets. Smith and Wessons had no safety catches. When you drew one you expected to shoot it.

Two men to each of the four external doors tied up eight men. Another was detailed to stay with Gill in the van – Farnworth's idea, but what an excellent idea – leaving fourteen officers, Sandy included. Now they took a much closer look at the twin oak doors.

No glass, so they had to send a man back to the van for a lump hammer, which they used to break the big mortise lock in the centre of the doors. Inside they found themselves in a small and claustrophobic reception area, with a frosted glass sliding panel set into the wall, like the money window in a cinema foyer. A few yards further and they climbed three steps onto a bare and wide landing area, which was the main ground floor reception area.

It was possible to make out some kind of tiled pattern by brushing away the dust with your shoe. Deep enough to call dirt, this was the most impressive thing about it. It covered all the horizontal surfaces in one even deposit. And not a single human footprint was to be seen, not even in the reception area, the hallway or the visible first half-dozen treads of the main staircase.

Farnworth summed it up tersely. "Move cautiously – and let's have no heroics."

Outside, Sandy had noticed the time: 3.55 p.m. Now, it was already dark. After a moment's reflection, Farnworth detailed two men to each side corridor, each group with a handset and at least one armed officer to each couple. Then, slowly and with a sound like a cricket in his ear which must be his ear-bones knocking, Sandy led the group of ten remaining men into climbing the stairs.

The building was virtually soundless: it seemed to swallow the patter of their footsteps. *Just when you thought Jack Hell was extinct . . .*

Hell was human. Hell had a man's name. Sandy could readily believe that hell could lie deep in a complete and stagnant silence, permeated by infinite terror. *No expense spared . . . to bring Jack Hell back for your amusement.*

Under daylight, the staircase would have been illuminated by windows, one to each floor and set into the wall on the first right-angled bend. A part of him still struggled to make a whole of the fragments: something vital to understand, beyond this aura of controlled and silent menace. He could get so far as to see, like one of those old black and white dream sequences from a thirties' film, the frightened boys, the vague figure of the receiving matron, the vaguer and more disturbing spiritual presence of the mother. Grey eyes. Tears. Wild grief, terror as could hardly be imagined, the terror of a handicapped child in such unfortunate circumstances.

At mid-flight and then again, just before the first floor landing, he stopped the column of men, listened upwards, with the impatient Tom cackling noiselessly at him, because he looked like a doubting parson.

Nothing, apart from the half-digested echoes from below. Then Jock's torch picked out footprints on the first floor landing.

He told them all what to do in a whisper. The problem was that there was hardly a single clear print in the mass of impressions. A well-trodden path, crossing and recrossing the landing area, spreading down the left and right hand corridors and up into the next stairwell.

It was the same arrangement as before, one armed sergeant, three constables, divided into pairs, one pair to each of the corridors.

On the bend where they encountered the window, he stopped to inspect one isolated print which was small enough for a boy's foot. He drew a circle round it with his forefinger, so that nobody would step on it. In the prickling silence of contemplation, he thought he might have heard something. If it was something, then it definitely came from above, something at the very limits of discernment. His imagination? Instinct screamed not very likely! Held them all still and listened again. Nothing. Just that foreboding silence, as if the building were holding its breath.

But there was something, something which had nothing to do with the younger brother – or maybe it had to do with everything. Sandy was thinking about the black lock of hair: hair from the head of a baby.

The brother was only another fragment. Put the brother aside and think again . . . Sandy's heart was thumping so hard it was shaking his chest. The force of imagery had increased tenfold between floors. Bamford had been leading them on all the time. Bamford had intended them to find the house . . . the house with its very convenient death certificate . . . Just as he had sent them the series of clues in the form of parcels and notes . . . *Mag the Magician!*

The footprints here were a mountain stream, the staircase cascades, the corridors tributaries.

There was a small pool which had gathered under a window and he crossed to see how it opened onto a perfect view of the approach road. Through a cleared pane, he saw the cars below, part melted by the mist into a white-spuming furnace. Somebody else had cleared the windowpane.

Turning back towards the next stairwell and the last, his torch played over a further rise of prints: the mountain stream took its origins from above.

The men were nervous because he had stood for a while and thought about it again. Questions – why bother now with questions? Why – because these questions were important to the man who had set them. And that man was very near now. That man was a breath away and he was extremely dangerous.

They would have to control their nervousness. Compromising with three men to this level, they lost Alan Farnworth here. It left Sandy with just Tom and a detective constable for the final ascent. He moved even more warily than ever, stopping to clean a pane in the smaller and squarer window that decorated this last angle. A faint turquoise line must be the junctional zone of fading horizon. He turned back to the trail, scratched his forehead: he tried desperately to see into the strange juxtaposition of intelligence and malevolence that was the mind of James Bamford.

His mother devoutly religious: they had found her Bible:

a Vietnamese child, devastated by napalm: *he had his floosies . . . got in the way . . .*

Tom's patience was always the most likely to break. It didn't surprise Sandy when he made a bolt past him and was already a couple of treads ahead of him, his gun in his hand and directed upwards.

"Come back, you idiot."

"Not bloody likely. I'm for climbing these dancers to-night."

Only he understood that the clown was in a sweat and was desperate for a cigarette.

He managed to get a restraining grip on the back of Tom's overcoat, but Sandy was in pain and Tom was pulling like a demon. It was as much as Sandy could manage, to hug the wall to their right, on the clockwise spiral.

"I heard something, Tom. I heard something at the head of this staircase."

"Come on then and we've got the bugger."

It was all wrong. He sensed more than saw something, a blur against the wall, above the limits of Tom's leading torch.

He was pulling Tom back, his mouth opening – but the shout was overtaken by the lightning. The dark exploded in a brilliant blue flare and his ears were deafened by the roar of thunder, followed by a sort of animal screaming, which seemed to fill the whole air and only slowly diminish and focus until he realised it was Tom: Tom was doing the screaming.

Tom was falling down onto him, his weight pressing him back down the stairs. He had to shout to the constable below to prop him or they would all have gone like skittles. There was an unreal moment of calm, during which he tried to grasp Tom firmly by the shoulders, only to find that his fingers were slipping in a warm moistness which was Tom's blood.

"Injured man – Sergeant Williams shot!" It was Alan Farnworth's voice, shouting into his handset at the level of the second floor landing. Then that same voice was addressing the men appearing from their searches of the corridors. "Come on – everybody down – everybody down to the second floor. On the double!"

Sandy was already halfway down the second flight of stairs, with Farnworth's disembodied voice now above him and the building all of a sudden raucous with the running and shouting.

Sandy shouted back up to Farnworth. "Put men on the stairs. Let's keep him bottled up there. Let's give him no chance of running."

"We'll hold him at second floor level!" shouted Farnworth, who immediately began to organise this.

Sandy was gasping when he reached the reception area, from carrying Tom between himself and the detective constable, who was called McGrath. He called a halt here to get his breath back and he spoke brusquely to the men already covering the ground floor landing.

"Keep the place in darkness. Make sure those outside watch the first floor windows as well as the doors. And that includes windows on the gable ends. Check if they've used the van radio – see if they've called an ambulance. And tell them we're coming out. Get them to cover us when we come out of those front doors."

They rushed Tom out though the main doors. He helped to carry him, expecting any moment the sound of gunfire from a window above and the blow of impact about his head and shoulders. They almost threw Tom into the back of the van and then Sandy climbed in after him, covering him over with two tartan rugs and then kneeling down next to him on the hard metal floor. McGrath found the first-aid box and was rummaging through, trying to find some big dressings, while Sandy prised the heavy overcoat open, so he could inspect the damage under the van's interior light.

"Tom – for pity's sake!"

The spray from the twin barrels of a shotgun had taken

him about the left shoulder. There was a hole in his neck over the shoulderblade from which white shards of broken bone were poking, together with the pumping gush of a ruptured artery.

Tom was trying to talk, and Sandy put his head down to hear the whisper.

"Couldn't have planned it better – six months on sick – an early bloody pension!" the clown tried to cackle in his ear.

"What about the ambulance? Call them again." Sandy was lurching onto his feet, then surging forward into the front of the van. "Call them up again and hurry it – and order a couple more, for God's sake. And get hold of somebody in authority at the casualty department and explain the situation. What the hell are you waiting for?"

"I think he just died, boss." The two men in the front – two men who did not include Gill amongst them – were staring back into the rear of the van where McGrath was leaning over Tom.

"Died! This awkward bugger – when he thinks he's just cracked it! Don't kid yourself – just tell them to get their skates on with that ambulance and stop wasting precious seconds."

You used your imagination and what did you achieve? Tom's lying here in a heap in front of him. He bent down again and checked there was still a heartbeat.

"Hold on, Tom!" There was blood on his ear and the side of his face from Tom's shirt.

What the hell was keeping them? Where was that damned ambulance?

Sweating then; he had never sweated like this in his life. The waiting was unbearable. He hadn't felt his own pain at all when carrying Tom. Now it came back with a merciless vengeance. He noticed it snowing in earnest: it was snowing like a bitter February.

No expense spared . . . to bring Jack Hell all the way back . . .

Sandy was speaking urgently again to the two men in the front. "Get on to your boss and see if we can get more marksmen – marksmen with infra-red sights. As many as you can get. We need to cover all of those upper storey windows. And give everybody a warning again over the radio. No lights. Warn everybody again about the lights." Sandy's neck was swelling in huge welters of pain with each heartbeat. He touched his lip with the corner of his hand and saw blood, Tom's blood. "Warn them about every ten minutes, Sergeant. No lights unless I say so. And warn them he might possibly use a boy as a shield."

Who was kidding who? A boy somehow alive in the centre of all this madness? Stick to what he knew: *to bring Jack Hell all the way back for your amusement!*

He rubbed his bloodstained hand across his forehead. He felt responsible.

Yet, without the boy, why should Bamford be here at all? Answer that question. Without the boy, what was the point of the entire exercise?

He was outside the van, still shielded by its bulk from the high windows, and his face was burning. He was wiping Tom's blood from his face, using snow and his handkerchief. He felt worse than he had ever felt in his life. Even the breakdown of his marriage hadn't made him feel this bad. Tom desperately injured. Tom might die. Sandy took a huge breath. He needed strength now. He needed some deep core of strength to fall back on, to draw on very deeply.

Then he caught sight of Gill, crouching along under the wall, making his way towards the entrance of the main building. Sandy only recognised him from the halo of reflection that was his fair hair. Even as he was wondering what Gill was up to, there was the welcome sound of the ambulance's approach, the swish of tyres and the low voices of the men who were guiding it up the approach road without lights.

"What more can we do for him?" Sandy was outside the

wall now, watching them lift Tom into the brightly lit interior.

"Move fast, that's what," murmured the driver's assistant. "And cut down the bleeding. You could let a man go with him in the ambulance, so we take it in turns to keep a thumb on the artery all the way to hospital."

Sandy watched it all unfold before his eyes, hardly able to blink. The ambulance doors closed but he could still see Tom's face, yellow like tallow wax, and so much orange all over the place which was his blood.

It was stupid and unprofessional but his mind wouldn't work as it should: shock – the shock of Tom's being shot. There was a faintness in his legs as the ambulance left. Leaning against the outer face of a rust-stained pillar, he stared through the rose bushes drooping under burdens of snow; five minutes later he heard the bell and saw the light flashing. Out of shooting range – Tom was out of it.

He had to work it out, what to do.

He had risen through the ranks faster than anybody in his division ever before. There was a reason for that. Until he had made chief inspector – he had stopped rising at chief inspector. And there was a reason for that too. A reason Julie had sensed; had sensed and had not liked. Above chief inspector you stayed largely in your office. Superintendents tended to push paper.

He had lit a cigarette under cover of the wall. Now, turning on his heel, he drew hard on it. It was so cold he couldn't taste it. It was so damned cold the blood was not flowing in his tongue. Organise. Rationalise. Just one thing remained absolutely vital, the possibility that the boy was still alive. That was still fundamental. Be patient? Maybe they ought to wait for the daylight? Wait for the cold, hunger, the uncertainties of dying?

"If I could be of help, Woodings?"

He had forgotten Gill, who must have come outside the wall and had been standing there watching him. Now he looked at him, at the dim outline of the man: was he imagining it or was Gill looking just a little too wild and dishevelled?

"Keep out of my way, Gill."

"I could try to talk to him."

"Talk to him?" Sandy tossed the remains of his cigarette into the snow underfoot and laughed softly.

"You're considering going back in there alone, aren't you? Well, that's daft and you know it. You'll end up in the next ambulance. Do you imagine that you'll be able to move a foot in that building without his knowing? Haven't you realised what that building is to him? Here, all about here, you have entered his labyrinth. You must have felt it, you know him as well as I do. You'll be entering the heart of a nightmare – and the nightmare is itself in the mind of a madman."

Mad? If Bamford was mad, who had driven him mad? Did Gill think he was so stupid he didn't know the real reason he was here?

"He called himself Mag. He spoke to me and he called himself Mag!"

"So what?"

Sandy wished he could see Gill clearly now. He wished he could see into the man's eyes.

"I think Mag means Mag the Magician. So what does Mag the Magician think he's doing, Gill?" Sandy had taken Gill by the lapel of his sheepskin. He shook him once then detached his hand as if the contact burnt him. Sandy was already running, crouched over, through the gates and back into the armoured van in the grounds.

He was ordering the sergeant in charge to get hold of Farnworth, who was still in the building, holding the second floor.

But Gill had run into the van after him. Gill was following him.

Sandy turned on him furiously, shouting. "Why kidnap

the boy in the first place? That's what the whole thing is about. You know, don't you, you bastard? The kidnapping of the boy was the one really important act and you haven't said one word about it. Because you know. You've known the reason all along. And I think I know it too. I really do think I can guess the reason too."

"No heroics, Woodings! The boy is dead. Take the boy out of your considerations."

Alan Farnworth was suddenly coming through on the radio. His voice was high-pitched. It was very urgent. "Is that you, Sandy. Listen to me – we've got a hell of a problem. I've had to pull the men back down to the ground floor. The mad bugger has poured petrol down the main staircase. The whole place is reeking with petrol fumes. I'll tell you, it was all I could do not to put a match to it myself . . ."

29

Pausing inside the building again: one advantage he must have was the fact that Bamford couldn't predict his movements. He had no certain route planned. He had also entered the building alone, contrary to Alan Farnworth's ordered opposition and, even more importantly, in direct contradiction of standard police practice. But then he was never really alone, was he?

Sandy Woodings smiled drily at the thought. He should be maximally nervous now. This was the moment of greatest danger and yet, although he was sweating freely over his face, he felt a sense of inner calm. He knew it was deceptive.

To his left was the main staircase where Tom had been shot. Bamford must have emptied a couple of gallons of petrol over the top because the fumes of petrol really were steeping the entire building. No stun grenades here! One match . . . To his right the first of the long corridors, which had been partially explored by Farnworth's men and which he now knew led to a second and smaller staircase, the building's fire escape.

Feeling his way, it seemed longer than he had expected. He kept to darkness most of the time, only now and then a quick muted stab with his handkerchief-wrapped torch. There was a stink of mildew underlying the smell of petrol, becoming stronger as he went further along the corridor, so bad already that he felt a sickening rise in his stomach.

He found himself on a spiral staircase, small and narrow.

Here were the footprints on the staircase which Farnworth's men had discovered and which led to one of the side rooms. A nerve-jangling electrical thrill ran down his arms into his fingertips.

He removed his shoes here, but he found his stockinged feet stuck like frost to the frozen wood, so he put them back on again. He had to straddle his legs across the rungs because there was less noise from the rotten wood bending. Funny how he could still smell it – on the staircase the stench of mildew was even stronger. He told himself to slow down. Not to make Tom's mistake.

Pushing himself in front like that, Tom must have been addled – unless he had heard the sound and knew what was waiting too! Sandy thought about that now, halfway up that first flight of stairs. He considered that and he felt cold sweat extend onto the back of his neck. The least he owed Tom was to take it easy now, to stocktake at intervals.

He paused on every third rung, listened, probed with all five senses. Nothing from above – nothing at all from the reaches of darkness. He waited a while longer, still listening. Then he heard it: from a floor below, the pad of stockinged feet.

As predictable as night followed day. *The boy is dead, Woodings.* He felt another wave of electical tingling, down his arms, from his neck into his chest, pricking up goose flesh over his belly, contracting his balls . . .

The wall was emulsioned all right, not blue but a mould-mapped shiny glossy green. Even as he stared at the wall, it came to an abrupt end. The stairs had only taken him up a single storey.

Moving across a tiny square landing he went through into another corridor. Nothing like the main corridor, it was much shorter, barely wide enough for two persons. A room led off it so he side-stepped into the room, finding himself in what had obviously been a dormitory. There were pieces of old iron bedstead against the walls: rusting metal, coated with grainy black filth, the stuff spiders left behind on their cobwebs. He listened carefully again: Gill was moving silently.

Leaning against the wall between two windows, he listened again, heard nothing. It was beginning to worry him. He moved on, arriving at the door back into the corridor, where he counted to ten and was taken by surprise on the stroke of his last count by the crackle of the loudspeaker system, the sound of fumbling, a matter of getting used to the microphone, then that familiar voice with its strong Bolton accent.

"Bamford! Listen to me. This is Chief Inspector Farnworth speaking. We want no further trouble. So why not call it a day now. It's all over. Give yourself up and nobody else will come to any harm."

Sandy passed through the door, brushing the filthy wall of that narrow corridor, before moving into another of those small square landings. He started the ascent of another spiralling staircase.

Probably it had only taken him minutes. In his pocket he carried not only his Smith and Wesson but also a small radio transmitter, which was part of his plan for when he encountered Bamford face to face. Down there in the cool of night his plan hadn't seemed so very bad. Now he was glad he hadn't had much time to think about it.

That disembodied voice again . . . "Think about what I'm saying to you, Bamford. You must be hungry? The boy must be half-starved? You must be frozen near to death, the pair of you?" He stopped as before and listened. An unfortunate child, backward . . . but likable? Now that was a new shock wave. Likable – you didn't come back to a place you didn't like, did you?

That coursing, expanding, tingling again: much bigger: right down to his toes this time.

Maybe Gill wasn't so predictable after all? Gill was an additional complication Sandy could have done without.

He was doing well, climbing virtually noiselessly. Then, at the top of the second staircase, the gun in his pocket made a loud clunk against a door jamb. He whispered, "Damn!" and took the thing out, felt its weight, transferred it to his other pocket and moved the torch to his left hand. He padded across another of those tiny unventilated landings and through another grimy closed door.

Then it was suddenly a lot worse. The throbbing pain was mauling his neck and left shoulder: his heartbeat wasn't just in his chest but had moulded itself to his entire upper body. His heart was hammering against the sides of his skull, against the back of his neck, his chest seemed to expand and contract with each huge beat. Change pattern! He decided against the dormitory on this level. The corridor was quicker and he followed the footsteps through the door at the far end, beyond to another spiralling staircase, darker than ever, set deep into the masonry, as if it had bitten its way in using its own wooden teeth.

This was the last staircase. Bamford's footsteps had led him all the way. Only it wasn't just Sandy himself being led, was it? He didn't care as much about caution as he had earlier. The thrusting of his heartbeat made delicacy impractical. And he thought the noise of the gun banging on wood had made the precautions pointless anyway.

Another dormitory, another door, but no staircase. There were many footprints here, like the upper floors on the main staircase. He tested doors which led off the landing, trying the one nearest to him, his revolver-clutching hand raping space in a linen cupboard. His eyes were wide and staring in the mask of his face as he opened the identical door next to it, another linen cupboard, but . . . blue! He had almost pulled himself away but now he jerked the door open wide and stared. In that moment, his senses registered something else, something above the pounding heartbeat: he could smell burning. That smell caused an acute irritation over his chest wall: a prickly burning sweat, in the shape of an inverted triangle. He was absolutely still outside the single remaining door . . . a door which must open into a room which faced the front of the building.

Think now! But he could smell burning. He could smell it stronger. Good God almighty! Try to get the plan absolutely clear. Try to quell the first nauseous burst of panic. Try to get his plan foolproof.

But instead he was putting two and two together: *Gill isn't behind me. And the building is burning!*

With his hand shaking, he took the transmitter from his pocket. He was holding it fiercely despite the neuralgic pain in his left hand. He had to perform a trick with the other hand, opening the door, holding the gun, directing it as best he could along the line of vision that would be the torch's beam . . .

Dead . . . dead! Take the boy out of your considerations! His toe was kicking wood into darkness, his finger was compressing the button on the transmitter, causing the spotlights on the cars below to be directed suddenly at the top storey windows. Dazzling – the light in the room was dazzling as the door opened. A smaller dormitory, he was inside the dormitory, in his nostrils a welter of rancid human smells. No Bamford – all in that split second, his head turning – no Bamford! Only an intense pain to the back and the right of his head, only pain – followed by nothingness. Blackness.

30

When Christina arrives she will be wearing a black T-shirt, blue denim skirt and her sunflower gold earrings. He can hear the flames now. There is a waterfall sound as they rush up the top flight of the central staircase. When Christina comes . . . Soldiers sweating. Soldiers with smoking cigarettes jutting from half-Spanish faces already set into the lined repose of cruelty. His heart hammering. His heart is hammering now. Did his heart ever cease from that hopeless screaming hammering. Terror so horrible and so naked . . . Christina coming with her mother from the village protest meeting about a poisoned well. Christina . . . terror. Searing, roaring, terror which, for the remainder of his life, will metamorphose to loneliness. A loneliness so utter and complete that his world will pivot about this terrible hour. And the fire is roaring already. The whole of the main staircase . . .

Wake up, Mister Policeman!

He is losing the cement of time. Parts of him expand and dissolve, his body has blurred its shape in this awesome shifting vortex? "Come on – wake up!" Only a sharp tap. A tap to stun. While against the crackle of tinder-dry wood erupting into a bonfire, the soldiers who will murder Christina talk and joke nervously. And he waits, as he has waited over a million nightmares, handcuffed to an iron rail in the open back of their truck.

Time has started to rotate. Time whirling. Time against which he has prayed and blasphemed. Time is merciless.

Mister Detective is groaning. Only a light tap, to where it matters. He is groping with clumsy hands. His fingers touch something familiar: a trousered leg. Now he is realising, he knows where he is and who is standing over him in the semi-darkness. Whose shotgun is pressed against his bewildered brain.

"Wake up! Time is running out."

Goodbye Christina! Goodbye Baby Blue!

Mister Detective has a head which is hurting him. The pain in his head makes it difficult to think. But thought will come, thought is rapidly clearing. He is working it out logically now, that the man with the shotgun will have taken his gun from where it fell. His adversary won't mind now if he sits up out of his uncomfortable position, where the side of his face was lying on bare floorboards. He does so slowly, but nobody is fooled. His mind is already alert. His mind is racing. He says something surprising, as if the memory of that moment, of the brightly illuminated room before the spotlight was shot out, has fixed an indelible image on the backs of his eyes.

"Blue walls! Blue emulsioned walls!"

Time is gyrating, spinning, tearing at the molecules at the periphery of his being. His existence at the eye of this hurricane will be brief. Nothing to hold him. His soul longs for the black zero of suffocating darkness.

"Listen to me, Bamford. The boy is not your brother."

Words are useless. Yet words fashion themselves inside a mouth that is already dissolving into the storm. "No time, Mister Detective. No arguments. No discussions."

"Your brother died here. He died in this room?"

He ignores the intention which is to keep him talking. Talk to him: give yourself time. His voice, as he moves to the pillar of wall between two windows, as he glances abruptly out to see that it is headlights and about a dozen torches that are responsible for the half-light, is slurred as if drunk.

"People will fight evil, Mister Detective. It's the one thing that gives us hope for the future. Something in us that will recognise it for what it is. Something sickens at the very recognition of its stench . . . "

"I'm listening, Bamford. I understand what you're saying. But the boy is innocent." Mister Detective must be listening to the inferno too. For his voice is cracking and high-pitched and his face, too, is a mask of sweat. Sweat in which his two eyes shine, like the eyes of a wild animal, sparkling with a furtive alien life. "For the love of God, Bamford! The place is a bonfire!"

Oh yes. The boy *is* innocence, Mister Detective. What else but innocence could bend the needle!

The detective's voice contains the whiplash of panic. "What came out of that detention centre was damaged. They took your sanity, Bamford. You can no longer distinguish real good from evil. Is there enough of you left to understand?"

He can see the smoke now coming under the door. The policeman must see it too. The policeman is balancing on his toes, his eyes scanning the darker shadows of the room. Glittering eyes now that have swung back onto his own face, which like the policeman's, is a mask of sweat.

"To punish Margaret Stephens – is that what it's all about? Let you down badly, did she? Loved her and she let you down."

He is being rent asunder in the maelstrom.

"Poor Maggie – when the going became vicious . . . The deaths on the campuses finished Maggie."

"Don't you think she's suffered enough, Bamford? Don't you think she's been punished enough?"

Gill has done this: he knows this for certain. Gill, who will be squatting out there where it is safe, with his gun on the side door. His voice is little more than a whisper. "Is it possible, remotely possible, that a seed may be sown in one time and harvested in another?"

"For God's sake, the whole building is burning!" The policeman paces himself, knowing he will have to rush him. He listens, choosing his moment, knowing that in that moment he will almost certainly die.

"If the need is desperate enough. If the need is so very desperate. As a man might go down on the black earth and pray in the eye of the hurricane. The intensity of the wish is prayer, isn't it? Prayer. Just prayer. To any power that will listen. To make any promise. Could that prayer pluck a seed of innocence from a moment of pure evil . . . find a small fragment of eternity? What do you believe, Mister Detective?"

Now he plans his rush. A determined spring. But the butt of the shotgun catches him in the belly and he crashes to the floor again, on his hands and knees.

"What do you want, Bamford?" his voice is a scream, against the maw of the inferno.

"Work it out, Mister Detective."

"The woman . . . the woman who died in Latin America."

He has to hold his breath. He cannot answer.

"Murdered by a death squad. That woman was special." The detective is coughing, squeezing the words out against the choking smoke. "She was somebody special."

"My wife. Christina was my wife, Mister Detective."

The policeman has found a handkerchief and is holding it against his nose and mouth, coughing, his back against the wall adjacent to the window. "But that isn't all, is it, Bamford?"

Once more he refuses to answer.

"A child? There was a child. There has to be a child?"

He is falling back against the wall. His soul is disintegrating into a billion spiralling motes, tearing, rending, dissolving, into the black hole of time. He is coughing violently, despite the fresh air that struggles through the window, where he shot out the spotlights. *Christina coming. Christina with her black hair parted in the middle and the two braided plaits all the way to her waist* . . . Innocence will be raped first and then murdered. His Christina with her beautiful black hair, made luxuriant by her state. He will see the pure white line of her parting throughout the hell that follows, as she thrashes and mills in the hour-long agony . . .

"The lock of black hair. It came from a child. Half-American Indian. Black hair from a half-American Indian. A child, Bamford! You lost a child!"

His voice is a deep-throated roar from the lips of death. His voice is the billowing into infinity of a soul that has already exploded into the cyclone. "My son was born into his mother's blood, Mister Detective. His grandmother cut the lock of his hair. After he was dead. When she buried him with his mother. Two innocents in the one grave. The Hindus say it is the highest state of grace. To die without taking a breath. Without a name."

Realisation flooded Sandy's brain. Gill had debriefed Margaret Stephens all those years ago. He must have wrung every morsel of information from her . . . information about Bamford. He had fed that information . . . Oh, my God!

Sandy had only half-anticipated the truth. But there it was. Naked and terrible.

Yet the past was over. He could do nothing about the past. And there was another innocent. A child that might still be alive. Had to be to make it all worth the agony. His eyes had already scoured the room. A very large room, full of smoke and shadows. But Bobby Stephens was not in this room. How the hell could he be anywhere else but in this room? A huge room. Those flickering shadows were deepest in the wall and corners most distant from the big front windows. Windows with round tops in the front wall . . . One smaller window in the gable, the wall he was now leaning against, and directly opposite him was the black buttress that contained a large open fireplace. Nothing in the fireplace, except some gas rings under what looked like a makeshift roasting spit . . . *Time – God grant me time!*

"Why did you let me live, Bamford?" He was moving even as he spoke, edging along the gable, with his back to the wall.

Silence. Awesome, debilitating silence, during which, with a heart that was galloping, Sandy felt pity for this man. Bamford appeared to have lost his voice since that horrible description of the murder of his wife and child. But even as he wondered, Sandy sensed the answer. He sensed it with a further slide into raging hell, as the smoke continued to thicken, the noise of the fire – the panic-engendering roar – had so rapidly escalated. A perverse logic. All the way down the line.

"Why, Bamford?" but even his voice in asking had a pallid tremulousness.

In the half-light, Bamford's face was directed towards him with a ghostly opalescence. With the shotgun almost aimlessly directed towards the floor, Bamford was gazing down at something in his right hand. Something shining, metallic . . . Even at twenty feet away, Sandy could detect the change that had taken place in the man's sweat-drenched face. The object was placed, with a curious twisting of that head and shoulders, onto the floor, given a shove, slid across the floor and ended no more than a few feet from where Sandy was crouching. His own Smith and Wesson revolver.

Sandy's heart was pumping so fast and hard it was a continuous thundering in his brain. *A reason.* No time to think. Time only to react. To sense everything he had ever learnt about this man and to let his deepest gut reaction dictate. He turned abruptly from the revolver. He had been manipulated all the way down the line. But he was nobody's self-appointed executioner. He didn't care if Bamford was watching him now. He was stumbling across the floor, finding the wall that contained the fireplace, feeling the powdery plaster of that wall – the blue-emulsioned plaster – fumbling along in the choking dust and the malevolent stuttering darkness. He was clawing his way down the wall, away from the windows, deep into the shadows.

"Bobby!"

A poor weak shout, muted by the threatening panic, the feared hopelessness. Was it his imagination or did the crackling roar sound louder? The fire must be directly on the other side of this wall. The fire had already raged through floors, along the tinder-dry, dust-coated corridors, until it was no more than feet away.

"Bobby Stephens! For God's sake, lad!"

His ears wouldn't listen for anything now but the howling of the fire.

But his heart pushed him on. His heart felt the wall through palpitating fingertips. Felt for the change that must take place. Tapped . . . was tapping. An echoing hollowness. Was he imagining it? He could hear no echo. But he was feeling it. He *was* feeling an echo. Damn it, but it was a door. Another of those linen cupboards. And that was what he was after. He knew – he knew there had to be another of those linen cupboards!

He was down on one hand and two knees scrambling away rubbish. Tearing away the five missing cushions from the suite at Clarissa's house. A pile of old blankets, which smelled of old sweat. Something which crashed and tinkled when he hurled it which must be a thermos flask. Boxes filled with empty cans and wrappers from sweets and chocolates. A basin full of water brought in presumably from the melting snow. All part of the mound in front of the door to the cupboard. A man-made mountain. His hand tore away a transistor radio, which crashed against the far wall. Toys . . . Toys! He had almost thrown it but now he held it, he held onto that tiny figurine for grim life. Tried to see it. Could only quarter see it. But he knew what it was. He had bought something very similar for Gerry. A science fiction warrior from *Star Wars*.

He had found the handles and was tearing back the twin doors, forcing aside whatever rubbish was still left at the base. A huge cupboard for the dormitory.

A pounding tearing pulsation in the back of his head where he had been concussed. There was a hot sensation, blood under pressure, blood running down the back of his head, from the exertion of clearing the doors, from the monstrous excitement . . . That blinding flash of pain radiating into his shoulder, his reawakened neck. All one mass of crimson-lurid pain, which he was ignoring, which he was walking through, his eyes opened wide as saucers.

Three black pools in the deep grey shadows. Feeling. Feeling with instinct as much as violently shaking fingers. Three separate bundles of rags. Not rags. Blankets. One of the black pools was changing shape, was clambering into a conical base, with a tottering debility. He could smell him. He could smell the terrified boy!

"Jesus help us!"

"I cut my hand on the knife. I cut my hands all over. But I cut myself out of the stockings with my own knife."

There were swags of torment in every inch of bending. He picked up the trembling bundle and registered no weight. "I hid it . . . hid my knife . . . from the van . . ." Faltering a moment, he hitched up the bundle to geet a better grip. His head groaned. Darkness wallowed about him in titanic waves.

It was no good carrying him like a baby. His left shoulder simply said no. But there wasn't time to think it out. The dormitory was already an oven. Within minutes it would become a furnace. He guessed that whatever lay beyond every internal wall was now in flames. He was forced down onto his hands and knees, dragging his living bundle under

312

him, sheltering the child, like some dazed and faltering kangaroo. He skittered through thickening smoke towards the door. As he reached it, there was a dull explosion, followed by the tinkling of glass. Now he saw brilliant fireworks swirl about the windows, vivid orange sparks and talons of burning wood.

He could see Bamford.

The man was only ten feet away, a huge scarecrow shape, pressed against the wall between two windows. In the eerie glow of the sparks, he was squatting on his haunches, his pallid face white in the black halo of hair and beard. There was still a vitality deep in those black reflecting pupils. Sandy almost shouted, "Go on! Get the hell out! Take your chances." But something in the depths of those staring black pupils dissuaded him.

Without letting go of the boy, he scrambled across the floor to find the plastic basin full of water. He doused a filthy blanket with the water, threw Bobby over his right shoulder and then, huddled under the water-soaked blanket, he grabbed the hot door handle.

He was through the door.

Unbearable heat. Murderous heat. He couldn't breathe at all. He couldn't see. He was fighting his way along the corridor, feeling walls, past the other linen cupboard, the landing at the top of the uppermost flight of stairs. He was descending crabwise, with his shoulder pressed before him to the oven, his feet stumbling and tottering.

The very stones appeared to be burning. His fingers jumped away after a moment's touch, touched, touched again, stone that would bake meat. The next corridor, a bigger and wider corridor. The square landing. His hand prickled like ballooned orange skin. A poisonous pocket of air pitched him down onto the topmost steps of the next flight of stairs. Steadying himself, he clawed his way downwards, two or three steps at a time, lurching from wall to banister, pitching himself through onto the next corridor.

His shoes must be melting. Only a matter of minutes before his feet were blistered. He forced himself on again into a solid curtain of pain, choking heat and smoke. Ahead it was rapidly worsening. Ahead was a searing roaring wall of flames. The blanket had passed the stage of steaming. Over the dome that covered his head and shoulders, it was smoulding, charring. The last staircase was on fire.

He shouted out in the crackly voice of an old man. "Farnworth. Farnworth – for Christ's sake!"

No answer. How could they possibly hear him? They would be huddling outside the grounds, watching the bonfire from the far side of the boundary wall.

"Alan! Help us! The bottom flight of stairs. We're trapped above the bottom flight of stairs!"

He threw himself over the boy, on the small square landing. The blanket was on fire over them. Above them a whoofing thud which was the staircase above erupting into conflagration. A cataract of poisonous fumes welled down, bowling along rooms and corridor, hitting them with the solidity of rubble. White smoke rose up from below, a seething tide, as heavy as the sea. White smoke . . . White smoke . . .

"Run for it, man! Make a run for it!"

He had thrown off the blazing blanket. He couldn't breathe. He could hardly see. Shapes. The shape of a tunnel. The tunnel was the staircase, smouldering, almost aglow. He hurtled himself, with his living bundle, through the rectangular mouth of that tunnel of baking white suffocation. Hands were pulling him on. The hands of many, dragging him at breakneck speed through the white spuming pit of hell. Hands were trying to take Bobby from him but he wouldn't let him go. His skin was a prickling hive of needles, daggers. Snow! They were rolling him in the snow, throwing snow over him, rubbing snow into the scorched flesh of his hands, his face, the fissured lips, the ballooned and closing eyelids.

"Let me sit up. Just let me sit up, will you." He tried to demand it, but his voice sounded puny from lungs that felt full of razor blades.

"You're some lucky devil, Woodings!" That was Farnworth. That was Alan Farnworth's voice from only inches away.

"The boy? How is he?" His voice was squeezing itself through the worst sore throat he had ever had in his life.

"Minus a bit of hair and one eyebrow. Better than you are by a long chalk. You crazy man!"

A whining sound in his ears: a vehicle reversing through water, coming closer. The water was melted snow. An ambulance . . . It was the ambulance driver and Farnworth who were taking him, one to each arm. "Duck your head down, mate!"

"Gill did it, Alan. Gill must have put a torch to the place."

"Gill's disappeared. Slipped away. We never saw him again after he went in behind you."

Sandy knew Gill would have escaped, but it didn't stop him muttering fiercely, "I hope he never got out. I hope he's still in there, Alan!"

He was sitting on the couch and refusing to lie down. Bobby was in the ambulance with him. He could smell the acrid smell of burnt hair. The skin on the backs of his hands felt like raw melon. He could taste blood in his spit.

"Tom – Tom, Alan?" His voice was almost gone. They had closed one of the doors at the back of the vehicle. The ambulance was already moving.

"If you're asking about the sergeant who got shot," a strange voice, a Lancashire accent, "he made it at least to the operating theatre."

The ambulance attendant! Sandy was trying to ask the ambulance attendant more about Tom, whether he was heading towards the same hospital, whether Tom could die . . .

"Calm down now, sir. Save your breath. You're going to need it."

Tuesday, March 27th

I think, my darling, we have invented everything – as we invent rules. Boundaries. Time. What is possible. What is impossible. Because I want it to be possible for you. Everything. Let blossom the dark rose . . .

In the out of hours schoolroom doubling tonight as writer's workshop, under the harsh glare of fluorescent lighting, a fat elderly woman stands up to read aloud her story. Her bottom is so disproportionate it must surely be hormonal. She reads it passionately and cheerfully, seven handwritten pages, double-sided. She has confided to Maggie over coffee that the typewriter is a mechanical block to her. And Maggie can understand why. Her story is too warm. It is a complex structure, three-dimensional, and hopelessly entangled in love and humour.

Normality, my darling Jimmy, is something you take, greedily, you wrap your two hands about it.

Mrs Marsh – which is this lady's name – has helped her grandchildren set up the stage for the Christmas play. This is the basis for her story. Now she sings for us: a few lines from "Jesus Christ Superstar". You see how crazy love is? How mundane . . . how impossible?

Mrs Marsh is trapped at the top of some rickety stepladders. Below her the stage is spinning. Spinning as Maggie's world is spinning. Not round and round, but a twisting, whorling waltz, into and out of the darkest spheres of her overexcited brain. *Mr Woodings called again today, love.* As he calls weekly or fortnightly. She looks forward to these meetings, when she can welcome recovery by the hair growing on his shaven head. Maggie thinks: two days. This is the longest she has been separated from Bobby since he came out of hospital. Transferred from the burns unit after only twenty-four hours. A full week on the children's ward, where she had lived in with him, slept there so she could get up at any time of the day or night and look, touch, reach out . . . Was it all nearly three months ago already? Oh, but three months is not so very long. And now she must survive a week without him – dear Lord! A week is a sheer cliff face. *But you are dead? Is it possible that you are really dead?*

Placed centrally on one of the two opposed coffee tables is a margarine tub containing two pounds twenty pence. Eleven contributions, in tens and twenties. For the coffee, which appeared in an odd variety of cracked and chipped cups and mugs. For the twice-yearly magazine, *Write-Speak*. For the privilege of sharing vision with the six-year-olds who painted the pictures which adorn three of the four walls. Always the truth. Always beautiful. THIS IS MY HOUSE. THIS IS MY MUMMY AND DADDY. THIS IS BABY. Opaque posters on different coloured papers. TOMMY CAT IS MY CAT.

Can Mrs Marsh have finished her story already? She is discovering her chair, pinkly embarrassed, bathed in the gentle rain of appreciation. You see how it will be, my dear. Nothing that could strictly be termed applause in this writers' workshop. Not from any lack of charity, nor indeed any lack of talent, but taboos, my dear. Taboos she readily understands. Consideration, encouragement, kindness.

A young man – she recognises the intensity of a probationer – stands to his feet, with tears already in his eyes. John, who has the rounded shoulders of long-standing group responsibility, takes the typescript from his hands and reads it for him. The young man's wife has given birth to their first child, a daughter. He has wrenched his experience out of his heart, in words and tears.

On the second of the coffee tables stands a plump glass bottle with pebbled sides. It holds five crocuses, their cut ends in water. Another little act of love, they mirror the young man's tenderness: purple, yellow, white and blue.

Will she also break down when it comes to her turn? An almost unbearable spiralling twisting force, says no. Her poem is not brilliant. She is proud only of the feeling and not the artistry. *I don't ask your forgiveness: only let me go*.

Because I too stumbled on into my own dark forest. Only my torment was the dull matt black housewife's tale. I never pretended to your gift of understanding. I sweated blood for two nights over this poem which doesn't even scan. When you're not clever, does your heart expand to compensate? Forgive me: for I have forgiven you.

A West Indian with dreadlocks sounds out his angry young man's song. Her turn next. His will be a short exposition. How much can you elaborate on anti-materialism? Shoot down millionaires. Shoot down the people who ride about in nice cars. Yet his poem has such a lively pretentiousness, he makes her laugh. When he intends perhaps to make the world cry.

Grief, humour, terror, confusion: it is required to prove that love can be born from darkest night as from the lily-white day.

They are waiting for her. *I am the only stranger to this circle*.

For a moment panic suggests a horrific change of plan. To tear her clothes and rend her hair, kneel down naked in flesh and spirit and confess everything. Every crime she has committed, has not committed, could ever in her wildest dreams think of committing. Just to lose herself in that sweet welter of abasement. I don't know the truth. The truth is incomprehension. The past devours us. If you deny the impossible then you declare a limit to love. Are they showing signs of impatience? No – only a natural and good-natured curiosity. Your back bends. You curl about your centre. You shelter the womb which can take no more. Your left hand searches behind you for the backrest of the chair. You are already on your feet and rising. Magic is the force that drives you now. Magic will hold back the tears that threaten. Magic is communicable? Magic can bridge the possible and the impossible. Your mouth opens. If they will excuse the flaws. If they can only understand . . .

BOLTON

Artful Jack
Kills titans
Opens a single great wound
Grotesque nostril
In the fleshbase of chimney
Turns on the slow
Brick-red chute
Death by nosebleed

Smoky capped forest
Of childhood
Resistant to acid rain
Now mortality is underlined
One church, a mill
A terraced row.

Who'll grieve thee, old lady?

Dumb suffering Victorian
Fallen Queen
Too proud to ask
Where demand was your right
Some greater respect

At what stage
Should we have raised our hands?
As uneasily we trailed voyeur's feet
Ever backwards

Frank Ryan

From tumbling dust-groaning
Accrington-red blood tide
Crackling tears at the bones of our ankles.

Who'll pity thee
Dirty old town?
Cotton heart broken
Where girls played Fairy Foosteps

What time is it, Miser Wolf?

Against that same red brick
Of mills and houses
And cobbled streets

OTHER TITLES BY FRANK RYAN
AVAILABLE FROM SWIFT PUBLISHERS

IN FICTION

- SWEET SUMMER   ISBN 1-874082-01-4   Price   £5.99
- TIGER TIGER   ISBN 1-874082-25-1   Price   £6.99

- THE SUNDERED WORLD (HARDCOVER)
                       ISBN 1-874082-23-5   Price £16.99

- THE SUNDERED WORLD (PAPERBACK)
                       ISBN 1874082-24-3   Price   £6.99

IN NON-FICTION

- TUBERCULOSIS; THE GREATEST STORY NEVER TOLD (HARDCOVER)
                       ISBN 1874082-00-6   Price £16.99

If you would like to know more about these and other exciting Swift titles, visit our interactive website at:

www.swiftpublishers.com

These titles may be purchased by credit card from our website or, by post, by sending a cheque or postal order (not cash) for the stated amounts to:

Swift Publishers Ltd, PO Box 1436, Sheffield S17 3XP, UK.

Please add £1 towards postage and packing for single orders. If you order more than one book, please add an additional 50p per additional book. Applies only to orders to be delivered to addresses in the UK, Ireland or Europe. If outside these territories, please enquire about availability by letter or by e-mail to: *enquiries@swiftpublishers.com*